Book II. & The First Parable of God's Final Grail and Biblical Testament

THE BOOK OF DEATH
VOL. 1
BLOOD SKY DAWNING
Final Testament Parable

Anointed by Christopher Lee Cain & Scribed by Melissa Anne Cain:
The Second Coming of Jesus

CHRIST
& Mary Magdalene

www.thebookofdeath.net
www.theroyalembassy.org

Dedicated to Humanity

<u>Book II. & The First Parable of God's Final Grail and Biblical Testament</u>
<u>Testament</u>
Inspired by actual experiences

BLOOD SKY DAWNING

INTRODUCTION

GOD'S COLD WAR ENDS

THE FIRST OF GOD'S FINAL TESTAMENT BIBLICAL PARABLES CHRONICLING THE FINAL WAR OF HEAVEN & HELL, & DISPELLING THE LONG-ENGRAINED FEAR OF DEATH BY ILLUMINATING THE TRUTH BEHIND THE PURPOSE OF HUMAN LIFE.

On the eve of the Day of Revelation, the Cold War between God and Satan is over; and the august, grandeur lives of Earth's elite echelon cataclysmically collide as the execution date for the brutal murder of Jesus Christ, and the rising Rebellion of Satan, eclipses the horizon.

Now, with open warfare re-instated, Judgement is imminent; and humanity chooses either God or Satan when The Second Coming of Jesus Christ returns upon the modern world to fulfill God's Final Prophecy, gather the Chosen, build the Divine Army, and reclaim his Queen.

Consequently, in the Prince of Darkness' desperate bid to defeat God, Eternal Salvation is at stake as Satan uses his one chance incarnate to hold humanity hostage and steal the only soul who can tip the scales of victory by making her his bride—Dr. Madeline Knight, The Second Coming of Mary Magdalene.

From New Orleans to Salem, Chicago to Cincinnati, to Haiti and back again, eternity and extinction converge, and only the Faithful will survive when the top leaders of the Final War of Heaven and Hell descend and ascend upon the earthly plane. And unless Madeline defeats Satan in the battle to reclaim her namesake, she will never reunite with The Second Coming of Jesus Christ, and succumb to the same fate as the condemned souls he returned to save.

1

ISLAND IN THE SWAMPS

The swamplands of southern Louisiana were, and always will be, a place of mystery and danger inhabited only by indigenous unknowns living their entire lives in a predator-infested, Spanish-moss-covered paradise with no doors. Even though each year thousands of tourists captivated by the idea of a thrill flock to the multitude of tours promising to deliver on their desires, they never truly experience the raw nature behind the swamps' deceitful veil of temptation.

With alligators, black bears, cottonmouth snakes, and coypu river rats the size of small dogs, the "American Jungle" beyond the shores remains untouched by the outside world. Past the eerie waterways and rotting swamp shacks, generations of masterfully hidden secrets and supernatural happenings are abundant, protected, and rarely if ever understood.

The unnerving intimidation of the swamps is the foremost attribute allowing the Deep South to remain on its own isolated, unattainable plane, even though the bustling, gothic, archaic metropolis of New Orleans flourishes only miles away.

Sunday, April 13, 2014 – 1:00 a.m.

Northeast of New Orleans deep within the Honey Island Swamp along the rugged shoreline and through the gnarly cypress trees and brush, dozens of flashlights were visible in the darkness. Armed men with dogs were on the hunt, trudging through the forest and wetlands as they searched for a human target. Dressed in chest-high rubber waders and heavy yellow jackets with reflective striping, they embodied the essence of wild animals. Ruthlessly excited and naively engrossed in capturing a suspect they had never seen, not one man ever stopped to think about the dangers surrounding him.

Outside the swamps, these men were civil servants of the law who controlled unruly citizens. Inside the swamps, the lawmen had turned into bloodthirsty nimrods who craved the rush of the kill. Transformed by the primal nature of the wilderness absent on the urban streets of New Orleans, they were, in those moments, even more vicious than the carnivorous animal predators they failed to realize were also hunting them.

Police airboats appeared and soared over the untouchable waters with huge spotlights tracking the perimeter, while a helicopter hovered in the misty night sky illuminating the view from above. Consumed and entranced by the chase, the officers forgot the promise that had really led them to become so enthralled in a sport that was inherently unnatural. Instead, they darted every which way without the slightest understanding of their manipulation or the concept of a goal, led only by the mob mentality lifetimes of displaced thought had them accustomed to by the proxy of social heredity.

And it had all been instigated by a single man—a man who could manipulate human nature with the simple snap of his fingers; a man who took it upon himself to portray a helpless lamb as a raving wolf in the eyes of desperate men with guns; a man who had selfishly taken advantage of the effects handed down from generations of "the followers of the flock," as he liked to call them; a man who had knowingly placed his victims in a position where some would never see their families again, while he waited safely on the shore.

Undetected by the searchlights and escaping in a different direction, the object of the hunt appeared in the water through the steaming mist. Blood-spattered with her face beaten and bruised, Madeline Knight, thirty, was beautiful, tall, and athletic with light caramel-brown skin and long wavy brown hair in a ponytail to her waist. Thigh-high in water, she waded through the marsh dressed in a tight black military cargo leather jacket and black leather combat pants. She wore a long shimmering black-crystal Saint Benedict rosary around her neck, and carried two shiny handguns, one in each of her bloody gauze-wrapped hands.

For the first twenty-nine years of Madeline's life, she had only lived for the present time, for the earthly world, and for the desires she wanted. She had pushed the horrors of her past so far out of her mind she merely survived despite them instead of heeding prophecy as a result. Years of denial could have made any human cold, and she had hopelessly waited for a better tomorrow that never came. But one treacherous week of earthly Hell had changed her entire life, even though the events leading up to that week were, as usual, long and tedious with the ever-present threat of impending doom. In the back of her mind, she always knew her day of reckoning would come; she just didn't know how, or where, or when.

When Madeline reached the deepest part of the marsh, her perfectly-shaped body encased in dripping wet leather arose from the duckweed-covered waters and, like the rosary, glistened in the moonlight.

After securing her weapons in the tactical leg holsters strapped to her thighs, she navigated through a thick forest of trees and brush. Once on the other side, she could see a small swamp island through the hazy fog in the center of an expansively deep river. No more than twenty feet in diameter, the island looked like a serene oasis with only a single tree rising from the center of a grove of low-lying vegetation. It was the second place she was to go, the place that would mark the beginning of her long-awaited freedom.

Over the loud buzzing of the cicadas in the trees above, and over the rows of hissing snakes coiled on the shore refusing to enter the very waters they inhabited, Madeline could still hear the sounds of the men who hunted her; but fear them she did not. The sincerest sense of calm washed over her body, and only one thought came into her mind—the last words Vodou Priestess Haloise had said to her: "It is a mortal sin to forget the end of your life is always on the horizon. Whether or not you choose to accept that fact will either determine your fate, or lead you to your destiny."

For Madeline, it was far more one than the other. Now, there was a Queen's Ransom on her head, and she finally knew who she was.

As she made her way into the river with sparkling eyes no longer of this world, even the predators of the swamps were nothing more than yellow watchful eyes parting to make way for her exit.

2

SALEM HOUSE

Twenty years earlier . . .
It was the hottest day of the year in Salem, Massachusetts, in the summer of 1993. The early morning breeze barely relieved the sweltering heat as it blew over Madeline's tender soiled face while she worked in the family yard with her brother, digging out irrigation ditches. The previous day's temperature had reached 102°, which was far above the moderate climate average for the beautiful coastal city nestled in the Massachusetts Bay. And that day, Monday, threatened to be no different. The short period of darkness from the night before had only slightly cooled the temperature when the sun rose again, hot and heavy.

Madeline and her brother, Maxwell, nine and eleven years old respectively, woke up at 5:00 that morning to begin their day's chores. Regular summer vacation camps and activities had already started for the other children in Salem, but not for the eldest two offspring of the Jackson family. Madeline and Maxwell's parents, Charles and Claire Jackson, didn't believe in vacations or fun of any sort, including playing with other children. But considering Madeline and Maxwell were the only multiracial students with frizzy unkempt hair and secondhand clothes in a white upper-class school, they were outcasts in their neighborhood from the start anyway.

Madeline and Maxwell had already gone through their house and closed all the windows in the Jacksons' eight-thousand-square-foot estate on the big corner lot across from the cemetery. The house didn't have air conditioning, so to keep it cool during the summer they were required to open the windows at night and, without fail, promptly close them before sunrise the following morning. They never had to close the drapes, however, because they were rarely opened to begin with.

Before their father had left for work that fated Monday morning, he had given Madeline and Maxwell their usual chore list for the day; yet that time, there was only one task on it. The previous summer, Charles and Claire Jackson had 150 yards of irrigation ditches, one-foot-wide by three-feet deep, dug around the perimeter of their house with the objective of installing sprinkler piping. But the Jacksons never finished anything when it came to the beautification of their home, and the seasons came and went without having completed the job. Heavy rainstorms had caused the ditches to fill back in with dense clay dirt, and Madeline and Maxwell's task for the day was digging them all back out.

"And," as Charles had said, "the job better be finished before I get home from work or tonight it's going to be another beating!"

The Jackson family home was undisputedly the largest on the block and also the most unsettling. It bore a disturbing resemblance to the Salem Witch House, and many passersby believed it to be haunted. And although it sat in the center of Salem's primary upper-class neighborhood, there were no homes on the empty lots bordering the dark-gray three-story residence, and no fences separating the property lines. An invisible, impenetrable wall of protective energy encased the house and guarded it from outsiders at all times.

Even though the rest of the exclusive neighborhood had an abundance of beautifully maintained estate homes with impeccably manicured yards, the Jackson house was the opposite.

With distressed and worn wood siding, the house looked dreary and lacked any adornments. The front door was made of solid wood and painted the same dark foggy gray as the rest of the house, and all the windows were small and dirty with diamond-shaped lead window frames barely filling out the spaces they occupied. Apart from the large weeping willow trees cloaking the house in a dark cloud of shade on all sides, there was no additional landscaping or grass; the yard was a rock-free, meticulously groomed field of dirt.

The Jacksons never decorated the exterior of their home for the holidays, and no trick-or-treaters or carolers ever came to the door. Members of Salem society despised the Jackson house because it made the entire neighborhood look bad, but regardless of public opinion nobody, influential or not, dared to say a word. Charles Jackson was, after all, the chief of police among other unknown endeavors, and a large intimidating African-American man of great stature who stood six feet four inches tall.

The condition of the Jacksons' house wasn't their only idiosyncrasy causing strife amongst the local residents. In the predominately white town, having a wealthy mixed-race family with a young white mother only fueled the already persistent rumors circulating about the Jacksons, the most debated of which was the legitimacy of their financial prominence. Neighbors and associates wagered on how a police officer with a stay-at-home wife could possibly afford such a huge house in the most expensive part of the city. The implication was that a large family inheritance from the mother's side had accounted for the Jacksons' financial stability and political influence. But such speculation was only grossly fabricated hearsay. Nobody knew the truth behind what really went on within the Jackson household; nobody outside the family except Charles' only confidant had ever stepped one foot inside the house; and nobody was aware that apart from their children, Charles and Claire Jackson didn't have any other family.

Madeline and Maxwell had spent the previous day, Sunday, cleaning out the garage. Hoping to impress their father by completing their chores before he got out of bed, they had woken up earlier than usual. Unfortunately, their attempt to avoid spending the entire day working in the hot sun while he watched over them like the dictator he was, proved to be worthless.

After Charles had discovered his older two children working before he'd instructed them to do so, he was anything but pleased, and the gesture only increased his motivation to implement a stricter labor policy than before. He demanded they immediately remove all contents from the well-stocked one-thousand-square-foot garage and proceed accordingly under his instruction. Madeline and Maxwell subsequently spent the entire day with no food or water scrubbing the cement floor and organizing until 10:00 that night. In addition, because of his children's blatant disregard for his supreme authority, Charles warned them the next day, Monday, would be even more grueling.

And it was. After waking Madeline and Maxwell, Charles first had them wash and wax his police cruiser, and then gave them their orders for the day. Then, as soon as he left for work, they began the insurmountable task of digging out the irrigation ditches. Claire and their younger sister, Gabriella, were still sound asleep inside the dark cool house when Madeline and Maxwell retrieved their tools from the garage and wedged themselves into the ground to begin. As a frail girl of only fifty-five pounds and small for her age, Madeline could barely lift the full-size shovel and felt defeated before she started.

By 3:00 that afternoon, Madeline and Maxwell hadn't even made it halfway around the backside of the property. And although they were tired, dirty, hungry, and parched from thirst, Claire still hadn't come out of the house or invited them in to eat. Adding to their discomfort was the embarrassment brought on by the groups of kids from school that constantly rode by on bicycles teasing and taunting them. Their work, after all, looked more like corporal punishment than a child's chore.

Unlike Madeline, Maxwell was big for his age, and after years of hard work and soul-crushing abuse had become unusually strong. His overwhelming fear of his father, however, had also caused him to become unwaveringly obedient. When he looked over at Madeline, who was struggling to lift a huge piece of clay, and saw her drop her shovel and throw herself onto the ground in protest, he became enraged.

"Get up!" Maxwell yelled. "We only have half-a-day left and we have to finish. I'm not getting in trouble again because of you!"

"I can't!" Madeline cried. "I'm done! I don't know why you even bother. We'll never finish this—it's impossible! Remember yesterday? No matter what we do or how hard we try they will always find something wrong with our work and make us do it again or punish us for not doing it right. It took the tractor guy a whole day to dig these the first time. We can't finish this!"

Without responding, Maxwell continued his work in vain. He wasn't going to stop, and Madeline knew it—he never did. He would work forever to avoid defying their father and the consequences that came with it. But Madeline couldn't bear the thought of him trying to do it alone, so she was determined to stick it out. She loved her brother more than anything—he was her only friend. And although she may have been small, she was feisty, and even though Maxwell was two years older, she always looked out for him. Reluctantly, she picked herself up off the ground, walked to the water hose and turned on the spout, then dragged it over to where Maxwell was working so he could take a drink. She drank some as well, recovered her shovel, and lowered herself back into the ditch.

Moments later, they heard the alarming sound of items being thrown and furniture breaking coming from inside the house. Maxwell stopped and looked up curiously, but Madeline knew what was happening and dread shot through her body. She wondered if she had hidden it well enough this time, or if her mother had somehow found it again. But there was nothing Madeline could do to stop it now, so she just kept working.

Perched in a second-story window, Gabriella, five, pulled back the drapes and peered down at her working siblings with a sense of wonder and satisfaction. She wore a beautiful floral dress lined with lace, and played with a profusion of toys laid out on her tea table. Her lavishly decorated bedroom had gold wallpaper with pink-and-pearl ribbon striping and oak chair rail molding set halfway up the wall. A queen-size canopy bed topped with a fluffy pink quilt and dozens of teddy bears and porcelain dolls dominated the room, and her walk-in closet was stocked with hundreds of new dresses. It was pure extravagance. She, too, heard the sound of thrashing coming from the attic, yet remained unfazed. She gobbled away at her snacks and drank her lemonade while continuing to watch her brother and sister as they suffered in the heat.

Past Gabriella, through her bedroom door, and down the hallway was an old set of stairs leading to the third-story attic. At the top were two open doors, one to the left and one to the right. The bedroom to the left was Maxwell's. Scarcely furnished and undecorated with plain white walls and no windows, it was in shambles. His twin-bed mattress with no box spring had been thrown off its rusty frame, and all the blankets and sheets had been tossed into a pile on the floor. The only other piece of furniture, an old raggedy unstained wooden dresser, had all its drawers pulled out and the sparse contents heaped into the same pile on the floor.

Across the hallway was an identical bedroom, also undecorated with plain white walls, no windows, and few furnishings. It belonged to Madeline. Claire Jackson was inside, and that day she was on a rampage. Looking for something specific, she furiously tore through her eldest daughter's room like a human-tornado. And just as she had done in Maxwell's room, she smashed everything she touched and tossed it into a pile on the floor.

Claire was a strikingly beautiful woman of thirty-three, trim and curvaceous with porcelain-white skin, high cheekbones, sparkling emerald-green eyes, and platinum-blonde hair parted on the side and pinned perfectly into loose bouncy curls. She always stained her sultry pouty lips a bright crimson-red, and looked frozen in a glamorous 1940s neo-retro time capsule. It wasn't any wonder all the jealous women in town constantly gossiped about the mysterious Claire Jackson and her "disheveled" children. But, remaining true to protocol, not one of them ever dared say anything to her face.

Although Claire was a stay-at-home wife, there was nothing domestic about her appearance while inside her house. On that particularly hot Monday, she wore a pair of high-waist mini-shorts with a red-plaid print, a white chiffon blouse tied just under her breasts, and red high-heel pumps, all expensive. After pulling out the last of Madeline's dresser drawers, she dumped the remaining contents onto the ground and screamed out in pain when one of her long red manicured nails snapped off.

"Ouch!" Claire screamed. "Where is it? There's nothing you can hide from me!"

She stopped her mission of manic destruction and took a moment to regain her composure. She could smell it. After peering around in careful abidance of her markedly alert senses, she turned her head sharply to the right. Her eyes settled on a large black-and-brown teddy bear, two-and-a-half feet tall, sitting in the corner of the bedroom.

She stormed over to the bear and picked it up off the floor, violently ripped open the back seam, jammed her hand inside, then felt around through the stuffing until her eyes widened with anger. She pulled her hand out revealing a pink-and-gold beaded Saint Benedict rosary. Fuming, the pupils of her eyes glowed red and the religious artifact smoldered and ignited flames in her hand.

She ran out of Madeline's bedroom, down the stairs, rounded the hallway past Gabriella's bedroom, and burst through two huge French doors into her own.

The Jacksons had spared no expense on the furnishing of their marital den. The master bedroom was decorated dark and elegantly with black mahogany crown molding and beautiful red-and-gold wallpaper. Despite the feverishly hot temperature raging outside, a large fireplace with a shiny black marble mantel blazed next to an enormous, leopard-fur-covered four-poster bed.

As soon as Claire reached the fireplace, she flung Madeline's rosary into the coals and watched as it disintegrated into crackling flames.

Relieved, she walked to the window, pulled back the drapes, and looked down at Madeline and Maxwell, who were still working in the yard. She had warned them countless times and they knew better than to bring such blasphemous materials into her house. "How dare you defy me again!" Claire seethed, the red glow still in her eyes. "This will not go unpunished!"

She looked up from her children to spot Charles' Salem City Police cruiser coming up the driveway, and smiled wickedly. She hurriedly made her way down the front set of curved stairs to the entry foyer just in time to open the door for him.

Charles, forty, was a clean-shaven, devastatingly handsome black man with a gleaming shaved scalp and piercing black eyes that never looked back at the person standing opposite him. He wore his immaculate police chief's uniform every day, rain or shine, gun, black belt, handcuffs, and all. The row of shiny polished gold buttons adorning his heavyset uniform glistened under the flames of a candlestick chandelier as he stood in the dimly lit entryway.

A perpetually angry man who never liked to be bothered when he first came home from work—really a man who never liked to be bothered at all—Charles was uncontrollably subdued and entranced when it came to his seductively beautiful young wife; he could not resist her.

Claire draped herself around her husband and kissed him passionately. After arousing him, she pulled away and looked disapprovingly to the back door, behind which Madeline and Maxwell were working.

Madeline and Maxwell, hearts pounding loudly as they sensed their father's return, simultaneously stopped working and froze in fear. They knew what was coming.

Charles burst through the back door heading straight for Maxwell, seized him by the back of his hair, and with full force slammed him to the ground. Maxwell clawed at the dirt trying to escape, but Charles ripped him up by the arm, snapping the bone in half as his son let out an agonizing scream; a scream Charles instantly silenced by ferociously smashing Maxwell's face open with his fist, blow after blow, until splashes of blood saturated the ground next to where two of Maxwell's teeth had fallen.

Waiting in the house with the drapes pulled back so she could see, Claire stood in the window motionless, watching the brutal attack. A look of pure pleasure washed over her face.

Madeline threw down her shovel and charged toward her father, who stood over Maxwell ready to continue his assault. "No, stop! Get off him!" she screamed, lunging out to grab at Charles. But it was too late; he turned around and side kicked her with his heavy boots squarely in her ribs, which cracked loudly as her tiny body caved in and she flew backward to the ground unable to breathe.

Claire continued to watch through the window patiently. The moment she saw her daughter collapse in pain the sadistic gratification she loved so much aroused the senses of her body like an aphrodisiac. It had been an entire month since the last beating she ordered had materialized, but she always knew it would only be a matter of time before Madeline disobeyed her again. And for Claire, the days in between had been an agonizing wait full of pent-up desire now proving to be worth every minute. But she never imagined her release would taste so sweet.

Charles, however, was just getting started and eager to finish his duties in a private location. He took Maxwell's broken arm in one hand, grasped Madeline's long hair in the other, and dragged them both facedown through the dirt into the house. He then hurled his children through the kitchen door, slammed it shut behind them, and took off his belt. Claire turned to where they entered.

As the sun set over the gravestones in the cemetery, the white drapes covering the Jacksons' windows glowed a fiery red and the horrific sound of whipping and screaming echoed in the street as the vicious beating of Madeline and Maxwell continued.

3

PRIVATE PARTY

New Orleans, Louisiana
Monday, April 7, 2014 – 2:00 a.m.
Madeline's heart started to race. Gently at first as the initial sensations of anxiety filled her body from top to bottom, and then pounded harder and faster when fight-or-flight reflexes dominated her nervous system and the familiar feeling of lightness in her head penetrated her spine and sickened her stomach. When copious amounts of adrenaline discharged from deep inside her abdomen, it froze her ability to breathe and finally tore her from a ghastly nightmare.

Jolted awake, screaming, drenched in sweat, and frantically sucking air into her lungs, Madeline struggled to regain equilibrium. Panicked by the realism of a dream that had infiltrated her physical body, she couldn't yet remember who or where she was. As the comprehensibility of present-day life washed back into her mind, she sat up in bed and clutched the sterling-silver white crystal Saint Benedict rosary hanging around her neck—a gift for her upcoming thirtieth birthday from the one person who knew she needed it: her closest friend and mentor,

Vodou Priestess Haloise.

Distressed and alarmed by the hellish nightmare she'd just endured, Madeline threw off her luxurious white Egyptian cotton sheets and down comforter, slid open the top drawer of her champagne-finish antique-mirrored nightstand, and pulled out a shiny black Colt .45 semi-automatic handgun. Not a gift; a necessity she never left far out of reach. Disoriented, she looked up at the alarm clock, and realizing the early hour shook her head disappointedly.

Catholic saint and Haitian Vodou protection candles were situated in every corner and lined every shelf, illuminating the bedroom. The soft light from the delicate flames covered everything in the impeccably decorated sanctuary in a warm yellow glow. The only color in the room besides the whites and polished metals was the original exposed red brick wall behind the bed, which extended to the fifteen-foot ceiling. Crucifixes fitted with the Saint Benedict devil-chasing medal, known for its power and protection against the entry of evil, hung over every door including the bathrooms.

Madeline slipped out of her king-size bed wearing light pajama pants and a white tank top as her long wavy hair fell messily around her broad shoulders. With gun in hand, she walked out of her bedroom, down the long candlelit side hall, and into the parlor. After disarming the security system, she unlocked the front door, looked over the balcony into the courtyard below, and checked up and down the open-air hallway. To her relief, she didn't see or hear anything out of the ordinary, just the familiarly loud sounds of the lively New Orleans French Quarter nightlife.

Ever since childhood Madeline had dreaded the inevitable curse of sleep and the nightmares that accompanied it. And although content with the necessity to live alone, she wanted the comfort and protection she felt from the close proximity to the laughter and enjoyment of others living in the Quarter provided. It was never quiet, never stale, and New Orleans police officers constantly patrolled the streets day and night. Which was the exact reason she lived there.

Once satisfied nothing was amiss outside her home Madeline locked the door, rearmed the security system, and walked back down the side hall to the kitchen. The rest of her traditional prewar apartment matched the bedroom in decoration and style, and was also lit by a multitude of twenty-four-hour burning protection candles and adorned with Catholic crucifixes and Vodou artifacts. With high ceilings, brick walls, ornamental French fireplaces, heavy crown molding, and long luxurious drapery with Old World charm, it was a choice piece of real estate immaculately decorated with modern art, large-framed mirrors, and custom-made neutral-toned furnishings.

In the kitchen, Madeline knew exactly what she wanted. It was the same thing she wanted every night—the only source of relief that calmed her nerves and helped her get back to sleep. She opened the freezer, took out a large frosty bottle of Russian vodka, twisted off the cap, lifted it to her lips, and indulged in a long series of seasoned gulps. Afterward, she began her nightly ritual of making a strong drink consisting of three-fourths vodka and some festively colored traditional New Orleans hurricane juices, including passion fruit, orange, lime, simple syrup, and grenadine. She dropped in a few cubes of ice and a blue straw, and then climbed the slender spiral staircase leading to her rooftop deck.

In the French Quarter balconies and decks were the most coveted features of the many townhomes and apartments overlooking the bustling streets below. Tenants adorned their beautiful wrought iron railings with as many flowers and plants as they could hold, as displaying a green thumb in the Quarter was almost as important as a well-developed collection of Mardi Gras beads. Madeline didn't have a green thumb or a balcony, but she did have a spacious rooftop deck with a splashing fountain and resort-style furniture. And she liked it that way—nobody could see up, but she could see down.

From behind the two-foot-high brick enclosure topped with a short iron railing Madeline sat back in her chair gazing out at the downtown skyscrapers and meticulously restored nineteenth-century buildings surrounding her. The second the liquor hit her veins and calmed her rapidly firing nerves, she finally felt free and fantasized about what it would be like to participate in the festivities below.

Now thoroughly enjoying her cocktail in the warm spring air, Madeline couldn't help but remember the excitement she had felt when first arriving in New Orleans five years prior. Due to incomprehensible casualties beyond her control, she'd left medical school in Chicago and finished her doctorate in psychiatry at a private New Orleans university. Soon after graduation, New Orleans State Psychiatric Hospital accepted her application for residency in their children's ward, giving her a clean start and a career and life-changing opportunity. However, as hard as she had worked to get in, her boss, Dr. Harold Fields, constantly reminded her that: "Everything worth having in life comes with disadvantages, and unpleasant sacrifices will always have to be made."

But Dr. Fields' reminder had been late in delivery. Amid the cruel and unfortunate experiences Madeline had endured over the course of her life, it had been engrained long ago that personal sacrifice was the only key to survival.

A rain cloud burst open in the sky overhead and pleasantly sprinkled Madeline in a light shower. Rain in New Orleans was rarely predicted, but rather expected almost daily in the late spring and summer months.

Madeline loved the rain and believed it washed away her emotional baggage and distress. To allow herself to feel the cool water on her neck, she tied her long hair into a loose bun on the top of her head, revealing several black-ink tattoos written in Aramaic and Hebrew script. She had one covering every major scar on her body. The largest extended halfway down her spine, one covered the outside of her right ribs, another traced the line of her left shoulder, and three others were visible on the backside of her right forearm and left and right wrists just below the creases of her palms.

Madeline wished she could sit and relish the rain for as long as the passing storm would allow, but she was drunk again and soon her private rooftop party would fade away into another lost night. Work was now only hours away.

———

Outside Madeline's front door an eccentric woman relentlessly knocked as hard and loudly as she could with her fist. Not receiving a response, she interchanged pounding with incessantly pressing on the buzzer.

Rosette, fifty-five, a heavyset Creole woman with a thick accent, stood waiting impatiently. Born and raised in New Orleans, she had been a member of a highly regarded housekeeping company, that serviced the Uptown elite, for over thirty years. Working in the French Quarter was new to her and a longer drive than she preferred. She didn't much care for wasting her time sitting in rush hour traffic—or waiting for Madeline to come to the door.

"I swear," Rosette said, "if that girl keeps up with this nonsense she can learn to do her laundry herself!" She took out her cell phone and dialed Madeline's number numerous times once again, to no avail.

Inside her bedroom, Madeline continued to sleep while the television and disk-player still on from the night before continued to replay the menu screen of a movie. Combined with her alarm clock, which had been going off for an hour, the loud buzzing and knocking at the door finally forced her out of comatose and into the day. She fumbled for her phone, pulled it out from under her pillow, and looked to see who was calling.

"Great..." Madeline grumbled, reaching out and slamming off the alarm clock, which now read 9:00 a.m.

She sat up in bed severely hung-over and disheveled. The romantic date she'd shared with herself on the deck only hours before had left her painfully debilitated once again. Disappointed in herself, she looked over at the empty bottle of vodka sitting on her nightstand next to her gun and a full bottle of water. "Good job, old girl. Way to kill it," she said, picking up the water and downing it completely in one attempt. Now only wearing a tiny pair of black lace boy shorts, she got out of bed, tied on a black satin robe, and headed to the parlor.

When Madeline sheepishly opened the front door, Rosette, who was unamused by her tardiness, glared back at her with the look of disapproval and irritation. "I see you've had another late night," Rosette said, stepping into the apartment and closing the door.

"Early morning," Madeline replied. It wasn't the first time she was behind schedule, and neither of them expected it to be the last.

Rosette was used to working for the older wealthy put-together women who lived in Uptown and Old Metairie—not for young resident psychiatrists living in the wild French Quarter who couldn't get their life together. Madeline never understood why Rosette tolerated her behavior, but for reasons she would never know, Rosette always came back. Rosette knew Madeline had a pure heart and had worked for her consistently for over two years. She also knew Madeline didn't have any family, at least not any she'd heard of. Madeline never talked about anything personal. Plus, Rosette was a woman who'd spent her entire adulthood working in the private residences of her employers; she knew when to ask questions, and when to remain silent and observe strategically.

However, even with all of Madeline's shortcomings Rosette adored her. Having only sons herself, five to be exact, Rosette had always longed for a daughter and felt a loving responsibility for Madeline. Rosette wanted to provide Madeline with some sort of outside support, because despite Madeline's age and intelligence, she was uniquely childlike when in the safety of her home. Also, she paid well and didn't have a bunch of messy spoiled children to navigate around. Rosette could work a whole day in a peaceful environment and then go home early to her sick husband. Still, she always wondered how a young single woman could make such a mess in only three days, especially when she cleaned every Monday and Friday. But that was Madeline, and after a childhood of violent domestic-slavery, housework was no longer on her agenda.

While Madeline sat at the kitchen table reviewing a stack of patient files and nursing her excruciating headache, Rosette walked over, poured them both some coffee, and sat down beside her. "Listen, my dear," Rosette said, "I understand you're going through a hard time in your life. Even though you never talk about it, your lifestyle speaks more clearly than your words ever could, and I don't know how much longer you can go on living like this."

Madeline looked up surprised, feeling ambushed by Rosette's uncharacteristic intrusion. "You have no idea what I'm going through, Rosette," she said, embarrassed. "Nobody does. I'm a grown woman and the last thing I need or want right now is a lecture from you."

"Maybe not, but the road I see you going down is dark and it's dangerous, and a woman in your position surely knows better. All I can say right now, is you're lucky people don't know what goes on behind these doors."

"Not necessarily."

Madeline stood in her large walk-in shower under the hot and steamy water; it felt invigorating as it ran over her toned body loosening her muscles and recharging the morning. Aside from her recent drinking binges, she'd always maintained healthy eating habits, which wasn't easy to do in a city where the abundance of decadent food and strong drink was the top attraction. But Madeline never went out, and she wasn't a party girl—she only drank at home alone.

While brushing out her hair, Madeline started to struggle with a thick knot in the spot hanging over her breasts. It quickly became a stressful means of frustration and her mood took an instant shift for the worse. She yanked furiously at the knot as her heart beat faster and her breathing increased in intensity, brushing so hard she scratched her skin deeply as she ripped the comb through her hair.

"Matted rat's nest!" she cried, as clumps of hair collected in the drain.

After finishing her shower, Madeline stood in front of the mirror in a plush white robe. She wiped the condensation off the glass and stared intently into the reflection of her big dark-brown eyes and soft narrow features, breathing deeply as she calmed down. Ethnic hair care and curl straightening products lined the sink, as well as several bottles of prescription pills.

While combing her hair into her signature tight bun, Madeline noticed a light stream of blood slowly trickle from her hairline; she dropped the comb and quickly wiped it away with a white hand towel. Several more streams of blood promptly appeared and dripped profusely from her forehead, splashing onto the white limestone countertops. Her heart pounded loudly, and her vision started to blur as she frantically attempted to stop the now-gushing blood from saturating her face, body, and robe. As panic turned to low-toned petrified screams, she ripped off the robe, threw it onto the floor with the bloody hand towel, and ran out of the bathroom.

The towel and robe lying on the floor were, in reality, completely clean without a single trace of blood.

4

MODERN ASYLUM

Late again, Madeline was still reeling from the effects of her bloody hallucination. She veered her black Mercedes Benz ML350 SUV into the parking lot of New Orleans State Psychiatric Hospital screeching to a halt. But the instant she put the car into park she regained control of her emotions and switched to a face of impenetrable professionalism. Her job was her life, and despite the personal torment she suffered when alone, her patients took top priority when she was inside the NOSPH compound.

New Orleans State Psychiatric Hospital—NOSPH—was the country's newest and most controversial mental health research facility, built with government funding after the last major hurricane hit Louisiana. Intelligence-classified and heavily protected, it was the most coveted hospital for new psychiatrists to obtain a residency in the United States, and the most prestigious. Since its inception, management only included the oldest and wealthiest psychiatrists and physicians in New Orleans. And because the members of administration all shared aristocratic ties, they were easy to control because they spent most of their time controlling themselves. Old Southern money and old Southern doctors were synonymous.

However, because NOSPH was a government research satellite, its recruiters only sought the most exceptionally trained and influential young doctors in America. The purpose of management was to ensure funding continued to pool in, and verifiable results continued to pump out. The South may have run NOSPH, but the money came from Washington, D.C.

Long gone were the days of the gothic insane asylums constructed in the 1800s under the Kirkbride Plan. Originally built with the "intentions" of improving inpatient quality of life, the resulting medical care actually provided within the gigantic long-winged monstrosities was the opposite. The mentally ill were treated like animals, and the asylums became an evil playground where doctors and staff grossly abused the unrestricted power they held over their helpless patients. Overrun with torture, neglect, chastening punishments, and inhumane scientific experiments ending in premature deaths, most of the "haunted" Victorian-era institutions were eventually abandoned, condemned, or demolished.

After centuries of scrutiny, the modern mental health system gradually rebuilt its facilities and reputation, regaining the trust of society. Psychiatric care hospitals began to petition the government for the best technological advancements available and opened locations in some of the most beautiful parts of the country. With the unsavory realities of the business carefully hidden once again under new policies, the general field of inpatient psychiatry became an ideal career path to secure employment.

But a new hospital with high-tech medical equipment and generous funding wasn't the reason Dr. Madeline Knight came to NOSPH. She was an undercover Psychiatric Exorcist with an unconditionally-singular focus expressed through pure determination, and NOSPH was the best environment to conduct her own research in an undetected, discreet manner.

She grabbed her briefcase of patient files and the full-size black Prada backpack she kept filled with personal belongings and sundries, and headed in to begin another long day.

Protocol for entering NOSPH was like checking into a prison, and the rules applied without fail to both visitors and employees alike. Everyday Madeline had to submit to a tedious security check. If personnel didn't enter through the emergency medical hospital on the first floor, which had keyed elevator access to the doctors' offices in case of a patient or staff injury, they went through main security. Additionally, every employee, patient, and visitor also had to pass through a second individual security station outside each specialty ward.

Madeline wore a white doctor's coat over a particularly ill-fitting heather-gray pantsuit and a white button-up shirt fastened at the wrists. She simultaneously slid her access card outside the glass doorway to the children's ward as the security attendant buzzed her in. Through the first door and past the security station and lobby was another door leading into the nurses' station.

The nurses' station was the central hub serving as a liaison between the patient housing section to the left and the private doctors' offices to the right. Mounted in every corner including hallways and break rooms were cameras with 360-degree views visible from the multi-screen surveillance panels in both the security and nurses' stations. The only areas without video monitoring devices were restrooms, patient sleeping quarters, and the doctors' private offices.

When Madeline entered the nurses' station, head nurse Sherrie Monroe speedily met her at the door.

Nurse Monroe, in her own mind, was the undisputed definition of a modern Southern belle with New Orleans flair. She was thirty-six and looked every bit of it, and her years of endless hours spent in tanning salons gave her heavily foundation-covered face, which was always one shade lighter than appropriate, a slightly older appearance. Her hair was always dyed a perfect shade of yellow-hay blonde—Old Metairie girls never bleached—and cut just below shoulder length. But the color of her lipstick changed daily to whatever was new and trendy in her latest issue of *Southern Glamour Magazine,* and her thick black eyeliner was omnipresent.

It was Nurse Monroe's breasts, however, that were her most appealing, well-known feature. Even with her petite small-framed body, they were soft, large, and completely real; a full D-cup and she wanted everyone to know it. Hence, she always wore her uniform with the neckline cut just a little too low. Plus, she was a charlatan-daddy's-girl always taken care of financially to a minimum point that, despite her ability to achieve her nursing degree, she found herself forever stuck in the past days of her youth. Never fully embracing the responsibilities of adulthood, she was a perpetual teenager with a full-time job—as required by her father—and constantly on the lookout for a husband.

Nurse Monroe's father was the president of South State Medical Board, which had final say on anything medically related in the state of Louisiana. Therefore, despite Nurse Monroe's daily appearance and reputation for entitlement and unsavory behavior, it wasn't surprising to anyone she'd secured the position she had. But her blatant disdain for Madeline was nothing short of apparent, and everyone, including Madeline herself, was well aware of it.

"Miss Knight," Nurse Monroe said smugly, handing Madeline a stack of files, "we were expecting you over an hour ago. Here are your charts for this morning's rounds and a list of new patients admitted from the evaluation wing." She leaned in and noticeably sniffed Madeline, who still smelled of alcohol, and made a sour face toward the other nurses, who quietly smirked while watching what was known to be a regular morning exchange.

Without responding, Madeline took the paperwork out of Nurse Monroe's hand and quietly walked away past the other five all-female nurses who refused to acknowledge her presence formally. As soon as Madeline walked into the doctors' wing and the door closed behind her, Nurse Monroe walked over and started gossiping with the others.

———

Outside a patient recovery and confinement room, two of the

psych techs Madeline worked with closely on a daily basis, Ross and Jack Lee, walked toward her both smiling warmly. Whereas Madeline struggled to establish positive working relationships with the nurses, she excelled with the techs and aides.

Ross, fifty, was a large African-American man with kind eyes and a full gray beard he kept tightly groomed. He looked more like a bouncer than the quick-to-act caring psych tech he was, but his profession wasn't just a job, it was a calling. His mother, an old New Orleans Voodoo priestess, had been unjustly committed for life to a state psychiatric hospital when he was twelve. The disturbing negative environment he'd witnessed during the few visits allotted each year to see her propelled him into a career in psychiatry that would give him firsthand control over inpatient quality of life. And the children's ward at NOSPH was the location he thought he would have the greatest impact. He and Madeline had only become friends in the past year, but had always shared similar ideas about patient care.

Then there was Jack Lee, thirty-nine, gorgeous, cool. He was just under six feet tall with a robust muscular build, long wavy dark-brown hair slicked behind his ears, brown eyes, cream skin, and a chiseled face with a strong square chin. He always wore a silver Saint Benedict medal under his scrubs on a chain around his neck and had full-sleeve tattoos. Jack Lee's tattoos were pure creations of sophisticated body art—meticulously shaded black-ink images of wild animals, American Indian symbols, a wooden cross, and a solar-white dragon; all masterfully floating inside perfectly constructed thick black tribal lines, and always visible because of the way he rolled up his sleeves displaying toned forearms.

It wasn't Nurse Monroe's childish high school behavior that made Madeline, a self-sufficient intelligent doctor, feel like a geeky girl of sixteen; it was Jack Lee. He was "The South's Most Talked About Man," and undisputed King—a predominant modern New Orleans legend and everyone knew about him. Including Madeline. Her energy had always been strongly drawn to him, and she felt an unusual closeness seemingly derived from a Heavenly dream. But she kept her distance—her past was littered with secrets surely to offend a man of Jack Lee's inalienable stature.

Turn away, quick, Madeline thought as he approached, *before he sees you staring at his muscular body and broad chest. Stop it, Madeline! You're lusting over your psych tech. Stop it right now—it's unprofessional!* But there was only one-way for Madeline to describe Jack Lee: bad-boy dreamy. And she was careful to hide her feelings for him well.

Born in Louisville, Kentucky, to the wealthy elite, Jack Lee had been a psych tech at NOSPH for the past three years, and his current choice of profession confused all who knew him. He was a gifted sportsman within the international equestrian and fencing federations, and had been since his elementary academic years spent in private Catholic schools. Combined with a Catholic-Jesuit and Baptist higher education resulting in a Master's in Religious Education and a Doctorate in Philosophy and Theology, he could have had his choice of any career he wanted and quickly escalated to the top of the Pyramid of Power.

But Jack Lee didn't measure the worth of his accomplishments by social status or the size of his bank accounts. He held a deeply rooted self-realization of his Holy significance, and even as a child and professional scholar his teachers and professors had always encouraged his canonical call to the service of God; Jack Lee's true identity was a publicly known fact, especially in New Orleans and Louisville, where his namesake was widely considered and contemplated, yet never contested.

Jack Lee was an anomaly—he appeared stoic and unapproachable on the outside, yet was innately calm and observant on the inside. Those intrigued by his genealogy, reputation, and alternatively-striking appearance found themselves only bystanders, as Jack Lee, currently unwaveringly single, kept his private life untouchable. But, he was a teacher by nature, and his presence was strongly recognized in whatever space he occupied. He was like the Ether—permeating through, inside, and around the elements he encountered, yet undetectable to the naked eye.

However, the singular commitment immovably fixated within the purview of Jack Lee's own eyes, was and always would be, Madeline Knight.

"Morning, Dr. Knight," Ross said, handing her some paperwork. "Gotcha some incident reports from the graveyard shift. And what an active shift it was!"

"Good morning, Ross, Jack Lee," Madeline said, all business. "How's our boy Christian doing today?" She took the reports from Ross and peered into the room where Christian Peters, nine, was calmly sleeping.

"As good as you might expect, considering," Jack Lee answered. "They brought him in early this morning. He's not talking, but he's lucid."

"Okay," Madeline said, "I'm going to do a preliminary examination and then I have a conference call with Administrator Hamilton to determine placement."

"Placement?" Ross asked, surprised. "Where's he being sent? I figured he would be in our hands for at least a couple of months."

"You know how it goes. I have to prove he's a test case before I can get an approval. If I don't, he goes to a group home after recovery. I'll update you later this afternoon."

Madeline's office was executively furnished and, as an extension of her home, was also adorned with religious artifacts. It had a large comfortable leather couch with sleeping pillows and a blanket draped over the side. Two palm trees in planters sat in the corners, and there was a large armoire with clothing and additional personal items to the right of the door.

She spent most of her free time in her office and had decorated it accordingly to suit her frequent overnight stays, which were permitted because patients never went into the psychiatrists' offices at inpatient institutions. Instead, doctors tended to their patients either in a medical examination room or in a child-friendly playroom where the doctors could have nonthreatening activity-based sessions and view family visits through a two-way mirror.

A big window behind Madeline's desk provided a panoramic view of the beautifully landscaped grounds of the interior courtyard gardens where nurses and techs managed the outdoor therapy for patients of all ages and conditions. Some patients sat alone and gazed at the same spot for hours, some participated in group activities like playtime, yoga, or gardening, and others required physical assistance to simply walk around and enjoy the healing qualities of the sun.

Madeline sat at her desk diligently filling out Christian's examination report and waiting for her 2:00 p.m. conference call with Administrator Hamilton to ring through.

Dr. Florence Hamilton, forty-seven, was not a fan of Madeline; she ran a tight, orderly, disciplined program in strict accordance with the rules and regulations set forth by the board. She had no interest whatsoever in renegade methodology, and if she had to fight to receive additional funding for a cause, she promptly dismissed the request in favor of avoiding a rift. Her official job description was Chief Administrator of Patient Health and Finance, but she was stationed at NOSPH for one reason—to maintain aristocratic order.

Her husband, Walker Hamilton III, eighty-seven, was a billionaire real estate trust magnate who owned half of New Orleans, including the Walker Hamilton Country Club, which channeled, controlled, and sifted through anyone hoping to join or remain in New Orleans high society. He was a conundrum: one of the most loved, reputable, and humanitarian philanthropists in the city, yet true old money born of the founders of the South.

Contrarily, while Administrator Hamilton was born with a genius brain and a breakneck wit, she was also born to a poor white family in the backwater Louisiana swamps. Her ability to graduate from medical school and rise to the top of the social register was the miraculous result of her marriage at age sixteen to the man forty years her senior. And her ultimate goal of erasing her noticeably less-refined genealogy was achieved by decades of cosmetic surgeries combined with the luxuries of extreme wealth, resulting in her infamous doll-like beauty.

However, even with her strained dedication to perfecting a refined Southern ladies' vocal style, mannerisms, and etiquette, the remnants of her native tongue still seeped through every so often when she found herself in distress.

Dreading the call but eager to argue successfully to retain Christian as a patient, Madeline hastily answered the phone when it rang. "Good afternoon, this is Dr. Madeline Knight."

"This is Dr. Hamilton," Administrator Hamilton said in a thick sophisticated Southern accent. "I have on my desk paperwork requiring a signature to admit a Christian Peters, transferred last night for evaluation. Is this recommendation a request from the Family Services office?"

"No, Dr. Hamilton, it's a request from me. He's a nine-year-old patient of mine who is currently recovering from anal reconstructive surgery and multiple life-threatening skull fractures."

"I'm not sure why I have to remind you of this again, but you know perfectly well we don't admit patients to this facility based strictly on abuse-related injuries. This does not fall under our jurisdiction and I will not waste precious taxpayer dollars to pay for it. Now, I want a report showing his ability to function in a group environment on my desk first thing in the morning. Is that understood?"

"I did a thorough psychiatric examination of him this morning and based on my evaluation, he most certainly does fall under our jurisdiction. General housing simply won't do."

"Resident Knight, this is a long-term psychiatric hospital for children with diagnosed disorders, not a rehabilitation center for children of dysfunctional families. It's not where he belongs."

"I'm sorry, Dr. Hamilton, but based on the nature and history of abuse by his father, I feel this is exactly where he belongs. I respect your opinion as administrator, but I'm confident Dr. Fields will back my recommendation and provide a federal referral in his name."

"Well, I suggest you get that referral to me before the end of the day, Resident Knight. Good day." She hung up before Madeline had the chance to thank her.

The phone immediately rang again. "Hello, this is Dr. Madeline Knight."

It was her boss, Dr. Harold Fields. "Madeline," he said. "Come over to my office ASAP!" He hung up before she had a chance to respond.

Madeline was alarmed. She hadn't mentioned her preliminary diagnosis of the Peters case to him yet so that couldn't have been what he wanted to discuss, and she knew it. Regardless, her behavior over the past few months indicated that whatever it was, it wasn't going to be good. She had worked under Dr. Fields for three years and he had already extended her plenty of clemency during that time. Something in his tone warned her this was going to be different.

Madeline knocked on the door to Dr. Harold Fields' office and entered without invitation. Dr. Fields, fifty-nine, was six feet tall, clean cut, and handsome. He had a thick head of silver hair perfectly feathered-back and lightly sprayed, pale-white skin, and regal, pronounced aristocratic features. He had meticulously preserved his looks throughout the years with his usual "members only" clubhouse athletic excursions, but the bitter effects of stress had left him slightly weathered. And his nasty and expensive divorce from Dr. Angelica Fields had left their private practice liquidated.

Initially an adult psychiatrist, after his divorce Dr. Fields rebuilt his entire career around becoming one of the top authorities in the country on child psychiatry. After years of dedication to repairing what he thought his ex-wife had destroyed, South State Medical

Board made an unexpected decision to name him Chief of Child and Adolescent Psychiatry at NOSPH. A position that afforded him maximum perks with minimal effort. He reveled in his new station of authority and intended to show his ex-wife up with an even younger new wife and the international recognition to go with it. And Madeline Knight was the exact breed and flavor he was looking for.

Sitting at his desk with a frustrated look when she walked through the door, his eyes brightened the instant he saw her. There was always the thick air of sexual tension accompanying his interactions with Madeline, but she was careful never to reciprocate.

"Madeline, come in," Dr. Fields said. "That's an interesting suit, certainly leaves everything to the imagination." He looked her up and down still satisfied with what he saw. "Anyway, I've never been one to beat around the bush, so let's just get right to it." Madeline apprehensively stepped further into the room. "Certain, shall we say, accusations, attacking both your work and personal life have been brought to my attention."

"What a surprise," Madeline said. "I thought it was our patients' care that was top priority around here, not the incessant ramblings of certain hospital staff. You accepted my residency because I was top of my class, not most popular. I'm sure—."

"Stop talking," he said, cutting her off by closing his hand together mimicking a mouth. "That's not what this is about, and you know it. It's been three years of this behavior and I can only turn a blind eye so many times, which when it comes to you, I usually do. However, at this point, your job is unofficially on the line. Why don't you close the door and sit down?"

Madeline changed her tone and closed the door, then quietly walked over to his desk and took a seat. She knew exactly where this hearing was going. "Everything is completely under control," she said. "You have nothing to worry about. I only have a year left to prove my research findings so I can actually make a difference with these kids and I fully intend on completing them."

Dr. Fields stood up from his desk and slowly walked over to where Madeline was sitting. She shivered wincingly as he inched closer to her chair, his perverted energy encroaching as it violated her space. She could smell his cologne. It gave her a headache. It smelled profusely like the cheap aftershave her father used to wear. Still mildly hung-over from the previous night, the scent churned her stomach and made her nauseous. She kept her eyes pointed straight-ahead when he stopped behind her chair and suggestively rested his hands on her shoulders.

"If you play your cards right with me," he said, "you won't have any problems with that. Have you given any thought to my proposition?"

"Probably not in the way you intended."

"Hmm . . ." he said, pausing. "I spoke with Dr. Garrison last week. You've been skipping your mandatory treatment sessions. Being as his office is only two floors up, it shouldn't be tremendously difficult for you to find."

"I appreciate his help, but I think twice-a-week is a little much."

"Not considering your background." Dr. Fields smiled softly, took his hands off her shoulders, and walked back over to his desk. After sitting back down, he picked up a thick folder and tossed it to Madeline.

"Who's this?" she asked, relieved the subject was about to change to a topic not involving her personal life.

"A new patient coming in on Wednesday—Administrator Hamilton instructed me to handle it myself, but I told her I thought it would be right up your alley. If you think you can handle it?"

"What are the details?"

"Go over the file," he said sharply. "You'll find the two of you have a lot in common. I had to bypass the higher authorities to hand this to you, so don't screw it up. But if you do, well, there are always other career alternatives."

"Such as?" Madeline asked, looking up at him and waiting for the drawback.

It was the moment he'd been preparing her for. He hadn't called her into his office because he cared about her work performance or the therapy sessions she'd been skipping. Those were just cheap tactics he used to put her on the defense before asking for what he really wanted.

"Fascinating you should ask," he said. "As you know, the annual Future of Child Psychiatry Committee's conference is in New Orleans this week. I'll be out of the office most of the time giving lectures and meeting with distinguished doctors from around the world. I've been asked to give the keynote address at Thursday night's gala, and I would love for you to accompany me—not as a member of my staff, but as my date. This benefit is going to mean major exposure for our entire department, and I want you there beside me."

Madeline was speechless; he had sneakily slipped this one in knowing her arms were down. He'd been propositioning her in one way or another since the first time he interviewed her for her residency. But even though his lascivious behavior was getting more frequent and taking on a more serious tone, she usually just laughed it off and changed the subject knowing how to play his game. She'd expected a hearty verbal assault for her missed therapy sessions and chronic tardiness when he called her into his office, not a request for a public date.

"Harry…" she said nervously. "I don't know. I'm not sure I'm ready for something like that. What would people think? They say enough already. I mean, I'll be there of course, the whole staff will be. But I just can't say in what capacity."

"Well, perhaps you'll figure that out by then," he said coldly.

"If we're through here, I need to make my afternoon rounds." Madeline rose and started toward the door.

Dr. Fields stood up and called after her scornfully. "Dr. Knight! What you do or don't do when you're not in my facility is none of my concern. When you reek of it when you are, it becomes not only my concern but my problem as well. Be at your session tonight. Are we clear?"

"Perfectly."

5

THE SANDS

A petite young woman dressed in a floral linen robe over hospital pajamas stood in her room staring vacantly out the window. She had tight curly black hair cut into a short pixie, piercing dark-green eyes, thin bow-shaped lips, a perfectly shaped nose, and light caramel-brown skin now deficient of pigmentation. Her disposition lacked maturity and poise and her tiny underdeveloped build appeared childlike, however the slightest sign of age was apparent on her face and she was void of any emotion.

The walls of the room were constructed of large light-gray concrete blocks and looked as cold and dreary as the rainy Midwestern weather outside. A twin bed with a metal headboard was to the left of the window facing the door, neatly made with a white sheet folded over a dark-gray wool blanket and a single white pillow.

An old burnt-orange leather suitcase covered with stickers from the cities of the world lay open on the bed, although the young woman had never visited any of those places. Inside the suitcase were a few articles of clothing, undergarments, socks, and one pair of shoes. There was a small desk and wooden chair bolted to the floor on the right side of the window with dozens of black-and-white journal notebooks stacked neatly on top of it next to a pile of drawings.

"It's time," a nurse said, coming through the door accompanied by a psych tech who carried a pair of padded handcuffs. The young woman turned around slowly, walked over to the nurse, and calmly held out her delicate hands.

The trio then walked down a long hallway corridor with black-and-white checkered flooring and mind-numbing florescent lights. They proceeded through a security station and entered an elevator on the other side. When the elevator door opened on the first floor, they were greeted by two armed bailiffs in crisp olive-green uniforms. The bailiffs took the young woman into custody, escorted her into a State of Illinois mental health court, and sat her in front of a panel of several psychiatric doctors, social workers, and a judge.

The room was silent as the judge flipped through the stacks of paperwork each doctor individually handed to him. It felt like hours before he cleared his throat and addressed the young woman in handcuffs who sat quietly before him.

"Gabriella Jackson, twenty-five years old," he said. "You were remanded to this psychiatric hospital five years ago and are here today to discuss the terms of your release. Due to your recurrent hallucinations, combative behavior, and complete disregard for superior rules and regulations, it would be my recommendation, as was recommended by your attending physicians, that your stay here be extended indefinitely. Despite that disturbing fact, forces greater than myself have negotiated your immediate release. Therefore, you are free to go. I pray God watches over your soul."

He pounded down hard with his gavel to seal what was for Gabriella a long-awaited judgement. The doctors who had protested her release cringed in their seats when a bailiff removed her handcuffs and she smiled victoriously.

———

Madeline sat patiently in the lobby outside the office of Dr. Arthur

Garrison, M.D./PhD. She was deep in thought considering the possible repercussions attached to refusing Dr. Fields' invitation to the gala. She had no intention of going with him. Apart from being absolutely repulsed by the idea to begin with, she already had enough trouble with the bevy of female nurses who already hated her and resented working under a younger woman. Publicly flaunting at the gala what they would surely perceive as a sexual relationship with their boss would only escalate their contempt.

Many women at NOSPH and throughout New Orleans society in general considered Dr. Fields to be a top bachelor, and countless had attempted to seduce him after his divorce. Not only was he from excellent pedigree, but his social status alone would catapult even the lowliest ladder-climber to the top of the register. His ex-wife was a younger, beautiful, well-known psychiatrist, and a born-and-raised New Orleans medical socialite. And nobody wanted to replace Dr. Angelica Fields more than Nurse Sherrie Monroe, whom Angelica had gone to school with and known most of her life.

However, to Nurse Monroe's disappointment and disgust, it was Madeline, not she, who was to be Dr. Fields' coveted prize. A fact known to all who'd witnessed the obsessively flamboyant affection he showed to Madeline, which he made no particular effort to hide. He regularly overlooked her frequently occurring and widely reported "inadequacies," and blatantly showered her with compliments at every opportunity. But only in public— privately, he liked to keep her on guard and under his control.

Administrator Hamilton had warned Dr. Fields about his behavior multiple times, which he had impolitely disregarded; as far as he was concerned, he was his own boss and Administrator Hamilton was a figurehead who wore her title by default.

It was getting late, and after a long and tedious workday Madeline was ready to go home. She had managed to avoid three weeks of her therapy sessions without reprimand, and wasn't looking forward to a forced return.

To maintain anonymity, she always made her appointments for

the last hour on Dr. Garrison's schedule, and his floor was empty save a janitor and administrative secretary closing down for the day. Contrary to Dr. Fields' earlier statement, Dr. Garrison's office wasn't only two floors up; it was across the emergency entrance driveway in an adjoining wing with minimal security on the sixth floor, while Dr. Fields' and Madeline's office was on the fourth. And aside from both departments sharing the same janitorial team, they had absolutely nothing in common.

Dr. Garrison's division consisted of psychiatrists who handled outpatient adult psychotherapy cases mandated by the state. His patients included anything from officers of the law required to use their weapons in the line of duty, to state employees avoiding legal action for disciplinary offenses. And then there was Madeline.

Dr. Fields had informed Madeline upon hire that she was required to undergo therapy because he believed all psychiatrists needed to take advantage of the mental health resources available to them. And that usually the reason new psychiatrists initially chose to enter the field was because of a personal or family history of mental illness or abuse. Being a man of incredible psychoanalytic ability, Dr. Fields had easily recognized such traits in Madeline and had given her no choice in the matter.

She had been seeing Dr. Garrison monthly since her residency began, but had since been required to see him twice-a-week for the past six months, and wasn't particularly keen on the arrangement. She didn't want anyone knowing about her past and took creative measures to hide the truth about it. Nevertheless, clever psychiatrists have a way of getting even their most stubborn patients to talk, and Dr. Garrison was no exception.

"Hello, Madeline," Dr. Garrison said, startling her. "Sorry to keep you waiting. Come on in."

Madeline stood up and walked into his office without speaking. He closed the door, took a seat in a large brown leather wingback chair, and kicked his feet up on the matching ottoman in front of it. Madeline made her way to a long mustard-colored suede sofa adjacent to him, and stretched out her legs.

Dr. Garrison was a short plump man in his mid-sixties with pale skin and rosy cheeks. Bald on top with a wreath of bushy gray hair on the sides, he wore a daily uniform of round tortoiseshell glasses and a multi-colored argyle sweater-vest. His office was scholarly and traditional with dark cherry wood paneled walls and rows of shelves filled with medical, psychological, and theological books he often suggested for home reading. Behind his large antique glass-topped oak desk and leather swivel chair was a window covered with heavy twill drapes he kept closed during all sessions to create a dark library-den effect. He was a simple man who had no plans for retirement as long as his health and patience allowed him to continue with his practice.

"It's been a long time, young lady," he said. "I'm not usually accustomed to placing calls to my patients' supervisors, but you left me no alternative."

"Well," Madeline replied, "I'm sure Dr. Fields enjoyed the opportunity to solicit you for information about my progress, so, no harm done."

"You need to return my calls, Madeline. These are still mandatory sessions and you need to stay in compliance. I'm here to help you. And you know perfectly well this is all confidential. How have you been feeling lately?"

"Pretty much the same, I guess."

"Any side effects from the new dosage?"

"No. I transitioned fine."

"Did you transition, or have you decided to supplement with other methods of self-medication?"

"I'm taking my meds." She hadn't taken her medication since the last time she saw him. It wasn't helping anyway. It was making her symptoms worse.

Dr. Garrison decided to switch topics. Madeline's medication had always been an uncomfortable subject and he didn't want to continue to pry about it if he expected to make some degree of progress. "When we left off last time," he said, "you had begun to tell me about a series of recurrent nightmares from your childhood."

Madeline felt the anxiety surging up in the back of her neck. This was the line of questioning she knew he would push, which she'd been dreading. They weren't only nightmares from her childhood; they had been plaguing her every night of her life as long as she could remember and increasing in severity over the past six months.

"Yes," she said apprehensively, "the nightmares where I was trapped in Hell—with his presence pulling me toward him, night after night."

"Who was pulling you toward him, Madeline?"

"Satan."

Dr. Garrison sat up slightly in his chair. Madeline had mentioned experiences involving "Satan" during her last appointment; however, he had concluded her portrayal must have been a religious superstition or perhaps based on imagery she was using to suppress horrific memories she was unable to explain. He knew they were making headway and wasn't surprised when he didn't see her again for their next session, and had intentionally given her space before calling her back in.

"How did you know it was Satan?" he asked.

"I can't explain it; it's something you just know."

"I need you to try, Madeline. Can you describe the dream for me?"

Madeline's muscles tensed, and her chest tightened. A warm flush washed over her body, it became harder to breathe, and a familiar sense of fright began to take over. "It's like being engulfed in a sandstorm," she began. "There's sand swirling all around stinging your face and burning your eyes, and never-ending dunes blending in with the sky. There is no sky! You search for the exit, but there's no way out . . . and you can't feel or see anything . . . except fear . . . and him!"

"What is the worst dream you can remember? How old were you?"

The contents of Madeline's memory she'd desperately tried to hide and forget fully resurfaced and the words poured uncontrollably from her mouth. "I was eight," she said, her tone rising from a whisper to a cry. "When I woke up, I was lingering somewhere between the dream world and reality. It was like I was stuck inside my wall, paralyzed. The Sands were all around me, but I somehow knew I was still in my bedroom—I could see the other side. My body was completely inverted upside-down against the wall. I was kicking and screaming trying to escape and get back into my bed, begging for my mother to help! But she was just standing there in the doorway, staring at me!"

"What about your father, Madeline? Did anyone else in the house see what was happening to you?"

Madeline lay quietly for a moment, remembering. "Yes. My sister, Gabriella, she was there too. She just stood there in the doorway next to our mother. Neither of them did anything. They just lingered there, expressionless, just staring at me!"

———————

As Madeline walked to her car, her depressive state plummeted further than before. Every time she submitted to a session with Dr. Garrison, she found herself dangerously exposed. She hated talking about her biological family, but in therapy, it was unavoidable—her history with them had defined the current circumstances of her life. She was sick from the stress and needed to get home as fast as possible, mix a drink, and erase the filth of the day.

Driving home, Madeline couldn't shake the debilitating anxiety she'd felt while explaining the details of her nightmare to Dr. Garrison. She'd never divulged her experiences to anyone outside her family and had an ominous feeling about the consequences of making such an amateur mistake. Lately, the dreams were getting more frightening and vivid in nature, and spilling over into the day. She knew something in her world had shifted yet couldn't decipher what had changed or why. But she knew releasing the details verbally, to a third party, was sure to result in another increase in the magnitude of her dreams' severity.

She turned onto Interstate 10 and headed back to the Quarter. As cars sped by on the congested five-lane freeway, her heart began to pound harder and louder until a painful ringing erupted in her ears and her vision blurred. A massive sandstorm tornado appeared in the road ahead engulfing her car and blinding her view. She couldn't see anything in front or to the sides and checked the rearview mirror but saw nothing except clean glass—not even her own reflection. The cars once occupying the packed freeway had disappeared and a whiteout of never-ending sand blasted her car.

Suddenly the ringing in her ears turned to a grainy screeching howl, her blood pumped excruciatingly through her veins, and she couldn't catch her breath. The form of Satan appeared in the middle of the road ahead, disappeared, and then reappeared blocking her way. She tried to scream and slammed on the brakes as her car approached, but no sound came out and the pedal hit the floor with no reaction. She swerved evasively to avoid the terrifying image in front of her and skidded off the embankment gasping for air.

After the car jerked to a halt, she tucked her chin into her chest and put her arms over her head, sweat dripping from her brow and blood still pulsing. When the screeching subsided she looked up, the Sands had cleared, and the city buildings had reappeared with lights glowing in the night as usual. She found herself turned around on the edge of an off-ramp with cars whipping by once again, honking at her as they passed. She instinctively searched for her emergency flask of vodka, dug it up from deep underneath the passenger seat, took a long hard swig, then got back on the road.

When Madeline arrived at her apartment in the bustling French Quarter, hot tears streamed down her face. *I'm going crazy!* she thought, petrified and shaken. She parked in her reserved space in the lot across the street, looked over, and saw Gabriella standing motionless on the steps to her building with two bags of luggage, just staring at her.

6

THE WARNING

Madeline sat in her car with a death grip on the steering wheel immobilized by shock. Her brain had not yet alerted her body to move, and all she could feel was the sting of tears mixed with sunscreen and the pulsating around her swollen eyes. Confusion saturated her mind and the anxiety dominating her body only moments before had transformed into an overwhelming sense of anger and alarm.

Gabriella continued to stand on the steps waiting nervously, and her lingering uncertainty of what Madeline's reaction to her would be caused her poker-faced expression to change to one of unease. It was 8:00 p.m. and she'd been waiting in front of Madeline's building for hours hoping she hadn't miscalculated and that it was indeed the correct address. And after spending five years living in a controlled environment, the French Quarter had been a scary first-experience back out in the real world. Strange people had come and gone all night asking her for prostitution, money, or drugs; however, the majority were just heavily intoxicated persons creating annoyingly useless havoc.

But despite the fright of the circus surrounding her, Gabriella had never seen anything like New Orleans and had to admit it was a mind-blowing place to wait. All the brightly colored Old-World buildings with gas-flame lanterns and decorated balconies full of people were beyond enchanting. There were endless strings of neon lights and bands playing live music in the streets, which she could see and hear from every direction. Horse-drawn buggies circled the block at least twice an hour soiling the streets and crewed by tour guides who shouted out random historical facts about Voodoo queens and jazz to their fascinated passengers. The scent of fried food and other culinary concoctions permeated from the many restaurants she'd passed along the way with menus written in an English language she didn't understand. And it was all mixed in with a rich selection of elegant townhomes and apartments with lush gardens and waterfall ponds visible through ornate iron gates as she walked by. One of which she was currently standing in front of.

Well, she's obviously done well for herself, Gabriella thought, looking at Madeline's shiny new car. *All her years of hoping, dreaming, and desperate attempts to stay in school must have actually paid off.* But Madeline's finances weren't Gabriella's main concern. She hadn't seen Madeline in over five years and knew her sister most likely wouldn't want anything to do with her, not after what she'd done. Coming to New Orleans was a risk, and she worried her visit could go horribly wrong and she'd be forced to sleep in the very place she stood.

Madeline finally summoned the clarity for confrontation and stormed out of her car, slammed the door, and dashed across the busy one-way street heading straight for her sister. "Gabriella!" she shouted. "What are you doing here? How did you get out of the hospital? You know you're not supposed to be anywhere near me!"

"Calm down!" Gabriella said, surprised; this was not the soft-spoken, loving, and protective sister she remembered. "I had nowhere else to go when they released me. I need your help. Can you please just listen to me for a minute?"

Madeline looked around and noticed a New Orleans Police Department officer in his cruiser eying them from across the street. Hers was one of the more residential sides of the Quarter where citizens of means lived, and the officers usually stationed themselves in the area to ensure visitors didn't bother tenants. New Orleans liked to take care of its natives and he was watching the exchange carefully, ensuring nothing unsavory occurred between the young doctor and the homeless-looking girl on the steps.

Madeline quickly tamed down her demeanor. She didn't want to turn an already sensitive interaction into something volatile; she knew the level and style of antics Gabriella was capable of and a peaceful exchange was not among them.

"Unbelievable!" Madeline said. Gabriella looked so pathetic just standing there even thinner than she remembered and so pale. "Just pick your stuff up and get inside. The last thing I need right now is you making another scene."

Madeline unlocked the barred gates leading into her building and reached for a piece of Gabriella's luggage, attempting to remove the meager belongings from view. When she picked up a black computer bag, Gabriella snatched it back so snappily and hard the shoulder strap gave Madeline a friction-burn on her arm.

"Ouch! What's wrong with you?" Madeline yelled. "Fine, pick it all up yourself, but get moving!"

"I'm sorry!" Gabriella said, picking up the rest of her luggage.

Madeline scanned the street to see if anyone else was watching and then shuffled Gabriella inside.

As they passed through an arched walkway and out into a lush and tropical courtyard, Gabriella was mesmerized. It was like entering a secret garden. The ambiance was overwhelmingly stunning, and everything was draped in palm trees and banana leaves, hibiscus and magnolias, and countless other varietals of flowers and foliage she couldn't even conceive of. The four stories of balconies lining the interior perimeter were lit up like an executive hotel, and the grounds were meticulously manicured and paved with dark-red brick lined with Spanish tiles. On each side were two large rectangular ponds filled with koi fish, and dressed with delicate arches of spraying water illuminated by blue lights.

And the centerpiece highlighting it all was a grand three-layer twelve-foot marble fountain mounted on a brick pedestal in the center of a shallow turquoise pool. It looked like paradise and Gabriella was captivated.

"Gabriella! Let's go," Madeline said, snapping her back to reality. They stepped into a small antique elevator and headed to the fourth floor.

"How do you afford all this, Belle?" Gabriella asked.

"Don't call me that! And it's called work, Gabriella. Something you've never been particularly accustomed to. Not to mention the hefty baggage I dropped five years ago."

"Well, so much for you forgiving and forgetting."

"Yeah, I wouldn't count on that."

Madeline unlocked her front door, disarmed and then rearmed the security system, and then slid three additional surface bolts.

Relieved to be indoors, Gabriella walked into the parlor and tossed her luggage onto the floor as comfortably as if she'd been there a thousand times. But, as she looked around at the generously displayed religious paraphernalia she became unexpectedly uncomfortable. "Looks like you're still as superstitious as ever," she said, walking around the room admiring the fine furnishings and running her fingers over the locks on the door. "And still not taking any chances with security."

Madeline didn't respond. She didn't want any part of whatever it was Gabriella was selling. It wouldn't be worth the cost; it never was. But uncovering Gabriella's motivations would have to wait, at least a few more minutes. Madeline turned away abruptly and walked back to the kitchen. Gabriella trailed behind nervously.

Madeline stopped at a large oak bar cabinet set up between the kitchen and living room, fully stocked with ice, spirits, mixers, and expensive heavy crystal glasses. Without offering anything to Gabriella, she mixed herself a stiff martini, gulped it down, and then immediately prepared another. Her mind was racing, and she needed to slow it down. She felt stifled and couldn't stand to be in the same room with Gabriella any longer. She'd promised herself years ago never to feel sorry for her sister again. *What is Gabriella doing here? I thought I was finally free of her! She seems so nervous and desperate; this can't be good.*

"Look," Madeline said, refusing to look at Gabriella. "I really don't care what you think you have to say to me, but you're not staying here."

"Fine," Gabriella said, "I expected you to say that. I'll leave if you want me to, but not before you at least listen to what I have to say. . . Our parents found me. They called me at the hospital out of nowhere!"

Madeline stopped mixing her drink and listened intently without looking up. She felt instantly sick to her stomach and her bowels tightened. "What do you mean they found you—how?"

"I don't know how. Apparently, anyone can be found. It wasn't exactly easy to find you either, but I did. But that's not all, Belle. They reminded me of the warning and told me this was my last chance to either come back to the family or die!"

"Wait a minute! You want me to believe that after fifteen years they've suddenly decided to come back and carry out the warning they've threatened us with our entire lives? I don't believe you. This is just another one of your tactics to try to weasel your way back into my life and it's not going to work, not this time. You had your chance with me and you blew it. You spit on it! I put you away in a place where you could get the help and protection you needed, but that's it. I was done with you then and I'm done with you now!"

"That's not what this is, Belle, they were serious! I'm scared for our lives here and you should be too. Listen, I've changed. I'm not the same person I used to be. You have to believe that! I'm sorry for everything I put you through in Chicago, that wasn't me, that's not who I am."

"Well, who was it then? You destroyed my life and ruined everything I worked for. I had to leave the state! I changed my name and anything else I could do to erase my past and save the remnants of the life I had left." She walked over to Gabriella and stood right in front of her face. "You have been nothing but trouble since the day you were born so I'm not sure what makes you think I would ever trust you now."

"Because I want to be a family again! I can't continue to live like this—always wondering how or when our parents are going to come back and punish us for what we did to them. . . And I know you still live with the nightmares, because I live with them too!"

"You need to leave." Madeline grasped Gabriella by the arm and dragged her down the side hall and into the parlor.

"Wait! There's something else I have to tell you." Gabriella said, ripping her arm away. "It's about Max."

"Max? What would you know about Max?"

"He's dead, Belle!" Gabriella screamed. "Our brother is dead! Our parents told me he was killed in prison and that if I didn't want to end up like he did then I needed to do exactly what they told me to do."

"What do you mean he's dead?" Madeline asked, becoming hysterical. "You're a liar. You make me sick! You'll try anything to get what you want. You're lying! Now get your bags and get out!" Frantic, she picked up Gabriella's suitcase and headed for the door.

Gabriella reached for her belongings, pleading to change Madeline's mind. "I'm not lying! Why do you think I risked coming here? I know how you feel about me and knew you would tell me to leave. But our parents are coming after us whether you want to accept that or not. I need your help! You're all I have left. Do you remember the last time you saw Max—do you? You left him there in prison all alone with no hope just like you left me five years ago. Now he's dead."

7

CHICAGO

Tuesday, April 8, 2014 – 3:00 a.m.
While Gabriella slept comfortably on the living room couch, Madeline lay awake in her bed with the candles lit and glowing as usual. She'd fallen asleep for a short time only to be jolted awake by another terrorizing nightmare when her alcohol sedation had worn off. Lacking the desire to continue drinking, she was forced to deal with the distressful events and revelations of the day behind her. Grief-stricken, angry, and overcome by regret, she knew that regardless of her feelings about Gabriella she would once again have to assume the role of protector, and contemplated their options.

While reminiscing over a glass-framed photograph of herself and Maxwell, Madeline's agitation only compounded. It was the day of his college graduation and the last photo she'd ever taken with him. She had her arms locked firmly around his waist and they both wore luminous smiles. Maxwell was tall, handsome, and had the strapping muscular build of a quarterback. He and Madeline shared the same light caramel-brown skin and attractive, almost identical features known to all three Jackson children. With Maxwell preparing to enter law school and Madeline a premedical student, they finally thought their horrific past was behind them and that they could finally live the lives they'd always imagined.

Together as children Madeline and Maxwell had survived a rigorously militant lifestyle subject to daily punishments consisting of cruel and unusual methods of abuse. Their father had expected nothing less than perfection, and the likelihood of obtaining excellence in his eyes was an impossible feat. "Sacrifice is the key to service and obedience," was his motto; and sacrifice they did. Living in a world that rejected them by day and in the secret den of devils by night was tolerable only through hope, faith, and resilience. After a miracle disguised as a tragedy forced the immediate removal of all three Jackson children from their parents' household when Madeline was fourteen, they finally had a chance at survival. But having strenuously warned their children never to leave or betray the family, Charles and Claire Jackson, both exposed and humiliated, had vowed revenge.

Unfortunately for Maxwell his freedom had come too late. The torture he'd sustained proved too much to overcome, and he would never attend law school and he would never escape the life of misery inflicted by the parents whose evil had destroyed him. And that hopeful day, smiling with Madeline in his garnet-red cap and gown, would be the last time he ever saw his sister again outside federal prison walls.

As Madeline continued to stare at the picture, Gabriella's words rang over and over in her head: "Do you remember the last time you saw Max?" Of course, she did; she'd tried to forget. The experience had caused a landslide of grief that would torment her for the rest of her life.

Four months after Maxwell's trial and subsequent conviction, Madeline, twenty-three at the time and in her first year of medical school, had gone for her first and final visit. Maxwell had been officially sentenced to two life-terms without the possibility of parole in an Illinois federal penitentiary for a double homicide with special circumstances. If the death penalty hadn't been suspended in Illinois, he would've sat on death row. Instead, he was confined indefinitely to a level one maximum-security prison where most inmates sat in their cells twenty-three-hours-a-day with few exceptions.

But Maxwell wasn't like the other inmates; the warden had kept him away from the general population, and he received a wide variety of superior privileges unheard of for a prisoner of his caliber, including private visits. His cell was secluded in one of the abandoned buildings once used for executions, and that was where he had been the last time Madeline saw him—in a solitary chamber at the end of a locked maze of a dozen old barred prison doors, and down a long damp corridor lined with rancid-smelling empty cells.

Maxwell's confinement and the actions he'd taken to achieve it had been beyond Madeline's comprehension, and the only words she could remember saying to him were: "How could you do it—how?" He gave her the answer to her question that day, and she never went back.

Madeline sat up in bed, pushed the memory of Maxwell's graduation out of her mind, and set the picture on her nightstand. Channeling her aggravation, she sat down at her bedroom desk and began to meticulously disassemble and clean both her black handgun and her matching silver one.

She had never understood the justifications contributing to his special treatment while in prison, but for unspoken reasons the warden had granted Maxwell absolute protection in one of the country's most notoriously dangerous prisons—as long as he followed the rules. And while the notion of untouchable immunity was questionable, Maxwell's untimely death while under it was the most perplexing inconsistency of all.

Madeline had deserted Maxwell and left him all alone just as Gabriella had said, and now figuring out who or what was responsible for his death was the foremost thought on Madeline's mind. If Gabriella was right, and Charles and Claire Jackson were actively planning their demise, the prison where Maxwell died would be the first place to investigate.

After reassembling both guns, Madeline checked and adjusted the sights and simultaneously dry fired the triggers. She then purchased and printed a round-trip plane ticket to Chicago, secured a rental car, and dressed herself warmly. With a packed carry-on bag ready to go, she locked the black gun in her bedroom safe, grabbed her black trench coat, and blew out the candles.

After leaving a note for Gabriella on the kitchen table, Madeline quietly walked down the hall to the front door.

"Where are you going?" Gabriella asked sharply from behind, standing at the other end of the dimly lit hallway. She looked like a ghost in the long white nightgown Madeline had lent her to sleep in.

"I'm catching the first plane to Chicago," Madeline said. "It doesn't make sense what you say happened to Max. The whole point of solitary is protection; I'm going up there to find out what happened."

"What's the point of that? He's dead!"

"I need confirmation," Madeline said, grabbing her keys.

"Well, then I'm coming with you. I can't stay here by myself."

"No, you're not. Staying here is exactly what you're going to do. Trust me, you don't want anything to do with that place. Once you go in you can never wipe it off. Don't tell anyone where you are and don't tell anyone where I'm going."

––––––––

Later that morning, Dr. Fields sat at his desk enjoying a large cup of steaming black coffee as he listened to his voicemail. He was surprised to hear Madeline's voice on one of the messages.

"Harry, it's Madeline; I've got an emergency and won't be able to make it in today. I'm really sorry. I'll be in later this evening to check on my patients. Call my cell if you need me. Bye."

He was not pleased.

––––––––

Madeline stood outside the first set of sliding steel gates leading into the Federal Correctional Penitentiary of Eastern Illinois and clutched her rosary.

Housed inside were some of the most ferocious criminals in the country, all of whom were serving a minimum twenty-year sentence. The wicked energy of miserable hopelessness, ruthless violence, and pure evil radiated through the walls infecting all who came within distance. If someone worked at or resided in "East Pen," as the affiliates called it, was a family member of a prisoner, or lived within a 100-mile radius of the expansive historical prison, they regarded it as "Hell's Limbo."

Mentally transported back to the last time she stood in the exact same spot, Madeline's heart beat rapidly. Six years prior, she had fled the grounds with blood splattered on her face, in a full panic attack, crying and petrified by what she'd witnessed. This time, after the correctional officers invasively processed her through security and led her to the administration offices, she curbed the haunting memories of her past and braced herself for whatever she might encounter.

Irrepressible thoughts of unease, mostly about Gabriella, raced through Madeline's head as she waited outside the office of the security manager. Because the events following Gabriella's arrival had happened so quickly, Madeline hadn't been able to question her thoroughly on the details of her hospital release. The news about Maxwell's death had been so devastating that Madeline couldn't have conceived worrying about something so minor. And she had never seen Gabriella in such a fretful state of emotion; interrogating her further would have been unfeelingly harsh and counterproductive.

The sister Madeline remembered was selfish and cruel; always ready to do what she wanted, when she wanted, with no regard for her actions. The sister Madeline saw the day before was scared and frail, and she worried about having left her alone in New Orleans. But there had been no other option; Madeline had to keep her problems with Gabriella temporarily quarantined while simultaneously dealing with the more pressing ones, and she was confident Gabriella would be safe at the apartment until she returned that night. But, if their parents had found Gabriella while confined to a confidential psychiatric inpatient hospital, Madeline wondered if they already knew where she lived as well.

After a twenty-minute wait, a hard looking, ruggedly attractive man opened the door and walked up to Madeline. He was Japanese-American, six feet tall, and even though his tightly cut gray hair placed him in his fifties, he had a powerful physique and smooth sun-tanned skin.

"Dr. Knight? I'm Gordon Covey, the security manager for the prison," he said in a deep soothing voice. "We spoke earlier this morning regarding your brother, Maxwell Jackson. Come on in." He shook Madeline's hand and led her into his office, closed the door behind them, and pulled out her chair before sitting down across from her at his desk.

"Thank you for taking this meeting; you're a hard man to get ahold of," Madeline said. "I'm here to find out the details about what happened to my brother and collect his personal belongings."

"Well, to start, your brother was stabbed multiple times by another inmate during his transfer from solitary confinement. He was on the schedule for transport to an off-site undisclosed psychiatric unit."

"Why was he being transferred?"

Gordon picked up Maxwell's file already on his desk and opened the medical records section. "Hallucinations, suicidal behavior, and complaints of possession."

"So, why not treat him here?"

"We didn't have the ability to handle a psychiatric case of his magnitude. It was the only option without transferring him out of state. Unfortunately, I can't help you out much as far as belongings go, because he was killed almost five weeks ago. Anything unclaimed after thirty days, including the body, is sent out for disposal."

Madeline hadn't thought Maxwell's death could have hit her any harder, but it just had. Blood rushed to her head and her face turned hot. "Can I see the file?" she asked.

Gordon handed Madeline the file; he felt sorry for her. It wasn't every day a young attractive woman came into his office to collect the belongings of an inmate already sent out to a potter's field. *She looks so young,* he thought, *far too young to be a doctor.*

Madeline flipped quietly through the thick file, carefully scanning every page unsure what she was looking for. When she pulled out Maxwell's visitation log, she was shocked to see her parents had been to the prison multiple times to see him during the past six years. But six months before his death on March 6, 2014, their visits stopped.

"What?" she asked herself quietly. "We swore never to speak to them again—why would he agree to see them?" She turned to Gordon, "You've got to have some sort of surveillance videos showing the stabbing. Can I see them?"

"Dr. Knight, your brother was serving a life sentence for the brutal murders of his own wife and child. Even behind these doors there's an 'inmate's code of conduct.' It was common knowledge he was being transferred out of the facility. Nobody was surprised by his murder; it was a random stabbing."

"Please just show me the videos."

———————

Gordon snuck Madeline into the prison's security surveillance room and locked the door. No one outside his office was allowed inside without proper clearance or a warrant, but he wanted to help if only to provide her with closure. He searched through the media library and recovered the disk recording of the day and time frame of Maxwell's murder.

When he placed the disk into the audio-visual playback system, eight screens with different views powered on, and Madeline watched intently as he tracked forward to the moments before the incident.

Maxwell finally appeared on the screen, and they watched as two armed guards escorted him through the cylinder-shaped general population level in wrist and leg chains and wearing a bright-red jumpsuit with his number on it. Two rows of inmates, also in chains and wearing orange jumpsuits with similar numbers, passed Maxwell going in the opposite direction. Suddenly, an unchained inmate appeared clinging to the side of the central sniper's tower. With superhuman speed, he jumped into the air over the guards, paused mid-flight, and brutally plunged a jagged-edged knife into Maxwell's right side and multiple times in his jugular. Afterward, the murderer vanished faster than he'd appeared, and the guards stood by motionless as chaos among the prisoners erupted, watching as Maxwell convulsed in a pool of his own blood.

"Oh, my God!" Madeline shrieked. "Rewind it and pause on the murderer's face—I want to see who it is!"

Gordon played the video again but couldn't get a clear view of the murderer's face, only his inmate number. He typed the number into the computer and initiated a records search. "That's weird; we have no record of an inmate with that number. And I've never seen him before," he said, thoroughly confused and continuing to search.

Madeline looked in closer at the screen, expertly took over the controls of the sophisticated monitoring device, zoomed in tighter, and switched the main screen view to the camera catching the view from the front. Her eyes widened in horror and she put her hand over her mouth to stop from screaming when she recognized the face of the man who'd slain her brother.

Madeline closed her eyes as dark forgotten memories from her childhood flashed through her mind. She remembered a gigantic man named Stefan, the inmate on the video who'd stabbed her brother, at various stages throughout her life, always with her father. She recalled Stefan riding in the passenger seat of her father's patrol cruiser, sitting next to him during a department dinner party, and posted at his right side while standing at the podium after receiving his coveted police chief's badge.

It's Stefan! Madeline thought. *My parents really did have something to do with this; I never should have left Gabriella at home alone!*

Madeline needed to leave Chicago and get back to New Orleans as soon as possible. Careful not to alarm Gordon or indicate she knew the man on the screen, she gently touched his shoulder. "I have to go," she said. "This has all been very difficult for me and I have a lot to think about. Thank you again for everything you've helped me with."

"I'm sorry I couldn't do more."

"Actually, you can. Would you mind making me a copy of my brother's file?"

Gordon paused; he knew he shouldn't. *This girl is gonna get me into a lot of trouble,* he thought. But, he picked up the file and went out to make her a copy.

Madeline ejected the surveillance disk and slipped it into her jacket.

8

72 HOURS

Back in New Orleans and frightened for Gabriella's life, Madeline bypassed the elevator and raced across the courtyard and up the stairwell to her apartment. The helplessness she felt on the flight back from Chicago had been agonizing, and although she'd called the house multiple times to check on Gabriella, there had been no answer. Already dark, the three flights of stairs seemed endless as every possibility flashed through Madeline's mind, none of which was positive.

The past twenty-four hours had been a constant tug-of-war between Madeline's conflicting emotions regarding Gabriella's return to her life and the death of her brother. After five years of navigating the hardships of the healing process and attempting to rebuild a shattered life, Madeline had finally found strength in the adversities of her past. Now, after only one day, everyone and everything she had so adamantly eradicated from her conscious mind had ricocheted back with striking force.

When she reached her front door, she found it closed but unlocked and the alarm deactivated. She'd left explicit instructions for Gabriella on how to operate the security system, and this discovery only aggravated her level of concern. When she entered the apartment, every room was dark except for a hint of flickering television light coming from the end of the hallway. Witnessing the gruesome details behind her brother's death at East Pen had drastically altered Madeline's state of mind, and she decided to proceed with caution . . . and protection.

Madeline now knew her parents posed an imminent threat to her life and continuing to hide in denial was no longer an option. She had dedicated the past fifteen years to preparing for the day she might be forced to face them again, and it was time to put her training to use; without hesitation, her survival instincts subconsciously clicked into action. She kept a second silver-plated Colt .45 semi-automatic handgun in a holster secured to the underside of the entryway table. She quietly removed the gun, slowly opened the top drawer, and pulled out and expertly loaded the clip.

As Madeline moved cautiously through the parlor and down the side hall with the gun held securely at her waist, her breath became steady and she was prepared to use it. When she reached the end of the hallway and proceeded into the kitchen, the smell of burning food engulfed her nostrils and the sight in front of her halted the investigation. The entire house was trashed; the kitchen utensils were in disarray, food was scattered all over the countertops, and several pots boiled over on the stove, burned and black.

The fire alarm began beeping loudly as Madeline dashed to the stove, turned off the burners, and ran into the living room where she found Gabriella.

Gabriella was unconscious and hanging halfway off the couch dressed only in a tank top and panties, covered in vomit. Empty bottles of alcohol were strewn all over the floor.

"Not again!" Madeline screamed, rushing to Gabriella and checking her pulse; it was faint, her skin hot and sweaty. Madeline looked over to the coffee table and saw several open bottles of prescription pills with Gabriella's name on them.

The blaring fire alarm turned into howling sirens.

———————

Madeline sat in the lounge of New Orleans City Hospital's emergency room, poring through the details of Maxwell's file while awaiting an update on Gabriella's condition. She had never seen or read anything like it. Years and years of a person's life lost in the disorganization of a prison's poorly kept records system. It was nothing like the meticulously kept paperwork she maintained for her patients, and she had to piece the details together page-by-page before she could make sense of anything.

The most provoking section was the transport logs detailing the times Maxwell had been in and out of East Pen during his incarceration. He had appeared at a Chicago courthouse for more than a dozen appeal hearings, which had ended the same month their parents stopped visiting him. The file didn't reveal any of the details of his case, only the transfer records for processing between East Pen and the Cook County jail for holding. The name of his lawyer was also missing from the file, as Maxwell had retained private counsel and not a court-appointed attorney like the one he had for his first trial. *How could Maxwell afford the retainer and monthly billings?* Madeline wondered. *He was broke.* She put the file into her backpack and continued to wait.

Madeline was extremely distraught over Gabriella's overdose, and hours had gone by without word from the hospital staff. The last Madeline had heard, Gabriella was in critical condition with her stomach being pumped, and Madeline's distress was quickly turning into fear-driven rage. Their parents resurfacing was creating a fatal-domino-effect, and Madeline decided it was time to either disappear again or fight. What either choice would entail she did not yet know, but she needed to assemble before the end of the night, and knew exactly who to seek for help. After receiving an update on Gabriella that was the first place she would go.

Meanwhile, she still had work to do outside her personal plights. Her financial and personal needs had just doubled, and someone had to finance the impending storm; with Gabriella immobilized, it was Madeline's responsibility to do it. She looked at the missed calls list on her cell phone and saw Dr. Fields had unsurprisingly been trying to reach her all night. "Lovely," she said, dialing her voicemail and playing the messages.

The sound of Dr. Fields' coarse voice snarled at her over the recording, "What happened to you today?" he screamed. "This is outrageous! You had better make it in to see your new patient tomorrow or I swear it's over for you!"

The last person Madeline could afford to cross at that point was her boss, despite her plethora of private struggles. His flagrant flirtations were hard to bear, but Dr. Fields was big time in the world of child psychiatry and Madeline was still his resident—he currently held sole authority over the future of her career.

In an era where professionals of every kind jumped onto the bandwagons of reality television and personal exploitation, Dr. Fields' methods of self-promotion could compete with the best of them. His literary agent had been looking for a publisher for his book on childhood schizophrenia for a year, and his invitation to give the keynote address at the conference gala nearly ensured a large advance and a fully-funded deal. Which was not only good news and international exposure for him, but also for every doctor working on his team. With or without Gabriella, Madeline refused to give up what she had built. Her research findings and methods of treating undiagnosed patients alone would put New Orleans on the psychiatric map. She would have to ease any tension existing between herself and Dr. Fields, but not tonight.

She put her phone away, pulled out the file he'd given her the day before on her new patient, and looked through the previous doctors' notes. "Savannah DeVears, age seventeen," she read quietly. "Multiple suicide attempts, overdosing on medication while under psychiatric care, and a history of cutting—nothing uncommon. Why does he want me to have this case?" She closed the file, thinking, *Harry loves to play his sick little games, I'm sure this is no different.*

The reality was, every time Dr. Fields found himself with

writer's block he tossed one of his resident doctors a case so convoluted they would have no chance of solving it. He told them afterward it was to "keep them guessing and alert," and then secretly put the results into his book. Plus, he liked to keep his doctors under his control, which he achieved by keeping them mentally and emotionally out of control. He was a cold calculated leech who fed off other people's struggles.

After two more hours of waiting, the emergency room nurse arrived with an update on Gabriella. "Miss Knight—," she said.

"Dr. Knight," Madeline corrected. Madeline knew she looked young for her age and wasn't in the mood for a runaround. She wanted the facts about Gabriella's condition, not the usual brush-off given by nurses already overworked and understaffed.

"I'm sorry; Dr. Knight. Your sister is currently under sedation as her blood alcohol content was dangerously high at thirty-one percent. Obviously combined with her medications this overdose could have been fatal. We're going to keep her in ICU overnight, but she should be fine."

She should be fine? Madeline thought. *She should be dead with those numbers!* "I'd like to go in and check on her, what room is she in?"

"She's in treatment room number four."

"Thank you. Can you please send down the on-call psychiatrist?"

"Yes, Doctor."

Madeline walked through the double doors separating the waiting room from the emergency center and down the corridor past the trauma units to the treatment rooms. She pulled back the blue curtain to room number four and peered in. Gabriella was hooked up to multiple IVs, a breathing tube, and a catheter; Madeline was grateful she was under sedation.

"What a mess, Gabriella; what were you thinking?" Madeline said, sitting down on the chair next to the bed.

She blamed herself. Gabriella had a history of incidents resulting in hospitalizations more life-threatening than this, and the responsibility Madeline had always felt for Gabriella played at her conscience. *Gabriella is right about one thing,* she thought, *all we have is each other. I'm not going to allow her to end up like Max.*

Madeline retrieved a plastic bag out of her backpack full of the medications she had collected from the coffee table. She knew how her sister worked: once released Gabriella would be completely uncontrollable again. Madeline needed to know the circumstances under which Gabriella had been discharged from the psychiatric facility in Illinois. But for the moment, Madeline's top priority was keeping her sister safe. She looked across the hallway at the emergency psych holding rooms and formulated a plan.

"I'm going to figure out what's really going on here," she whispered to Gabriella. "You're not getting out of here for at least seventy-two hours. You'll be safe from our parents and from yourself."

A doctor wearing a white coat over a suit and tie opened the curtain and entered the room. He was thirty-nine years old, six feet six inches tall, slender and in shape with slightly tanned white skin. If it wasn't for his poorly selected wardrobe and disheveled disposition, Madeline thought he might have actually been attractive. Instead, his medium-long, slightly greasy dark-blond hair was pulled back into a low ponytail, he was unshaven, and his eyes were hidden behind noticeably smudged glasses. But he was hopelessly mesmerized by Madeline the moment he saw her.

"Hello, I'm Dr. Nathan Raines, the on-call psychiatrist this evening. You asked to see me?"

"Yes," Madeline said, rising to greet him. "I'm Dr. Madeline Knight. I'm a resident over at New Orleans State Psychiatric Hospital in the children's ward. My sister was brought in this evening, Gabriella Jackson."

Dr. Raines was struck senseless. *A doctor and she's beautiful? No way!* he thought, unable to stay on topic. "You must be working under Harold Fields, then? I did my residency with him."

"Yes, actually," she replied, uninterested in his personal affairs.

"Anyway, I found her passed out on the floor when I came home this evening."

"I'm assuming then you'll be attending his keynote address at the gala this Thursday night?"

"Yes, Doctor, but back to the point. I don't think this was just an overdose. She has a history of this type of behavior. It was a suicide attempt and I need you to place her on an involuntary seventy-two-hour psychiatric hold. She was just discharged from an out-of-state inpatient facility. I found these." She handed him the bag of pills.

He couldn't keep up with her. "Wow. Okay, yeah, you've got it. Can you get me her other medical records?"

"Yes, as soon as I can. Thank you, Doctor; I've got to go. Goodbye."

Madeline pulled back the curtain and left, closing him in behind her. Before he could make sense of the enigma he'd just witnessed, she had already strutted off down the corridor and out the exit doors, leaving him stunned and stimulated.

9

THE VODOU PRIESTESS

With Gabriella safely mandated to City Hospital's psychiatric ward for a minimum of three days Madeline could now confront any impending dangers without interference. After leaving the hospital, she drove into an Upper Ninth Ward neighborhood called the Bywater. Settled along the edge of the Mississippi River, the distinctively recognizable subdistrict of New Orleans was colorfully reminiscent of French, Spanish, and Caribbean colonial architecture. Although less than a mile from the French Quarter, the Bywater felt worlds away and was the ultimate sanctuary for true New Orleanians, old and new.

Madeline parked outside a beautifully decorated double shotgun duplex renovated into a single residence. By day, the house radiated light off its bright turquoise-blue exterior wood paneling and vibrant yellow and pink trim. By night, it glowed—illuminated by strings of lights flickering off the abundant green foliage and flowers wrapped around the yellow columns on the front deck. With a white picket fence encasing a lush tropical garden, it was the most enticingly magical house on the street, belonging to the most famous woman in the neighborhood—Vodou Priestess Haloise.

Priestess Haloise was another modern New Orleans legend and a longtime New Orleanian of Haitian descent. She had spent most of her life traveling back and forth between her house in Louisiana and her grandmother's home in Haiti, which she had recently inherited. Having dedicated her life to the acquiring of religious knowledge and the understanding of spirituality, she used her influence in both countries to remove the stigma attached to the different forms of Vodou and dispel the negative connotations falsely and negligently imposed on its name.

Long before the colorful shops in and around New Orleans sold the commercialized version of Louisiana Voodoo to tourists and local enthusiasts, international Vodou was a dominant religion in many countries and cultures around the world. Its origin was based on the universal belief in God the Creator and the mastering of the natural forces of the spiritual plane in a multidimensional reality. But for Priestess Haloise, modern Vodou was a hybrid combination of the ancient African and Haitian religions and her secondary religion of Roman Catholicism.

Priestess Haloise's grandmother had sent her to a Catholic academy in southern Louisiana when she was five years old, and she was raised almost exclusively by strict Catholic nuns. By age sixteen, Haloise considered taking vows, and grew to emulate the nuns' discipline and poise through a life of dedication to prayer and the practice of chastity. But after a mission back to Haiti at age eighteen she decided to stay, attended university there, and took up the study of her native religion for the next seven years. Haloise returned to New Orleans ordained a Haitian Vodou Mambo, taking the title of Vodou Priestess in the United States. Highly educated and steadfastly dedicated to charitable service, she became one of the most respected and sought-after religious healers and clairvoyants in the world. While especially praised in the Bywater, her popularity and wide appeal had her known only as "the Priestess" all over New Orleans.

But Madeline's connection to Priestess Haloise went far beyond notoriety. Madeline had considered making a home in New

Orleans for most of her life and had moved there with the hopes of finding her place in a multicultural city that embraced a combination of religions. As a child, Madeline had never been fully able to develop her religious awareness because of its banishment by her parents. But she nourished herself as needed by secretly stopping into the Immaculate Conception Church of Salem each day on her way home from school. And coincidentally, a church was where she had met Priestess Haloise—at the Saint Louis Cathedral in New Orleans. They both attended the late morning mass every Sunday and shared an immediate kinship, and Madeline began seeing Priestess Haloise for spiritual guidance regularly ever since.

Eager to get inside and see the Priestess, Madeline locked the car and ran up the sidewalk. It was close to midnight, but Priestess Haloise always did her most important work just before dawn and Madeline knew she would understand her late arrival. Madeline would have called ahead to announce her visit, but Priestess Haloise had never owned a telephone and only accepted in-person communication.

When Madeline opened the gate leading into the front garden she felt an instant shift in the energy around her. She hadn't felt such positivity since the last time she saw Priestess Haloise more than a month before. With the severity of her nightmares progressing and the resulting toll on her body increasingly debilitating, Madeline had retreated to the safety of her apartment and abandoned the outside world except for work. When she reached the porch and knocked softly on the front door, she regretted waiting until then to reconnect. Priestess Haloise was, after all, her closest friend, and after years of companionship they had become family.

Priestess Haloise opened the door with an uneasy smile on her face. Usually a serious woman, it was a sign of worry not satisfaction. Priestess Haloise was sixty, but had glowing chocolate-brown skin as smooth as she had when twenty years younger. She was medium height with a slender build and had completely gray hair in thin braids down to her waist. Never adorning herself with flashy beads or headdresses, she always wore a neutral-colored chiffon wrap dress that trailed to the floor and a white silk scarf swathed around the top of her head. She was naturally beautiful and conservative and always kept her full lips stained a rich coral matte. Her only accessories were seven gold hoop earrings in each of her ears and an omnipresent white crystal rosary around her neck identical with the one she had given Madeline.

"Miss Madeline, it's been a long time. Come in." She hugged Madeline long and hard before closing the door behind them.

Feeling safe and vulnerable the moment she walked into the house, Madeline's emotions erupted, and she couldn't contain herself before the words plaguing her mind poured from her mouth. "Haloise, something terrible is happening!" she cried. "My past has come back to destroy me just as you predicted it would!"

Priestess Haloise remained quiet but her smile faded, unmasking a stoic gaze as her senses began to attract a world of knowledge she had never before conceived. When she hadn't heard from Madeline in several weeks, she knew something serious was brewing and that eventually Madeline would resurface and come to her for guidance. Priestess Haloise had prepared herself for that moment and anticipated its arrival with a strong premonition it would drastically alter both their lives after passing. She put her arm on Madeline's shoulder and led her past the living room, through a beaded doorway, and into her candlelit prayer room.

"I'm going to read the spirits," Priestess Haloise said firmly.

The prayer room was a visual masterpiece exquisitely decorated with meticulously preserved Haitian heirlooms of the finest variety. Heavy royal-blue satin drapes tied with gold tasseled ropes covered the windows and bunched gracefully on the floor. A grand chandelier, far too large for the room, hung from the ceiling coloring everything beneath with the glistening rainbow lights from its hundreds of crystals. The wall on the left had floor-to-ceiling oak bookshelves filled with hundreds of ancient Vodou scrolls, Bibles from multiple religions, and a wide array of historical theology and Eastern and herbal medicine books. And set against the right wall was the heart of the room—her altar.

Unlike a public altar on display at a museum or central location—visited all day and containing the many offerings from the people who pray at it—the Priestess' private altar was a spiritual sanctuary. It was the sacred place in which she prepared all rituals and where her personal prayer and meditation occurred.

The altar consisted of a top and bottom tier made of marble and covered with crisp white canvas. The top tier had a large wooden crucifix raised from the center surrounded by several oil paintings, statues of the saints, and dripping white candles. The bottom tier held vials of oil, jars of herbs, and bags of healing powders and roots with a stone mortar and pestle to grind them. And two large crystal carafes of holy water used only for the blessing of the house sat to the side of a large gold offering bowl.

Beautifully organized and in perfect harmony, the entire room encompassed the essence of positive energy-charged spirituality. And it all revolved around a gold silk covered table where Priestess Haloise performed all her rituals and readings.

Madeline sat down and waited patiently while Priestess Haloise retrieved a small leather bag containing chicken bones, crystals, and alligator teeth, which she carefully spread around the table before taking a seat across from Madeline.

"Now tell me, child, what has transpired?" Priestess Haloise asked.

"My sister showed up on my doorstep yesterday and told our parents had found her," Madeline began. "She said they told her our brother was dead, that he'd been killed in prison, and that she was to come back to the family or suffer the same consequences. I flew to Chicago to find out what happened and found not only was he dead, but my parents had orchestrated his murder. We've been hiding from them for fifteen years. She's afraid for good reason, and so am I."

"How do you know your parents were involved?" Priestess Haloise asked as she began to sift through the artifacts and set them in order on a gold plate.

"Because I saw the prison's security tapes showing the murderer. I recognized him as a longtime associate of my father who had obviously infiltrated the prison system. And my parents had visited my brother multiple times during his incarceration. He had sworn never to contact them again, so I couldn't believe it!"

"Why do you think your parents would come after you now after so much time in silence?"

Madeline looked away from Priestess Haloise and felt her body painfully tense with anxiety once again. If she was going to seek the Priestess' help, she needed to be completely honest with her. Madeline had kept her secret for years, having made a pact with Maxwell and Gabriella never to tell a soul, and had adhered to it without exception. It was a disturbing fact about her childhood so shameful she could barely fathom speaking the words. The inhumane nature of her life under the rule of Charles and Claire Jackson was so devious and twisted American society would never have believed it. And Charles and Claire Jackson had carefully designed it that way. But after seeing the grisly manner in which Stefan had savagely executed Maxwell, Madeline had made a promise to avenge his murder, and now she had to take the first step toward keeping it.

"My parents are Satanists," Madeline said cautiously. "When we were children they practiced secretly and taught us the laws of the Darkside. I refused to abide by their teachings, as you know I've always been close to God, but there was a price to pay for what they considered blasphemous. Disobedience meant violent beatings and punishments that lasted for days, even months if the offense was physically harmful. But despite their difficulties with trying to convert us, they made the extent of our expected allegiance to the family abundantly clear. They said they could always 'rectify defiance' and therefore welcomed it. They enjoyed the process and believed the more viciously they beat us the darker and more enslaved we would become. The only unbreakable rule was leaving or exposing the family. If we did, they would consider us 'deserters,' hunt us down one by one, and kill us."

After a moment of silence, Madeline looked back up at Priestess Haloise and waited for her to respond, but she did not. She simply stood up, walked over to the altar, and lit a cigar. She then began a ritualistic Vodou cleansing consisting of blowing clouds of smoke over Madeline and the artifacts to remove all negative energy attachments and channel in the positive.

"Did you ever tell anyone?" Priestess Haloise finally asked.

"Yes, but only once about the beatings, never the truth about what they were. We knew the consequences if we did, and telling wouldn't have mattered anyway. Our parents had a mysterious way of interacting with the people who encountered them. My mother may have looked like just a housewife, but the aura around her was like a repellent. And aside from being the most intimidating man alive, my father was chief of police; it was the perfect cover for a man and woman who secretly controlled the city and had everyone in their debt. People on the outside happily dismissed what they didn't have to see."

Priestess Haloise walked behind Madeline's chair, cut off a piece of her hair with a razor-sharp bone-handle knife, and then sat back down across from her. "Give me your hands." She took Madeline's hands and closed her eyes for several moments before opening them. When she did, her expression had changed to one of confusion and concern, but she had no doubt the knowledge she had just envisioned was true.

She then prepared to explain to Madeline what she had somehow always known. "There is more danger to your situation than just your parents' vendetta against you," Priestess Haloise began. "It's about you. It's about who you are. I know this is going to be hard for you to accept or understand but you must trust me and open your mind to realities you cannot immediately see. An imminent shift in the power between the forces of Heaven and Hell is upon the earth, and you, my child, are in the middle of it. Sides are being drawn and the solidification of powerful alliances millions of years in the making is coveted more now than ever before."

Madeline pulled her hands back. She had known Priestess Haloise for years. She had accompanied her to Haiti every July for the past four summers and had never heard her speak about such things. "What are you talking about?" Madeline asked, growing agitated and uncomfortable. "This isn't about me; this is about my parents murdering my brother. If I'm in the middle of it, it's not because they want my soul; it's because they want blood!" She stood up and walked over to the altar. "Everywhere I turn, the nightmares of my past continue to haunt me. I've been running from the horror inflicted by my parents since the day I was born, and I'm done with it. Their sins go far beyond the lines of good and evil, and it's time to take my life back. I'm going to find them before they find me and make sure they spend the rest of their lives paying for what they've done!"

Priestess Haloise had expected Madeline's response and knew there was no way to reach her at that point. Even she didn't fully understand the information she had just extracted and would need to investigate her scrolls to find additional evidence before advising Madeline further. But, before allowing Madeline to leave, Priestess Haloise wanted to prepare her for what she might encounter on her own.

Priestess Haloise went to the bookshelf, picked out an ancient Vodou book titled *Demonology and Protection*, and gave it to Madeline.

"Remember why you do the job you do," Priestess Haloise said. "Save the mind to protect the soul. If you're going to go after your parents, you have to do it according to the instructions in this book. Their souls have already been taken. Do this the right way or you will lose your soul as well.

———————

Exhausted and distraught from her day, Madeline looked dreadful as she put her keys into the top drawer of her entryway table and looked at herself in the mirror hanging above it. She lit several protection candles as she walked through the kitchen and into the living room. She had forgotten about the shambles her apartment had been left in hours before, and empty alcohol bottles and junk-food wrappers still covered the coffee table and floor. "Welcome home, Gabriella; seems the years have found you unchanged," she said, taking out a large garbage bag and reluctantly cleaning up the mess.

The black computer bag Gabriella had possessively yanked away the previous day lay open on the floor, sparking Madeline's interest. She picked it up and sat down on the couch. Inside were dozens of black-and-white journal notebooks, one of which she took out and casually flipped through. After focusing on a few random entries Gabriella had written about her daily inpatient life, Madeline disregarded it. Journaling was an integral part of patient ritual and rehabilitation, and although Madeline didn't utilize that method with her patients, she knew many other doctors who did. She put the notebook back into the bag, set it aside to bring to Gabriella the next day, and continued to clean the room.

After picking up a half-full bottle of vodka off the floor, Madeline was ready to numb the pain of the day with the first of her nightly series of cocktails. As she lifted the bottle to her mouth ready to indulge in a nice long drink, she stopped herself. *What am I doing? This is destroying my already screwed up life!* she thought, taking one last look at the bottle in her hand before smashing it against the brick wall and storming over to the bar cabinet.

She grabbed hold of the heavy piece of furniture and slammed it over violently. Bottles of liquor and crystal glasses shattered all over the floor.

10

SAVANNAH

Wednesday, April 9, 2014 – 8:00 a.m.

The next morning Madeline walked confidently out of the elevator and into the children's ward at NOSPH having selected her wardrobe to match her mood. She wore an expensive black tailored pantsuit and had her eyelids traced with thin black eyeliner and her lips stained rich coral matte. For Madeline, it felt like years since the last time she slid her access card and walked through the glass doors leading into what only days before had been the most important place in her life. Even with her hair in the same tight bun and Gabriella's black computer bag slung over her shoulder, it was impossible not to notice the transformation in her attitude and demeanor.

When the lock switched open to the security door leading from the lobby into the nurses' station and Madeline entered the room, the group of gossiping nurses ceased their chatter and gawked at her in astonishment. Madeline didn't even notice; she boldly passed by without speaking or acknowledging their stares and headed for the doctors' offices.

Nurse Monroe, however, surprised by Madeline's early arrival and unpleasantly moved by her glamorously sophisticated new style, immediately separated herself from the others. With a sly smile, she stepped in front of Madeline antagonistically and blocked her way. "Miss Knight, you're in surprisingly early today," she said loud enough for everyone to hear. "Did the bars close down early last night?"

The other nurses' jaws dropped. Talking badly about the doctors behind their backs was a daily occurrence—and Nurse Monroe had created a solid reputation for having a loud mouth and complete lack of social etiquette—but a flagrant verbal attack on Madeline publicly, despite the widespread lack of respect for her, was unheard of. The buoyant morning energy in the room froze with disbelief as everyone in witness waited nervously for Madeline's reaction. Everyone except Nurse Monroe—she was proud of her bold achievement and waited with joyful anticipation.

Without flinching or changing the focused expression on her face, Madeline sat the computer bag down, looked at Nurse Monroe, and silently and slowly backed her into a corner. Madeline's statuesque body towered over the petite Nurse Monroe. "The last time I checked it was Dr. Knight to you, Nurse Monroe," Madeline said, pointing first to herself, "doctor," and then at Nurse Monroe, "nurse."

Nurse Monroe tried to speak, but Madeline cut her off. Madeline's usually firm calm voice now carried an intimidatingly threatening tone. "You've gotten away with running your mouth off around here for years because of who your daddy is, but I don't care who paved your way," Madeline said, nodding slightly to the cameras in the ceiling. "All the cameras in here provide a false sense of security for overprotected, self-indulgent, desperate, infantile women like you because there aren't any cameras outside these walls—not in the streets or down a dark alley; not in the swamps or behind closed doors. And once those doors close behind you it's every woman for herself. You don't know me. You never have, and you never will. Remember that."

Madeline turned around and picked up the computer bag then

walked away past the shocked nurses' station.

Nurse Monroe, unable to move, glared after her speechless and humiliated with a vengeful look in her eyes. She wouldn't allow this to go unpunished.

––––––––––

Without any additional thought or emotion pertaining to Nurse Monroe, Madeline went to address her first priority of the day— her meeting with Dr. Fields. It was standard procedure for residents to confer with their supervisors before examining a new patient, however, based on Dr. Fields' irate voicemail from the previous night, Madeline knew the discussion would involve significantly more.

Dr. Fields would be out of the office most of the week attending the conference, which would provide Madeline with the freedom she needed to locate her parents and devise her plans accordingly. But he was furious about her unexcused absence the day before, and only one agreement between Madeline and himself would dissuade his anger and guarantee her a pass on any disciplinary action that might accompany it. Her ability to maintain her workload while simultaneously ensuring her and Gabriella's survival depended on his acceptance of such agreement, and his undivided cooperation afterward.

Madeline secured her bags in her office, pushed the thought of her parents to the back of her mind, then sacrificed her pride and knocked on the door to Dr. Fields' office.

"Who is it?" Dr. Fields asked.

"It's Madeline. May I come in?"

"Yes. Enter," he said, leaning back in his chair behind his desk. He contemptuously interlocked his hands behind his head with elbows extended. When Madeline walked through the door with Savannah DeVears' patient file under her arm he was ready to indulge in a long groveling-session sure to end in his favor. However, Madeline immediately subdued him with her unexpected new appearance and took full advantage of his conspicuous approval.

"Good morning, Harry; interesting read," she said, holding up the file. "Thanks again for assigning me the case."

"Wow, for once you're actually taking advice instead of giving it. That's a sexy suit. I like it," he said, exhaling audibly. "What happened to you yesterday?" He watched her lustfully as she closed the door and sat down across from him. He had encouraged her for years to add more "revealing-femininity" to her wardrobe, and this was exactly the look he had in mind.

"Nothing I can't handle," she replied. "It's all taken care of. How about I fill you in on all the details over lunch and we can discuss the arrangements for our date at tomorrow night's gala?"

Dr. Fields perked up in his chair and the creases of his lips turned up ever so slightly—the closest thing to a smile he was going to allow. And even though this change of events pleased him greatly, he went out of his way not to show it. "Nice to see you've finally given in to me," he said confidently. "I knew you would come around. I'm playing golf for the rest of the day, so I'll be passing on lunch. But I'll call you later tonight. I'm dying to know what you're planning to wear and to lend you my personal recommendations."

"Sounds great, Harry. So, exactly how much leniency do I have with this DeVears case? I was up all night doing a thorough examination of the file, and it's clear to me why you put me on it."

"Clear to you? This isn't a test case, Madeline. We're just pushing her through. Let me explain something to you. And I want you to listen carefully and keep your mouth shut while I do it. Your ability to understand what I'm about to tell you will either propel or extinguish your career at this hospital. Now, you know perfectly well we are a federally funded and controlled facility. And who runs the federal government? Politicians do. We do what we're told to stay under their radar, and in return, they stay out of our way."

"I'm not exactly sure what you're getting at."

"Because you're not listening. The little girl in the file you're holding is the second cousin of a very prominent man who has every assurance of his election to the governorship this fall."

"It says in the file she was rescued during the raid of a satanic cult compound."

"That's what both he and his team of advisers want the authorities to think. He needs to erase his connections to the family and keep their deaths a secret until after the election. While not exactly an easy task to accomplish, a mess like this going public would end his campaign before it was even necessary to have one. And the support he provides our organization would end with it."

Dr. Fields stood up and leaned forward with his palms on the desk, his tone now stern. "Every detail in Miss DeVears' file is true, except one. She didn't live at the compound; someone stashed her at it, along with the bodies and every other piece of evidence. Everything that happened to that girl and her parents happened behind the privacy of their own sweet southern Louisiana mansion's front door."

"Wait a minute!" Madeline shouted, standing up. "You can't expect me to—."

"I don't expect you to do anything; I'm telling you. She's so far gone there's no bringing her back now anyway. That's how we handle private cases at our level, Madeline. Get used to it. The board has instructed us to process her through the system in compliance with the judicial requirements for criminal psychiatric placement, and that's exactly what you're going to do. I put you on this case to collect details on her current condition, not to fix it."

Madeline's vision blurred then slowly came back into focus.

An echo now trailed Dr. Fields' words, "Think of this as an unregulated, undocumented opportunity to add to your research findings, and I'll give you all the rope you need. Just don't hang yourself."

––––––––––

While Madeline sat at her desk preparing for Savannah's first examination, her conscience went wild with emotional and moral contradictions. Dr. Fields had set an unbreakable precedent during their meeting, leaving Madeline to make one of two distinctly different choices. He had given her the freedom to study and experiment with Savannah's psychiatric care in any way she wanted, but the one stipulation was that Savannah needed to be transferred to the next hospital in the same condition she arrived in. No attempt to correct her illness was permitted.

But Madeline had already developed her own preliminary diagnosis the night before when examining Savannah's file. And her plans for treating Savannah involved more than just a processing evaluation with a predetermined conclusion. Savannah was the type of patient Madeline had built her residency around protecting. Simply passing Savannah on to a life sentence at a hospital for the criminally insane after merely collecting data for her own usage wasn't Madeline's understanding of a doctor's code of ethics. She intended to administer Savannah's medical care with swift ferocity in accordance with the methods devised over the course of her career—not the methods dictated by corrupt politicians scheming to maintain control of their political party.

Savannah's prior hospitalization records were from private institutions unaware of the expertly contrived facts about her case, and each had refused to give the diagnosis required for a judge to commit her to a criminal psychiatric institution. Now, the conspirators in charge of Savannah's care had used internal connections to force NOSPH to provide the diagnosis instead. But she was not to be healed in the process. If Madeline brought Savannah into recovery, Savannah would be able to reveal what had really happened to her, and that's exactly what the handlers managing the case didn't want.

Defying Dr. Fields by curing Savannah could mean the end of Madeline's residency. But she decided to continue with her original plan and deal with the consequences later.

Madeline met Ross and Jack Lee outside a patient evaluation room and retrieved Savannah's chart from the wall. "Alright," Madeline said. "Miss Savannah DeVears—what time did she get in this morning?"

"Actually," Ross answered, "they brought her in late last night around eleven, and so far, it's been an unpleasant experience for everyone involved. She's not talking or eating but somehow managed to land one of the night techs in the emergency room. One minute she's unresponsive, the next she's in need of sedation. These are the incident reports." He handed the reports to Madeline and her serious expression changed to one of disbelief. "Yep," he said, "those are all for her."

"Okay," Madeline said. "Here's the details as stated in her file. She's been in the system for three months, all private institutions. Police found her at a satanic cult up by the Arkansas border after receiving an anonymous phone call about a murder-suicide. Apparently, she watched her father put a gun in his mouth and pull the trigger. They took her to the hospital and the rape kit found severe signs of sexual abuse, including a recent abortion."

"Why did they bring her here?" Jack Lee asked.

"That's where it gets complicated," Madeline replied. "Aside from the fact she found some pretty clever ways to try to kill herself in the last facility, she also has severe schizophrenia accompanied by homicidal tendencies. She butchered her mother up with a hatchet after her father blew his head off. That combined with years of her father's sexual abuse against her, she now believes she is her mother. This is her last stop before she's committed to a north state prison hospital for the criminally insane."

"Interesting..." Ross said suspiciously. "That's a pretty conflicting diagnosis considering she hasn't said a word since she arrived. What are we supposed to do with her? We don't handle that type of patient in this facility."

Madeline took Ross aside out of Jack Lee's earshot. Other techs and patients continued to walk by in the busy hallway. "Here's the thing," she said quietly. "We're not supposed to be handling it. I've been told just to push her through. But between you and I, there's more to this case than what's in the file, and I think you know what

I mean. I need you with me on this one. It's going to take a lot more than medication and therapy to pull this kid back."

"You got it, Boss. Be careful in there. I'll be right outside the door."

———————

The psychiatric evaluation rooms at NOSPH were the most uninviting, uncomfortable locations in the building. Cold and lacking any entertainment or nurturing adornments, they were designed to keep new patients as calm as possible by restricting unfavorable reactions to overabundant stimuli. As a result, initially the patients usually became withdrawn and more depressed.

When Madeline opened the door to Savannah's room, an evil shiver ran through her body. She had already treated multiple patients in Savannah's condition and, disturbingly, more and more of them had been admitted to the hospital over the past six months. Madeline always campaigned to add them to her treatment roster, but the dark stale energy in Savannah's room reminded her of death, and she knew Savannah was going to be different from the others.

The room had a single hospital bed equipped with leather restraints and a portable chair and table with an untouched tray of food on it. Savannah wore baggy green hospital-issued pajamas and sat catatonically in a wheelchair by the window with both palms resting on her thighs. She was seventeen but looked much younger. She was shockingly frail, and her medical report registered her weight at only eighty pounds with a height of five feet two inches. Her skin was pale and white, and she had long stringy blond hair that hung to her waist because of the way she sat with her chin imbedded into her chest.

Madeline slowly took a couple steps toward her, careful not to alarm the extremely volatile patient. "Good morning, Savannah, I'm Dr. Knight. We only have a short time to make progress here so I'm going to get right to the point and skip all the redundant questions you've no doubt already been asked. How do you feel about that?"

No response.

"I hear you had a rough time last night," Madeline continued. "Being as we both know what's really going on here, I'll tell you right now that kind of behavior isn't going to get you anywhere. Now, what I need to know is this—how interested are you in saving your soul?"

Still no response.

Remaining cautious, Madeline stepped in closer and noticed Savannah begin to scratch at something on her right arm that was bleeding. "What's that on your arm, Savannah?"

That question invoked a response. Savannah slowly turned her head to the left where Madeline was standing, but continued to look down.

Making progress, Madeline decided to initiate contact and attempt a physical examination. Savannah's eyes followed her as she walked around the front of the wheelchair and stopped inches away between Savannah and the window.

Madeline then looked over what she'd already seen graphic pictures of in Savannah's file. Savannah's arms and neck were covered with dozens of bruises, scars, and cuts—some fresh, some scabbed over. Many were long deep slashes while others were sloppily carved words in a language Madeline couldn't decrypt. Two jagged scars were visible around Savannah's wrists from an extended period of time in restraints of either handcuffs or rope. And having long since healed over, Savannah couldn't have acquired them from her recent hospital stay.

In the place where Savannah was scratching in the crease of her elbow, an odd shaped scar similar to a cross was on top of multiple undecipherable tattooed images. Madeline had seen patients in worse physical condition than Savannah, but none who had been so grossly defiled.

Shocked by the extent of Savannah's injuries and the tense focus Savannah had suddenly awarded her, Madeline's heart began to beat rapidly. When she finally reached out to touch Savannah,

Savannah whipped her head up and stared with fierce brown eyes directly at Madeline, who flinched back.

An unexpected familiarity in Savannah's eyes instantaneously shocked Madeline with a bolt of fright. And after composing herself, she attempted to continue the examination while Savannah gaped motionless with her head cocked back over her left shoulder in a kinked position.

Madeline reached out again and gently took Savannah's wrist in her hand. Savannah's skin instantly blistered and burned, searing upon Madeline's touch. Savannah yanked her arm back and jolted painfully, jerking her head left and right, up and down. She stopped abruptly, looked at Madeline, and then hissed loudly and spat at her face. Madeline snapped her head to the side and Savannah missed, hitting the wall instead where a black stain instantly formed.

Madeline jumped back as Savannah stood up, overturned her wheelchair, and flipped the table and all its contents onto the floor. She picked up the chair and hurled it at Madeline with immense force, knocking Madeline back several feet to the ground. Savannah then screeched venomously and ripped at her clothes, tearing them off and revealing additional lacerations covering her body underneath.

Ross and Jack Lee rushed into the room and restrained Savannah.

"You'll hang for this you stupid snitch!" Savannah screamed at Madeline. "We're exactly the same! They're gonna string you up from the railing—you're gonna hang!"

Two female techs entered the room and helped to cover and restrain Savannah while she continued to scream obscenities.

Madeline struggled to lift herself up from the floor as the room began to blur.

11

BLACK BELT NIGHT

Savannah continued to scream in the background as Madeline burst out of the patient confinement room and into the bustling hospital hallway. Disoriented with her hair unpinned and vision still blurred, she ducked into the closest restroom, slammed the door, and locked it. Her heart beat louder and harder, ringing in her ears as she succumbed to a full panic attack.

As blood pulsed painfully through her veins and sweat seeped from her forehead, she paced back and forth desperate to regain control. A piercing pain shot through her chest, she struggled to breathe, and vertigo overcame her senses dropping her to her knees at the base of the sink. Her fingers and legs went numb as she struggled to grip the faucet handle, and after finally turning it on, she pulled herself up and splashed the cold water over her face, extinguishing the heat radiating from her body.

When she looked up from the sink, water ran red down her face and the reflection she saw in the tiny mirror was no longer her own, but that of a young Madeline. She was fourteen years old and staring into her bathroom mirror, the dripping water now replaced with bloody tears streaming from her swollen eyes. Her lower lip had been gouged open and split down the center and bright-red blood flowed down her face and neck, staining her white T-shirt, which was slit open in slashes lined with blood.

It had been another night of sadism at the Jackson family Salem house on Christmas Eve, 1998, forever changing the lives of every person present. Unbeknownst to Madeline and Maxwell, the lesson they were to learn that day turned out to be temptation and ownership, and they had failed it miserably.

Charles and Claire Jackson had charged Madeline and Maxwell with the responsibility of watching Gabriella that afternoon while they attended to business outside the home. And it had been a losing arrangement from the start. Gabriella was to stay inside and watch television while Madeline and Maxwell completed their chore for the day—collecting all the rocks from the dirt-covered two-acre yard and depositing them into a large tractor bucket to be filled before their parents' return.

Throughout the day, Gabriella had repeatedly snuck into their father's den and gorged herself with the silver-wrapped chocolates he kept strategically placed in a crystal jar on the bookshelf. Charles always kept the jar full, and the children were under strict orders never to eat the delicious contents. He knew the exact count, and Gabriella had shamelessly helped herself to more than half.

When Charles and Claire returned home that evening, Claire went straight upstairs to soak in the bath, while Charles first inspected the yard work. After careful examination, he reluctantly accepted the task had been completed to his specifications. He then angrily retreated to his den where he first checked the level of the crystal container and identified the chocolate transgression. His unmistakable roar erupted from the dark lair at the front of the house demanding all of his children's immediate attendance. He then informed them that the wrongdoing was the fault of the older children who had been in charge and failed to prevent it. Therefore, he would reflect the necessary punishment solely on the two guilty parties and not the actual perpetrator.

He sent Madeline and Maxwell to wait in their separate bedrooms until he arrived to administer their lashings—fifty each. He then sent Gabriella to the master bathroom to fetch her mother, and proceeded to unbuckle his black police belt—his favorite method of punishment because of the way its woven leather effortlessly ripped open the skin it struck.

Claire enthusiastically rushed downstairs with Gabriella, sauntered over to her husband, and seductively pulled off and handed Charles his belt. He then folded it in half, grasped it in his right hand, and climbed the two flights of stairs to the attic.

Maxwell was always the first to receive his punishments and Madeline was always forced to wait in her bedroom across the hallway for hers. She crouched behind the door in debilitating anxiety, anticipating the beating to come and dreading the horror of listening to Maxwell's screams while she awaited the same fate. Her heart began to race as heavy footsteps resonated from the airshaft and Charles reached the top of the stairs and opened the door to Maxwell's bedroom.

Madeline's vision blurred and sweat dripped from her forehead when she heard the words she'd been dreading snarl out of her father's mouth. "Turn around," he yelled to Maxwell, "take your pants down, pull off your shirt, and put your hands over your head on the wall!"

Even at sixteen Maxwell dwarfed his father by two inches and seventy-five pounds, yet still did as he was told. Ten seconds later, the sound of cracking leather mixed with Maxwell's shrieks of squealing pain filled the hallway and echoed down the rear stairwell and throughout the house.

Claire and Gabriella calmly sipped diet colas at the kitchen table.

When Charles had the Salem house built years earlier, he had refused to install handles and hardware on any of the interior doors, including bathrooms, as privacy was not a luxury he permitted his family. And Madeline peered through the hole in her door watching angrily as he continued to whip Maxwell repeatedly.

She had fantasized for years about what she would do the next time her father beat them but had never found the courage to carry out her plans. Her parents saw their children as property—disobedience by means of escape would not be tolerated.

Charles Jackson never just spoke to his older two children; he screamed and yelled with every breath and only referred to them as "offspring." He didn't allow them to laugh, smile, consume sweets, or wear fashionable clothes. And he didn't consider them to be humans worthy of an opinion, love, or happiness, and reminded them of that regularly. Madeline and Maxwell's years of lifeless existence under his rule eventually poisoned their relationship and drove them to opposite means of coping. Maxwell struggled with his need for subservience; eventually expressing his discontentment through drugs and violent behavior toward the only people he had control over. Madeline struggled with her need to extricate herself from their unbearable circumstances and expose their parents for what they were. She would eventually risk her chance at a future to achieve it.

And that day, crouching behind her bedroom door, something inside Madeline snapped. She sprang up from the floor, ran across the hallway to Maxwell's bedroom, and as if the words had come from someone else's mouth, demanded her father stop the attack. Stunned and unnerved by her unprecedented disobedience, Charles screamed at her to get back to her room. But it was too late; she was already invested. She charged forward directly at her father and leapt onto his back, attacking him courageously and ripping him away by clawing her fingernails deep into the flesh of his neck.

Charles pulled at Madeline's arms, but she wouldn't release. He dug his feet in and swung around forcefully, propelling her off his back and across the room so powerfully, she smashed headfirst into the wall busting through the sheetrock and cutting her eye and ripping open her lip.

Dazed with her head ringing, blood gushed from the gashes on Madeline's face as she pushed herself back, jumped up, and ran blindly from the room.

Steps behind, Charles chased her into the hallway with eyes glowing red in an enraged-blackout-pursuit. With his belt now open in his hand like a whip, he thrashed psychotically through the air tearing at Madeline's delicate skin with blistering might.

She ran frantically down the stairs barely able to see through the blood and swelling around her eyes. After missing a step on the steep splintered boards, she tripped, flying outward and tumbling to the bottom. Once on her feet, she wiped the blood from her eyes, grabbed hold of the grandfather clock in the second-story hallway, and slammed it to the ground behind her stalling his path. She then ran down the front staircase, rounded the corner past Charles' den, and sprinted through the foyer.

When Madeline reached the dining room headed for the back door, Claire stood in front of the wet bar in the butler's pantry outside the kitchen blocking her escape. Charles had already made it down the rear stairwell and was heading toward them. Madeline screamed at Claire, begging for help and attempting to hide behind her. But Claire stepped away, exited the pantry, and slammed the door before Madeline could follow, putting her back in her father's reach.

Charles stood in the entrance ready to strike, and Madeline turned to run, but Claire had already locked the door.

Making one last attempt, Madeline launched forward, maneuvered past her father, and ran up the rear stairwell, but still she couldn't escape. He rushed after her, whipping madly and tearing open her flesh, lash after lash with precise aim. The force of the belt stained the pristine white walls with long black scuff marks all the way up the stairwell, down the halls, and throughout the master bedroom where he had her cornered.

Madeline finally submitted to his will and held her arms up on the bedpost.

After Charles had enforced her original punishment of fifty lashings, he tossed the belt onto the floor, turned around, and silently walked back to his den.

Madeline limped into the bathroom bleeding and in pain. Maxwell never came back out of his bedroom, and no one came to check on her.

As Madeline splashed cool water over her stinging face and neck, thick welts began to protrude from the gashes across her back, arms, and legs. While lost in her reflection in the tiny mirror—the only mirror allowed in the house—the reality of what her life would be like from that point on flashed through her mind, and she made a decision.

Madeline cleaned her face the best she could and then walked out of the bathroom past the rear balcony where she looked down and saw her mother on the couch. Claire was relaxing with a glass of champagne, high again off the intoxication of her children's beatings. Madeline then walked back into her parents' bedroom, picked the belt up off the floor, and took a pair of her father's handcuffs from his closet. She took the items to the top of the front stairwell and secured the belt around her neck by looping it through the buckle as she had practiced countless times before. She then connected the makeshift-noose to the solid oak railing, handcuffed her hands behind her back, climbed over the balcony, and jumped.

Sitting at his desk, Charles heard the sound of a loud thud, turned around, and saw Madeline through his doorway hanging with her legs flailing, slipping into death. He sat and watched for a moment more, then reluctantly rose to cut her down. Before he reached her the railing snapped and Madeline fell unconscious to the floor.

Still looking into the bathroom mirror at NOSPH, Dr. Madeline Knight finally recovered from her panic-attack-fueled flashback. She wiped the water off her face with a paper towel, repinned her hair into a perfect bun, and walked back out the door unnoticed into the bustling hospital hallway.

12

MR. & MRS. CHATSWORTH

Madeline remained calm until retreating into the privacy of her office, then locked herself in and drew the shades covering the window in the door. The lingering effects of her panic attack continued to incapacitate her body, and she was aching to ease the tension. Breathing deeply, she ran to the couch, threw off the pillows, reached far under the back crease, and retrieved a half-pint of vodka. But just before the alcohol hit her lips, she realized the severity and repercussions of the mistake she was about to make and promptly dumped the entire bottle into one of the tree planters.

Savannah's examination had escalated far beyond what Madeline had expected, and Madeline was grateful no additional patients were on her schedule until early evening. She was making a late afternoon visit to Gabriella at City Hospital, but needed to complete a vast amount of personal research beforehand—research that would help her to move forward with the first phase of her plan to locate and expose her parents.

Madeline had transported Maxwell's prison file and stolen video from the surveillance room at East Pen in Gabriella's computer bag. She took them out and made copies of each item before putting the originals back in the bag and stashing it in her office safe. The video footage of Stefan killing Maxwell and the visitors' log showing her parents' consistent contact with Maxwell while incarcerated was the only evidence she had against them. To prove her parents' involvement in orchestrating the hit on Maxwell, Madeline would have to be able to connect them irrefutably to Stefan. And she had no doubt that wherever Charles and Claire Jackson resided, Stefan wouldn't be far away; he never was. Therefore, the first task Madeline needed to accomplish was finding her parents.

She mentally disconnected from her duties at the hospital, sat down at the computer, and prepared to do a search. After fifteen years of no contact, she had no idea where they lived or where to look, and decided to work her way back from Salem and establish a connecting trail of activity.

Because NOSPH was a federal research hospital, its network connected to a national database with access to the contact information of every active human being with a social security number in the country. Madeline logged into the system, entered her security code, and typed her parents' names, birth dates, places of birth, and last known address into the search engine. An immediate NO RESULTS appeared on the screen.

"Great. Big surprise," Madeline said.

She hadn't expected finding her parents to be easy; aside from the East Pen visitors' logs, Charles and Claire Jackson had been without a sighting for fifteen years. But Madeline had assumed there would at least be a fragment of traceable information, even if just financial. But there was nothing. No credit cards, no mortgage, no rentals, no tax returns.

Madeline had made no attempt to keep track of anything connected to her life in Salem. The memories of her past were like a black hole of destruction residing in the deepest niche of denial she could manage. She had avoided any evidence of its existence out of fear its evil would suck her back in and she'd never recover. But Priestess Haloise had warned her of the hazards of denial, and prophesied that the second Madeline declared herself free from her past it would resurface. Well, Madeline had considered herself free, and her past did resurface—with a callous, tactical depredation.

After thinking for several minutes, Madeline looked over at the large metal file cabinet in the corner of her office. It contained the medical history files for every patient she'd ever treated, and the only people with access were Dr. Fields and herself. Giving away patient information without proper authorization or a warrant could cost a doctor his or her medical license. Breaking into a doctor's records at a government research facility and stealing them was a federal offense. Consequently, Madeline's office file cabinet was where she hid her most valued and damaging secrets, as well.

She entered a four-digit number into a small lockbox bolted to the wall next to the cabinet and took out a ring of keys. She then unlocked the bottom drawer, reached into the very back, and unlocked a hidden compartment with a different key from her personal chain. She pulled out a three-inch-thick brown leather file holder labeled: Annabelle Jackson.

Madeline was hesitant. She sat at her desk for a few moments and contemplated her decision to move forward. She realized opening the file would force her to remember who she really was and where she had come from. The task of convincing the people around her she was always "Dr. Madeline Knight" was much easier than believing it herself. Despite graduating with honors and surpassing the best young doctors in the country who had also applied for her residency, truly accepting there could be life beyond Salem was significantly harder. If Madeline had ever thought she could outrun her past and live a normal life, that fantasy was about to be destroyed.

She unwrapped the ties around the buttons securing the cover and removed several labeled folders. The first contained legal name-change documents approved in the state of Louisiana five years prior confirming Madeline Knight was born under the name Annabelle Jackson. In the next file were all of her personal identification documents for both names, including two passports, two social security cards, and a birth certificate.

As Madeline sifted through the various folders and loose paperwork documenting the last fifteen years of her life, she set several sections aside for later use. The first was from her stay at a Salem hospital under her birth name, Annabelle Jackson.

When Madeline tried to hang herself at age fourteen, she had only survived because the railing couldn't support her weight and broke before she asphyxiated. But she had still suffered life-threatening injuries as a result. Her neck had snapped from the initial whiplash and she had sustained multiple cervical fractures requiring major surgery. A long incision was made vertically along her spine and several pins inserted, and later removed. In addition to her neck, after falling more than twelve feet to the hardwood floor, Madeline had landed on her right forearm causing a severe compound fracture of her ulna, also requiring surgical repair.

Following her recovery from surgery, her doctor had placed her on a suspended seventy-two-hour psychiatric hold and suicide watch. During that time, social workers and city officials had questioned her about how the other injuries not associated with the hanging had occurred. But after the brutality of her last beating, Madeline had a new understanding of her parents' sadistic indifference to her life. Therefore, for good reason, she remained silent and refused to reveal where the lacerations on her body had come from.

But the balcony hanging wasn't the first time Madeline had attempted to take her own life while living in her parents' home. Charles and Claire Jackson had severely punished her for it on all previous occasions, and her blatant disobedience with her final repeat offense and resulting hospitalization infuriated them greatly. They had initially contemplated letting Madeline die that last time, but knew they didn't have the authority. Therefore, confident they'd trained her well enough not to implicate them in her injuries—and not wanting a dead body to dispose of on Christmas Eve—they had gambled on her silence and called an ambulance. It had been a risky move, and they had intended to monitor her hospital recovery closely.

However, after a concerned nurse decided to record all of Madeline's phone conversations, a disturbing call between Madeline and her mother raised the already-present level of suspicion against the Jacksons. As Claire Jackson had tried to convince Madeline to come home by shaming her daughter into taking responsibility and portraying herself as the victim, Madeline had erupted in anger with a shocking verbal rant. She had screamed obscenities and declared how much she hated her mother and hoped that Claire died. Madeline had said she would never come home again and accused Claire of organizing their beatings and allowing her and Maxwell to endure endless pain. Afterward, Madeline had refused to accept any more calls from her parents. The nurse played the recording for Madeline's primary doctor—a man already in opposition with the Jacksons and unmoved by their political authority—and he banned them from any further contact pending an investigation against them.

With Madeline's increasingly destructive, unpredictable behavior, Charles became uneasy about the possibility she might talk and sent in his only confidant, Stefan, disguised as a maintenance worker to warn her of the consequences. Stefan's dark methods of coaxing had never failed to provide results, and he designed the encounter to convince Madeline to remain diligent in her silence.

Instead, she slit her wrists the following day with a sharp rock she found in the hospital exercise yard. But the injuries weren't fatal. A nurse found her unconscious but alive, and after yet another failed attempt and recovery, Madeline decided her life must have a meaningful purpose she did not yet understand. She finally told her doctor about the physical abuse endured under her parents' rule, and never saw them again.

The second set of papers Madeline set aside was from the Massachusetts Department of Children and Families. They detailed the immediate and mandatory removal of Maxwell,

Annabelle, and Gabriella Jackson, ages sixteen, fourteen, and ten respectively, from the Salem home of Charles and Claire Jackson. The Department of Children and Families had placed all three children together in a foster home in Chicago, Illinois, to keep them far out of their parents' reach.

The third set of papers was copies of several newspaper clippings from the *Salem City Chronicle*, which ran in early January 1999, with headlines reading:

After Beating and Suicide Attempt - Children Removed From the Home of Police Chief and Wife; Salem City Police Chief Steps Down; and *Newspaper Reaches Out to Ex-Police Chief for Comment – Family House Abandoned*

Madeline laid out a yellow pad of paper and a pen, picked up the phone, and restarted her search with existing evidence even the Jacksons couldn't destroy.

The Department of Children and Families was her first call, and she decided to use her birth name on the file.

"Massachusetts Department of Children and Families, Julie speaking, how may I help you?"

"Hi, my name is Annabelle Jackson," Madeline said, "and I'm looking for some information on a case."

"Is it for a family member, student, or ward of the state?"

"Neither. It's my own, and it's almost fifteen years old. The case number is SAMA-414-1972."

"Please hold." Madeline waited a few moments before the receptionist returned to the line. "I'm sorry, Ms. Jackson, we don't have any records of that case number."

"What? That's impossible. Check again. It's under Charles and Claire Jackson of Salem, Massachusetts."

"I'm sorry, but we have nothing listed under those names. Goodbye."

"Wait! I have an original copy right in front of me. An entire case file can't just disappear—!" The sound of a dial tone rang in

Madeline's ear. "Hello? Hello?" She quickly accessed another line and dialed the next number, this time using her current name.

"Salem City Hall, records department, Betty speaking, how may I direct your call?"

"My name is Dr. Madeline Knight, and I'm looking for current information on a former police chief named Charles Jackson."

"Ma'am, I have never heard of a Chief Charles Jackson. There's never been anyone in office by that name. Goodbye." Another dial tone.

"This is insane!" Madeline yelled, dialing a third number.

"Federal Correctional Penitentiary of Eastern Illinois, inmate records, how may I help you?"

"My name is Dr. Madeline Knight. I'm the sister of a deceased inmate, Maxwell Jackson. I need to obtain the official security clearance information collected from all of his visitors so as to inform them of his death. Is that something you can help me with?"

"I'm sorry; we've never had an inmate here by that name."

"Don't con me like that!" Madeline screamed. "I was just in there yesterday. I need to speak to Gordon Covey in the security department, right now!"

"I'm sorry, miss, but Mr. Covey is no longer with us. He was killed in a prison riot yesterday afternoon—."

Madeline hung up the phone, cutting the operator off midsentence. If Gordon was dead, she knew it was a result of her conversation with him at the prison. She sat at her desk scared, bewildered, and sick with guilt. *How can the existence of an entire family and the legal evidence of what they've done just disappear?*

She paced around her office unsure of what to do next. Clearly, Charles and Claire Jackson were in hiding and superseding the boundaries of identity tracking technology to stay that way. But their recent behavior indicated they had resurfaced. And Gabriella was the last person alive Madeline knew who'd spoken to them. Perhaps there was something in Gabriella's State of Illinois psychiatric hospital records linking her to their parents' location?

Madeline forged a patient medical records request form on her office letterhead with the approval signature of "Gabriella Jackson," signed her own name as the attending physician, put it in the fax machine, pressed send, and called the recipient.

"Patient records, how may I assist you?"

"This is Dr. Madeline Knight over at New Orleans State Psychiatric Hospital. I just faxed over a records request form for a Gabriella Jackson, and I need that information sent back right away."

"That shouldn't be a problem, Dr. Knight, but unfortunately for an out-of-state nonemergency request it can take up to twenty-four hours to obtain clearance. I'll fax the records to your office as soon as I receive approval. I could have them ready in as little as ten minutes, but it could take until tomorrow afternoon."

Madeline hung up still without any concrete clues pointing to her parents' location. There was a knock on the door.

"Dr. Knight?" asked Cristy, one of the nursing assistants.

"Who is it?" Madeline asked, having already recognized Cristy's annoying baby-voice, but stalling as she remembered the door was locked—an NOSPH policy violation during shift hours.

"It's Cristy."

Madeline quickly got up and opened the door.

Cristy was standing there with her hand on her hip ready to facilitate an agenda. She was five feet three inches tall with a thin boxy athletic build, tanned-white skin, shoulder length hay-blond hair with no layers, and a plain oval face with gray eyes. She wore little makeup, which was surprising considering she was one of Nurse Monroe's closest friends from high school. They both constantly bragged about their old days as head cheerleaders and campus cronies, and current drunken and sexual escapades. Cristy was also the office snoop, and far below average on the intelligence scale. But contacts afforded jobs at NOSPH, and she was there to stay.

Cristy had been present for the encounter between Madeline and Nurse Monroe earlier that morning, and had volunteered to scope out Madeline's current level of agitation and report her findings back to Nurse Monroe. But Madeline wasn't going to entertain additional gossip perpetuating what she considered a dead subject. Having already made her point clear to Nurse Monroe, she now intended to make the same point clear to Cristy.

"I've been trying to get through on your office line, but it's been busy all afternoon," Cristy whined.

"Well, I've been busy all afternoon," Madeline replied. "If the necessity to contact me for assistance with pressing hospital matters exists, you are more than well-versed on the workings of the facility paging system. So, what is it exactly that requires my haste, post, haste attention?"

"City Hospital is on line two," Cristy replied, muddled and confused. "Anyways . . . they've called several times and said it's urgent, regarding your sister. I didn't know you had a sister—."

"Thank you, I'll take the call." Madeline shut the door in Cristy's face and answered the phone.

"This is Dr. Madeline Knight."

"It's me!" Gabriella yelled. "I've been calling all morning; where are you?"

"I can't talk right now, Gabriella—I already called the nurse this morning and told her I would be coming in to see you later this afternoon. Get some rest and I'll see you then. I need to go."

Just as Madeline hung up, a fax came through. She waited eagerly as one hundred pages of records from the Illinois state hospital system piled up in the dispenser. She scanned through the pages looking for something helpful. When she found the emergency contacts section, the information it contained was more confusing than anything else she'd encountered that day. The only names listed were:

PARENTS – PASTOR MILTON AND PALAMIA CHATSWORTH, CENTRAL CHURCH OF ENLIGHTENMENT, CINCINNATI, OHIO

Madeline had never seen or heard either name before, and dialed the phone number listed without hesitation or expectation as to what she might discover.

"Central Church of Enlightenment, pastor's office, Gwen speaking, how may I help you?"

"Pastor Milton Chatsworth, please?" Madeline asked hesitantly.

"He's not available right now. Can I take a message?"

"No. . . . Is Mrs. Palamia Chatsworth available?"

"Mrs. Chatsworth doesn't take unsolicited phone calls. What is this regarding, ma'am?"

"Her daughter—Gabriella Jackson."

"One moment please, I'll transfer you."

Madeline could barely breathe as she waited. *Who are Pastor Milton and Palamia Chatsworth?* she wondered. Then an eerily familiar voice she hadn't heard in over fifteen years came over the line—her mother's.

"This is Palamia Chatsworth; how may I help you on this blessed day?" Mrs. Chatsworth/Claire Jackson asked. "Hello? Hello?"

Horrified at the sound of her mother's voice, Madeline slammed down the receiver. With her heart racing, she went back to the computer determined to find an answer. She hurriedly typed CENTRAL CHURCH OF ENLIGHTENMENT into the Internet search engine and RESULTS FOUND appeared on the screen. She clicked the first article on a local Cincinnati newspaper's website, which read:

"THE NEW PILLAR OF OUR COMMUNITY- Mayor-sponsored inauguration and ribbon-cutting ceremony for the grand opening of the new Cincinnati Central Church of Enlightenment is scheduled for Friday, April 11, 2014, at noon. Come and meet our new pastor, Milton Chatsworth, and his wife, Palamia, in time for Sunday's first mass!"

A fancy publicity photo at the bottom of the page glorified Madeline's father all decked-out in a beautiful pastor's robe, smiling with his arm around her mother.

"My parents are pastors?" Madeline shouted. "You've got to be kidding me!"

13

PLAN OF ATTACK

Visiting hours at New Orleans City Hospital's psychiatric ward wouldn't begin for another ten minutes. And Madeline could hardly contain her fury as she paced the packed visitors' waiting room mumbling out loud, completely unaware of the scene she was creating. She had deferred her remaining patient evaluations to the next morning's schedule and fled NOSPH early before driving straight to the hospital to confront Gabriella.

After days of no sleep, Madeline was running on pure second-wind adrenaline fueled by a disturbing sense of wrath she had never before felt and never wished to feel again. Expelling the sin from her body before its presence controlled her was almost as vital as extinguishing the root of its cause. The thought of her father's sure-to-be-devious masquerade as pastor of a church was enraging, and she needed to decipher exactly how much information, if any, Gabriella knew about the situation.

It was impossible for Madeline to comprehend how years of sacrilegious torment at the hands of the two most sadistic individuals she'd ever known had culminated with the welcoming of those same individuals as leaders of the most prevalent new church in the Midwest. She was disgusted, and before leaving her office had researched the church in greater detail. After contacting city hall and a local newspaper in Cincinnati, she'd uncovered a surprising amount of information, all of which was almost as unbelievable as the upcoming inauguration itself.

Pastor and Mrs. Chatsworth—as Madeline's parents now called themselves—had emerged from obscurity as two of the most influential members of Ohio society with strong political connections on both a city and state level. The mayor of Cincinnati had tried for years to build the city up to a new standard of modern living and reign as a major political force in the United States. And the introduction of the Chatsworths fit in perfectly with his plans.

The mayor was the brother of a prominent Republican senator who was working his way up to a presidential bid. Together they had decided to bring back the old methods of combining the powers of religion, business, and politics to strengthen their chances against the competition. As a result, their family had invested millions of dollars into constructing the new Central Church of Enlightenment, as well as the Chatsworths' rectory estate compound.

In addition, the Central Church of Enlightenment itself had somehow raised enough capital to buy out three of the major newspaper organizations in Ohio. And they had constructed a commercial printing plant and new corporate headquarters on the church grounds, which was already producing a best-selling publication. County legislation had also approved the building of a new kindergarten through twelfth-grade academy across from the main worship center. Therefore, parents residing in the greater Cincinnati area now had the option to send their children to a private nondenominational religious school free of tuition, which also offered live-in accommodations for qualifying students in need. It wasn't surprising the Chatsworths were so highly praised; their organization not only promised Cincinnati spiritual guidance, but education, national recognition, and hundreds of new jobs as well.

Madeline, however, couldn't believe the ruse. The glossy

publicity photo she'd seen of her father wearing a billowing black satin robe and stole adorned with a white clerical collar and hanging cross was enough to induce another vial outburst of expletives. The image of Pastor Chatsworth's phony bleached-white smile—one she'd never witnessed a day in her life—with his arm around his falsely-sanctified wife, was both cringe-inducing and wickedly deceiving at the same time. Now supposedly every Sunday he would stand in front of thousands of parishioners, all hungry to find meaning and direction in their lives, and preach about the forgiveness of sins, importance of family, dangers of domestic abuse, and the grace of the Lord. It was a clever charade the new Milton and Palamia Chatsworth had going—the powerfully handsome and strapping black pastor joined by his beautiful, angelically-alluring white wife; what a treat. How could those poor unsuspecting souls ever deny them?

For Madeline, the hurt from the pure injustice of the whole spectacle was boiling up inside ready to explode. Maxwell her beloved brother was dead—murdered by their parents after they'd already denied him the opportunity for a decent life. And then there was Gabriella, who sat in the city psychiatric ward having barely escaped with her life after being institutionalized for five years because the trauma from her childhood had made it impossible to cope. Whatever beliefs Madeline held about her parents' everlasting threat of a "deserter's extinction" had been replaced by pure indignation and the undeniable desire for retribution. Not just for the sins against her family, but also the sins against the herds of innocent people being sucked into the Chatsworths' cunning subterfuge of ecclesiastical asylum.

"Dr. Knight?"

A familiar voice brought Madeline back from the rotating screen of distressful thoughts dominating her mind. She looked up and saw Dr. Nathan Raines standing in the doorway outside the nurses' station. *Wow, personal attention from the attending psychiatrist? I guess it pays to be a doctor!* Madeline thought, picking up her bags and heading for the door.

Despite her straight-shot mission to get in and interrogate Gabriella, Madeline couldn't help but notice Dr. Raines had somewhat cleaned up his previously disheveled appearance. He still had five days' worth of stubble protruding from his patchy beard, but his now clear lenses revealed intoxicatingly iridescent hazel eyes. And with his clean, shiny hair pulled back into a dreamy man-bun, his golden locks made him look like a Greek Titan turned polished surfer. This time, it was Dr. Nathan Raines who had mesmerized Dr. Madeline Knight.

Even amid her current state of turmoil, the sight of a man like Nathan Raines caused a foreign tang of blush to warm Madeline's body. Her sham of a personal life had always been a bothersome reality, but adverse circumstances had robbed her of such indulgences and survival was always given first seed. Apart from her secret attraction to and harmless daydreaming about Jack Lee, for Madeline romance was just another sensory impression toward which she was consciously immutable.

"I heard you were waiting and thought I would come out and bring you back myself before it gets busy in here," Dr. Raines said.

"I didn't realize the doctors here greeted visitors personally," Madeline replied. "I guess the city hospitals are a bit ahead of the rest of us."

"I wish that were true. No, I started my shift early and figured I'd give you the royal treatment. Follow me." He led Madeline through the security checkpoint bypassing procedure, and through the newly admitted patients' holding room.

The city hospital psychiatric system was nothing like the federally funded, top-of-the-line research and inpatient facility Madeline worked in. It was a processing center that evaluated patients brought in under a seventy-two-hour involuntary psychiatric hold. And it was a terrifyingly unpleasant place to be.

If a doctor hadn't admitted a patient under special circumstances and transferred them into a private hospital room for continued medical care—like Gabriella—he or she had most likely been arrested by the police, examined for injury, and deposited into the holding area. If a patient was brought in by ambulance and deemed physically sound, he or she was taken into the same room, but only after spending approximately twelve hours shuffling through the emergency medical system. And after being discharged by emergency, such patients waited another twelve hours for a psychiatric doctor to determine whether to issue a commitment or release them back into the world that had caused the confinement to begin with.

Similar to being held in a county jail, once a person became entangled in a city's psychiatric system they were locked in with no control over their human freedoms until release. And many types of people had found themselves in such an unfortunate predicament: homeless schizophrenics found wandering the streets, recently released persons with mental illness unable to maintain themselves on the outside, and those deemed a suicidal threat. But one-fourth of the patients were heavily intoxicated citizens who'd experienced a bad day, or days, that kept getting worse.

The processing ward looked like a small bus terminal except for the row of highly coveted, semi-comfortable chairs that reclined into beds. With more patients than beds, occupancy was first-come, first-served. And breaking the unspoken rule of respecting whose chair was whose could surely erupt into a psych-tech-involved resolution with a couple shots of chemical restraints. It was an active place to work and an even more surreal place to be contained. Some patients wandered around making a ruckus, some slept, and some waited in the phone line trying to contact outside help. Others just sat patiently refusing to touch their one-time bag lunch, aware they'd made a huge mistake and hoping for an immediate release as soon as they had the chance to meet with a doctor and make their case.

Madeline had worked in a city hospital system during medical school, and as she walked through the holding room on her way to visit her own sister, the experience brought back both sad and embarrassing memories. After all, Madeline knew how it felt to sit on both sides of the glass wall separating doctors from patients.

"So, how is Gabriella doing today?" Madeline asked as she and Dr. Raines passed through the holding section into the hallway leading to the patient recovery rooms. "She called me early this afternoon demanding my immediate presence and the delivery of personal goods, so I'm assuming she's somewhat in the clear?"

"She's in the clear," Dr. Raines replied, "but we're still running her blood work and trying to raise her electrolyte count to a safe level and minimize the damage. She'll be on intravenous fluids and a catheter for the next twenty-four hours. Her kidneys are in good shape, but she put them through quite a marathon. We'll continue to flush them out."

"Have you examined her personally?"

"Not yet. The morning psychiatrist did a preliminary interview after emergency transferred her in from ICU. But she was just coming out of sedation and it wasn't particularly productive; she had no idea how she got here. I was planning on meeting with her later this evening after her next physical exam." He stopped walking outside a closed door. "This is it."

Madeline realized that as soon as she entered Gabriella's room the truth of her life would erase the unexpected feeling of calm she felt with Dr. Raines, and those moments of subtle relief would become a distant memory. *Sad I should feel a trip through a city psych ward with an attractive doctor to be a pleasant break from reality.* "Well," she said, "thank you for taking the time to walk me back. I need to go in and see her now."

"Would you like me to come in and try to talk to her while you're here?" he asked, wanting to extend the encounter.

"No, thank you, Doctor."

"Nathan," he said smiling, hopelessly entranced by the light dusting of freckles on her perfectly-shaped nose he couldn't take his eyes off; he reached out and gently touched the tip. "You have the cutest little freckles, you remind me of—."

"Yes, well, thank you, Nathan, but I'm sure Gabriella would request my exclusion from any conversations she has with you anyway. She wouldn't want to be cheated out of the opportunity to present me with a skewed version of her status should the need arise. But thank you just the same."

"Okay, well, if you have any questions feel free to give me a call. Until then, I'll just look forward to seeing you tomorrow night at the gala?"

"Indeed. Good-day, Doctor—I mean, Nathan."

————

Gabriella was lying in bed gently sipping an orange juice through a straw and watching television when Madeline walked into the room. She looked surprisingly well considering the condition she was in the night before. But then again, it wasn't exactly Gabriella's first encounter with drugs and alcohol; she had enjoyed her fair share of both long before her run-ins with the laws that prohibited them—even while locked in the state psychiatric system.

She was pleased to see Madeline and instantly clicked off the television, but the smile on her face faded the second the door closed, and she realized her sister's enthusiasm didn't match her own. Because, although Madeline was relieved to see Gabriella alert and no longer attached to a breathing tube, the anger she felt about their parents had returned the moment Dr. Raines had left. She was troubled about Gabriella's current medical condition, but right now she only wanted answers.

"Dangerously rough night you had there, huh?" Madeline asked. "I guess five years didn't teach you a thing."

"Yeah, well, I really don't think you have much room to talk, do you?" Gabriella replied, sitting up sluggishly. "Considering it was your cabinet I drank out of. Anyways . . . where've you been? I called you hours ago."

"Some of us actually have to work." Madeline tossed Gabriella a small duffel bag full of bathroom items and some clean loungewear she'd taken from her office armoire. Already on the opposite side of town, she hadn't had time to travel back to the French Quarter just to scavenge up her own expensive belongings to adhere to Gabriella's always-lavish tastes. She'd already submitted to that scenario more times than she cared to remember.

Before Gabriella's five-year commitment in Chicago, every time Gabriella ended up back in the hospital after one of her many episodic psychiatric benders, Madeline had found herself a slave to visiting hours and the facilitation of Gabriella's needs. She didn't have a life outside taking Gabriella's calls, coordinating with Gabriella's social workers, and running to the hospital twice-a-day to visit an ungrateful sister who never appreciated or cared for her presence anyway. It had quickly become a destructive way of life Madeline had left behind for good reason.

Gabriella opened the bag and sifted through the contents before looking up unsatisfied. "Where's my computer bag? I told you to bring it! What am I supposed to do in here all day without my stuff?"

"That's the least of my concerns—and right now, 'stuff' is the least of yours!" Madeline began to pace frantically around the room. "I know you were telling the truth about Max, but he didn't die in prison, he was murdered! Our parents sent someone in there and had him killed and I have the evidence to prove it!"

Gabriella momentarily forgot about her missing trinkets and raised the back of her bed to sit up. "What evidence?" she asked. "What are you talking about?"

"At this point, that's my business, not yours!"

"What? I don't think so, Belle! You need to tell me what's going on. I thought we were supposed to be in this together?"

"So did I! But at the moment, I'm under the impression you're not being as forthcoming as you claim to be." Madeline stopped pacing and stood at the foot of Gabriella's bed. "I worked for hours this morning trying to locate our parents. I checked everywhere using every resource I had, and every record of our family's existence had been erased. Would you like to know how I finally found them?"

"How?" Gabriella asked cautiously, trying not to aggravate her obviously temperamental sister any more than she already was. Gabriella knew better, considering the last time she pushed Madeline past her breaking point she didn't see her again for five years.

"In your hospital contact records! He's a pastor in a church? Why would you keep something like that from me? Are you grifting me again?"

"Belle, listen—."

"No, you listen! You better give me one reason why I shouldn't just walk on all this right now. You think people are so easy to find? I'll be so far gone what's left of me won't even be a ghost!"

"Hey! You can just stop right there. I understand you still have certain feelings about what happened between us in the past and you're frustrated right now, but don't take your issues out on me! I used the only money I had to come here and make amends for what I did. And I'm not exactly in the best situation myself right now, so stop making everything all about you. I have no idea what you're talking about, Belle. Our parents never mentioned anything like that and I sure as hell never put them on my contact list. I didn't have control over my own food and drink schedule let alone over who came and went. So, slow down for a minute . . . I seriously have no idea what you're talking about."

Madeline tried to calm herself down; she hadn't intended to take her frustration out on her sister. "Alright, alright. I'm sorry, Gabriella. I feel like I'm going insane right now. This whole situation is way beyond anything I expected. It's crazy! Right now, I don't know what to think or who to believe."

"It's fine. Trust me, I understand. For once, I'm not the only one in the dark. Okay, what do you mean he's a pastor? They threatened me with their warning, but that just doesn't make any sense. What did you find out?"

"That our parents have somehow become the managing pastors of some huge new church in Cincinnati, Ohio," Madeline said tiredly, slumping down into one of the chairs.

Gabriella sat quietly for a moment thinking about what she'd heard, then fearfully erupted, "Well, no wonder they're coming after us—they need us all dead because they don't want anyone knowing their secrets. We have to figure out what to do!"

"I already have. If you can believe it, the entire city is throwing them a huge welcoming ceremony on Friday. Every major news station in the country will be there to cover it. And when they do, everyone in attendance is going to be in for a big surprise. I'm flying to Cincinnati evidence in hand, and when the cameras start rolling, I'll be right there waiting to expose our parents for the frauds and cold-blooded murderers they really are."

Gabriella jumped up to get out of bed, but the medical tubes attached to her body pulled her painfully back down. "You can't go up there alone—you'll get yourself killed! Listen, you said yourself they erased all our files and that the whole city is supporting their cause. Nobody will believe you if you show up on your own; I'm going with you. You'll need my help and someone to back your story. When am I getting out of here?"

"You're not. You're under a seventy-two-hour hold. You know that."

"And you know I didn't try and kill myself! It was an accident. You're a big fancy doctor now, right? So, get me out of here. I have to go with you!"

"I can't, Gabriella; you're not under my care. And right now, this is the safest place for you anyway. I'm really sorry, but that's the way it has to be. As long as our parents have no contact or access to you, I'll have a chance to ambush them before they make their next move. I have to go."

"Fine," Gabriella said sadly, "if that's the way it has to be."

"It is." Madeline was beyond fatigued and needed to rest and refocus. Knowing her parents were busy preparing for their big celebration would at least allow her some time of her own to regroup. She stood up somberly and walked to the door.

"Belle, wait!" Gabriella shouted after her. "If you're really going to do this on your own, then be careful. They're capable of anything and I don't want you putting yourself at risk, not for me, and not for Max. I don't want to be without you again."

Madeline opened the door and left without looking back.

14

MEETING WITH THE DEVIL
IN
THE PASTOR'S DEN

Cincinnati, Ohio

The course of creation for the Central Church of Enlightenment—the CCE—had been a constant source of wonder and speculation for the inhabitants of Cincinnati, and the owner had made great efforts to design it that way. With religious affiliation amongst Americans at an all-time low and the growth of nondenominational churches on the rise, the CCE was hitting its market at precisely the right time. The strong accuracy of those facts, however, had no bearing on the reality that generating interest in church-related religious activities was the most difficult obstacle threatening its success. Especially in modern times where fame, wealth, and materialism were the desires of highest priority for the majority of the people in the world. But the mastermind behind the CCE had taken such desires into consideration and cleverly used them to its advantage.

As with any new business venture involving a reconstituted idea, it was of uppermost importance that the CCE rendered their anticipated clientele in awe of their product's appearance. The fruits of this concept were wisely obtained by the initial tantalization of having the church's construction commence at sundown and promptly retire just before sunrise the following day. So captivated by the excitement generated from wanting what they couldn't see, nobody ever questioned the reasons for the secrecy. The newspapers diligently assured that the "construction under cover" was to avoid interrupting the daily quality of life enjoyed by greater Cincinnatians in the struggling to be up-and-coming city. But the CCE property covered more than fifty acres in an uninhabited industrial neighborhood near one of the entrances to Cincinnati's famed abandoned subway system. Therefore, the construction didn't actually disrupt the city's daily operations at all, but rather attracted them.

The question of whom owned the project was also a great ambiguity triggering assumptions, but miraculously nobody knew the answer. The city had gone through years of political elections and public office transitions since the CCE's inception, yet not one official ever knew the actual details behind the mysterious project. Furthermore, the demolishing of the existing buildings on the church's property had begun several years before the official announcement explaining the intentions for the land.

Contractors and suppliers from around the country had flocked to Cincinnati to secure a chance to bid on the project, but all materials were to be purchased from local vendors only, and all subcontractors had to have licenses registered within city limits. The newspapers called it "The Rust Belt Economy Boost." But still, nobody knew the identities of the chosen subcontractors and suppliers, also creating another hot source of speculation. Rumors circulated throughout the construction industry about who'd won the bids for the jobs, but the CCE project managers never confirmed names and only allowed one company to work on their contracted phase at a time. Regardless, thousands of people had obtained jobs during the decade spent working on the massive church compound, and the city considered the additional employment a Godsend. Which was another great tactic implemented by the mastermind behind the CCE.

Because Cincinnati had the misfortune of leading the nation in population decline, it was imperative to regain the more than two hundred thousand citizens it had lost over the past fifty years. To do so, they needed to jumpstart their failing economy, and the job creation provided by the new church had been a welcome stimulation. Also, adding a visually mesmerizing piece of architecture sure to generate additional tourism at no cost to the taxpayers was a profitable perk as well. And while Cincinnati was already home to a diverse array of architectural styles both prewar and modern, the Central Church of Enlightenment was a combination of both and a work of art like the world had never seen.

Historically, commemorative buildings were erected to pay homage to the founders of an industry or a revered political figure, but not the Central Church of Enlightenment. Press releases distributed from unknown publicists were absolutely clear that the new church was built to pay homage to the city and citizens of Cincinnati as a whole, and that its offerings were available for enjoyment and praise by any resident or visitor wishing to take part.

The CCE was practically a city within itself. With high fencing made of polished iron surrounding the grounds on all sides, after the grand opening the contents behind the walls would be left open for all to see. The best time of the year in Ohio was spring, and the church had planned its opening to take full advantage. Widespread gardens and perfectly manicured parks displayed the finest arrangements of indigenous horticulture and made up every square foot of property not supporting a structure. The hundreds of magnolia and cherry trees lining every street were in full bloom and displaying an overwhelming abundance of white and pink blossoms. Dainty white fragrant honeysuckle tubes with yellow stamens draped the iron fences, and the bulbs of purple-blue chionodoxa and white-yellow daffodils lined the ponds, playgrounds, and benches. Combined with expertly trimmed square hedges of bright-yellow forsythia lining every street and walkway, the results were breathtakingly magical.

Private security patrolled the grounds day and night, and until the grand opening, temporary barricades were set up two blocks from the actual property obstructing the street entrances from all sides. But the image the public could see was absolutely magnificent. The CCE Academy across from the church had the size and amenities to rival the finest of universities, and even the church itself looked nothing like a traditional basilica.

The architectural plans had been drawn-up using a combination of old prints gathered from the late 1920s, and combined to give every structure on the grounds a historical feel with a modern flair. In a part of the country flanked with beautifully sprawling Catholic and Presbyterian cathedrals, before the Central Church of Enlightenment's construction extravagant nondenominational religious establishments in Ohio were unheard of. So, to assist in its universal appeal, outwardly visual extravagance was exactly what the CCE thrived on.

The actual church was fashioned in the way of modern French Art Deco and reminiscent of the Cincinnati Carew Tower. The front of the building resembled a skyscraper consisting of three connected assemblies of the same design. The tallest was in the center extending twenty stories high with two equal-sized replicas extending fifteen stories high on each side. The roof-mounted silver cross perched in the center hypnotically lured in its admirers like Sirens. And because the entire structure was completely encased in polished-copper rectangular panels and had no windows except the thirty-foot crystal double-entry doors, the whole church shined like gold in the sun. Hence, a carefully crafted name plaque reading: *"The Golden Monument."*

Madeline's initial research on the CCE hadn't provided her with the slightest inclination as to the mammoth size or importance of what her parents, Pastor and Mrs. Chatsworth, were now the celebrated ordained leaders of. Her instantaneous anger and disbelief had caused her to focus on nothing more than how the two people responsible for the destruction of three lives could possibly have become religious clergy. She had no idea the CCE had caught the attention of the national and world media, all sighting the rarity that such levels of excitement would be surrounding a religious affair in the United States. Or, that the church had generated a titanic amount of publicity and attention specifically highlighting its grand opening. All of which assured Friday's inauguration ceremony would mark not only the climax of a long-awaited, highly anticipated extravaganza, but the bringing of refreshed life to the city as well.

However, unbeknownst to the millions of spectators engaged in the heaps of enthusiasm circulating around the Central Church of Enlightenment on the outside, corruption and deception simultaneously erupted from the inside. For the people of Cincinnati, the Golden Monument symbolized the promise of a healthy and happy future filled with prosperity and rebirth. But in actuality, it was the first location on the earthly plane where the separation of humankind from Heaven and Hell would inevitably collide.

The interior of the Golden Monument was strikingly different from the exterior. It had been carefully designed to entrance parishioners upon first entry, and therefore to maintain the highest shock value no photographs had been published and no one outside the CCE mastermind had seen it. It was two days before the unveiling and the entire building was completely empty and eerily silent. No music played, no candles burned, and not a single worker hustled about or prepared for Friday's gargantuan celebration. Quite odd considering the vast size of the clerical compound was bigger than a Catholic seminary.

Inside the main worship hall, it was dark and lit only by rows of dim track lighting, which could be cleverly adjusted for brightness according to the desired mood. Dark mahogany wood paneling with heavily detailed crown molding covered the walls floor to ceiling. And six colossal exposed-wood beams extended from the creases of the walls and met in the center of a one-hundred-foot dome, which housed a single circular skylight filtering in the only light from the outside.

Aside from a large silver cross—identical to the one on the roof—hanging over the altar, nothing inside the church represented anything holy. And in stark contrast to the excessive adornments of the exterior, the interior of the hall was luxurious without extravagance and modern, sophisticated, and vast.

There was enough space to seat over ten thousand people in the coliseum-style arrangement, which positioned each row higher than the one in front of it, designed for optimum viewing pleasure. The pews were made of polished piano-black wood covered with a thick gloss and lined with soft black leather cushioning. And two levels of balconies encircled the room and lined the altar, adding standing room for an additional two thousand members of the congregation.

The grand doors leading into the hall opened. A towering bony gentleman dressed in a pressed black-and-white butler's uniform and carrying a large antique silver tray entered the room. He had pitch-black eyes, pale-white wrinkled skin, bloodred lips, a long angular face, and white hair slicked back into a tight chonmage topknot. He walked with the precision and sternness of a military bandmaster down the garnet-red carpet-covered main aisle and up to the front altar.

He proceeded up twelve steps onto the preacher's platform and walked to the back of the altar where glass shelves filled with large crystal goblets lined the walls. He picked up six of the goblets with his long white-gloved hands and placed them onto the tray. He then turned around and exited the altar to the right entering the sacristy room, which housed all vestments, sacred vessels, and hundreds of carafes of red wine. He placed the tray atop a medieval wooden table and filled three of the goblets with one varietal of wine and three with another.

He then picked up the tray, exited the sacristy through a rear entrance, and walked down the hallway past the church offices and dressing rooms. At the end of the hallway, he reached into his pocket and retrieved a gold skeleton key, unlocked a heavy wooden door, and entered. He locked the door behind himself and continued down a long narrow hallway displaying no signs of the modern architecture adorning the rest of the church. It was dark and shadowy with flames from burning kerosene lanterns flickering off red-and-gold wallpaper.

When he reached the end of the hallway, which slanted downward as he walked, he descended seventy-five steps of a dark spiral staircase with a gentle red glow radiating from the base. Two massive French doors made of solid oak greeted the butler at the bottom of the seemingly never-ending helix, and with a tight fist, he knocked hard three times, paused, knocked three times more, and the great doors slowly opened inward. He entered, and with a loud thud, the doors closed securely behind him.

Inside a grandiose dimly lit office, Pastor Milton Chatsworth—formerly Charles Jackson—sat behind a large stone desk. Fifteen years of elapsed time hadn't added a single line to his smooth face or around his intensely penetrating black eyes. His youthful good looks remained intact with the only revolution in his appearance being his police chief uniform's replacement with a heavy black satin General's jacket. The collar of which extended to his chin and parted in the middle, displaying a shiny clerical collar made of polished titanium. The construction was seamless without a zipper or button, and with fabric stiff as metal, Pastor Chatsworth's jacket resembled a fitted piece of polished body armor.

Stefan, Pastor Chatsworth's only confidant, protector, personal soldier, and handler for life, wore the same uniform in dark gray without the clerical collar. He was eastern European with black eyes, sharp facial features, thin lips, and razor-cut blond hair. He had a thick scar extending from the crease of his left lip to the bottom of his left ear, and stood seven feet tall with ginormous hands and bulging muscles. He anchored himself silently at attention behind Pastor Chatsworth's right shoulder, while Palamia Chatsworth—formerly Claire Jackson—stood behind Pastor Chatsworth's left.

The years had been kind to Mrs. Chatsworth as well, but the young mother once exuding a glamorous retro beauty had grown into a fiercely striking woman. Her clenched jaw and cold-white skin showed the decades of struggle she'd endured to arrive at her current station of power. And the omnipresent look of sadistic pleasure once filling her eyes now resembled the impenetrable focus of a decorated officer awaiting the declaration of war.

Her platinum-blonde hair was pulled back into a sleek elongated up-do extending from her head, with a polished titanium band matching her husband's lining the base of her crown. Her full lips and eyebrows were as pale as her face, and the only color highlighting her features was a dark-brown blush on her high cheekbones and wide eyelids. She wore the same General's jacket as Pastor Chatsworth, with a matching skirt cinched at her tiny waist and hanging to the floor.

Higher up on a pedestal, opposite Pastor Chatsworth at the front side of the desk, sat the same terrifying being Madeline had evaded in the Sands—the Devil himself. Satan the Prince of Darkness, perched in a raised red-velvet wingback chair, faced his two most powerful Generals awaiting their report on the progress and status of his next attack. He was dressed in a black colonial aristocrat's formal suit lined with gold, a white ruffled shirt, and a ruby-red silk plaid waistcoat. He had a shiny silver watch attached to a long fob, the time of which he checked incessantly; the hands ticked loudly every time he flipped open the case. With large sparkling silver eyes and dilated red pupils, he looked like death incarnate. Fitting, considering his image of what man should be was nothing remotely close to the original beauty of its being.

His appearance was more of a version of what he would have designed man to be had he only the power over such creations, which his wretched soul was adamantly sure he would one day possess. He looked neither young nor old and his hair was neither long nor short but rather a dark skin of silky black fur covering his head like an animal. There was no muscle to his mass but the thickness of his bones was clearly visible through his transparent, opaque skin. As were the throbbing purple veins of blood transporting the life force he needed to function but not to feel. He had inhabited a body he himself created, and used it at will to walk the earth during his last desperate endeavor to achieve his one and only goal: renegotiation of his punishment of condemnation to an eternity of banishment and torture burning in the Lake of Fire and Brimstone, as imposed by the Divine Wrath of God. And time was running out before that day arrived.

Through the dark ring of shadows enclosing Satan and his Generals, the butler emerged with the tray of wine and set it down in front of the Prince of Darkness. "Here you are, my Lorde," he said in a deep British accent. "The two wines you requested for sampling and approval prior to first mass. I have filtered them and added the sedatives accordingly. Are there any additional requests I may provide?"

"Nothing further, Lavoy," Satan said, eyes pointed straight-ahead burning into Pastor Chatsworth, who waited patiently for Satan's Butler to excuse himself.

After Lavoy disappeared into the darkness, Pastor Chatsworth waited to hear the loud crash of the oak doors and then prepared to begin the speech he'd been waiting with anticipation to deliver. The last fifteen years of his life had come down to the execution of a meticulous equation consisting of whit, charm, and perseverance; the implementation of which now hung on final approval from the evil, immortal authority he'd served for as many lifetimes as he could remember.

"All of our hard work is finally paying off," Pastor Chatsworth declared proudly. "In just a few days' time, the first of your new churches will open, marking the beginning of a new era. Our goal is to bring in as many souls as possible and send them back out to do our bidding. The entire city is at our fingertips and everyone is in line and under my control—."

"Your control?" Satan roared, refusing to grant Pastor Chatsworth the luxury of impressing him prematurely; he had his top General on a sharp hook and would keep him writhing there. "Need I remind you that the spitting of empty promises about 'goals' simply will not do? I want concrete details with the numbers to back them up. Sides are being drawn as we speak; their King has returned, and my time is running out! Millions of years of my research have made up the words to your sermons and it will be my manipulations coming out of your mouth. All must be in order for Friday's inauguration in preparation for Sunday's first mass."

Pastor Chatsworth quickly remembered whom he was sitting in front of and his enthusiasm faded. He may have been the face of the acerbically cruel CCE operation, but he was in no way the true authority. He stiffened his back, lifted himself up higher in his chair, and retired the proud sentiment he'd foolishly permitted to infiltrate his demeanor.

"Lorde and Master," Pastor Chatsworth said. "I can assure you after fifteen years of my dedication to this cause, despite certain setbacks, we have devised a surefire method to convince the cities of this country that bridging church and state is the only way to achieve great power. By selecting the Central Church of Enlightenment's nonreligious specific organization as our launching pad, we have finally found a way to surpass the Baptist, Presbyterian, and Catholic churches combined in both control and financial gain on U.S. soil. The rest of the churches of the world will soon follow."

Satan was pleased. "Excellent, Chatsworth," he said. "If you make good on your promises, you will be rewarded by becoming the first of my loyal Generals to achieve a status such as this. On Sunday, you stand to take control of the first of one thousand churches under construction across the country with high-ranking men of darkness disguised as their leaders. And when your church opens successfully, the powers I am giving to your bloodline only will enable you to facilitate the actions of all leaders beneath you. I've waited millenniums to catch the God-fearing race so off guard they would become putty in my hands, but I never imagined it would have been so easy. Less than one hundred years after taking control of their wasted minds through the very technologies they themselves created, I have absolute power over the main port cities of this country. By initiating our strike from the hidden core of Cincinnati, the synapses of my plan will begin to fire from the center of the eye and ignite the cells of all posts awaiting my orders."

Satan leaned back and smiled impishly. He was especially entertained by the sound of his own voice and deliciously proud of himself for having delivered the speech he had ordered Pastor Chatsworth to prepare. "Come Sunday," Satan continued, "when the parishioners are shuttled in like cattle and the doors close behind them, their souls will be mine for the taking. Your son's sacrifice was only the beginning."

Mrs. Chatsworth flinched ever so slightly at the mention of her son, yet she did not speak. Her husband's submissive behavior was nauseating, as was the entire charade. Although she had her own ideas of how to aid in the progression of their church, she had begrudgingly decided to allow the terms to play out as Satan wished. She was confident that if his original plan should go wrong, her reserve strategy would ensure her emergence as his true liberator and her status as a mere General would become a distant memory.

"Our son was a disgrace!" Pastor Chatsworth replied. "He was nothing more than a drug addict who defiled the family. He was worthless. I was happy to sacrifice him for your cause."

"As you should have been," Satan declared. "I have told you countless times that the weak will not be left to stray and no deserters will be left alive. I have ample confidence in my plan to exhaust the Heavens of every believer by crushing all faith in their mighty Lord and Savior before his fortieth year has passed. Generations of temptation facilitated by my army have finally made the souls of God's children ripe for the taking. The majority of the world is already under my influence, and it is only the strongest believers who remain to suffer the final wrath of my devices. And it is the strong who will allow me to condemn all Earth to the same fate as I have been. When the Son's Queen is mine, and God is left with nothing except the spoils of the very souls he created, He will have no choice but to buy them back!"

Satan picked up a goblet of wine and drank it down completely; the dark-crimson liquid visibly flowed down his throat igniting a bloodred glow in his once purple veins. "I have needed your eldest daughter since the day she was born," he said. "I have continued to administer great pains to obtain her, but she has proven to be quite the challenge. And nobody knows that more than the two of you. Don't let her slip away again!"

"Yes, Lorde and Master," Pastor Chatsworth said. "I made the rules clear long ago and I will take pleasure in carrying them out to completion."

"Silence!" Satan roared, pounding his fist down on the desk like a gavel, shaking the room and rattling everyone in it, including Stefan, who stood like a statue of stone. The remaining goblets toppled over and shattered; the wine flooded the desktop and flowed onto the floor. "It is I who made the rules and not the other way around. You have a job to do and I suggest you get to it. We have less than one week left. All bloodlines must be accounted for and in line for the transition. Period."

Satan stood up, his immense size towering over the three subordinates before him. "If you hadn't failed me years ago in Salem my mission would have been exceedingly more progressed. I told you to turn your children's souls not beat them! You had the world in your hands in a sleepy city protected by my shelter and you destroyed it. You're both lucky you possess the one thing I need in addition to your absolute devotion. The only reason you're still here, and not burning in the depths of Hell, is because I invested fifteen years of the precious time I have left in cleaning up your mess and erasing your past. That will only happen once. Any further problems will not be tolerated. The consequences of another failure will be worse than you could ever imagine. I have given you the promise of eternity reigning in my kingdom. The alternate outcome will be the opposite. This is your last chance!"

15

CLEANSING

New Orleans, Louisiana
Inside a narrow acrylic-glass booth at an indoor-outdoor tactical training center and gun range, dressed in a black tank top, fitted black casual cargo pants, and boots, Madeline fired off round after round with her black handgun. Sleeping had seemed an impossibility, and she needed to release the anger consuming her mind and the negativity influencing her judgement. Plus, she didn't want to be alone with her thoughts and risk succumbing to another alcoholic escape.

The sound of the range was deafening, as the facility was always full of customers, day and night. In the fifty-booth park, the money expelled in a single hour on ammunition alone was worth tens of thousands of dollars. Southern states have always touted their gun enthusiasts, and New Orleans was no exception. Gun shops were a widespread amenity, and it was a fashionable pastime for arms bearers to sharpen their skills and show off expensive new toys at the most exclusive locations.

Madeline, being not only a woman but also a young attractive woman, wasn't welcomed in her club fondly at first. After years of regular membership, she still received disapproving stares from men who had never seen her before—or any woman with a gun for that matter. But regulars who knew her had learned to either ignore her presence or respect it, as she was clearly an expert marksman, and every round she fired at the human-shaped target was a dead-heart center.

Raised by a high-ranking officer of the law with military connections no civilian could ever understand, Madeline was never a stranger to the company of firearms and knew how to handle all-manner of weapons by age seven. But for Madeline and her brother, Maxwell, to join their father at the local gun ranges, state law had required them to pass a hunter safety course and acquire licenses, and their father had signed them up immediately. Not only were they the only children in the class, but Madeline, the only female, had completed her written and physical tests without error at only eight years old. On the day of graduation, she went to the range to put her now-legal skills to the test, and even then she had the best precision-shot in the group—which only humiliated and angered the seasoned police officers administering the school. But being a strong woman in the center of her father's cutthroat world was always part of life for Madeline Knight.

Charles Jackson had demanded his children grow up to be soldiers, and a militant life was exactly what they led. He had bred Madeline and Maxwell for admittance to West Point Military Academy and the Annapolis Naval Academy respectively, and had structured their daily routine to replicate boot camp. Madeline and Maxwell had each undergone several private educational tours of a fully operational, at-sea-and-active Navy missile cruiser before entry to high school. And between weapons training, martial arts, Morse code, foreign languages, and superior intelligence, Madeline and Maxwell were highly evolved, disturbingly abused diamonds in the rough. How they would individually choose to express those talents, no one had known.

Charles had debated embracing a United States military career himself when younger, but had decided that becoming a police chief would provide more freedom with the same rights.

Moreover, he had considered himself to be the General of his own army, and Madeline and Maxwell were his star cadets whom were to take command of the two largest military organizations known to man. However, due to failings all his own, his plans fell through and left him with nothing more than a ravenous regret and the taste for revenge.

But even as an adult, Madeline had adamantly kept her weaponry and tactical training skills polished and tight—she always knew one day she might need them.

She continued to lose herself in the noise of the range, blasting off more rounds with her silver handgun, and every shot was now a dead-head center.

As the sun began to set over the Mississippi River, Madeline finished off the last of her ammunition and expertly unloaded, disassembled, and packed up her gear. Because even though she had been avoiding going home, it was time to prepare for the inevitable task of confronting her parents in Cincinnati. The prospect was daunting, and she knew the outcome would end the course of her life as she knew it.

Earlier in the day after leaving City Hospital, Madeline had hoped to take advantage of an afternoon off and garner some sleep ahead of the grueling days to come. But she hadn't been able to bring herself to return to her apartment, as acknowledging her home in New Orleans had felt like staying immersed in a life no longer her own; a life she had hopelessly cultivated to exude the image of success; a life she now realized never existed at all. Her previous motivations outside her career had always revolved around establishing a home filled with all the feminine luxuries her parents had denied her. Those same luxuries were now mocking her in the cruelest way possible; nothing but bits and pieces of a dream long lost—cold, taunting evidence of the useless waste her material wealth had become from its use as a substitute for nirvana. How could she possibly go back home now?

With her parents' reemergence, Maxwell's murder, and the responsibility imposed by Gabriella's return, Madeline's life had been irrevocably altered. The necessity to proceed with a new stance was an undeniable fact with no way to escape the efforts required to sustain it. But the shame of the person Madeline was by means of blood-family-association haunted her more than the pain of her ailments. She had tried for years to forget her past, ran from it, buried the incomprehensible truths of the abuse, injustice, and torment. But twenty-nine years spent concealing the damage had finally broken capacity, the floodgates had burst, and the contents behind them were widespread and rushing.

Madeline's mind swirled in every direction as she drove the fourteen miles from Harahan to her apartment. The endless blocks of poverty overrunning the minority neighborhoods separating the shooting range from her next destination of an Uptown health food store became more apparent than ever before. As she sat in the evening traffic congestion on St. Charles Avenue in the Garden District of New Orleans, her eyes opened in a different way. Her unobstructed conscience now revealed the blatant injustices she'd never seen, or rather chosen not to see. She had made that same drive more than one hundred times before, but with her rose-hued veil now removed, she forced herself to accept her environment as it really was.

Like everything else in Madeline's life, her single-sided perception of the beauty of the Big Easy began to dissipate as if never in existence, and her two days of sobriety left her stranded in the remnants of her once-flooded soul. The self-inflicted illusion she'd lived amongst was now undeniably revealed by the potent rays of sunshine gleaming through the breaks in the passing clouds of the storm. Now, all Madeline could see was the abundant separation between rich and poor, black and white, and educated and ignorant.

The thoroughfare of St. Charles Avenue was elaborately draped in succulent foliage, trappings of prosperity, and the decadent restorations of a proud history. While only a few blocks north or south, there were thousands of African-Americans born into generations of poverty congregating in forgotten sections of a city looking past their existence. From one side of New Orleans to the next—off the well-traveled tracks of the famed trolley and recreational areas designated for college students and tourists—the poor continued to inhabit unsanitary dwellings settled in the remains of a disastrous hurricane. They had never been properly liberated by a city that flourished amongst their stagnancy and demise.

The evidence was everywhere Madeline looked; one restored building was overshadowed by one hundred more never repaired from the sieges of water they'd been engulfed by. New Orleans was an occupied ghost town, drowned out by the sound of howling tears and haunted by the thousands of poor New Orleanians who had died in horror while begging and praying for the ruling class to save them.

Madeline was sick to admit she had contributed to the problem as selfishly as the officials governing the state-of-affairs. She had come to New Orleans for culture, religion, and prosperity, while never using her acquired prosperity to build up the community from which she'd happily took it. Her work as a psychiatrist had always come from a place of love and public service. But her one-track mind clouded by work-by-day, drink-by-night tendencies had allowed her to ignore the reality of the world around her. Meanwhile, the cries for help emitting from the sea of destitution and violence draping the city in a blanket of slums had been pushed aside to make way for those who refused to hear them.

Madeline detested herself for it. She had buried her past under the existence of those less fortunate, never realizing the oversight. The Law of Compensation had delivered the worst of its promises, and she had received from life exactly what she'd contributed.

She abruptly turned off St. Charles Avenue, headed north to Claiborne Avenue, and took the fast track home. The easiest reaction would have been to perseverate over her mistakes, but it wouldn't have eased her guilt or corrected the problem; she had work to do and needed to complete it before morning.

Madeline always knew her life had a special purpose and was

determined to discover exactly what that purpose was. Everything she'd endured up to that point had prepared her for the next phase of knowledge, and what Priestess Haloise had taught her about the necessity of tribulation finally made sense. Madeline didn't know what direction her life would take after returning from Cincinnati, but for now, New Orleans was the best place where as a psychiatrist she could truly be of service. She intended to remain a dedicated New Orleanian, and through any means possible give back what she had taken.

Everything outside Madeline's residency at NOSPH was in complete disarray, and maintaining the career she had built was as important as obliterating her external afflictions. She had become a psychiatrist to save the minds of her patients to protect their souls, and to resume her calling she would first have to cleanse her own. She had always believed she needed to become someone else to survive in a world that never understood the extent of her personal suffering—how wrong she had been. The only way to find the peace and freedom she longed for was to eliminate the havoc of her past while continuing to develop the achievements she had earned to secure a prosperous future.

When Madeline returned to her apartment, she prepared to implement a spiritual cleansing of the entire house. Her years of solitary withdrawal had left every room in a thick fog of negative lifeless energy. And despite the beauty of the meticulously decorated rooms and profusion of powerful religious adornments, the deeply seated pain and emotional trials of her life had blocked any possibility of positive nourishment.

Adhering to the same ritual she'd witnessed Priestess Haloise perform on multiple occasions, Madeline wore her rosary around her neck and washed each room with the smoke of burning Haitian sage. Afterward, she opened all the windows, turned on the ceiling fans, and allowed the light breeze from the warm night air to wash through the house and replace old stagnancies with new vitality. Finally, she misted every doorway with freshly blessed holy water and lit new candles. She felt a revival of spirit and energy never experienced outside of Haiti, and was determined to keep it flowing in abundance.

After taking a long shower, Madeline prepared a Spiritual Cleansing bath. She filled the tub with hot water and Haitian herbs, flower blossoms, and leaves, then shed her white robe, stepped in, slid down, and fully submerged herself under the surface.

———————

Madeline sat down at her desk and scanned through the book of *Demonology and Protection* Priestess Haloise had given her the night before and had strictly warned her to follow. Priestess Haloise had taught her that everything happening in the world was predetermined to manifest, and that through extensive research and meditation a reliable precedent to justify or predict all events was available for guidance. Priestess Haloise had prophesied a time when the chronicles of the earth—past, present, and future—would collide, forming what she called the "Era of the Ether."

Every book of Vodou scrolls Priestess Haloise owned she had either transcribed herself or obtained by inheritance from her grandmother, Mambo-Josephine, a great Vodou Mambo in Haiti. The only material Priestess Haloise cemented into her own modern self-authored scrolls was events she had both predicted and validated with passages from the *King James Holy Bible*. Priestess Haloise was a Catholic and an ordained priestess; she had to make sure both methods of spiritual guidance worked together harmoniously.

The Haitian Vodou scrolls acquired from her grandmother, however, were of different origin. They documented spiritual methods handed down through multiple generations, and contained secret rituals never revealed to anyone outside her village or family heirs. Mambo-Josephine's scrolls contained laws and occurrences involving demonic possessions and exorcisms performed within her religious community, and could only pass them on to Vodouists chosen to propagate their practices. She had entrusted them to Priestess Haloise years before her death.

Priestess Haloise's mother had died just before giving birth, and Priestess Haloise's grandmother had raised Priestess Haloise alone. Mambo-Josephine had continually taught Haloise about the first War in Heaven and warned her that life was a constant battle over the souls of humans. She told Haloise that because of Satan's rebellion against God and his Angels—long before the Creation of Man—until the End of Revelation the human soul would never be safe while evil and deception continued to manifest on the earthly plane. And it was the duty of God's chosen Messengers to offset the fight by protecting the souls at risk of Satan blocking their paths to salvation ahead of the Final War of Heaven and Hell. Priestess Haloise had taught that same philosophy to Madeline.

Madeline sat and thought about what Priestess Haloise had said the night before about an "imminent shift" taking place between the forces of Heaven and Hell. *What did she mean?* Madeline needed answers, and she needed them before she ventured north to confront Pastor and Mrs. Chatsworth. Her mission to expose her parents' involvement in her brother's grisly murder and lifetime of satanic secrets was no longer her sole focus. The stakes had gone far beyond her personal interests. It wasn't only her and Gabriella's lives at risk, but also the lives of the thousands, possibly millions, of people Pastor and Mrs. Chatsworth would surely condemn by exposing them to their vile existence.

Madeline continued to study *Demonology and Protection*, steadfastly underlining multiple passages and crosschecking each with her own *King James Holy Bible*.

She read aloud to herself from *Matthew 10:16*, " 'Behold, I send you forth as sheep in the midst of wolves: be ye therefore wise as serpents, and harmless as doves.' " That was exactly what Madeline felt like—a sheep amongst the wolves. She always had. Her life had been a constant mission to protect the world's victims against the dominating force of opportunistic assailants without morals. The road had started with Maxwell and Gabriella, and led into child psychiatry and medicine before thrusting her back to her siblings once again. Now that roster would include a flock of Cincinnatians she had never even met.

Madeline took out a box containing her own Vodou scrolls collected throughout her years of study and travel to Haiti and examined them. She knew there had to be something to corroborate the shift Priestess Haloise had predicted besides her personal connection to it.

"In the new era," Madeline read from a Vodou scroll, "Satan will try to overtake the holy temples of the world and fill their pulpits with men of darkness impersonating the cloth." She then scanned through her Bible stopping at *Matthew 7:15-16.* " 'Beware of false prophets, which come to you in sheep's clothing, but inwardly they are ravening wolves. Ye shall know them by their fruits. Do men gather grapes of thorns, or figs of thistles?' " *Is this the shift Haloise was talking about?* Madeline wondered. *If so, are we progressing toward the Era of the Ether?*

Madeline looked back in *Demonology and Protection,* still confused as to why Priestess Haloise had been so adamant about following its terms. Madeline underlined the keywords that caught her attention:

"DEMONCIDE"; "TRANSFIGURATION"; "FOLLOW EXACTLY OR LOSE YOUR SOUL TO THE DARKONE"

She continued reading and stopped at a section titled *"SIGNS OF SATAN'S SOLDIERS."* The symbols she saw of an upside-down cross, a Baphomet Sabbatic goat, a downward-facing pentagram, and the drawings of hands and fingers depicting the Devil's horns and the numbers 6-6-6 were recently familiar to her. The book explained that if the symbols were worn or gestured individually, their bearer could attempt to justify the meaning of their blasphemy by saying the symbols represented an unrelated affiliation in an attempt to deceive their accuser. But when a carrier wore or gestured the symbols in conjunction, the significance would be impossible to disguise or disregard because his or her purpose would be to make their true allegiance known. And *Demonology and Protection* was clear about what such an allegiance would mean: varying degrees of demonic possession resulting in the creation of a Human Portal, which Satan could then use at any time for specific demonic operations.

"Where have I seen these before?" Madeline asked. She took Savannah's patient file out of her backpack and pulled out the pictures taken of Savannah's injuries upon admittance to the hospital. Madeline viewed each of the photographs of the convoluted scar on Savannah's arm from every possible angle. Under closer examination, Madeline found the tattoos underneath the burn to be a hidden combination of every satanic symbol she had just seen in the book. "I knew it! Tomorrow I'm going to find out just how far gone you are."

Despite the consequences, Madeline wasn't going to disregard Savannah's case, especially after everything she had both witnessed and read over the last three days. Her research findings compiled from patients displaying the same symptoms as Savannah, combined with her own personal experiences, provided all the confirmation needed to continue with Savannah's treatment. But Madeline would need to confer with Ross before Savannah's next session the following morning.

After phoning Ross, Madeline organized all of her evidence for the Central Church of Enlightenment's grand opening: copies of the newspaper clippings from Salem and every folder from her childhood records, Maxwell's inmate file, and the prison surveillance video showing who was responsible for his murder. She felt confident, prepared, and recharged with unabashed determination.

Madeline's faith in God and the resulting spiritual guidance had given her the strength to endure a childhood that had demanded the opposite. And it was that same faith now providing her with the strength to confront the Chatsworths.

She packed her bags and printed out a round-trip ticket to Cincinnati. "Ladies and Gentlemen, meet the real Pastor and Mrs. Chatsworth!"

16

JACK LEE

Saturday, April 13, 1991
Fair Grounds Race Course, New Orleans, Louisiana
To the worldwide spectrum of dedicated members of the equestrian community, Louisiana is celebrated as "the Southern center of competitive Thoroughbred racing."

Fair Grounds Race Course in New Orleans was the third-oldest racetrack in North America and held its first races in the mid-1800's. It was home to the Hamilton Derby, the mid-April final preparatory race on The Road to The Kentucky Derby; the race if won by Jack Lee would give him, on his seventeenth birthday, his first chance to qualify for the biggest race in the world, held in his hometown of Louisville in the Bluegrass State—The Kentucky Derby.

For the 1991 Hamilton Derby, the two youngest professional jockeys in the United States would run head to head: Jack Lee, known on the track as "The Kentucky King," and his oldest childhood friend, Prince Onyx, known on the track as "The Southern Prince."

Jack Lee was to ride his ghost-white Thoroughbred filly named Blue Salvation. Blue was one of the rarest horses in the world, one of the only dominate-white-gene champions in racing, and infamous for scaring her competitors clear off the track. She was favored second at the Hamilton Derby, but only a win would allow her to qualify for Kentucky.

Onyx—the son of a European princess and a New Orleans astrophysicist who'd inherited billions from the pharmaceutical industry—was to ride his pure-black Thoroughbred colt named The Emperor. The Emperor was favored to win the Hamilton Derby, but he, too, required the win to qualify for Kentucky. Adding to Onyx's motivation was his recent growth spurt and struggle to make weight, which almost guaranteed his dreams of winning the Kentucky Derby would both begin and end that season.

The weather that day called for a downpour, but Blue Salvation had won all her races in the slop. But the rain had always made The Emperor timid, and Blue Salvation was his team's number-one-feared opponent.

When the starting pistol fired, Jack Lee and Blue burst hot out of the gates in the blinding rain, holding the rail and the lead into the last corner. It was uncharacteristic for a calculated female horse who'd always waited in the back assessing her route, determining her needed exertion, and then powering forward in the last stretch. Onyx and The Emperor were holding on tight, less than a nose-length behind on Jack Lee and Blue's right. But as the young riders exited the last corner, Blue surged forward once again, dropping into a never-before-accessed gear, leaving The Emperor behind with the rest of the pack.

With no challengers in sight, less than a quarter furlong from the finish, just as the announcer started to call Jack Lee and Blue's historical win, Blue crumpled over her weight and speed with a devastating breakdown. She visibly shattered two ankles as her twelve-hundred-pound body tumbled to the ground, launching Jack Lee off her back.

Onyx and The Emperor took first place.

Jack Lee suffered a broken collarbone and a concussion. But

Blue Salvation died instantly on the track—her heart had exploded.

Jack Lee and Blue's trainer was known for running clean, and for a steadfast policy against doping. And Blue Salvation was not a horse who needed encouragement. She'd tested negative for drugs the night before, but her autopsy contradicted those results.

Someone had given her a massive dosage of amphetamine juice mixed with a cocktail of cocaine minutes before she'd gone from stable to gate—a dosage six times the lethal amount. That someone had to be one of only a handful of trusted caregivers or friends allowed access to the twenty-four-hour-a-day, armed-security-protected million-dollar horse. And that someone—seventeen-year-old Prince Onyx—had been caught on camera.

Blue Salvation, the most cherished companion, partner, and family member Jack Lee had loved and trained since the day she was born three years earlier, was buried at the finish line inside the Fair Grounds paddock, and Jack Lee never wrapped his knees around a saddle again.

————————

Thursday, April 10, 2014 – 5:00 a.m.
Fair Grounds Race Course, New Orleans, Louisiana

It was barely dawn at Fair Grounds, and a thick mist covered the track. The sun hadn't yet peeked over the horizon, and the grandstands were empty, dark, and silent as Jack Lee leaned against the guardrail inside the paddock, alone, watching the seemingly disorganized morning routines. But the stables were as active as ever, and more horses worked the track at one time than on any race weekend.

"Morning Workouts" at the track were the most intimate, magical, and exhilarating time for those who had devoted themselves to the lifestyle. The comradery developed and revered among owners, jockeys, trainers, staff, and their families in those early hours of the day was the most contagious and memorable aspect of the job. It was the haven Jack Lee unfailingly went to every morning to remember—but other than Blue, it was the only part he missed.

After Blue Salvation's death, despite his parents' urging for him to come home to Kentucky, Jack Lee had decided to stay and finish high school at the live-in New Orleans prep school he and Onyx had both attended. But despite their proximity, Jack Lee verbally shunned Onyx with silence and completely disregarded Onyx's existence within his world. And although their families' long history of friendship, combined with an unsolicited financial settlement, left Onyx exonerated from any repercussions for his murder of Blue Salvation, Jack Lee's cold war with his betrayer had only just begun.

After their twelfth-grade graduation, Onyx studied in New York and London, while Jack Lee stayed on and completed his entire undergraduate, graduate, and doctoral degrees at the local Catholic-Jesuit university and Baptist seminary in New Orleans. Jack Lee was forever connected to the city where he had felt his earthly life shift from a direction of competition, to a direction of deeply-connected spirituality. And his ever-strengthening awareness of his connection to God reassigned his energy from the companion he'd lost, to the Divine Mission he was to embark upon with the companion he was left destined to find.

Throughout college, Jack Lee's decision to focus on religious and theological studies was directly related to the question of his true identity, which constantly lingered on his mind. He spent every free moment inside the school cathedral connecting to God and preparing himself for the transfiguration yet to come.

Still, Jack Lee's sharp good looks and single status had the collegiate girls he encountered continually engaging him with romantic enthusiasm. But Jack Lee had no interest in meaningless interactions. He was certain the only woman he knew was the partner to his soul would eventually appear. His intuition told him he'd find her in New Orleans, and he intended to stay there until they reunited.

Unfortunately, when the day of Jack Lee's doctoral graduation arrived, he remained a bachelor. Anxiety crushed his hope as he walked the stage for the last time; he received his final degree that day but felt he was leaving empty-handed.

He had unfinished business in New Orleans which included a cold war left to settle and a bride left to claim.

Jack Lee's parents, however, adamantly required him to return home immediately after college, and earn back both his costly tuitions and his inheritance by joining his younger brother, Maximus, in perpetuating the family equine-breeding empire. Jack Lee's extended education had been burdensome to his father, who was beyond the capacity to continue without adequate successors. He'd instilled such need in both of his sons since their births, and Jack Lee was forever caught between pleasing his father, his internal connection to the Higher Power, and his current distaste for the industry of which his family held the market share.

Eventually, to his father's embarrassment and fury, Jack Lee swore no part in the occupation he forever blamed for Blue Salvation's death—unless their organization made significant changes; and despite Jack Lee's love for his father and dependence on his father's approval, even the enticement of early inheritance and instant political influence could not sway him. Jack Lee wanted his definition of true life, not his father's. And Jack Lee knew he owed the world an everlasting accomplishment resulting in increased life to all, which extended beyond the confines of the wealthy and privileged world he had grown to detest.

Believing a lesson in destitution would realign Jack Lee's priorities, his parents allowed him a six-month volunteer station serving poverty-stricken adolescent eastern Kentuckians. However, the experience only bolstered Jack Lee's undeniable consciousness of an earthly call to a greater Holy existence. And while his always-inherent pull toward the service of God was not intended for the priesthood, he knew a reign infinitely higher in Biblical significance awaited.

Such a course of life, however, did not resonate with his parents' plans to perpetuate their financial legacy which had required strenuous, tenacious competition to achieve. The blood-family-propagation of their multi-generational conglomerate was of absolute necessity to remain in power.

Handlers forced Jack Lee to remain in Kentucky and implemented a strictly organized strategy to confirm his allegiance and prepare him for reintegration. But still, Jack Lee's moral and philosophical opposition to the behaviors and lifestyles of the upper-class community in which he was immersed kept him from social acceptance.

Finally, an involuntary arranged marriage was instated to nullify Jack Lee's continued insubordination. And despite his initial refusal, out of fear and respect for his father—a man immovably and deceptively controlling—Jack Lee submitted.

And so, for several more years Jack Lee lived despondently under his father's rule in a lifeless marriage; a marriage to a woman whom shamelessly flaunted her serial-adultery. But despite his misery and diminished self-confidence, Jack Lee continued his life as a dedicated scholar, preparing for his Divine Mission, and believing faithfully his day of emancipation would soon come.

And it did, but not without harmful compensation. On Jack Lee's thirty-third birthday, his father's untimely death in a gruesome car crash left Jack Lee lost and distraught. After the funeral, the family dynamic instantly shifted, as his mother and brother joined alliances, leaving Jack Lee to his own devices for the first time in his life. But consequently, he found himself with the personal freedom he'd forever desired. Within months, lawyers filed a mutual petition for Jack Lee's divorce, which was uncontested and swiftly granted.

However, for Jack Lee, what he thought was freedom predictably morphed into unbearable loneliness and crippling depression. He saw his birthdays as a punishment and a curse, and his father's sudden passing had left a cavernous void and a labyrinth of confusion. Jack Lee had failed to grant the wishes of his father and had buried the best of himself while attempting the task. Guilt combined with extreme co-dependency upon his father's now nonexistent direction and control sparked an unbridled down spiral of self-destruction.

For a full-year, Jack Lee extinguished his pain and self-loathing under a gushing spout of alcoholic shame—a breathing, and punishing, and callous shame that swallowed him up, day after day, until his life was a revolving nightmare of sickness and decay. The cycle was unyielding, and the weeks turned to months, and the months turned to a hopeless existence with no means left for escape. And as the liquor consumed him, he felt his Divine Mission slipping away.

Then one night, Jack Lee went driving, searching for his relief. As he sped down the dark and winding tunnel of flashing scenes that bludgeoned him with every mistake and indecision of the past, the faster he drove. And the faster he drove, the more he left behind. Faster and faster the trees flew by, faster and faster—until the suffering abruptly stopped!

When Jack Lee opened his eyes, his car was wedged in a ditch, totaled with the radiator steaming and the airbag deployed—he should have been dead, but miraculously he felt no pain. He exited the vehicle and, surrounded by a cold wet fog, climbed up and out of the steep embankment. The dark country road was empty and eerily silent, and the fog hovered static and gray under the surreal power of the full moon. And then he saw her.

Lost and afraid, Madeline emerged from the mist, making her way through the deserted forest searching for a way out. With pale translucent skin and thick curly hair flowing to her waist, she wore a ghostly white wedding gown of fitted sheer lace. Jack Lee called out to her, but no sound emitted from his lips. He then ran after her desperately, but every stride declined to abolish their distance; an unseen force blocked him in, refusing his advances and separating him from his bride.

Then suddenly Madeline stopped. Feeling Jack Lee's presence behind her in the Ether, she slowly turned around and faced him. Despair and disappointment filled her eyes, and bloody tears streamed down her cheeks. Her expression was that of disheartened abandonment, and this realization sliced through

Jack Lee's soul. It was a look he'd seen before in Madeline, long ago—a vision he remembered well, and had promised her she'd never endure again.

"How could you leave me?" Madeline whispered. "Now I have to go…"

And then Jack Lee saw Satan, his number one enemy—the devious vessel of sin Jack Lee had suffered and jousted since the beginning of evil's time.

Wearing a dashing black-tie tuxedo, Satan emerged from the shadows of an archway of cinders burned into the trees. He then blocked Madeline's path and looked straight at Jack Lee.

"You've fallen from grace, Son," Satan said, smirking with victory. "And now the rib of your bride is finally all mine!"

Satan reached out to grab Madeline, but she flinched back and recoiled away. And before he could snatch her, two blinding yellow lights from over the hill gave way.

As the grill of a massive semi charged toward them, Madeline turned back to Jack Lee. "Come find me," she said. "You know where I'll be."

Madeline then stepped in front of the ghost truck.

Now, with God's stiff warning entrenched into his core and a new invigoration for life, Jack Lee was ready to begin his long-awaited transfiguration. A lifetime of suppressing his true identity under the demands of social acceptance erupted as flames of fire. The roots of his lineage he'd felt on the inside for over three decades were now ready to be worn on the outside as badges of honor.

Jack Lee painfully dipped his arms in blood and black ink from shoulder to wrist. For forty days he sat under the needle, determined to emerge unrecognizable to the world who'd thought they knew him. Every image and tribal line Jack Lee had permanently engraved beneath his skin symbolized God's great warriors of generations past and eternally connected the blood veins of the souls of God's warriors yet to come.

On his thirty-fourth birthday, when the last session of his tattooing was complete, Jack Lee emerged from the artist's studio into a blinding white light and he fell to the ground, covering his head with his arms. After a few moments, all of his apprehension vanished, and he rose to his knees, staring into the light as the scenery around him disappeared. The Heavens opened, reclaimed his spirit, and re-filled it with all the knowledge and wisdom acquired through millions of years of existence before the Creation of Man. Between the flash of an instant, every question Jack Lee had ever asked was answered, and although he was no longer a scholar, he knew exactly who he was.

Jack Lee went straight to his mother and, wielding a mighty scepter of courage and trust, bravely informed her of his transfiguration and the namesake he bore—he was ready to begin his Divine Mission, publicly announce his presence, and proclaim the Word of God.

But his mother's reaction was confusion followed by intense antagonism and hate. And when she realized his sincerity of purpose and determination she warned him explicitly to reconsider his plans—any word spoken of his true identity would result in both of their demises, especially if her social reputation were to end in embarrassment.

Still, Jack Lee held strong. He would not deny God and go back into the cage of domination he'd lived in for so long. His mother was either for him or against him; in the New Era, there would be no fence left to ride.

Always a woman incapable of retreat or conceding defeat, Jack Lee's mother flexed her sovereign power and ratcheted the reigns. Her image as soft and nurturing was a carefully constructed façade. In her own mind, she was the legend behind the legacy; the fierce tyrant behind her late husband's illusion of strength—she was the cloaked monarch of the King's manor, and so she would remain. Cruelty, malice, and trickery were her most polished weapons, and with no patriarch alive to stop her, she put her arsenal to the test.

Jack Lee was her son, and she would control him. She sought

to eliminate his inheritance and implemented staunch financial and occupational constraints. Jack Lee was to never again speak of God or his Mission. He was to exhibit absolute subordination and emerge as the face of the family empire without further complaint, and operate in harmonious unity with his brother under her direction—if not, Jack Lee's eviction from the family compound and extraction from Louisville and their legacy would be immediately imposed.

Adding to the burning inflammation of the already disintegrating family dynamic, was Jack Lee's only brother from whom he'd always been estranged—the young Maximus, who was a burgeoning squire with a violent temper and a criminal mind. The younger heir wanted nothing more than to be the sole beneficiary of the wealth their father bequeathed, and played at their mother's affections and her need to maintain her social standing; Maximus asserted that he would not allow Jack Lee to embarrass them or take what they'd built. And Maximus knew undoubtedly that Jack Lee would choose moral deliverance over monetary asylum.

And Maximus had bet correctly. Jack Lee refused his mother's ultimatum and agreed to leave Louisville without a fight. But not before he gathered the media and made a televised public announcement of his true identity, which erupted in both praise and ridicule.

His mother hastily retaliated—she flatly denied Jack Lee's proclaimed birthright and namesake in a public outcry of her own, and her team of lawyers branded Jack Lee certifiably mad.

Maximus claimed victory.

Once removed from his mother and brother's plans of destruction, Jack Lee vowed to triumph over anyone else attempting to silence him. And despite his mother's innocuous threats of financial demise, his inheritance was irrevocable. She was merely a consort—the family empire was paternal, only to be transferred to male descendants. Upon the age of forty, Jack Lee would retain split control of every penny.

Until then, Jack Lee made his inevitable return to New Orleans in the summer. He was once again a lone wolf in the desert with a cold war in recession. But even at only thirty-four years old, his reputation preceded him. Word of his true identity and pending financial abundance had traveled far and wide, and he used the opportunity to carefully bide his time.

Jack Lee's long-standing reputation as a rising spiritual leader in New Orleans remained, as did his certainty that New Orleans was home to the companion he was back to claim. He had an open invitation to lecture at the educational institution of his choice, and he chose to return to the Catholic-Jesuit university of his pre-doctoral studies.

And that was where Jack Lee found her. In the flesh, sitting alone in the university church on the first day of the fall semester, was twenty-four-year-old Madeline Knight. Jack Lee knew her instantly, yet gazed secretly in astonishment. There was a bewildering aura about the young Madeline as she huddled in the elaborate domed cathedral—she wasn't praying, but rather clutching a rosary and shivering in fear.

When the church bells rang announcing morning mass, Madeline had immediately exited as student and faculty parishioners filed inside. Without hesitation, Jack Lee followed her cautiously as she hurriedly pushed through the crowd and out the doors. He trailed her throughout the campus until she crossed the street to the north stepping onto the campus of the adjoining nonsectarian research university, and entered the Department of Psychology.

Knowing his time with Madeline was not yet to be had, Jack Lee continued his distant observation of her for the next two years. And he shortly realized she wasn't congregating at the church in search of spiritual enlightenment—she was seeking protection. And although Madeline, like everyone else in New Orleans, knew of Jack Lee, she remained unaware of his presence or personal association with her affairs.

When Madeline's graduation from medical school arrived, Jack

Lee summoned his connections in her department and ascertained her residency location. He then immediately retired his professorship and sparked the lines of social gossip, once again, by taking the only job available in the New Orleans State Psychiatric Hospital children's ward: a psych tech on Ross' team.

Jack Lee and Ross had quickly developed a strong kinship because of their similar views and genuine desire to help troubled children. Additionally, the job was the perfect sanctuary for Jack Lee to keep a watchful eye on Madeline, and he relished the proximity to her his position at NOSPH provided.

But Madeline and Jack Lee's slight degree of separation was unavoidable. Moreover, Jack Lee knew the severity of Madeline's disposition and plights. And although the excruciating days of waiting for her tortured him, he knew the handicap of her distress was something only time and her own transfiguration could heal. The ropes from above temporarily tied his hands, yet he would wait close by until she won the battle reigniting the cold war.

And Jack Lee still had his desert left to traverse before the Swords of Fire would cut the twine and release him into battle. The opposing powers working against him did not cease their duties simply because he'd left Kentucky after slipping through the trapdoor of his mother's grasp.

Jack Lee's almost five years in exile had left his mother and Maximus in constant dissension. And as Jack Lee's fortieth birthday approached she wanted her first son, her property, back, and the fiscal control he would bring with him.

Maximus, two years behind Jack Lee in line for his inheritance, fought his mother for Jack Lee's continued estrangement and financial abandonment. Jack Lee had attempted to amend the parameters of their horse-breeding philosophy after their father's death. And Maximus knew Jack Lee's interest in their empire would be liquidated the second Jack Lee acquired it: effectively splitting their assets, land rights, and animal stock. And with Jack Lee personally in control of his fifty-percent and the remaining fifty-percent controlled by the estate trust manager, the odds practically guaranteed the manager's allegiance to Jack Lee's strategy.

Maximus had already squandered his allotment of accessible funds and had mortgaged his home to supplement the difference. Additionally, Maximus' uncontrolled temper had destroyed century-long business relationships, and combined with unsavory debts and domestic scandals, his improprieties had become embarrassing public knowledge.

Eventually, Maximus' desperation breached the surface of his tolerance. And after weeks of fruitless scheming to coerce and bribe the family lawyers, Maximus' brash attempted murder of the trust manager incited a nightlong manhunt. Now left with no amnesty or allies for the first time in his recklessly privileged existence, Maximus disgracefully gave up his fight and took his own life—and head—in a widely publicized shotgun-suicide ending inside the family compound.

Thursday, April 10, 2014 – 9:00 a.m.

As the sun beat down over Fair Grounds Race Course, and the heat stoked the New Orleans humidity, the Thoroughbreds completed their workouts. The annual Hamilton Derby was to commence on Saturday, and Jack Lee was looking forward to skipping it.

He tossed a delicate white rose on top of an already existing pile of fresh and rotting flowers next to Blue Salvation's monument, and left the track headed to work at NOSPH.

Less than a week remained until Jack Lee could return home to his abandoned family compound in Kentucky—just in time to pull his horses from the quickly approaching May 2014 Kentucky Derby, and for his Divine Mission to take full effect.

17

PORTAL
OF
POSSESSION

Thursday, April 10, 2014 – 10:00 a.m.

Jack Lee was on-post watching through the window of Savannah DeVears' room door, waiting for Ross, who was unusually late, to arrive. Nurse Monroe was inside taking Savannah's morning vital signs and preparing her chart. After Savannah's physical outburst the previous day, hospital policy mandated a psych tech had to be present for all future interactions. Savannah was strapped to the bed with restraints for her blood draw, and would be kept that way until after her morning session with Dr. Knight.

Not looking up as she burst through Savannah's room door, Nurse Monroe slammed into a disengaged Jack Lee, smashing the window in his face and instantaneously snapping him out of his daydream.

"Oh, my gosh—Jack! Are you okay?" she shrieked, then realized it was the perfect opportunity to initiate a seduction, as she frequently did. She deliberately pressed her breasts against his chest as she leaned in. "Why don't you come over to my office and let me take a closer look at that? Maybe get a little ice to make it better?"

"No, no. It's all right; I'm fine. It's not the first time I've had a door slammed in my face," Jack Lee said, backing up and taking the chart out of her hand. "Thank you for your concern, Miss Monroe."

"I love it when you call me that, Jack Lee. It makes me feel like Marilyn," she said, in a breathy voice while shaking her bouncy blond hair gently from side to side.

"Ah, yes. Well, speaking of Marilyn, here comes Madeline. Excuse me, Nurse Monroe."

As Madeline walked down the hallway toward them, Nurse Monroe, forever scorned by their embarrassing encounter in the nurses' station, scowled, and walked away.

Madeline was now dressed in an even edgier style than the tailored suit she'd worn the day before. She'd replaced her white doctor's coat with a casual fitting three-quarter-sleeve double-breasted black tuxedo jacket, which she wore unbuttoned over a white silk blouse with a pair of dark-blue designer jeans and nude patent-leather pumps. With perfectly smudged black eyeliner, nude gloss, and the same tight bun, she looked both chic and powerfully professional at the same time. If it weren't for her security nametag, she would have looked even less like a doctor than the first time Jack Lee saw her sitting alone in the university chapel. But he was just as taken.

Wow—even more beautiful! Jack Lee thought as Madeline approached. *Come on, man, be cool. Be cool! Don't let her catch you checking her out. Eyes straight ahead. Keep your distance just a little longer.*

"How's she doing today?" Madeline asked.

"Good, so far. She's all yours, Doc," Jack Lee said, handing her Savannah's chart.

"Thanks. Where's Ross?"

"Haven't seen him yet. It's odd, he's usually in his office an hour or so before my shift starts." He looked up and saw Ross turn the corner and start down the hallway toward them. "Actually, scratch that. Here he comes now."

"Perfect, stay handy."

Ross walked up to Madeline with a black pouch similar to a doctor's medicine bag in his hand. Jack Lee hung back and waited to the side.

"I met with Priestess Haloise this morning," Ross said to Madeline quietly, "and Savannah has definitely been infiltrated. If she's not already under a full-demonic possession, she will be soon. I have all the items I need."

"I figured as much," Madeline said. "The satanic tattoo on her arm is only given after years of preparation. I pulled all her medications yesterday afternoon, so you'll be working with the cleanest slate I can provide."

"Well, let's get to it. Today I'll prepare the room during your exam. After you leave, my job will be done privately and never discussed."

"That's the way it's always been." Madeline pulled her sterling-silver white crystal rosary adorned with a Saint Benedict medal out of her jacket pocket and put it around her neck.

Ross turned to Jack Lee. "Stay outside and keep watch. Don't come in the room unless one of us calls on you specifically. And keep the doorway clear; nobody comes in."

"You got it," Jack Lee replied. He waited for Madeline and Ross to walk into Savannah's room then closed the door and locked it behind them.

———

Whether coincidence or fate, the cosmic connection linking Madeline and Ross to Priestess Haloise had turned out to be a pleasant surprise and not a premeditated affair.

Ross had worked at New Orleans State Psychiatric Hospital since its opening, however his New Orleans ancestry traced back to the French slave trades of the early 1700s. With more than 300 years of African Vodun traditions in his bloodline, Ross was privy to the innate secrets and knowledge only found within the original religion both Louisiana Voodoo and Haitian Vodou were derived from. His lineage was a genealogy rarely found in New Orleans, and one giving him an honorary senior "crowned" status amongst the priests and priestesses of both communities.

He was never ordained a Houngan—Vodou priest—as he practiced privately and liked to keep it that way. But his reputation as one of the most regarded healers in New Orleans had those in need constantly calling on him for services regardless of his official status. And it was a result of his service to the community outside NOSPH that he came to know Priestess Haloise. After meeting through the social grapevine of local Vodou and Voodoo practitioners, Priestess Haloise's interest in Ross' profession working with children with mental illness led them to begin working together on various cases. Most of which involved clients brought to Priestess Haloise for help after a psychiatric misdiagnosis had provided no relief.

It was only after Ross—in search of healing botanicals unavailable in New Orleans—had accompanied Priestess Haloise on her annual mid-July trip to her home in Port-au-Prince, Haiti, that he discovered her close relationship with Madeline. Madeline had made the trip as well, and initially their joint presence caused much alarm for both. Neither had anticipated additional company, and adding to the discomfort, Madeline was a doctor under whom Ross worked. But any negative reservations faded after their first few days together, and they discovered the full extent of each other's inherent good nature.

The striking similarities of their pasts—both having family members committed to long-term psychiatric hospitals who'd influenced their career decisions—became apparent during the long conversations they shared about childhood and hardship. The wisdom acquired during the sacred three-day festival they attended at the holiest site in Haiti—a cleansing under the sacred powers of the Saut d'Eau waterfall—had culminated in a pact to intertwine a spiritual and holistic approach with the future treatment of their patients at NOSPH. And by the end of the two-week excursion, Ross, Madeline, and Priestess Haloise had cultivated a bond that would link them inseparably for the rest of their lives.

Long before graduating medical school Madeline had dedicated her psychiatric residency to compiling research findings that confirmed the separation between demonic disturbances and a legitimate medical diagnosis. Because of the trinity created on the trip to Haiti, her findings began to include not only her research, but also the intelligence acquired from the cases Priestess Haloise and Ross had worked on individually, making Madeline's treatment techniques increasingly effective.

Dr. Fields' desire for Madeline romantically wasn't the only reason he allowed her such leniency; she also produced consistently high numbers of patients treated with documented positive results. He had accepted multiple awards and secured millions of dollars in extra funding for his department based on her results, which was a main contributory factor to his invitation to speak at the conference gala. Therefore, not only was Madeline required to represent Dr. Fields at the gala as a trophy date on his big night of recognition, she was also required to stay quiet about why he was being recognized in the first place.

When Madeline entered Savannah's room, she first walked over and stood next to the bed. Ross began working in the background, blessing the room and ensuring all items he needed were in place before Madeline completed her examination.

Savannah had straps securing her chest, arms, and legs, and was lying motionless with her head facing the wall. She made no acknowledgement of the intruders altering her space.

After setting a large needle and a bottle of droperidol on a tin table adjacent to the bed in case the use of chemical restraints became unavoidable, Madeline reviewed Savannah's medical chart. Even though Savannah's behavior the previous day had been terrifyingly unexpected, Madeline was still eager to administer a second session. Now that she had definitive information explaining the meaning of Savannah's markings, she was positive her initial diagnosis of a demonic disturbance was accurate. And the condition appeared to be progressive. But Savannah's markings weren't the most enticing element contributing to Madeline's interest.

Savannah's retaliatory attack after Madeline's hand had burned Savannah's wrist was territory Madeline had not yet encountered with any other patients. But a similar incident had happened to Madeline before, and the incident with Savannah brought to the surface a forgotten memory from when Madeline was eleven: her mother's refusal to touch her after she too had been seriously burned by Madeline's hand.

After reviewing the notes detailing Savannah's activities from the previous night and past morning, Madeline found that Savannah was still refusing to respond to any verbal contact. She still wouldn't participate in her own food consumption, and the night nurse had placed her on intravenous fluids and nutritional supplements. Also, despite Madeline's removal of all psychiatric and anti-psychotic medications the day before, Savannah didn't show any signs of withdrawal from her plethora of prescription pill consumptions. Even strapped down, she looked as calm as death except for the fact her eyes were wide open.

Savannah didn't move or blink and her body hadn't responded to any of the neurological tests Nurse Monroe had administered. But despite the moist and balmy texture to Savannah's skin and excessive sweating, her vital signs were stellar. Her heart rate, pulse, blood pressure, and oxygen levels were all well above average function—close to that of a highly trained athlete. Her previous medical history had shown her to be consistently below the requirements for normal health. So far below normal she was under constant medical surveillance and had spent a week in a medically induced coma until her body had reached a healthy equilibrium. Plainly stated, at that moment Savannah appeared to be a completely different person.

"Despite your behavior yesterday, Savannah," Madeline said, "I'm still here to try and help you save your soul."

Ross walked over and cut off a lock of Savannah's hair, put it into his bag, and continued to bless the room. Even with Ross' intrusion, Savannah still didn't move or respond to Madeline's statement.

Madeline continued. "I know that to receive the detailed markings inside your elbow you would've had to endure years of torture and satanic teachings which resulted in the successful implantation of an external entity. I know—."

"You don't know anything," Savannah said in a barely audible raspy voice while still facing the wall.

"What did you say?"

Savannah slowly turned her head and looked at Madeline. The pupils in Savannah's eyes beamed bright red and her voice was now demonically distorted. "You don't know about anything except for the sting of a cold black leather belt whipping your back!" Savannah hissed, her eyes widening further as she noticed the rosary around Madeline's neck. "You can take your rosary and go hang yourself! That worthless piece of trash won't be able to protect you where you're going—her soul is already mine. I'm the King! I'm the King! He's coming for you too—you're gonna hang! Blood is gonna gush from your head, you holy rolling snitch!" She turned to Ross. "Witch Doctor! There's going to be hell to pay— you're all dead!"

Savannah started to thrash back and forth with superhuman strength. The brackets to her arm restraints snapped off the bedrails and she lunged out at Madeline and scratched at her face, which was just out of reach.

"Ross, hold her down!" Madeline screamed, reaching for the needle.

Ross rushed over and tried to restrain Savannah, but she was seething viciously, and her strength was too much for him to control. She dug her nails deeply into his arm tearing his skin open in four deep gashes, and blood splattered across the wall as he ripped it away.

Savannah cackled loudly and thrashed wildly, kicking her left leg free. Madeline stuck the needle into the bottle of droperidol, filled it, and stabbed it into Savannah's right thigh instantly sedating her.

Inhaling deeply and catching her breath, Madeline looked up at Ross. "This is over; finish what you started. I'll send in Jack Lee."

————————

Madeline sat in her office penning out her report on Savannah's session. Contrary to Madeline's beliefs, the report would have to conceal the genuine nature of Savannah's sickness with a parallel diagnosis, and Madeline grew more agitated with every word she wrote.

She knew there was nothing more she could do to help Savannah, as Savannah's fate was now at the mercy of Ross' ability to complete a successful extraction. If Ross could help Savannah, Savannah would have a chance at recovery after she was transferred to the psychiatric facility for the criminally insane—her next destination regardless of her departing diagnosis. If Ross couldn't help Savannah, she had a lifetime of earthly hell awaiting her future—or at least what was left of her did.

Madeline had spent years observing the treatment policies of patients under demonic possession, and not one attending psychiatrist had ever referred one of them to a priest for an exorcism. It wasn't part of procedure in government-run psychiatric organizations, and Madeline had no reason to believe Savannah would be an exception—especially considering the family and political ties she came from. After Savannah's release from NOSPH, her status would be "walking-dead" as far as the public was concerned. Madeline had no choice but to remain confident she had done everything possible to save her.

Although the task of diagnosing Savannah was complete and NOSPH would now only be monitoring her physical health until transfer, Madeline was still horrified by Savannah's verbal assault against her personally. The evil premeditation behind the nasty utterances Savannah had so ruthlessly expelled from her mouth was as hard to deny as the obvious state of her possession. *How could Savannah have known the details about specific tragedies from my childhood?* Madeline wondered, unable to just write the report the way Dr. Fields had requested and be done with it.

Never before had a patient under possession, or any other impairment, referred to Madeline with accusations aside from physical appearance. Major inconsistencies still existed in Savannah's case beyond her medical status, and the available details weren't adding up to a sure conclusion. Or perhaps the details were adding up, and Madeline couldn't yet acknowledge the truth about what she inherently knew was plaguing her. Either way, Madeline feared an unidentified force of evil was closing in, and that whatever unclean spirit, or spirits, had infiltrated Savannah, had targeted her as well.

Madeline knew she would have to investigate the issue further after compiling more evidence. But first, Ross had to complete his exorcism and consult with Priestess Haloise to interpret the results. So, staying true to her promise to maintain her position at the hospital, Madeline moved on to her next commission and filed the stalemate concern of Savannah into her mental-inbox of to-dos for later review.

After all, it was Thursday, and a demonically possessed patient wasn't the only looming catastrophe causing Madeline's contention. Tonight, she would emerge as the publicly admissible date of the great Dr. Fields, visibly on display for not only her department, but for the entire psychiatric medical society to see.

Unfortunately, Madeline knew the whole charade was both unavoidable and essential at the same time. Dr. Fields had made it perfectly clear that joining him at the gala was the only acceptable response to his "request." And with her job at risk and the imminent need for time off work on the horizon, staying in Dr. Fields' favor was a top priority.

Madeline actually thought attending the gala with him might assist in the execution of her plans. Every doctor from the children's ward was partaking in the conference's closing luncheon the following day, Friday, during which time she planned to be in Cincinnati. And she hoped Dr. Fields would be too engrossed in his post-gala bliss to notice her absence. She would navigate her way around him sexually of course, as she would never let his slimy hands anywhere near her repulsed body. But she still had to play a willing hostess for the night regardless of her personal feelings.

The only encouraging prospect softening Madeline's distaste for the evening to come was that Dr. Nathan Raines would also be in attendance. Even with everything else going on in her life, she couldn't stop thinking about the handsome doctor and the romantic desire he had rekindled inside her. But that wasn't the only reason she was looking forward to seeing him. She knew a positive relationship with Dr. Raines would also ensure her continued control over Gabriella's hospitalization, as he was officially the primary doctor in charge of Gabriella's care. Gabriella's sole focus was getting out of the hospital, and Madeline needed to halt her discharge until she returned from Cincinnati, if she returned at all. Gabriella was in no condition to take care of herself, and Madeline couldn't afford to allow an early release to make Gabriella's psychiatric situation worse and risk her sister losing her life.

Madeline planned to make a dramatic appearance at the gala that night, and it needed to play out seamlessly if the finicky array of obstacles dominating her life were to remain in balance. She had a twofold task ahead of her: pacify the demands of the insatiable Dr. Fields while simultaneously making herself irresistible to the deliciously charming Dr. Raines. She had a new gown sure to accomplish both.

She locked up her office for the day and headed out to prepare.

While walking past Dr. Fields' office, Madeline noticed the door was slightly open. He wasn't supposed to be on the hospital's schedule that day, which he'd confirmed when they spoke the night before. She poked her head through the door to investigate.

Nurse Monroe was in the office with Dr. Fields reviewing paperwork. She had her body strategically placed over his desk with her cleavage overtly exposed as she giggled and touched him suggestively. Madeline lightly tapped on the door and entered the room, much to the delight of Nurse Monroe, who was quite tickled to have been caught by Madeline in her questionable position.

"Excuse me, Dr. Fields?" Madeline asked, unfazed by her colleagues' fraternizations. "Sorry to interrupt, I didn't realize you would be in today."

Nurse Monroe buttoned her shirt and looked up with a prematurely triumphant smile. But she was the only one amused by the encounter—Dr. Fields hadn't even the slightest twinge of either pride or embarrassment regarding their behavior. He already had Madeline exactly where he wanted her, and if Nurse Monroe wanted to try to thwart the situation with an over saturation of sexually-fueled attention, that was fine with him.

"I had to stop in and sign a last-minute transfer release," he replied, getting up and taking his one-wood driver club from his golf bag. "I'm headed to the golf course for the rest of the afternoon. Gonna brush up on my swing—show the out-of-towners how it's done." He got into perfect tee-off position and began to sleazily wiggle his hips. "Hey, Madeline!" he cooed. "Are my gyrating hips distracting you?" He swung.

Madeline didn't respond. Nurse Monroe stared shocked.

"Okay, fine!" he pouted. "Support my golf skills from the clubhouse next time. How are things progressing with your little assignment?"

"Just fabulous," Madeline said sarcastically. "I'm actually heading out for the day myself. What time is the car picking me up tonight?"

Nurse Monroe leered back at Madeline in surprise as the look of repulsion washed over her face. She had no idea Madeline would be accompanying Dr. Fields to the gala; nobody did. And Nurse Monroe already had a surprise of her own organized for him that night. She stepped back from his desk, once again humiliated by Madeline's antics.

Dr. Fields just smiled. "The car will pick you up at seven o'clock sharp."

———————

Madeline needed to ensure the rest of her body did her gown justice, and so she had scheduled herself a manicure, pedicure, body scrub, and facial. She hadn't visited a spa in months, but the majority of women attending the gala were the wealthiest, most glamorous, and most pampered in all New Orleans. Madeline had regrettably allowed her personal grooming habits to disintegrate amid the deep depression she'd fallen victim to over the past few months, and wanted to look as polished as possible.

After her treatments, Madeline sat quietly in the swivel chair of a swanky hair salon's styling station as her longtime stylist, Letitia, painstakingly picked through Madeline's tangled matted hair.

Letitia, the most sought-after stylist in New Orleans, was a beautiful half African, half Puerto Rican American, who was trendy lesbian-cool. Her book was constantly full and she only took the most high-profile appointments, mainly consisting of local celebrities and the professional football and basketball player's girlfriends and wives. Madeline was none of those things, but Letitia looked forward to trying to pry out of Madeline's head that which she could never quite figure out. And Letitia was hopelessly smitten with the half-black stunner who used to come in and have her hair relaxed and trimmed unfailingly every four weeks.

With Madeline's lighter complexion and narrow features, she could have passed for a woman of almost any exotically ethnic race. But she was proud of her black heritage and had made its presence clear to Letitia upon first meeting, because for good reason, Madeline only allowed stylists sharing her ethnicity to touch her hair.

"I haven't seen you in a while, girl," Letitia said in a thick Southern drawl. "What-cha got, a special occasion tonight?"

Madeline just nodded. The all-too familiar feeling of panic rushed through her body with every additional stroke Letitia made with the comb. The pain from the tangles was almost unbearable and Madeline was beyond embarrassed—her hair was in worse condition than ever and full of tough knots, several of which had to be cut out. It was true; she hadn't been in the salon in over six months, not since her emotional stability began to unravel. And when it had, brushing out her waist-long hair was an impossible feat, hence the omnipresent bun she used to conceal the evidence.

After Letitia finally worked her way through the last of the tangles, she took out a cast iron curler and began to straighten Madeline's hair.

Madeline's heart started to pound and her vision began to blur. Becoming more irritated and uncomfortable, she subconsciously jerked her head away and the curler seared her ear causing her to begin screaming uncontrollably.

The pain of the burn instantly propelled Madeline into a full hallucination mirroring the traumatic occurrence from when she was eleven years old. She looked up at herself in the mirror and no longer saw Letitia behind the swivel chair, but saw her mother, Claire Jackson, instead. Claire was holding a sharp wire-bristled comb, which she tore ferociously through Madeline's matted hair.

Flabbergasted by Madeline's behavior, Letitia jumped back and watched in disbelief as Madeline continued to scream and pull at her own hair. The other customers and stylists in the salon stopped and watched in fearful astonishment.

Madeline, still engrossed in the hell of her public hallucination, shrieked in agony while whom she saw as Claire Jackson smiled with pleasure and continued to savagely rip out huge clumps of Madeline's frizzy hair. Blood rushed down Madeline's forehead in thick streams as the wire bristles gashed open her skin, exposing her skull and drenching her clothes bright-crimson red.

Madeline then saw her father, Charles Jackson, appear in the mirror and enter the salon dressed in his police chief's uniform. He unbuckled and took off his black leather belt and folded it in half in his hand. "You had better stop your whining or tonight it's going to be another beating!" he growled, raising the belt into the air.

Madeline's screams turned into furious huffs of rage as she turned around and swatted at her mother. The anger in Madeline's eyes intensified as she clutched Claire's arm in her hand and twisted it so tightly her mother's skin blistered, burned, and caused the room to fill with smoke.

Back in the reality of the salon—as Madeline's hysteria continued—Letitia seized Madeline by her shoulders, desperate to calm her down. The external contact jolted Madeline out of her hallucination and she threw Letitia off, knocking Letitia back several feet painfully to the ground.

Humiliated and still engrossed in the physical effects induced by the episode she'd just endured, Madeline grabbed her backpack and ran out the salon door.

———————

Sitting safely and quietly in front of her bedroom vanity mirror, Madeline was a visual and emotional disaster. Her eyes were puffy and swollen from crying, and tears continued to gather in the corners of her eyes and stream down her reddened cheeks. Rosette—whom Madeline had called on her way home from the salon—silently stood behind Madeline, gently combing out Madeline's hair and pinning it up into a formal style.

Madeline picked up one of her prescription pill bottles, took out two pills, and popped them into her mouth.

18

THE GALA

The annual Future of Child Psychiatry Committee's conference was the most important meeting of the year for all professionals working in psychiatric medicine. Research findings and new laws outlining the required care procedures for children had a trickle-down effect, and doctors working with adults also wanted to have the opportunity to voice their say. It was the first time the conference had come to Louisiana, and New Orleans' medical society was proud to accept the honor. It was a monumental affair, and distinguished doctors and medical students from around the world had flown in for the weeklong conference, which consisted of multiple seminars, lectures, and training workshops.

The FCPC Gala was the largest medical fund-raising celebration of the year and the most talked about and anticipated event of the FCPC Conference. As a nonprofit organization, the purpose of the gala was to raise the financial resources needed to continue research efforts the following year. And because the Future of Child Psychiatry Committee didn't receive any government funding, it relied solely on private donations, and the gala was its main source of revenue.

It wasn't the average five-hundred-dollar-a-ticket dinner either;

it was a prestigious affair costing $25,000 for each person just to sit down. Overpayments were highly encouraged, and the concept of free admission did not exist—all guests planning to attend, VIP or not, paid in full before their names were printed in the official announcement.

The goal of the night was to make money, and unless an attendee was a special guest of a speaker, to receive an invitation the gala's curators thoroughly investigated the financial prominence of prospective invitees. But not just for high net worth; the deciding factor was what a prospective invitee's reputation was for spending their net worth . . . on hefty donations.

The curators had the duty of selecting guests reduced to a perfect equation. They had publicized the event so cleverly within the industry that persons "lucky enough to attend" felt fortunate to be there, and not obliged. The entry list wasn't limited to just psychiatrists, however; the selection committee considered all major players in the fields of medicine, politics, sports, and entertainment. And if a well-known doctor or member of high society was excluded, the oversight was considered a blatant snub with embarrassing consequences.

The Hotel Raphael in downtown New Orleans had been the venue selected to host the 2014 FCPC Gala, as it was undeniably the most elaborate, exquisitely beautiful, and newest hotel in the city. With Old World glamour mixed with traditional Southern ambience, the finest interior decorating and furnishings, and supremely luxurious amenities with services to match, the choice had been easy to make.

When Madeline arrived on the arm of Dr. Harold Fields, nobody present could have possibly imagined only hours before she'd been in crisis, practically immobilized, and unsure if she would attend. Fortunately, Rosette had dedicated several hours to rescuing Madeline from unpresentable despair, and Madeline stepped out of the black limousine looking absolutely stunning.

She wore a striking black floor-length gown of heavy jersey and sheer lace, which draped her stately curves in a fitted silhouette with a short mermaid train. It had a high-collar neckline fastened with satin buttons, fitted-lace cap sleeves, low-cut lace paneling all down the open back, and a shimmering black corseted waistline. She carried a black-sequined handbag, wore ankle-wrapped black stilettos with a silver heel, and had her hair in a demure French twist with lips stained bright orange-red. Madeline never wore jewelry, but with her artistic wrist and neck tattoos controversially visible for the first time, she was the portrait of graceful elegance with an edge.

Although Madeline had viewed arriving with Dr. Fields as less than thrilling, it pleased her to see he looked more handsome than ever. Dressed like a prince in a full-dress black tuxedo with tailcoat, gray double-breasted waistcoat, satin-gold tie, and paisley handkerchief, his bold fashion choice was as daring as hers, and they were by far the most attractive couple of the night. As they walked up the red carpet, through the front doors, and into the hotel foyer, Madeline's dress flowed perfectly with every step and heads turned as cameras flashed.

Dr. Fields had an entirely different outlook on his position; he felt great—like a celebrity—and held his head up like the renowned gentleman he now officially was. Not only was everyone viewing him in awe, but he was finally with the one woman he'd been trying to acquire for three years. The only pleasure exciting him more than the feeling of Madeline's arm tightly interlocked with his was that his ex-wife was already there when they arrived. All of society knew Dr. Angelica Fields was engaged to the most notable, wealthiest surgeon in the city, and Dr. Fields had made sure they both received an invitation.

Dr. Fields and Madeline slowly waltzed through the lobby and into the courtyard garden where the other guests were gathering for drinks and passed hors-d'oeuvres. True to New Orleans style, the courtyard decorations were a lavish display of fountains, candles, lights, blooming foliage, and a miniature symphony playing under an illuminated domed stage.

While Dr. Fields and Madeline made the rounds greeting and being greeted by the high rollers in attendance, Nurse Monroe's NOSPH entourage sneered at Madeline and muttered about her unexpected arrival with the boss. Nurse Monroe had been furious about what she considered a bold act of disrespect toward her specifically, and had chosen not to embarrass herself further by announcing it to her followers. From Nurse Monroe's perspective, Madeline's shrewd audacity to touch a man far above her social class was sickening, and Nurse Monroe didn't want to pay Madeline any more attention than she was already attracting on her own. Instead, Nurse Monroe stood silently on the sidelines internally fuming with insane jealousy and plotting her next move.

When Ross saw Madeline, he melted with the sentimentality of a proud father. He had never seen her look so lovely or confident, and he was already aware of her arrangement with Dr. Fields. She hadn't wanted to shock Ross at the last minute and had informed him of her obligation to play hostess preemptively. He understood her position, knowing she'd only gone along with one of the many games Dr. Fields played so well.

Ross walked over to Madeline and greeted her with a gentle kiss on the cheek. "You look beautiful, Dr. Knight," he said with a smile.

Jack Lee was speechless—in many ways. He, however, did not know Madeline was going to show up with Dr. Fields, and could feel his face turn hot with disappointment. His heart dropped into the pit of his stomach, and a sickening feeling of anger he wasn't accustomed overcame his senses. He could barely take his eyes off Madeline's beauty or stop himself from punching Dr. Fields in the face, all at the same time. Although he knew their day had not yet arrived, Jack Lee had still dreamed about seeing Madeline at the gala all week. He'd imagined himself leading her onto the dance floor, stealing her heart away into marriage, and whisking her away from the crumbling ethics of the world and everyone in it. Including Dr. Fields, who had ruthlessly crushed those dreams the moment Jack Lee saw him with Madeline, and Jack Lee couldn't bring himself to acknowledge her as she passed by.

But Madeline was as struck by the sight of Jack Lee in a tuxedo as he was by her in a dress, and his lack of enthusiasm confused her. Feeling unusually bold, she stopped right in front of him. "What's the matter, Jack Lee?" she asked playfully. "Suddenly 'The South's Most Talked About Man' has nothing to say?"

A King and a Knight; match made in Heaven. But, not today, Jack Lee thought, pointedly avoiding her eyes. He gently shook his head covering his pain with a smile, and walked away just as Dr. Fields stuck his hand out to him expecting another welcoming compliment.

Although Madeline didn't see Dr. Nathan Raines standing across the room at the bar, he saw her—and all the commotion instigated by her entrance. He'd been watching the room all evening waiting for her to arrive, and with her unexpected appearance, he'd barely recognized her at first glance. When he realized the woman at the center of the attention was the fast-talking, slightly offbeat, and seemingly aloof young doctor he'd met only days before, he was as captivated as everyone else. But the sight of Madeline in a glamorous gown was quickly retired to the back of his mind; she was apparently the date of Harold Fields, and that discovery left Nathan blinded with an infuriating rage.

A sharp rod of anger struck him hard. But unlike Jack Lee, anger for Nathan Raines was a sensation he was more than accustomed to; especially when it came to women, and more specifically, when it came to Dr. Harold Fields. Nathan turned away and shattered his glass with his bare hand.

Even though Dr. Fields was more than aware of the strife he was causing, he continued to flaunt his latest conquest and held on to Madeline's arm possessively. Reporters and admirers pursued him from every direction and he loved every minute of it. NOSPH had distributed several press releases announcing his speech, all boasting that his research department had "redefined the boundaries of child psychiatry." And the gala had more news coverage than ever before.

After Dr. Fields' colleagues had finished showering him with compliments and ceased fawning over his date, the reporters took their turn to shout out questions.

"Dr. Fields! How does it feel to be speaking tonight in front of all these prestigious guests?" asked one.

"I hear all the major networks are asking you for interviews! How does it feel?" asked another, stepping over the reporter preceding him.

"I'm sure you'll get that book deal after this!" shouted yet another. That was the reporter who caught Dr. Fields' full attention, as it was the one comment he was hoping to hear and eager to address. He released Madeline's arm forgetfully and opened himself up fully to the interviewers.

Madeline happily excused herself and surveyed the room. But, before she had the chance to locate the one person she was hoping to see that night, she heard a familiar Southern voice calling out from behind in a sharp, condescending tone.

"Resident Knight."

Madeline turned around disappointedly and saw the one person she was actively hoping to avoid that night: Administrator Hamilton.

Dr. Florence Hamilton was tall, thin, and beautiful, with snow-white, doll-like skin and perfectly straight, shiny brown hair cut just above her shoulders. She looked like pure sophistication, everything she felt Madeline was not—a walking picture of perfect harmony in a shimmering midnight-blue Chanel suit and adorned with two million dollars' worth of diamonds. She had a strong distaste for Madeline, who she only ever referred to as "Resident Knight."

"I wasn't expecting to see you here like this," Administrator Hamilton said.

"Good evening, Dr. Hamilton," Madeline replied. "Well, as you know, due to your outstanding generosity the entire department is here tonight for Dr. Fields' keynote address."

"Yes, they would be. I was of course referring to your close proximity to the good Dr. Fields' arm and not your presence here as an employee." She looked Madeline up and down unimpressively. "That's a lovely dress you've mustered up; I have to say it suits you far better than a white coat. But, perhaps you should have considered wearing that high neckline in the back instead of the front, being as breasts aren't nearly as offensive as your Middle Eastern brandings. Anyway, I'm sure you're aware as hospital administrator I was against your handling of the DeVears case. Dr. Fields saw matters differently . . . and now I can see why. Good evening." She flicked up her chin and walked away before Madeline could respond.

Madeline was relieved. And she finally spotted Nathan Raines standing across the room at the bar, now with gauze around his hand. Even though he never looked up at her, she blushed ever so slightly at the sight of the most dashing man in the room.

Nathan looked even better than the last time she saw him. He was clean-shaven and without his glasses, revealing the full extent of his angular features and high cheekbones. His untied hair hung at his shoulders in shiny golden-blond locks, and he wore a sharp black-and-white tuxedo, having clearly chosen not to bother with a tie, as his shirt was unbuttoned just below his collarbones showing off smooth tanned skin.

Madeline started toward Nathan ready to make her appearance, but before she could get more than a couple feet away, Dr. Fields pulled her back to him.

"Where are you off to?" he asked. "It's time to take our place at my table. They're about to serve dinner and directly after I'll begin my speech."

Madeline smiled, careful not to show her disappointment. She took his arm and they proceeded out of the courtyard and toward the ballroom just as Nathan Raines looked up and saw them walking away.

The Hotel Raphael's Grand Ballroom was breathtakingly gorgeous, magnificently expansive, and decorated as beautifully as a royal wedding reception. Every table had gold chairs and crisp white linens topped with the finest porcelain, silver, and crystal, and were overflowing with vases of flowers bordered by floating candles and ice buckets chilling full bottles of champagne.

The ceiling was four stories high and painted to mirror a cloudy blue sky, which turned to midnight stars when the lights were dimmed. One dozen multi-tiered crystal chandeliers draped the entire room in a majestic rainbow of shimmering gold. And the guest tables surrounded a huge parquet dance floor, which lined a stage fixed with multiple overhead spotlights and a scholarly podium expertly displayed in front of a full-playing jazz band.

Everyone was in their seats—happily stuffed by the delectable four-course meal served by waiters in regal butler's uniforms—sipping champagne and eating cake as Dr. Fields' speech concluded:

". . . As an experienced leader in the mental health field, my researched-based recommendations and advanced treatment plans provide opportunities for children and youth diagnosed with psychological disorders, including childhood schizophrenia, and their families to live productive lives. I have laid out an effective program for the best practices, including: early detection of the physical signs and symptoms of children with emotional and behavioral disorders, advanced therapeutic counseling services, and comprehensive community-based supports. Together, with your ongoing charitable donations, we can establish a positive foundation and a movement toward Inclusion and Integration. Thank you!"

Dr. Fields exited the podium to the praise of the audience's applause and a standing ovation. Madeline made her way to greet him with the affections she knew he'd be expecting, but again congratulators mobbed around him blocking her way. Happy to be the last person on his mind at that moment, she spotted Nathan Raines once again.

Feeling nervous and slightly embarrassed, she braced herself for the task ahead and headed in his direction before the opportunity escaped her.

"Here we go," Madeline said. "Control the doctor, control his patient."

Nathan had returned to his post by the bar, disengaged from the happenings of the evening. He was unimpressed with the speech he'd just heard, and even more unimpressed with the man who'd delivered it.

"Wow, you make quite the statement in a tux!" Madeline said to Nathan as she approached. "Hardly recognizable outside your lab coat. What's with the hand?"

"I live on the edge. But, the only statement tonight is you in that dress," Nathan said with a short smile, barely looking up from his drink. "I didn't think you would have time to recognize me at all. Surprised he ever let go of your arm. Work obligation?"

"Not exactly."

"It's okay. I know how Harry works. You're not the first and you won't be the last."

"Thank God!" she said. They both laughed. "Anyway, I could ask you the same question. I didn't realize the city hospitals paid so well. Even I didn't have to come out-of-pocket for my fancy ticket. Complements of the old Southern money over at NOSPH. What's your secret?"

"Well, I was really just giving you a hard time about Dr. Fields," he said, concealing his distaste and remembering Madeline was unaware of the bad blood between himself and Dr. Fields. "But, if you must know, I happen to be an heir to what you love to call 'old Southern money' and my family receives an invitation to this gala every year, regardless of which city it's in. I've never been interested in enduring such disgusting displays of overabundance, because honestly, it probably costs more money to throw these parties than could ever be made in donations. But, when you said you would be coming . . . well, I went ahead and plunked down the twenty-five-K. Can I get you a drink?"

Madeline was blushing once again. *He can't possibly be serious, could he?* she wondered. Without his glasses, Nathan's sparkling hazel eyes were nothing short of intoxicating. She found herself lost in them and distracted by the way the light reflected off the different shades of auburn, brown, and gold.

"Yeah, a drink sounds good," she replied, contemplating. She instantly felt the familiar urge to order her favorite drink: a dirty martini straight up with a blue cheese olive. But she didn't. "I'll have a sparkling water with lemon, thank you."

"I like your style," he said, and then turned to the bartender. "Two sparkling waters with lemon."

After the bartender fixed their drinks, Nathan raised the subject of Gabriella before Madeline had the chance. "One of the nurses was checking on your sister right after you saw her yesterday," he said. "And whatever you two were talking about must have really upset her because she was in worse condition after you left than before you arrived. Her heart rate had soared, and she refused to disclose what was bothering her. She only demanded to use the phone, presumably to call you back. After she'd been de-escalated I tried to call you at your office to discuss her condition, but you'd already left for the day."

"Well, it looks like you have your chance now. What do you want to discuss?" Madeline asked.

"Honestly, I'm very concerned about her," he said, back in full-doctor mode.

"You should be," Madeline replied, knowing where he was going with his interrogation. She was going to have to do more convincing to keep Gabriella in the hospital than she thought.

"Madeline, she's made it overtly clear that she didn't try to take her own life. She said she didn't realize the alcohol would react the way it did with her medications."

"With a blood-alcohol content of over thirty-one percent I really don't think it matters, does it?"

"Maybe not, but listen to me; she's due for release tomorrow night and I think—."

"That's not a good idea! This is a patient who is a lot more complicated than she appears. As I mentioned in the ER, she was just discharged from an inpatient facility she'd spent five years in for the same reasons. And at this point, she's proven that a release wasn't such a good idea. Gabriella is a danger to herself and always has been. I've suffered through years of this type of behavior, and we both know a patient will say and do anything to get out of an involuntary hospitalization, which is why we rely on their family's input as well. I'm leaving first thing in the morning for a quick business trip, and I would be more than happy to work with you on a better treatment plan when I return. But Gabriella cannot under any circumstances be released before then, or before you've had sufficient time to really dissect her condition."

Dr. Raines stood there for a minute looking curiously at Madeline without responding. He was getting two very different stories, but that wasn't the strangest discrepancy about his dilemma. What bothered him the most was how sorry he'd felt for Gabriella during his first examination; she had seemed genuinely excited about getting out of the hospital and starting a new life with her sister. She had completely downplayed the severity of her previous hospitalization, and he didn't understand why Madeline would be going out of town when her sister was in such a helpless situation.

The whole dynamic felt increasingly odd, and he knew untold truths existed within the verbal depiction of their stories. He couldn't quite put together what those truths were, but knew it was pointless to ask before examining Gabriella's past hospital records himself, which she still hadn't signed a release for. And, even though his patients' needs were his first responsibility, his growing affection for Madeline was an equally deciding factor. She was both a family member and a psychiatrist, and Gabriella would be her sole responsibility after discharge. He didn't want to risk interrupting that balance prematurely, so he nodded a reassuring "yes" to Madeline's request. "I'll extend her hold an additional twenty-four hours pending receipt of her medical records," he said. "After that, I'll decide what to do."

"Thank you," Madeline said, satisfied she'd met her goal and quickly changing the subject. "Now, if you don't have any objections, I would love to enjoy this expensive 'display of overabundance' and forget about work, just for the night."

"Absolutely!" he said, relieved to be off the subject of Gabriella and on to the subject of Madeline. "Beautiful young lady," he asked with a gentleman's bow, "would you like to dance?"

Madeline had accepted Nathan's offer to dance feeling confident Dr. Fields' business affairs would keep him endlessly preoccupied. And he had been—more than an hour passed without Dr. Fields coming to look for her. By that time, almost everyone at the gala was sufficiently intoxicated and all inhibitions reduced to the lowest of standards, even for such "distinguished" guests.

But encouraging heavy alcohol consumption was part of the curators' plan. The husbands too drunk to restrain themselves had purchased all the high-priced auction items, including several expensive European import cars, one-of-a-kind pieces of jewelry, and first-class island vacations. Every time a man with more money than the man bidding before him thrust his paddle into the air, an even richer man aching to prove his wealth thrust his paddle right up afterward to beat him. And in that manner, the night had been a success: the wealthy men of the community had reestablished their financial hierarchy; their wives had reestablished their pyramid of social status and which matriarch was at the top of it; and the curators of the gala had more than exceeded their money quota for the year.

Ross had already left, as did most of the staff working early the next morning. Plus, watching drunk, rich men blow hundreds of thousands of dollars on items they already owned or didn't need was of little interest to them.

Jack Lee had left immediately after Madeline's arrival and hadn't stayed for any of the festivities—he had seen enough. It was a wise decision; if he had seen Madeline twirling around on the dance floor with Nathan Raines all night, the injury would have far exceeded the distress Dr. Fields had provoked.

But Dr. Fields had seen Madeline with Nathan. When he looked up from his diminishing court of instant friends—completely inebriated with scotch in hand—and saw Madeline dancing with his nemesis, he was not pleased. Even though it was perfectly customary, if not expected, to lend your date for a dance at formal affairs, Nathan Raines was off-limits. Scowling brutishly, Dr. Fields charged off to confront them, aiming to spear the woman who'd spit his hook in his hour of drunken limelight.

Nurse Monroe, looking particularly ravishing herself in a decadently expensive garnet-red strapless gown that displayed all her bountiful assets, had advantageously kept herself close to Dr. Fields the entire night. Now that her father, Dr. Monroe, had finally left, she felt confident in her ability to swing the attention her way and have the evening conclude in her favor. She had watched closely as the love triangle between Dr. Fields, Nathan Raines, and Madeline developed, and knew it was time to strike. Just as Dr. Fields rose to confront them, she expertly snatched him back by the arm and pulled him away to the dance floor.

———

As the evening wound down, Madeline came out of the ladies' room and spotted Dr. Fields and Nurse Monroe drunk, kissing, and all over each other as they sloppily stumbled into the elevator. Thoroughly amused, Madeline cracked a smile and headed back out to Nathan Raines.

———

When the elevator carrying Nurse Monroe and Dr. Fields reached the top floor, they continued their tryst in the hallway as Dr. Fields led the way to his suite. He'd reserved the luxury quarters the day

Madeline accepted his invitation to the gala, having planned to consummate their courtship with the passionate evening he'd been fantasizing about since the first day he met her. But Nurse Monroe was to be the only victor that night. Her careful planning and perseverance had landed her the most coveted spot in all NOSPH: Dr. Harold Fields' bedroom.

Once inside, Dr. Fields went to the in-suite bar to refresh his cocktail. And Nurse Monroe, not half as intoxicated as she pretended to be, located the do-not-disturb sign, secured it outside the door, and locked it.

Just as Dr. Fields lifted his fresh glass of aged scotch to his lips, she unzipped her red gown for his viewing pleasure. She proceeded to entice his desires further by performing a striptease. She gently unpinned and shook out her hair allowing it to flow down in bouncy blond curls, then sauntered across the room heading for her target.

Dr. Fields, now shamelessly aroused and void of all inhibitions, dropped his glass, shattering it in the sink. The moment she was within distance, overcome by his hazy moment of lust, Dr. Fields lifted Nurse Monroe's tiny body up onto the bar counter and proceeded to have scarcely-consensual sexual intercourse with the forbidden woman who'd strategically trapped him in her web.

Holding him in her arms afterward, Nurse Monroe smiled wickedly.

After a short-lived night of slow dancing and harmless flirtations, Madeline and Nathan couldn't hold back from each other any longer. They succumbed to their desires and left the hotel remaining an arm's length apart as they walked out the front doors.

Nathan yearned to pull her close as they waited patiently for the valet, but restrained himself as the few guests left waiting for their cars watched them both intently. Scandal brewed the moment his brand-new red Lamborghini Veneno sports car pulled up and he opened the passenger door for Madeline. Administrator Hamilton stopped outside her black stretch limousine and glared disgustedly as Nathan retrieved his keys from the valet, jumped into the front seat, and Madeline, the "half-black minion" she detested, sped away with New Orleans' Golden Boy of Medicine.

Once out of downtown, they cruised up the quiet streets of St. Charles Avenue. As the wind from the humid night air blew through Nathan's long hair, Madeline watched him wistfully from the passenger seat. They had talked all night at the gala deepening their already obvious connection, and now words were the last expression either of them cared to indulge; the radiating heat of their body language was the only translation required.

As they drove past the same Garden District mansions Madeline had admonished the day before, her emotional confidence began to plummet. The forward momentum of deliverance she'd forced herself into was in jeopardy of sliding into reverse. Confusion combated her desire and she questioned her presence there with him.

They turned off St. Charles Avenue and drove through a security station into Audubon Park Estates. After a short drive through the neighborhood, the car finally slowed to a stop, Nathan pressed a button in the dash, and two wooden gates opened inward. He pulled into a circular brick-paved driveway and parked outside a grand antebellum estate. Far too grand for a single man to live in alone, but he did.

Madeline stopped in front of the doorstep just before she entered. She looked up at the exquisite home and took a moment to wonder, *Can I do this? Can I really run back after a life I promised to leave behind?*

Nathan went inside to light up his dark and desolate mansion, and noticed Madeline hadn't followed him in. He went back out to her, took her by the hand, and led her slowly into the house.

———

Under the heavy luxurious sheets of a large Victorian bed, against the backdrop of dripping candles and paintings of priceless art, Madeline and Nathan slept comfortably in the early stages of what could become a beautiful love affair.

19

VICTORIA CHATSWORTH

Friday, April 11, 2014 – 4:00 a.m.

Madeline awoke the next morning tucked under Nathan's chin with his arms wrapped securely around her breast from behind. The soft air of his breath mixed with the sweet spice of cologne blew gently over her cheek as she lay watching the last candle's wick melt into ash. She felt so small inside the cocoon of his enormously tall and muscular body, and although the night had been platonic, the sense of safety and comfort was like nothing she'd experienced before and longed to feel again. The few hours of sleep had been the most restful, uninterrupted of her life, and if she hadn't set her phone alarm to vibrate, she would have slept in the ecstasy of Nathan's embrace for as long as he would allow.

But the warmth temporarily calming Madeline's nerves turned ice-cold when she remembered the Chatsworths, and what lay ahead. She forcibly disassociated from the unfamiliar comforts and accepted without complaint that her whimsical evening with Nathan Raines was but a fleeting mirage lost forever in the truth of life.

She had booked a 6:30 a.m. flight out of New Orleans to CVG Airport in Kentucky, and it was the only nonstop ticket available.

With a two-hour-eight-minute flight time, an hour time-zone change from central to eastern, and a rental car to pick up for the thirty-minute drive over the Ohio River into Cincinnati for the noon inauguration, she couldn't afford to be one minute late.

The Central Church of Enlightenment's ribbon cutting ceremony was Madeline's only chance to strike out at her parents publicly on a scale broad enough to provoke the interest and suspicion necessary to indict them. With cameras broadcasting the event both domestically and internationally, and with the eyes of every reporter, politician, and citizen present fixated on Madeline's every move, Pastor and Mrs. Chatsworth would never be able to escape their demise. Not after Madeline bravely stormed the crowd, took the stage, and presented the evidence exposing the Chatsworths' satanic blood-soaked past of conspiracy and lies. She would brand them as frauds implicated irrefutably in Maxwell Jackson's murder.

Madeline had formulated the perfect plan, and now her providence rested within the success of its delivery. But it wasn't the airtight schedule or risk of failure causing her skin to bite with a hybrid sense of fear; it was the fact that she was personally walking the wrath of vengeance straight into the den of the vicious filicide murderers who wanted nothing more than to see her dead.

Nathan was practically comatose when Madeline shimmied out from underneath him and off the bed. As quietly as possible, she tiptoed into the bathroom and called herself a cab, then slipped out of the shirt he lent her to sleep in and back into her dress, snatched up her purse and shoes, and headed for the bedroom door. Careful not to make even the slightest sound, she slowly pulled down on the long brass handle of the heavy carved-mahogany door. But when it opened smoothly without resistance and she was free to leave without explanation, she stopped herself.

As she gazed back at Nathan sleeping peacefully, taking one last look, a profound feeling of genuine sadness erupted from a place of emotion she'd repressed long ago. Leaving him without saying goodbye didn't seem like the best gesture considering the night they'd shared; she didn't want to leave him at all. But it wasn't the time to concern herself with the consequences of an unpredictable gateway she probably shouldn't have opened to begin with. So, reluctantly, she restrained herself from additional contact and made her way down two floors of dark winding stairwells and out the front door. She ran across the driveway, exited the property through a side service gate leading onto the street, and hopped into the waiting cab.

Back at her apartment, Madeline changed clothes and loaded her travel bags and evidence files. If everything went as planned it would be a quick round-trip expedition, and she ambitiously hoped to return to New Orleans later that night. But she knew such hopes were aspirations without high probability, and left a notarized letter naming Gabriella the beneficiary to her estate on the table for Rosette, should she not return.

For Madeline Knight, the time available to save both her and Gabriella's lives was quickly running out, and there was no choice but to continue her mission without hesitation or doubt.

After a traffic-free drive in her own car to the airport, she boarded her flight right on time.

Cincinnati, Ohio – 11:00 a.m.
The woman Madeline was before her plane left the ground in New Orleans was nothing like the woman she became when the Boeing 737 halted at the CVG gates in Kentucky. Her change in persona and demeanor was a potentially lethal hindrance not even Madeline herself could have predicted. The vision she'd seen of herself running up on stage and unmasking her parents for all to see had initially felt like the retribution she'd been waiting for. Now, as she drove through the entrance onto the property of the Central Church of Enlightenment, it was a feat she no longer knew she could summon the nerve to accomplish.

Before parking, Madeline wanted to drive by the front of the church and survey the layout to prepare her plan of entry. However, as she rounded the corner approaching the Golden Monument, the sight was so far beyond her mental range of understanding she regrettably realized how grossly she'd underestimated the difficulty of the paramount crusade ahead.

Hundreds of private security personnel dressed in CCE uniforms monitored the sidewalks and prohibited pedestrians from entering the streets out of order. The construction barricades once blocking the passage of traffic were gone and waves of cars passed through the gates without obstruction. Tens of thousands of residents and tourists wandered the grounds admiring the new staple of the community while waiting to attend the most publicized celebrity debut in United States history.

It was impossible to comprehend that only two days before the entire property was empty, calm, and serene, as it was now a media and entertainment frenzy. Out front of the Golden Monument, thousands of cars honked incessantly and weaved around one another unsafely, looking for parking. All designated lots were already at capacity and the traffic control team scurried to block off side streets for additional vehicle storage.

As the noon hour approached, the spectators began to line the streets with unruly and unusually eager ferocity, waiting for the blockades in front of the main lawn to open. Everyone present wanted to get as close as possible to the shiny golden structure, which had after years of community programming deviously denoted itself the "new promised land."

Ahead of the waiting parishioners and closer to the church but not yet on the grounds, hundreds of reporters and paparazzi photographers gathered outside the gates to the main hall's rear entrance and the Chatsworths' rectory estate. They were all hankering to capture the first pictures of the new pastor and his wife, whom to date had only been seen via publicity photos released by the CCE.

At the bottom of the steps leading to the church's enormous red-ribbon-covered crystal doors, a huge production stage awaited the Chatsworths' arrival. The backdrop was a gaudy display of superfluous decorations and flowers with mammoth clusters of red and gold balloons. Several twenty-foot projection screens to air the live transmission were installed behind the podium and at multiple locations around the five-acre valley of grass bordering the Golden Monument. And thirty-foot sets of speaker boxes with amplifiers continuously blared upbeat and hypnotic music expertly mixed by the CCE disk jockey.

There were two distinct seating sections for the landmark affair. To the left and right of the stage were the luxury climate-controlled VIP boxes set high above the lawn. Meticulously groomed butlers served red wine with imported cheese and tropical fruits to the one thousand guests already comfortably seated in their chairs. Behind the VIPs and spanning across the front of the stage and entire surface of the lawn, was the colossal standing section. With the capacity to hold two-hundred fifty thousand people, red and gold velvet ropes sectioned off the entire viewing arena ensuring even those not in high regard still felt as though they were.

Across the street on the CCE Academy school grounds, there were twenty circus-sized hospitality tents bustling with caterers, entertainers, servers, and staff. The CCE had prepared a gratuitous array of free food and festivities, which awaited the crowd after the ceremony, and alone had attracted thousands of extra guests.

Thirty minutes before noon the police security unit monitoring the perimeter finally opened the lawn for entry. Fully armored crowd-control officers ushered thousands of people onto the grounds accordingly, all of whom pushed, and pulled as they tried to get past.

Madeline was unable to navigate around the mobile police station now occupying the street, and temporarily parked at the end of the main block to calm her increasingly escalating anxiety. Her thought pattern and sense of focus were dangerously out of control. The staggering amount of money, resources, people, and excitement feeding into the inaugural extravaganza was a quantum-mind-warp pushing her closer to termination. *How could this ridiculous presentation possibly be in honor of my parents?* she wondered, praying she had somehow been wrong; that the Internet announcement had been either a mistake or illusion imagined in her time of desperation and quest for answers. But it wasn't. The Chatsworths' names were on banners and flags strung up and waving all around the compound. The unveiling was undeniably real and happening in less than twenty minutes.

When Madeline sat down on the plane in New Orleans, she had forced herself not to think about anything emotional that would threaten or hinder her capacity to complete her mission. But now, as she prepared for a moment that meant life or death, feelings about the people she loved most in her life were the only emotions she could contemplate. Romanticized thoughts about a future with Nathan and Gabriella rushed through her head. She thought about Priestess Haloise and Ross, whom had no idea where she was or what she was doing. Nobody except Gabriella would know what had happened to her if she never made it home again.

Only one week prior, Madeline had felt she had nothing to live for and held no real insight into the true purpose of her life. She had been on a course of personal annihilation, killing herself slowly one drink at a time. Living only through her patients and the occasional trip to Haiti with Priestess Haloise and Ross, both of whom managed to live on a spiritually satisfied level she herself could never attain.

But the circumstances of Madeline's world had changed dramatically in only five days. Gabriella had come back to repair the past and reestablish a family and it was Gabriella's words Madeline kept hearing: "I don't want you putting yourself at risk . . . I don't want to be without you again," Gabriella had said, just before Madeline had walked out the door without responding. And since Madeline hadn't been able to visit her sister on Thursday, Gabriella now sat alone in the hospital helplessly awaiting her return.

And then there was Nathan Raines. He was the first man

Madeline had ever opened herself up to emotionally, and she was uncontrollably drawn to him in a way she couldn't explain. They both shared the same dream of starting a private practice, and Madeline's residency was finally coming to a close. With a partnership including Priestess Haloise and Ross, and perhaps now even Dr. Raines, that dream was a real possibility.

For the first time in Madeline's life the future made sense—everything she thought she wanted was lying in wait on the horizon. And what was she doing? She was lingering in front of hundreds of thousands of rabid supporters and armed security guards all representing the very individuals she had come to impeach. What chance did she have? Her parents had gotten away with extortion, abuse, and pathological-trickery for years in Salem. And when their cover was breached, they had expertly and without dissension abolished their crimes as if never in existence. Charles and Claire Jackson hadn't just reemerged with new lives and identities, they had reemerged with the wealth and social standing enjoyed by few others with far less to hide.

Madeline began to think she must have been crazy to come to Cincinnati and challenge the two most treacherous individuals she had ever encountered. At that moment, all she wanted to do was turn the car around, drive back to the airport, gather what she could salvage from New Orleans, and run; start a new life, just like they had, somewhere else. She knew what her father was capable of; she'd seen the hate in his eyes when he wanted nothing more than to snap her neck; now there was no one to stop him from doing it. The Chatsworths had already concealed one murder; what bother was one or two more?

But that was the whole point—the reason Madeline had risked her life to come to this contemptible place of humiliation and danger. Murder! Pastor and Mrs. Chatsworth had maliciously and brutally slain her beloved brother, and they'd done it while he was sick, defenseless, and bound by handcuffs and chains. But the limits of their merciless rampage hadn't ended there; after they'd finished with Maxwell, they located Gabriella, also sick and defenseless, and threatened her with the same demise.

Madeline didn't need any more answers. She knew exactly why she came to Cincinnati. The Jackson children had spent their entire lives trying to escape a horrid past, and Maxwell was the first to lose the fight. Before leaving East Pen, Madeline had sworn to avenge his murder and end their parents' satanic reign of evil. And if the price of fulfilling that promise was her life, she was prepared to pay it.

With renewed clarity, Madeline resumed her original plan. After assembling a high-resolution zoom-lens camera, she photographed every person sitting in the VIP lounges, including the most crucial one of them all—Stefan. As he organized with the black-suit-wearing, earpiece-equipped executive security team, Madeline snapped as many photographs of him as possible. She now had the last piece of evidence needed and could officially link Stefan to the Chatsworths. With a look of disgust, she drove off and found parking several blocks away.

Madeline looked down at her watch—11:55 a.m. It was time. She tucked her backpack and cell phone under the front seat, exited the car, and tied her black trench coat over the same black suit she'd worn two days before. After slinging a leather messenger bag containing the evidence over her shoulder, she put on a pair of black sunglasses and headed toward the stage.

When Madeline reached the gates leading onto the lawn, the entire valley of grass was already packed and overflowing. The immovable wall of people surrounding the stage was as overwhelming a sight as the church itself. She stopped at the back and waited stone-faced for the first view of her parents in fifteen years. Her heart beat loudly over the clamor of the restless crowd and a feverish heat radiated from her body creating a separate aura of her own making. As the wetness from her raging perspirations soaked the pits of her arms and dripped down her forehead stinging her eyes, the crowd exploded with thunderous cheer.

The mayor of Cincinnati—a tall lanky bald gentleman with a pure-white mustache and a gray pinstriped suit—appeared on the stage. "Welcome! Welcome! Ladies and gentlemen of Cincinnati and of the world!" he shouted, silencing the crowd. "After years followed by months of brewing excitement and momentous anticipation, I am proud to introduce the new religious leaders and pillars of our community, Pastor Milton Chatsworth and his wife, Palamia!"

The Chatsworths appeared on stage smiling, waving, and dressed impeccably rich as the new First Family of Religion. Pastor Chatsworth wore a gleaming black Italian suit and his titanium clerical collar underneath a wealth of vestments that would make even a Cardinal envious. The man had no shame. Instead of a simple pastor's robe, he donned a red-and-gold velvet embroidered tunic with wide sleeves and a plaid stole. Mrs. Chatsworth wore a red plaid couture dress-suit with a high stiff collar and gold embroidered trimming, and white gloves. With her oversized white wide-brimmed ladies' hat with silk netting covering her eyes, she could see out, but nobody could see in. Stefan, in a shiny dark-silver suit with a security-surveillance microphone in his ear, surveyed the scene standing protectively behind his masters.

At the sight of her parents, Madeline's heart steadied. She clenched her jaw and squeezed her fists so tightly her nails dug into the soft skin of her palms. Her once uncontrollable apprehension transformed into the honed-in focus of a hawk stalking its prey.

Pastor Chatsworth raised his arms to quiet the screaming crowd, stepped behind the podium, and began his speech in an entrancing monotone. "I am standing here today not as a religious leader, friend, or neighbor, but as a fellow citizen dedicated to the rise and success of this great city!"

Once again, everyone cheered.

Except Madeline. With ears ringing so loudly she couldn't hear, she slowly made her way through the crowd; the vast sea of bodies before her parted effortlessly as she passed. Steadily quickening her pace, she carefully timed her attack to washout the scandalous effects of Pastor Chatsworth's speech the moment it ended.

But unbeknownst to Madeline, two executive security guards

fitted with the same earpiece as Stefan were also making their way through the crowd. One guard encroached on Madeline's right side, the other on her left, both slowly closing in around her as Pastor Chatsworth's speech continued, ". . . After bridging the vast waters between city and state, business and schools, church and community . . ."

When Madeline reached the side of the stage ready to strike, the two guards restrained her and dragged her out of sight to the back of the stage.

"And now," Pastor Chatsworth said, "we have a special surprise my wife and I have waited until today to share with you—something that makes me the proudest leader in the entire world . . ." Simultaneously behind the stage the guards ripped Madeline's sunglasses from her face, confiscated her evidence bag, and replaced her trench coat with a red-and-gold plaid embroidered stole. "I would like to introduce you all to your new associate pastor, our daughter, Victoria Chatsworth!"

Madeline's face flashed over every screen on the CCE compound and behind Pastor Chatsworth at the podium. With the guards firmly grasping her arms, Madeline was forcefully escorted onto the stage as the crowd cheered wildly.

Mrs. Chatsworth walked over to the front doors of the church with a large pair of scissors and cut the red ribbon just as Madeline, in complete shock, was briskly taken away.

20

CROSSROADS

Locked inside the pitch-black vestment closet of the Golden Monument's sacristy room, Madeline crouched on the floor underneath the hanging robes shaking uncontrollably. After a raging fit of hysterical fury, she had screamed and pounded herself into an exhausted state of mental anguish and distress. Once she'd realized the confines of her temporary prison were impenetrable, she accepted her fate and became unwaveringly certain the powers of evil would shortly escort her to a sudden death.

Twenty minutes later when the same two guards from the ceremony finally opened the doors, Madeline was drenched in sweat and immobilized by fear. Her disheveled hair hung over her tear-soaked face and her knuckles were bruised, swollen, and littered with splinters from an unsuccessful attempt at escape. She had shed her suit jacket while battling an unbearable heat radiating from the floor, and her now-ripped white silk camisole left her embarrassingly exposed.

After prying Madeline's interlocked arms from around her head, the guards bound her wrists in front with rope and lifted her limp body off the floor. They then proceeded to drag her unwillingly out the rear entrance, through the long dimly-lit hallways, and down the unrelentingly deep spiral staircase. At the bottom, the two French doors opened automatically without announcement, and the guards shoved her through the entrance and into a dark wretched-smelling chamber.

Once inside, the unmistakable terror of the Sands thrust Madeline into another irrepressible outburst of fright. She battled wildly in a last effort to free herself from her captors' grasp. But having already delivered their package to the specified location, the guards released her abruptly, turned around, and left. The doors slammed shut and locked behind them, leaving Madeline standing alone at the beginning of a cold dark tunnel.

Dripping red candles lined the floor on both sides and reflected off the polished-black obsidian walls arching just above her head. A galactic tide of distortion left her sense of space and balance in a ghastly atmosphere of confusion, and her hearing was lost amongst the deafening sound of a howling wind. Freezing air from an unknown source hit from every angle, frost-nipping her skin and providing an unfathomable depiction of the vast space surrounding her. The air temperature dropped below freezing, her lips went purple with frost, her skin white, and the tips of her sweaty hair hardened with ice.

As she tore at the ropes binding her wrists, the putrid smell of sulfur gas suddenly filled her nostrils, saturated her lungs, and churned her stomach. Instantly light-headed and faint, she fell to her knees and vomited on the floor.

Barely relieved from the intense nausea, Madeline tried to stand up, but the room spun, her vision blurred, and she slipped and stumbled to the ground, vomiting once more. After the last foreign substance had been expelled from her body, she found her footing and painfully adjusted to the lightness of a strangely unbalanced change in gravity. This time, it was no hallucination—Madeline knew she had entered another plane of dimension, and in actuality, she had.

With her vision restored, she untied her wrists and focused on the end of the tunnel, following a cryptic appeal which lured her forward and unafraid into the darkness. When she looked back down at the candles once flickering off the mirrored obsidian, the light had become part of the walls with flames now encompassing the entire tunnel like burning fumes of liquid gasoline.

When the flaming archway disappeared, and Madeline ventured out into the black openness of what lay ahead, she heard the loud crisp sound of fingers snap. A gigantic ten-foot-tall fireplace instantly ignited, extinguishing the cold, defrosting Madeline, and illuminating a grandiose lair tactically entrenched within a massive volcanic rock. The sweltering, glistening domed citrine geode, encrusted with millions of gold crystals, dazzled everything beneath in a luminous orange hue. And an expansive floor of black opal swirled in the form of a moving galaxy with its brilliant play of colors glowing under Madeline's feet.

Pastor Chatsworth stood in front of the blazing flames and turned around to face his daughter; his robes of worship now replaced by a quartet of necklaces constructed of quarter-size black diamonds, the longest extending to his waist. The jewels hanging heavily over his structured black-sheen Italian suit solidified the trappings of a finely dressed modern monarch. He wore two flawless five-carat white diamonds in each of his ears and a fifty-carat scarlet emerald armor-cross ring encased in yellow gold on his right middle finger.

The large lava-stone desk from the meeting with Satan was positioned atop a floating glass platform hanging in the right side of the lair, with a wide glistening curved-glass staircase leading up to it.

Mrs. Chatsworth sat in the chair behind the desk with her back to Madeline. She wore a liquid-silver gown covering every inch of her hands, fingers, and body, all the way up to her chin. The molten fabric sheathed her perfect figure so tightly it fused with her skin. Her hair was now tucked underneath an exquisite diamond-draped headdress, cropped on the left side and dangling over her right eye and down the outside of her cheek. She licked her bloodred lips and swiveled her chair around into Madeline's view.

For Madeline, the magnitude of the visual brilliance and otherworldly-extravagant ambience in front of her was both mesmerizing and utterly disturbing at the same time. But her adjustment phase quickly dissipated, and hatred and revenge smothered her natural instinct to question the scientific possibility of what she was witnessing. The mystical enchantments stimulating her mind all played second-string to the asphyxiating rage she felt at the very sight and chillingly close proximity of her parents.

"Stay back!" Madeline commanded, dripping wet in a fighting stance and shooting a quick series of glances around the room to locate an alternate means of escape.

"That is no tone to be taking with the loving parents from whom you've been astray," said Pastor Chatsworth. The sound of his voice echoed throughout the chambers causing Madeline's body to shudder with the same paralyzing fragility he'd always effortlessly inflicted at will.

Madeline spotted a brass rotary telephone sitting on a table to her left next to a luxurious gathering of red velvet furniture. She ran over and grasped the receiver, raised it to her ear, and dialed 9-1-1.

Pastor Chatsworth let out a cackling opus of laughter. "I wouldn't do that if I were you," he said. "Even if it were the police on the other end of the line, which it's not, I can personally assure you it wouldn't be me going out in handcuffs. Then again, you're already quite familiar with that arrangement, aren't you?"

Madeline heard a wickedly demonic voice on the other end of the line whose words she couldn't understand. She slammed down the receiver and ran toward the tunnel headed for the doors. Just as she entered the flaming passageway, Stefan stepped out of the shadows and blocked her exit. The sight of him instantly transported her back to the moment she saw him on the prison's surveillance screen. Real time paused, and the memory of Stefan mercilessly stabbing the jagged-edged knife into Maxwell's neck sent her into a violent outburst of physical attacks.

"Monster!" Madeline screamed, scratching his face and ripping at his hair. Her efforts were no use; Stefan was so large a man her assault was as worthless as the wings of a monarch butterfly flapping against a handler who'd clasped its abdomen in his fingertips. He gripped her wrists and pinned them behind her waist, hissed in her face, and flung her back to the center of the room.

Pastor Chatsworth nonchalantly moseyed over and circled Madeline repeatedly, dizzying the object of his unnaturally licentious fascination. He inhaled deeply and took in the intoxicating scent of his fugitive daughter. He stopped to the side of her right ear, leaned in closer, and exhaled hotly through gritted teeth. "You're looking more delicious than even I could have ever imagined," he said. "Our worshipers are going to love you. I had hoped to see your sister here as well to round-out our little family reunion, but we can get to that later." He crossed his arms behind his back and walked away.

"We won't be getting to anything later!" Madeline yelled. "My sister is locked away where you'll never find her!"

Pastor Chatsworth scoffed at Madeline's outburst nonplussed and continued to the other side of the lair.

"I know what you did to Max!" she screamed.

"You know nothing!" he said, whipping around.

Madeline slowed her breathing. "What was that stunt you played outside? What do you want from me?"

Pastor Chatsworth ignored Madeline's request and walked back over to his post by the fire. He wasn't going to allow her to dictate the terms of his performance, nor was he willing to relinquish the satisfaction provided by his absolute control over her. He had waited fifteen years for this moment, and after having captured her so spitefully, wanted to savor the event.

The open furnace of infernal fire dwarfed him as he hovered silently, entranced by the blaze. Leisurely waving his hand back and forth through the blistering flames, he proudly demonstrated his imperviousness to mortal dangers. "No need for haste, my little thistle-covered flower," Pastor Chatsworth said. "The forthcoming explanation of my devices will appease your thirst in due time." He looked up at Madeline with beaming-red pupils. "As you can see, Annabelle, or should I say . . . Victoria! Or better yet, what is it you're calling yourself these days? Oh, yes—Madeline. You're not the only one skilled at making a past disappear and creating a new future."

The time had come once again to deliver a speech he'd been long preparing. He would first break Madeline down and calm her nerves, and then tantalize her senses and capture her soul. But he knew she would have to offer it willingly, so he put his superlative talents as Satan's chief representative to work. "During your lost years," Pastor Chatsworth began, "your mother and I had to rigorously multiply the capacity of our powers to recover from the humiliation and obstruction your unfounded disobedience caused our family. And like all great leaders, we elevated ourselves from the depths of defeat and rose again to greatness in the eyes of our master. All the while harboring the vessel of your forgiveness in anticipation of the day your fruit would ripen."

Still highly on alert, Madeline looked up at her mother, who continued to perch stoically on the platform above. But Mrs. Chatsworth refused to look at her daughter and continued to stare past Madeline as if she didn't exist.

"We have created the first of the New Churches of the World," Pastor Chatsworth continued. "And, as you now know, a new life and identity for you to go with it. It's time to stop avoiding your destiny." He walked over to Madeline and handed her a large black-velvet jewelry box. His eyes widened with delightful expectation. "Open it."

"I don't want anything from you," Madeline said, stepping back away from him slowly. "Everything you touch reeks of blasphemy!"

"I said open it!" he roared. "I assure you I wouldn't offer anything but pain for your enjoyment. This is not a gift by me, but rather an offering from the new Ruler of all Humanity meant to solidify your allegiance to His Grace. Open it."

Madeline reluctantly took the box out of Pastor Chatsworth's hands, cringing at the sight of his perfectly manicured fingernails filed in the shape of pyramids and dipped in 24-carat gold. She looked back up and saw his lips purse with pleasure when she opened the silver-satin-lined box. Her eyes darted back down when a glistening light sparked her unexpected amazement. Inside was the most beautiful necklace imaginable. Each of the sixteen platinum-encased flawless white-blue diamonds creating the broad circle was one hundred carats. Worthy of a queen, it shimmered like the sun.

"My precious, precious Victoria," Pastor Chatsworth said, "Madeline Knight is an illusion. All your years lived in denial have been pointless. You thought you controlled your destiny, but you have never owned such power. Your place is within the Chatsworth Monarchy—a name to which heads will forever bow to and obey." He walked back and stood by the fire. "You should be expressing gratitude for the great lengths we have gone to save you."

Mrs. Chatsworth began to twinge in her seat. The thought of Madeline touching the necklace she had reserved for another had propelled her into a swelling state of internal madness, and the intense hatred she'd always felt toward Madeline rushed back with a burning flush of jealousy. She was fuming. Her eyes glowed red and her chest rose in and out while Pastor Chatsworth continued his schmoozing.

"We are, after all, a gracious, generous, and forgiving people," he said, his vocal tone rising with each additional pitch. "It is time for you to take your rightful place at the top. Every wish of unlimited desire will be yours for the taking. The true leader of the New World Order has chosen you to lead his herds of faithful servants. And they have all given their souls for the one task of worshiping you. Don't deny him. Don't deny yourself. No more nightmares. No more fighting an obsolete world that doesn't want you. Outside these doors, you are a slave; inside them, you will be a queen. Join us. Crawl out from under the rocks and stand in the sun!"

Madeline was impressed. In all her life, she had never heard such words of encouragement. Moreover, she had never heard her father praise her so admirably. But his lyrical prose wasn't the best of his enticements—since birth, the only gifts he'd ever offered her were a sound beating and the leftover scraps of his own indulgences. The man serenading her now was as recognizable as a stranger. Clearly, his lifetime of immoral worship and corruption had more than provided the life, luxury, and power he'd always coveted. It was surreal to realize and accept that everything he'd ever taught her was true. He had defied the laws of human existence and transcended time and space into the boundless In-Between. He had sold his soul to the Devil and all his dreams had come true.

Madeline now knew unquestionably that the Era of the Ether Priestess Haloise had predicted was not only real, it was already upon the world. Priestess Haloise had informed Madeline years before that once Madeline opened her eyes to the spiritual ways of the universe and became fluid within the merging planes, she could never revert to old methods of limited thinking. And Madeline's eyes were open, she had become fluid, and there had been a shift just as Priestess Haloise had prophesied only three days before. Also, as predicted, the conflicting forces initiating the shift had trapped Madeline in the middle. The only question left was whether she would choose to stand strong and embrace the sanctity of good or submit to the temptations of the ever-growing powers of evil.

She looked down at the diamond necklace in her hands—it truly was the most beautiful ornamentation she'd ever seen. She shook her head and smiled, closed the case, and then hurled it across the room into the blazing fire. Pastor Chatsworth's face went mad with fury when the box and its contents effortlessly disintegrated into a pile of red sand.

"Well . . ." Madeline said, sighing dismissively. "So much for the gifts of Satan; never more than sand through your fingertips. A convincing speech, I can see why he hired you. But now it's my turn to tell you who I am and what I stand for. I protect souls; I don't take them. I would rather live and die in a world that doesn't want me then spend one second with you hovering in the mirage of paradise outside the gates of Hell. You preach about having risen to the heights of greatness when all you've done is violate every natural law in existence with your crimes against the good of man, and heinous sins against your children." Madeline cut her eyes at Mrs. Chatsworth. "Watching with pleasure while we were beaten, humiliated, and neglected—you make me sick! The luxuries afforded by a lifetime of dedication to Satan count for nothing when you're dead. And when you are, I'll be watching not with pleasure but with pity, as the remnants of your dark souls disintegrate into ashes just like his gifts in the fire."

"You're making the biggest mistake of your life!" Pastor Chatsworth growled, exposing his gums and pointed teeth.

"The only mistake I've ever made was keeping quiet about you. I find it awfully interesting through all of this you have failed to even mention my brother. I know you killed Max and I won't be quiet this time!"

Mrs. Chatsworth had listened to her husband's failed attempt at handling a job he was no more suited for now than he was fifteen years earlier, and she'd heard enough. She intended to put an end to his worthless efforts at pacifying the disgraceful creation of her womb who should be bowing down at their feet, not spitting at them. With eyes still glowing red, she flew down the stairs in a hostile rage to where Madeline was standing.

"You ungrateful, treacherous, swine snitch!" Mrs. Chatsworth seethed. "You speak with such confidence when your insolence is piercing my ears like a squealing goat. Who the hell do you think brought you here? The precious sister you think you have safely stashed away—it was I who released her and sent her after you! Gabriella will be greatly rewarded for her loyalty and devotion to this family. We set our plan into motion long before the glimpse of revenge was even a twinkle in your eye. Murdering your brother was nothing more than a sacrificial trap meant to deliver you to me. He was on our side long ago, long before he failed us and became dispensable. It was your blasphemies that got him beat!"

"You're a lying snake!" Madeline screamed. "Gabriella may be trouble, but she's no traitor. And my brother despised you just as I do; he was pure, and kind, and you destroyed him! It was your evil that turned him into what he was. And when he refused your offer, just as I have, that's when you killed him!"

Mrs. Chatsworth scoffed and cracked a shrewd nasty smile. "Poor, poor girl, always running two steps behind. What your brother was or wasn't doesn't really matter at this point, but you had better get to know your sister really well because you will soon be working beside her. Does the New Orleans City Hospital psychiatric ward ring a bell for you? We know exactly where Gabriella is because she called and told us you would be coming here without her." Her face was now only one inch from Madeline's turned cheek. "Now you will produce my daughter and accept our terms, or you will die!"

"That's what you think. Does the name Gordon Covey of the Federal Correctional Penitentiary of Eastern Illinois ring a bell for you? Because I got to him before you did. And Stefan sure looked good in prison-issued orange. Now it's you who will be destroyed." Madeline stormed over to Stefan, who was still in front of the tunnel. "Get out of my way!"

Stefan turned to Pastor Chatsworth, who grudgingly nodded with his approval. He had to let Madeline go and he knew it. Stefan stepped aside, and she fled through the tunnel and out the now-unlocked entrance.

The black opal floor split deeply down the middle when Madeline slammed the doors behind her.

21

NURSE MONROE
ON THE HUNT

New Orleans, Louisiana

Dr. Fields' evening as the reigning social king of New Orleans had turned into a morning after of looming social disgrace. As he stared at his reflection in the large mirror of his extravagant hotel suite vanity, he scraped the soot of his memory and sifted through the details illustrating his transgressions of the night before. Between the pulsating bolts of pain from his throbbing headache, the few images he could remember flashed through his mind and provided no comfort whatsoever—especially when it came to the unscrupulous deeds a successful plan for damage control would require of him.

After an extended hot shower and a chemically equalizing shot of scotch, he looked over at Nurse Monroe still sleeping naked in bed and knew he'd made the second biggest mistake of his life. Avoiding sexual relations with Nurse Monroe was a survival strategy and lifelong commitment he'd implemented years before to combat her unrelenting attacks of calculated seduction. And even with all his efforts, her decade of shameless public flirtations had made him a regular target for unfiltered mockery at the Walker Hamilton Country Club, despite mortifying her father who was often present. But regardless of Nurse Monroe's consistent supply of ego-boosting female flattery, Dr. Fields had zero interest in humoring her romantically, and for good reason.

Nurse Monroe's father, Dr. Herman Monroe, was the president of South State Medical Board, and he and Dr. Fields had known each other all their lives. They grew up together in Old Metairie, went to the same Catholic preparatory school, and attended the same undergraduate college and school of medicine. Although they were more academic adversaries than close friends—having shared the high school title of co-valedictorian—they had maintained an unbreakable gentleman's agreement over the years. And that agreement involved the unlimited extension of favors within their individual ranges of capabilities, as necessary.

Because Dr. Monroe had reached his peak of success more rapidly than Dr. Fields had, Dr. Fields often found himself to be the member of the alliance requiring the favors. Therefore, during a time when Dr. Monroe seldom came calling, Dr. Fields had given Nurse Monroe the head position on his staff as a gift requiring no reciprocity. In fact, Nurse Monroe's presence at NOSPH helped Dr. Fields more than anyone else, as it afforded him opportunities he might not have enjoyed otherwise.

But bringing Nurse Monroe onto his team was the extent of Dr. Fields' use for her. Truthfully, he found her to be incompetent, obnoxious, and an ongoing liability. She knew her position was secure for life if she wanted it, and continuously behaved with the air of strict entitlement. Most of the time, Dr. Fields wasn't sure if it was he who ran his department, or Nurse Monroe. Her ongoing rivalry with Madeline, however, was the most damaging liability of all.

Dr. Fields had obsessed over Madeline since the day they met, and the constant interference from Nurse Monroe's own obsession with Madeline made it impossible to advance his acquisition. His desire for Madeline was so strong he had grown to hate Nurse Monroe and had been plotting Nurse Monroe's amicable dismissal for the previous three years. He'd been waiting patiently for the right circumstances to emerge, and his regrettable night with her after the gala had set him back significantly. But he was never a man willing to allow a pesky hindrance to keep him from his most coveted prize, especially if that hindrance was Nurse Monroe, and the prize was Madeline Knight.

Dr. Fields had a long-standing reputation as a man uncontrollably infatuated with the female gender, but only females of a particularly special breeding. The only vice overshadowing his undeniable fascination with exotic women of intelligence was his devious attraction to beautiful women suffering from psychological illness. And as far as he could tell, Madeline was both, making her the most potent aphrodisiac he'd ever experienced.

After discovering his sexual attraction to his female patients while in medical school, Dr. Fields had decided to complete his residency in adult psychiatry as a result. He loved the power he wielded over women in a fragile mental state, and always made sure to take on the youngest and most beautiful cases. He sought to mold each individual patient into his perfect version of a woman, and after further investigation found persons with a history of either physical or sexual abuse to be the most willing and enticing candidates.

The mischievously calculating Dr. Fields' young patients saw him as a god and savior, and he reveled in his ability to control the results of their therapy by hindering progress and ultimately keeping them sick. After months, sometimes years, under his care, his choice patients eventually succumbed to a doctor-induced medical crash. The sicker the patient was, the more attached and dependent they became. And that was exactly the way Dr. Fields had designed his treatment plans to be. After only a few years in practice, he had complete physical and emotional control over a harem of women under the age of twenty-five, all of whom he engaged sexually. However, knowing that participation in such vulgar activity with a patient was both a code of ethics violation and illegal, he became a master at finding crafty ways to hide it.

When he started his private practice—an adult outpatient psychotherapy center with his now ex-wife—it was the perfect cover. And although Dr. Angelica Fields eventually discovered her husband's villainous exploitations and infidelities, the blinding cloak of denial and shame combined with the vanity and greed of keeping their business, kept her quiet. And as the years passed, their practice grew, and they hired additional associate psychiatrists. The last of whom was a young resident named Dr. Nathan Raines.

After completing his residency, at the Fields' request Nathan had decided to stay on at the center permanently and accepted a salaried position. Shortly thereafter, he inadvertently fell in love with one of his patients, the beautiful Katarina Dubois. She was the twenty-one-year-old half-French, half-Hispanic daughter of a prominent Louisiana transportation tycoon, and by far the most desirable debutante in all New Orleans. Nathan immediately ended their doctor-patient relationship and went to Dr. Fields to request reassignment. Dr. Fields had happily obliged, praised Nathan for his ethical integrity, and looking for an even more devious challenge, took on Katarina's case himself.

After a year of dating, Nathan proposed to Katarina and she accepted. She was still seeing Dr. Fields professionally, however, to which Nathan tirelessly objected, and to his surprise, she was resistant to the point of outright refusal to cease. And because she'd originally sought psychiatric help to cope with the death of her mother and not a dual diagnosis, Nathan felt a year should have been sufficient time to resume life on her own without therapeutic assistance. But it was at that point Katarina's mental health bizarrely began to decline—as did her sexual relationship and preferences with her fiancé.

Nathan eventually went to Dr. Fields to discuss the situation, hoping to solve the problem amongst themselves as colleagues, and in the best interest of the patient. Unfortunately, Dr. Fields saw the matter differently and didn't meet the request favorably—he had no plans to relinquish Katarina, whom he'd been secretly having dangerously abusive sadomasochistic intercourse with for a year. Furthermore, he loved knowing the beautiful fiancé of his younger, wealthier employee was completely under his control, and his control only. She would never leave him on her own accord; he was certain of that.

Utterly disturbed and past his boundaries of tolerance, Nathan pledged to confront both Dr. Fields and Katarina during one of their sessions. When he burst through the locked door and into Dr. Fields' office, what he saw irreparably destroyed his life. The image of his innocent fiancé naked and in bondage with a ruthless Dr. Fields barbarically penetrating her from behind was seared into Nathan's conscious forever. And it was the last time he saw Katarina Dubois alive.

The shame and embarrassment of being caught by her fiancé in such a humiliating position combined with her inability to escape the grasp of Dr. Fields' control had pushed Katarina beyond psychological capacity; her father's maid found her dead in the tub the following morning with both of her wrists slit.

The incident sparked an outrage. News spread across the nation that not only was Katarina engaged to the heir of the wealthiest family in Louisiana, but she'd been seeing his boss for therapy. Dr. Fields' wife, aware of the truth behind the suicide, promptly filed for divorce, and everyone else involved took swift action to minimize any public embarrassment or legal repercussions.

Nathan, overwrought with agony and guilt, wanted no part in a conspiracy. But his family refused to have such a tantalizing scandal tarnish their reputation, and along with Dr. Fields called on their allies at South State Medical Board. All records of Katarina's therapy and death were secretly burned, and a joint publicist for both Dr. Fields and Nathan Raines carefully contrived and delivered a public explanation absolving them of any involvement.

The Raines family forced Nathan to stay in New Orleans under their watchful eye and gave him the position of Chief of Staff at

City Hospital as consolation. He was able to assume absolute control over every department, as well as continue his psychiatric practice. But, his hatred for his family, Dr. Fields, and the corrupt society supporting them, only brewed.

Dr. Fields, in a self-correcting transition into child psychiatry, was eventually given the position of Chief of Child and Adolescent Psychiatry at NOSPH. He was the perfect candidate for the job, considering he was deeply indebted to the organization overseeing it.

And Katarina's father, owing an old favor stemming from debts of his own, received immunity for all past mishaps and a generous financial sum in exchange for his silence.

Within two months, the entire incident was safely locked away into the exclusive vault harboring the hidden sins of New Orleans society. And it had all happened under the powerful umbrella of the highly influential Dr. Herman Monroe.

––––––––––

While Dr. Fields contemplated the impending consequences of his evening with Nurse Monroe, the post-gala morning after for her was the pinnacle of euphoria. When he walked out of the bathroom dressed and ready for the two o'clock luncheon, she was lounging comfortably on the bed basking in the knowledge that her siege of advancements had finally overpowered the resistance.

Nurse Monroe's life ambition—deeply ingrained by her mother before an untimely death—was to become a doctor's wife. She believed unequivocally that it should have been her on Dr. Fields' arm at the gala, not Madeline Knight. And regardless of the additional reinforcements needed to seal the treaty Nurse Monroe longed for, she would make sure the next time it would be.

She was perfectly aware that Dr. Fields felt nothing positive for her emotionally; but she didn't care. Being a nurse was nothing more than the chastening-shackle of her father's contemptuous punishment for her lack of social grace and higher education. But now, her latest victory had placed her one-step away from reprieve.

Dr. Harold Fields wasn't getting away with utilizing her body for pre-marital, erogenous pleasure and then continuing his life without obligation—she would see to that. He'd even ordered her breakfast via room service in a cheap attempt at nullifying his actions, but she was unimpressed.

Although Nurse Monroe didn't know the exact extent of the present favor owed between Dr. Fields and her father, she certainly knew who was on the receiving end of the arrangement. If a lifetime of living amongst prominent wealthy men had taught her one lesson, it was that when a man is facing extinction he'd pay whatever he has left for social and financial salvation. Even if the terms of that salvation meant a lifetime of servitude to the man who sold it. Well, when it came to Dr. Fields, that man was Nurse Monroe's father, and "daddy's girl" was ready to collect.

Nurse Monroe's plans were finally within reach, and for the first time in her life she had her target in the crosshairs from an elevated position.

As soon as Dr. Fields left, she had new clothes sent up from the hotel boutique under his room number, left the expensive breakfast he'd ordered on the silver tray untouched, and headed to work at NOSPH. But her agenda for the day did not involve tending to patients.

———

Nurse Monroe strutted into work looking and feeling great, now dressed in an expensive black tailored suit without her white nurse's jacket and wearing significantly toned-down makeup with bright orange-red lipstick. After passing through security where the guard met her with an impressed second glance, she walked up to the nurses' station where Cristy was organizing paperwork.

Cristy had also stayed late at the gala, but not as late as Nurse Monroe. Cristy was eager to get the rundown on the post-soirée events after her friend hadn't shown up to work that morning, and the wide grin on Nurse Monroe's face was evidence the details would be juicy.

"Someone is in a good mood this afternoon!" Cristy chirped. "It looks like you had a more productive night than I did."

"Hey, Cristy—you know it! Just like the old days. She may have brought him in, but I took him home!" Nurse Monroe scanned the relatively empty office and took on an authoritative tone. "Alright, I need today's patient schedules and the incident reports from the night shift. All doctors are out attending the convention's closing luncheon."

"Well, I guess it looks like you're the top dog today!" Cristy said, handing her a large stack of files.

"Now you're finally smartening up. Things are going to be a lot different around here from now on. Spread the word." Nurse Monroe took the files from Cristy and walked out of the nurses' station and into the doctors' wing.

After sneaking into the janitor's office, Nurse Monroe took the manager's set of keys, went to Madeline's office, and after looking around to make sure no one had spotted her, unlocked the door, went inside, and closed the shades.

Earlier, when Dr. Fields was in the shower at the hotel, Nurse Monroe had gone through his briefcase and stolen his ring of keys to the doctors' private files. And now she was going to take full advantage of her thievery.

She took Dr. Fields' keys from her pocket, opened Madeline's file cabinet, and flipped through the available folders. She wasn't exactly sure what she was looking for but was confident if she looked hard enough she would eventually find some form of damaging evidence to use against Madeline. Nurse Monroe was no fool; she'd been around doctors her entire life and knew that if there was anything they didn't want found, they stashed it in their private offices.

"I know there has to be something on you in here," Nurse Monroe said. "I've heard you and Harry talking; where is it?" She reached into the back of the bottom drawer and found Madeline's hidden compartment; it was locked, and the keys she had didn't work. She seized a letter opener from the desk, and with no regard for her vandalism, eagerly pried the lock open with fanatical determination. She stuck her entire arm as far back into the compartment as she could, felt around, and found it. "I knew it! Come to mamma," Nurse Monroe said, pulling out the only item inside: Madeline's leather-covered personal file.

Nurse Monroe was ecstatic. She sat down at Madeline's desk and meticulously perused through the contents of the file, closely examining every detail. When she discovered Madeline's hospital and name-change records, she had what she needed.

"Yep, all smoke and mirrors."

She closed the file, looked around the desk, and spotted a doctor's appointment card taped to Madeline's calendar. It read: *"Dr. Arthur Garrison, M.D./Ph.D. Monday, April 14, 2014 – 6:00 p.m."* She instantly recognized Dr. Garrison's name and knew his office was on the compound. She gathered the folders, took the entire file and appointment card, and left.

Nurse Monroe stepped into the elevator and pressed the button for the sixth floor. After the elevator doors opened, she walked down a long corridor passing over the emergency entrance driveway and into a mostly-deserted private office floor. When she found Dr. Garrison's office, she knocked softly on the door, and when there was no answer, she took out the janitorial manager's keys and let herself in.

After ransacking Dr. Garrison's patient files, Nurse Monroe found the one marked: *"Dr. Madeline Knight."* She then looked inside and found dozens of miniature cassette tapes labeled: *"SESSION RECORDINGS."*

She smiled. "You're mine now you little rat!"

22

HIGH
TREASON

Cincinnati, Ohio

Deep within the bowels of the Golden Monument, Madeline's refusal and subsequent departure had caused a split in more than just the opal floor. Pastor Chatsworth, sitting in his chair atop the glass platform, slowly clawed his nails into the stone desktop as he stared at Satan's empty throne on the pedestal opposite him. Mrs. Chatsworth paced in front of the fire, eagerly preparing her execution of the reserve attack she'd been concealing until precisely that moment. Neither had spoken since Madeline slammed the doors, and the question of who would call the standoff hung heavily in the air. They were in scorching opposition regarding the fate of their eldest daughter and had been long before implementing the plan to recapture her freedom.

After Madeline's final suicide attempt had shattered the Chatsworths' cover in Salem, their mission to re-establish the roots of witchcraft in a city where its existence would go undetected, disintegrated with them. Even though their service and allegiance to the rise of the Darkside had catapulted them to the top of Satan's ranks, their unprecedented failure had left no choice but retreat. The Chatsworths then disappeared into the underground sects of their cult and spent the next five years rebuilding their worth through rigorous training and grave seclusion. When Satan called on them to erect his new churches, their rebirth made them the perfect candidates to facilitate his physical incarnation and to become the first unknown faces of the False Prophet.

Although the Chatsworths' rank as Satan's top Generals and leaders of the Central Church of Enlightenment was the most coveted amongst all other Generals, it was also contingent on several stipulations. The overall success of the church was of most importance, but easily attainable if all contributing factors developed without discord. The CCE was already selling itself effortlessly, and future parishioners flocked to participate unknowingly in the blasphemies infecting anyone who chose to walk through the doors. Therefore, the Chatsworths only needed to maintain the church long enough to support and promote Satan's expansion plan for the other nine hundred ninety-nine locations awaiting his orders. However, to ensure a national launch the Chatsworths needed to fulfill the one requirement threatening to terminate everything Satan had built if not achieved. And that requirement was that all Chatsworth bloodlines needed to be converted and under Satan's control before the CCE's first mass.

But winning back the children lost due to their own miscalculations was the one obstacle blocking the Chatsworths' route to ultimate redemption. They were solely to blame for their barrenness, and disagreement about whose actions had caused their children's desertion was the main source of conflict between Pastor Chatsworth and his wife.

Pastor Chatsworth had always believed in the strict discipline and deprivation of his offspring as a means of control and preparation for their future as soldiers. Mrs. Chatsworth, however, had different ideas about what she felt was necessary, and took her husband's militant strategy to a level of cruelty that reversed its effectiveness. In actuality, she never wanted Madeline or Maxwell, and had only procreated to secure a commitment from her husband and obtain future advancement. Sacrificing her own pleasure to develop Pastor Chatsworth's protégées had never appealed to Mrs. Chatsworth's vanity, and caring for her children's needs was of little importance. But she eventually found an unlikely source of entertainment in the brutality and torture of Madeline and Maxwell, and it all stemmed from her outright jealousy and hatred of Madeline specifically.

Ever since Madeline's birth, the sight of the little girl whose beauty far exceeded her own sent Mrs. Chatsworth into an irate outrage of animosity and loathing. The reality that she'd given life to a superior being of opposition who emitted the Light of God was so unbearable she was on a never-ending quest for Madeline's extinction.

Unfortunately, Madeline's existence was the only achievement setting the Chatsworths' lifetimes of service to Satan apart from the rest of his notable officers. She was the one soul he was steadfast on acquiring out of the world he planned to overtake, and had made his orders explaining her treatment clear after the Chatsworths' first request for her dismissal: Madeline was to be converted, not killed.

To satisfy herself in another way, Mrs. Chatsworth exercised the only power she had and made sure Madeline never enjoyed a single day without humiliation and pain. Anyone who interfered with her plans to achieve that goal endured the same afflictions, and because Madeline's close relationship with Maxwell only festered Mrs. Chatsworth's disdain, his lifetime of torture mirrored his sister's.

Mrs. Chatsworth's abuse of Madeline and the joy it provided soon became a progressively addictive drug. The more brutal the punishments her husband inflicted at her command were, the more aroused she became, and the harsher she required them to be. But soon Mrs. Chatsworth's tolerance level required something stronger, and shortly after Gabriella's birth she discovered a renewed source of revenge. She relished the opportunity to shower Gabriella with the gifts and affection she refused Madeline, and loved the additional agony Madeline felt because of the blatant favoritism. It was a second tier of satisfaction on top of the physical abuse, and quickly escalated into another of Mrs. Chatsworth's full-fledged addictions. Gabriella eventually grew to emulate her mother, replicating the spite bestowed upon Madeline, and therefore adding a third tier to the levels of tormenting alienation Mrs. Chatsworth had established.

Eventually Madeline fell into a dark depression, and her last attempt at freedom finally provided relief from her parents' destructive control. The Chatsworths aborted their mission in Salem and paid a hefty price for their disobedience; and Satan lost his bid for Madeline's soul and demanded restoration. The damage to all three children, however, was unexpectedly extensive, and after the Chatsworths' years of banishment the task of reconstructing their family was long and tedious.

Maxwell had crossed over to the Darkside long before his removal from Salem, but the wicked extent of the cruelty and torture inflicted by his parents had wrecked him for eternity. Although he'd initially tried to utilize the teachings of the Darkside to build a family empire of his own, Maxwell's lack of self-control and maintenance made success impossible. He had been so grossly defiled and demoralized that his resulting violence, rage, and drug use dominated his ability to join the hierarchies of satanic power, and instead led him to murder and imprisonment. The Chatsworths, attempting to fulfill Satan's requirement for bloodline accountability, spent more than one million dollars of their own money to negotiate Maxwell's release from prison, but in the end, it was a verifiable waste. His deteriorated condition had made him useless as an associate at the CCE, and the Chatsworths had to find another container for his blood.

Gabriella was the easiest to reinstate, as the Chatsworths had known her location and kept her on the shelf all along. Promising to release her from the psychiatric facility Madeline thought she had secretly confined her to, along with the chance at revenge, was all the nudging Gabriella needed to return to the family. The only condition the Chatsworths imposed was she had to remain in confinement until they'd secured a plan to ensure Madeline's return as well.

But, obtaining Madeline was the hardest undertaking of all. So hard in fact, Satan himself had taken on the duty of her conversion after she'd demonstrated an unwavering refusal against him. And although he'd been tracking her every move since birth, his increased interference in the months leading up to Gabriella's arrival in New Orleans was the cause of Madeline's increased barrage of nightmares and demonic hallucinations; but still, he could not penetrate. A better plan was required, and luring Madeline in by murdering her brother and threatening the future loss of her sister was the ultimate victor. Maxwell was to be the sacrifice, and Gabriella the bait.

It was an ingenious plan resulting in Madeline's long-awaited appearance in Cincinnati and had opened the door for the Chatsworths' final act of temptation. But in the end, she remained unobtainable. Now they needed a final solution, and Mrs. Chatsworth was certain she'd found one.

She stopped pacing in front of the fire and decided she would be first to break the silence. Generally, she was adept at holding out the longest; but this time, to secure her supreme agenda she knew forfeiting her dignity was the only way to swing Pastor Chatsworth's loyalty her direction. Still in her flowing silver gown sans headdress, she sauntered across the room, stepped over the foot-wide crack in the opal floor passing by Stefan, and climbed the glass stairwell.

Her husband was deep in thought about the outcome of their future when she placed her palms delicately on the desk across from him and leaned in. "Do not grieve over the loss of Annabelle, my love," Mrs. Chatsworth said in a low sultry voice. "Be grateful for it. She is a bad-seed child who has continually poisoned our family's values. Must I remind you that all our years of hard work in Salem were obliterated by her struggle for control and attempts to halt our progress?"

Pastor Chatsworth lifted his fingers from the deep gashes in the stone and looked up at his wife; he knew her intentions and was prepared to dissuade any realization. "Despite the accuracy of your persuasion, my love," he responded, "we are both well aware of our orders. We've been over this countless times; why do you refuse to accept it? When he came to us with this opportunity he was clear what he wanted, and he wants Annabelle."

"I don't care!" she erupted. "I hated her then and I hate her now! We warned her repeatedly of the penalties of desertion. She is a treacherous snake sent to us from the other side; I've always known that. She's no daughter of mine. Bringing her back will only cause what's left of our family empire irretrievable harm. For or against us, she will always be a threat. We must kill her before she kills us!"

"Kill her?" he asked, standing up. "Are you out of your mind? All bloodlines must be accounted for! If we kill her, he loses her soul. Disobedience is not an option. Everything he has given us will surely be taken away. We will burn in Hell, not flourish beside him. I've fought centuries for an honor such as this, and I've never lost a soul in my life. I can convert her."

Mrs. Chatsworth knew it was time to take her seduction to the next level. Her husband would never disobey orders unless she convinced him it was in his master's best interest, even if in reality the interest was all hers. Madeline was the most revolting creature she'd ever observed; allowing her to live in the same glory as she did was a fate Mrs. Chatsworth would rather die than enable.

A beautiful woman herself, Mrs. Chatsworth expertly put her feminine wiles to work. She walked around the desk, took Pastor Chatsworth by the hand, and led him over to Satan's throne. After gently pushing him down onto the enormous plush cushion, she sat on his lap and wrapped her arms around his neck. "Listen, my love," she said, whispering into his ear. "I know how hard you've worked, which is why it's time you took your rightful place as his equal, not subordinate. I can assure you even our master has room to learn. Annabelle is the only soul who can corrupt his rule. She will never come to our side. We've always known that."

A dormant feeling overwhelmed Pastor Chatsworth's body and

the craving for the sexual attention his wife had withheld for the past five years overwhelmed his focus.

When Mrs. Chatsworth had first discovered that Madeline's return was Satan's final requirement in their arrangement to achieve a pardon from exile, she became withdrawn and vindictive toward her husband. Because even with the hardships accompanying her ostracism, life without Madeline had been absolute bliss, and she'd fought endlessly to convince Satan to reconsider his request and accept Gabriella instead.

To increase the chance of Satan's approval, Mrs. Chatsworth had secretly hired a team of handsome wealthy suitors in Chicago to prepare Gabriella unknowingly for her return and presentation. The plan was to restore Gabriella to the flawless package of irresistible beauty and poise of her upbringing, but it had backfired.

Gabriella's ten years away from her parents' organized lifestyle had her riddled with psychological problems from the start. While living with Madeline in Chicago, she was in and out of several psychiatric hospitals, never fully able to cope in the outside world because life with her parents had been designed for her pampering. The luxury and indulgence enjoyed in Salem was so deeply ingrained into the core of her being that old habits resurfaced without resistance. Once she'd tasted the offerings of Chicago's upper-class society, she indulged with rampant delight and exhausted herself with equally remarkable zest.

Working hard and attending college like her sister had never appealed to Gabriella. She wanted the materialism of an affluent lifestyle, but she wanted somebody else to provide it. She was a parasitic-hog by nature, and when her suitors began showering her with gifts and initiating her into their privileged world, she wasted no time gorging herself with everything provided. But she had no romantic interest in her ever-present male company, only in the new lifestyle of intoxication they provided. And she preferred to enjoy it on her own terms.

Pills, alcohol, and ecstasy were Gabriella's drugs of choice, and even though Madeline had warned her to stop, she only escalated. Late nights turned into early mornings and chaos ensued. Then, after a barrage of police-defused parties Gabriella had hosted in Madeline's absence, the college housing committee evicted Madeline from the apartment they lived in on campus, forcing a move to a menacing neighborhood. Shortly thereafter, Gabriella's repulsive behavior ultimately repelled her rich sponsors. Without their connections and financial support, she had to satisfy her addictions with a less-desirable crowd and stole from Madeline to make up the difference.

After overdosing one night at a party, Gabriella was dumped on Madeline's front porch unconscious and minutes from death. The damage sustained to Gabriella's nervous system from the ecstasy— one of the deadliest and falsely glorified drugs on the market—had completely disabled her ability to function. Unable to care for Gabriella alone, Madeline assumed a conservatorship and had her sister admitted to an inpatient neurological hospital where it took Gabriella several months to heal. But Gabriella's sadistic treatment of other patients, diabolical outbursts, and history of prior hospitalizations prompted her doctors, with Madeline's consent, to transfer her into the state psychiatric system where her lack of progress kept her entangled.

And four more years passed before the Chatsworths—always aware of Gabriella's location—required her assistance and began the yearlong process of organizing her release. And now that Gabriella was released, Mrs. Chatsworth was eager to reinstate her original plan and do away with Madeline for good.

Still on her husband's lap atop the glass platform, Mrs. Chatsworth firmly ran her fingers over Pastor Chatsworth's scalp massaging his head, and then took his face into her hands. "Killing Annabelle will show our ultimate loyalty, and we will finally be able to give Satan Gabriella in her place," she said, kissing him softly. "She is the daughter we raised to fulfill his every desire, and she is the daughter he should be honored to have." Mrs. Chatsworth got off his lap, sat on the desk in front of him, and opened her legs. When he rose to join her, she took his hand and guided it up her dress. "Not only will he understand, but he will be grateful and surely reward you with advancement beyond any aspiration you've ever dreamed of holding."

She had succeeded; Pastor Chatsworth was sold. He started to caress her body, befuddled with arousal. "You're right," he said, disrobing. "It is my time." He lifted her dress higher, put his arms around her waist, and kissed her lips passionately.

Mrs. Chatsworth then turned her head away while he indulged himself, and addressed Stefan, who continued to stand by the door unfazed. "Make sure Annabelle never makes it back to New Orleans," she said. "Kill her and bring me the body. Kill her or I'll end you and do it myself!"

———————

Madeline drove furiously toward the Cincinnati Suspension Bridge headed for the airport. Even though she was immersed in heavy traffic, she felt as though she were floating through time. Only hours before she'd been overcome by hopes, dreams, reservations, and regrets. And now, steaming with anger, the tunnel vision of her mind contained just one thought at the end of it: ripping Gabriella up by her neck and beating the truth out of her.

Madeline had tried to call the hospital to speak with Gabriella but couldn't get through; she had made Nathan Raines swear the night before to block Gabriella's telephone privileges and keep her sequestered from other patients and untrustworthy staff. At the time, Madeline had feared for Gabriella's safety and wanted to ensure Gabriella's survival should she never return. Now the only desire she wanted to ensure was that Gabriella never stepped foot outside a psychiatric hospital again.

Madeline screamed as a sudden force from behind smashed into her car and jolted her head forward violently onto the steering wheel. Swerving sharply, she looked into the rearview mirror and saw a black Cadillac Escalade SUV quickly closing back in with Stefan at the wheel. He rammed into her again with increased power, slamming her against the seat belt and knocking the wind out of her lungs. Gasping for air, she hit the gas, cranked the wheel, and cut through the traffic ahead.

Seething as foam sprayed from his mouth, Stefan stayed in range, his engine revved, and he easily overtook Madeline's tiny rental car. He pulled alongside, yanked the steering wheel, and crashed into her driver's side door, caving it in and forcing her off the road. She sideswiped a temporary construction guardrail and bounced back just as Stefan smashed into her again, sending her closer to the edge.

The bottom of Madeline's car thumped loudly as she mowed over a row of orange cones, which flipped up and cracked the windshield hindering her view. She veered around the cones, regained control, and maneuvered off the main highway and onto a service road running parallel to the river.

Still in pursuit, Stefan plowed into Madeline once again, clipping her car from behind and blowing out the left rear tire. She lost control and the car whipped around in circles as she fought the wheel, desperate to correct. Screaming, she spun off the road and flew over an embankment, lodging into a shallow ditch filled with water as the airbag imploded in her face.

———————

At that same moment in New Orleans, Priestess Haloise was knelt at her altar in prayer. Suddenly an unseen force from behind thrust her forward, smashing her head down hard on the canvas-covered marble tier and bloodying her face.

———————

Doused in white powder and blinded, Madeline struggled for awareness and unbuckled her seat belt. With her head throbbing from the intense ringing in her eardrums, every reflex in her body told her to exit the vehicle and run. She knew this time Stefan intended to kill her, and if caught that's exactly what he would do.

She tried to open the door, shoving hard to push it back, but it was caved in to her waist and stuck. She pulled her legs from the crushed frame and crawled to the passenger's side just as Stefan ripped the door off the hinges, grabbed her hair, and seized her up and out of the car in one swift motion. He punched her in the kidneys with robust brutality dropping her to her knees, then retrieved a thick leather strap from his pocket, wound it around her neck, and flexed his bulging muscles, tightening the noose.

———————

Priestess Haloise clutched her neck, dazed and entranced as she fell to the floor choking and unable to draw her next breath.

———————

Madeline leaned back and pushed against Stefan with all her weight, secured her feet on the doorjamb of the car, and thrust back as hard as she could. Her unusual burst of strength sent Stefan flying back off his feet into the mud, and she quickly loosened the strap and wrestled herself free. Once on her feet, she tried to run but Stefan lunged out, tackled her legs, and slammed her face-first to the ground.

With renewed authority, he grabbed her wrists and dragged her to the riverbank where he submerged her head backwards into the cold muddy water. Madeline's terrified eyes looked up at him as he tried to drown her.

———————

Priestess Haloise tried strenuously to rise from the floor, but the unseen force continued to pin her down with unrelenting weight. She jerked back in pain, clutched her chest, and the feeling of water filling her lungs left her unable to breathe.

———————

As the sun began to set, Madeline kicked wildly, scratching at Stefan's arms and fighting to free herself.

———————

"Madeline, Madeline!" Priestess Haloise gasped, as visions of Madeline's face flooded her mind.

———————

As water replaced Madeline's last breath, she released her hands and frantically felt for anything under the water she could use. After feeling a large sharp piece of steel, she clasped her right hand around the blade so tightly it sliced her palm to the bone. Then, with ferocious power she jabbed the spear through Stefan's left shoulder, gouging open the muscle and paralyzing his arm. Black blood gushed from his wound as Madeline burst from the river choking up the murky water and ran. Stefan let out a deafening roar, ripped the spear from his arm, and chased after her.

It was now completely dark as Madeline raced from the river's edge, across a busy street, and into a massive rail yard. The station was fifty tracks wide and illuminated by the headlights of dozens of trains combusting in the misty night. She sprinted up the tracks with paranormal speed, looking back as Stefan closed in. Without hesitation, she dashed in front of a charging locomotive, clearing the tracks with an elongated leap and leaving her assassin behind.

Stefan was unstoppable as he approached the passing train now separating him from the target. Effortlessly, he flew demon-like into the air, clung one-handed onto the side of a railcar, and climbed over the top.

Out of breath and convinced she'd escaped Madeline slowed her run to a walk. The cold wind from the train blew through her hair as the last car brushed past. She looked up at the sound of a demonic growl and saw Stefan perched on the roof.

He sprung out defying the opposing speed of the train and tackled her to the ground. He lifted her up by the back of her hair and spat black venom into her eyes, blinding her once again. He then kicked in the back of her knees, dragged her over the train tracks, and held her head down on the rail like a guillotine.

As another train charged toward them at full speed, Stefan's eyes glowed red and he hissed and roared, ready to enjoy the victory of the hunt.

Madeline eyed the train as it approached. She turned back to Stefan and ripped at his right hand, which was securely clenched around her neck. She then kicked her knee up hard three times crushing his scrotum and using the only human entity he possessed to take him down. She rolled him off, pulled herself up, and took off running.

Stefan stood up to recapture his prey, but he couldn't move; his ankle was caught in the switch.

Madeline glanced over her shoulder to gauge her position and saw him stuck in the tracks. She stopped.

The conductor sounded the horn and engaged the breaks, which burned as the train approached. But it was too late; Stefan was smashed.

Bloody, wet, and enraged, Madeline retrieved her backpack and phone from the wrecked rental car, gathered her suitcase and a first aid kit from the trunk, and taped her wound with temporary sutures and wrapped her hand in gauze. After changing into clean clothes, she put her gear into Stefan's parked SUV, climbed into the front seat, and sped away just as the authorities arrived.

Back on the road and headed to the airport, Madeline found Stefan's cell phone in the dash. Only one number was saved; she dialed it.

Mrs. Chatsworth lounged contented on her favorite red velvet sofa dressed in a gold-lamé robe, sipping champagne by the fire. She jumped with delight when she heard the brass rotary phone on the table behind her ring and enthusiastically answered it.

"Is she dead?" Mrs. Chatsworth demanded.

"No, but Stefan is!" Madeline said into the phone. "I suppose he figured it best to leave the wet-work up to you this time around."

Mrs. Chatsworth's joyful disposition vanished, and she crushed the champagne flute in her hand. "Annabelle!" she seethed evilly as her black blood dripped to the floor. "You always were a crafty little snitch. I've waited twenty-nine long years to end your useless life, and now I finally have the chance to celebrate your last birthday by slitting your throat myself. Enjoy this last victory. By midnight tomorrow, Gabriella will be freed and what's left of your rotting corpse will be devoured by Lucifer's beasts on your way to Hell!"

"If you want me dead come and get me!" Madeline countered, as lightning struck in the foreground and the rain began to pour. "You've called down the thunder, now it's time to reap the whirlwind!"

23

HIGHER
CALLING

New Orleans, Louisiana
Friday, April 11, 2014 – 8:00 p.m.
Exhausted and unable to move, Priestess Haloise lay motionless on the floor of her candlelit prayer room fixed in a trance and unaware of her current location. She had just endured the entirety of Stefan's brutal attempt on Madeline's life, and not by way of her clairvoyant abilities. She had literally wielded a power never before in existence, which had taken her out of her bodily self and into the realm of Madeline's spiritual aura. Priestess Haloise had physically felt every punch, kick, jolt, and strangulation, and had telepathically absorbed every emotion and thought transmitted from Madeline's mind.

After reading the spirits for Madeline on Tuesday night, the remainder of the week for Priestess Haloise had been filled with as many physically and emotionally trying revelations as Madeline's week had. Unable to escape the knowledge that a drastic metaphysical shift had initiated the opening stages of Earth's new era, Priestess Haloise had felt obligated to discover which elements had contributed to the catalyst, and what Madeline's role was as a conduit. Priestess Haloise had henceforth ceased all public religious ceremonies and healing services, remained within the confines of her home, and dedicated all strengths to determining what effect the change would have on humanity.

By Wednesday morning, Priestess Haloise had reaffirmed her initial reading that Madeline was caught between the ethereal forces of good and evil. And after tracing the roots of Madeline's spiritual lineage back to the beginning of Madeline's creation, Priestess Haloise found Madeline to be an elite soul chosen by God and immersed in the center of the impending Final War of Heaven and Hell.

And while history had never known a human to be called upon for aid in the everlasting rebellion of demons against angels, Priestess Haloise had extracted information supporting her theory that there may be no difference between the three species.

But Madeline's soul was not human; she was neither angel nor demon, and there seemed to be an unusual shield of protection keeping her temporarily safe on both sides. Priestess Haloise had felt overwhelmingly responsible for maintaining that safety, and had subsequently found herself unexpectedly privy to a never-before-accessed source of Divine information.

Vivid recollections of premonitions from Priestess Haloise's youth had suggested that the Final War would transpire during her lifetime. And her strong intuition contended that the core of the shift involved her as much as it did Madeline, and on a level beyond the ability to predict and facilitate discoveries. But the question of what Priestess Haloise's role might be had dominated her subconscious mind, and she consequently found herself overwhelmed by forgotten memories and un-invoked visions in support of her theory. The main problem with her quest for answers, however, was that her recent visions and memories didn't coincide with any events from her natural life, as far as she could remember. Instead, they had all originated from another time and place seemingly derived from a heavenly dream.

Priestess Haloise had finally reached the point in life where she believed herself to be comfortable with whom she had become. After a lifetime of celibate, unyielding service to all living souls and spirits, she thought she had found contentment and fully embraced her true calling. But following Madeline's departure on Tuesday night, an immense spiritual void had developed in Priestess Haloise's concept of her own existence. And as a woman of extremely organized thought and unusual psychic ability, that startling lack of understanding of her own lineage had left her deeply confused and in disruptive turmoil.

Having lived an unstable and tumultuous life during her early childhood in Haiti, Priestess Haloise believed there had to be missing information from that time which would explain her recent lapses in memory. However, because the lapses were so vast, she wondered how only five years of her life on the island could account for such detailed revelations remembered fifty-five years later. Therefore, late Wednesday night she had proceeded to scrutinize all paperwork inherited from her grandmother, Mambo-Josephine, which documented Haloise's life from birth to the present, in an attempt to piece together any inconsistencies.

Priestess Haloise's mother, Johanna, grew up with Mambo-Josephine in a small village outside the city of Port-au-Prince, Haiti, surviving on their own after the death of Johanna's father. The village was a religiously devout, closely integrated community, and while Vodou was practiced in most homes, the strict adherence to the laws of the Catholic Church was expected, including chastity before marriage. Consequently, when an unwed Johanna became unexpectedly pregnant at age nineteen, an outrage ensued amongst the townspeople. Both Johanna and her fiancé, Jean-Patrice, were left buried in shame and ridicule, even though unbeknownst to the public the child she carried was not his. It couldn't have been; Johanna had never engaged in sexual intercourse with Jean-Patrice—nor with any other man.

Publicly, Jean-Patrice rejected the child as his own, shunned Johanna, and verbally condemned her in agreement with the majority's belief in her guilt. He refused to acknowledge their engagement, stating he'd only courted her temporarily while determining her qualifications as a wife. But privately, he'd always loved and coveted Johanna immensely, and was distraught over her perceived betrayal.

To extricate himself from blame and restore his family's honor, Jean-Patrice demanded Johanna divulge the name of the unborn child's father. He intended to confront the perpetrator who he thought had violated his property and force that man to take responsibility. But when Johanna tried to explain the virginity behind her impregnation and teach Jean-Patrice of the gift she bore, he branded her a whore and a liar and became hysterically enraged by what he believed to be an attempt to defraud him further. In a blackout fury, he attacked Johanna blindly and clubbed her to death with a stone mortar in her mother's home. Afterward, covered in holy blood and tormented by demons for his crimes, he fled the village banished and in terror, and was found dead of fright shortly after.

When Mambo-Josephine discovered Johanna's bludgeoned body lifeless and abandoned on her prayer room floor, she sought the aid of their neighbor, a fellow Houngan priest who was also a surgeon. He performed an immediate birth by cesarean on the deceased Johanna, and the infant survived.

Upon viewing the newborn baby girl, the Houngan professed her a "born deity" and named her Haloise. He then declared the murder of her mother a Crime against God and warned the village that any future crimes against the child would result in their own banishment, and possibly eternal damnation.

As the early years of Haloise's life passed by, even with the loss of her mother she found herself powerfully drawn to the Spirit of the Lord in fulfillment of the Houngan's prophecy. When she turned five and was old enough to attend school, Mambo-Josephine sent her away to a Catholic boarding convent in Louisiana. Mambo-Josephine's goal was to continue Haloise's spiritual education in an American school while also keeping her safe from those who still questioned her legitimacy and origin.

The separation from her grandmother was a harsh struggle for the young Haloise, but always a soul of wisdom beyond her body's years, she understood the sacrifices necessary to secure global recognition of her religious significance. And although she would ultimately choose the calling of a Vodou priestess as the most humanity-focused intermediary to facilitate her pilgrimage as a healer and prophet, the worldly education and independence she gained from the separation and Catholic upbringing made her workings all the more valuable.

Throughout her childhood and into adulthood, Priestess Haloise never wondered or questioned who her father was. She always maintained a strong sense of identity through her ever-strengthening connection with God, and the internal love she felt as a result provided her with all the spiritual and emotional nourishment she needed. However, as the visions and newly recalled memories following Tuesday's reading with Madeline became clearer but not concrete, the content began to reveal an entire life with the father Priestess Haloise never had; and for the first time she began to wonder who he was.

By Thursday, Priestess Haloise had become certain that if she could answer the question of her legitimacy, the identity of her father would explain her position within the universal shift. And Thursday morning when Ross arrived in the Bywater to seek treatment advice for Savannah DeVears' condition, Priestess Haloise had embarked upon the first of the physical changes that would lead her to that explanation.

When she opened the door for Ross, her trusted and beloved colleague had dropped to his knees and bowed his head respectfully immediately upon sight of her. Initially embarrassed by his uncustomary greeting, Priestess Haloise had bid him to rise and asked him to join her inside the house. But Ross had declined, declaring his inability to cross the doorway as he was now on holy ground and already infected with the influence of an unclean-spirit. He explained to Haloise that the demonic entity embodying Savannah had done so with the specific intent of attacking both

Madeline and himself through the portal of Savannah's possession. The current weak status of the entity, however, had made penetrating Madeline's strong aura impossible. But the entity was steadily strengthening with the help of reinforcements, and had already infiltrated Ross' aura in a way he could not personally remove.

Although the severity of Ross' affliction had concerned Priestess Haloise greatly, she found herself without concern for her own susceptibility to contagion from the demon hounding him. A numbing sensation overtook her body, repelling the entity and rendering it powerless to affect her. Even Ross himself had felt the sticky residue and rotten odor of the demon diminish significantly in Priestess Haloise's presence, and therefore waited patiently on the porch for her to gather the supplies he needed for Savannah's exorcism.

When Priestess Haloise returned from inside the house, the numbness encompassing her body had advanced, causing all five of her senses to lose individual functioning power; her physiological capacity for perception now operated in a single state of hybrid awareness. She saw, heard, smelt, felt, and tasted the elements as never before, and the lenses of her eyes now reflected the subjects of the world without filter. She noticed the Red Plague Infestation-of-the-Damned now attached to nine out of every ten persons who walked by her house on the busy streets of the Bywater; a pre-apocalyptic plague sweeping the whole world only she could see.

When Priestess Haloise looked back down at Ross, who continued to kneel unaware of her new abilities, she now saw the cloudy-black mass of the unclean-spirit hovering over his aura. But the demon feeding off Ross' energy was different from the Red Plague she'd seen corroding the souls of the ninety-percent whose evil deeds had subjected them to such punishment. Ross' good nature had made him impervious to such penalties; his intruder was sent to corrupt, not punish. It was one of multiple satanic spirits contributing to the progress of Savannah's possession, charged with the task of dissuading Ross from his alliance with Madeline.

Ross had winced back in fright as Priestess Haloise instinctually placed her palm on his head, expelling the demon and forcing its entity to detach. Ross felt immediate relief and bowed his head in gratitude, then silently accepted the black pouch of artifacts she'd prepared and walked away.

When Priestess Haloise went back into the house, she knew she was no longer the person she used to be but was still unsure of whom she'd become. She had then spent the rest of that night and all-day Friday knelt in prayer at her altar waiting for the answer. After leaving her body and spirit open for an entire day of perfect meditation through silence, solitude, and fasting, her mind went void of all visions or memories and allowed only vibrations matching her own to flow through. The resulting transcendence had enabled her to endure the live experiences of one of only two people on Earth with whom she shared an unbreakable connection: Madeline Knight.

Priestess Haloise's ability to experience Stefan's attack on Madeline, through Madeline as it happened, had made it possible for Priestess Haloise to transfer an external surge of strength resulting in Madeline's superior power over her assailant. Priestess Haloise and Madeline had subconsciously combined forces on a high-frequency level of telepathy, which had manifested itself as tangible energy.

Madeline was still unaware of the miracle she'd experienced, and Priestess Haloise had never known of or exercised such capabilities. Priestess Haloise did know, however, that only one explanation existed for their miraculous feat, and that was Divine assistance.

The connection between Priestess Haloise's newly acquired memories of life with her father, the shift on Earth and her perception of it, and Madeline's role connecting it all was now impossible to deny. And the time had come for Priestess Haloise to summon the consulting forces of the spiritual world to understand the purpose behind that connection. Only then would she understand her role in the shift, learn the truth about her origin, and complete her transformation back into whom she always was.

And now, Friday evening, as Priestess Haloise's physical abilities returned following her participation in Madeline's attack, she slowly picked herself up off her prayer room floor and wiped the blood from her face. The numbness still present in her body now created a warming sensation that massaged her muscles making it effortless to move, and an atmosphere of heightened awareness left her concept of space and balance pleasantly fluid. While carefully adjusting to the new lightness of her walk, she meandered into the living room taking each step as though she were walking for the first time. The ever-present arthritis once painfully tormenting her bones had disappeared, and although she'd gone two days without food or drink, she found herself without the need for sustenance.

She retrieved a picture of Madeline from her living room mantel and put it in the gold bowl on the right side of her altar along with the lock of Madeline's hair. She then lowered herself onto her knees and scanned through several of her ancient Vodou scrolls, crosschecking her findings with the Holy Bible. And although she'd closely examined the contents of her books, scrolls, and papers hundreds of times before, this time she interpreted the words with renewed perspective.

"This transition involves more than just a shift in the spiritual lives of humanity," she said, writing notes in a new scroll with an ink-dipped calligraphy pen. "Earth's Era of the Ether is the collision of the forces of Heaven and Hell on the earthly plane, and it's happening at a phenomenal speed of unseen rotation. Who are you really, Miss Madeline? Who am I? And who are we together? I can feel your every breath!"

Priestess Haloise then prepared the room for a series of Vodou rituals to reestablish herself with her place of worship. With her body rapidly evolving in form, she needed to wash away the energy of her former self and allow the knowledge of the spirits to penetrate her mind as she now was.

First, she did a thorough cleansing of the room including: the lighting of fresh candles, a cigar smoke wash, the anointing of oil on all religious objects, and the liberal sprinkling of holy water. Second, she began her regular ceremony to summon the guiding power of the Spirits of the Saints. She played an old Haitian Vodou record to immerse herself in the sacred sounds of the highly religious tanbou drums, and then began an hour-long ceremony of ritualistic singing and dancing. For Priestess Haloise, performing this ceremony allowed the spiritual intermediaries of the Creator to work alongside her body so as to learn from them directly in a subconscious state.

But this time she didn't observe any of the usual sensations indicating the spirits' guidance. And she realized she would now be personally responsible for accumulating any additional intelligence she didn't already hold.

Priestess Haloise went back to her altar, retrieved the bone-handle knife, and cut an incision down her palm. After allowing her blood to pour into the gold bowl, she mixed it with Madeline's hair, lit the end of a sage-filled cigar, and blew the smoke into the bowl while closing her eyes. She inhaled deeply as the newly-mixed essence gust back abundantly over her face, and then looked up in astonishment.

"Oh, my child! You're not only coveted by the goodness of God, but by the darkest depths of Satan as well! But where do I stand in all of this?" She took out a bag of silver coins symbolizing the population of humankind and dumped them onto the altar. She closed her eyes and sifted through the coins with her fingers, and when she was finished only two of the coins remained in the original pile. "The numbers are now greatly favoring the side of evil—but why?"

She opened her Holy Bible and searched for something more. And while reading from *Revelation 16:14* she found the answer, "'For they are the spirits of devils, working miracles, which go forth unto the kings of the earth and of the whole world, to gather them to the battle of that great day of God Almighty . . .' It's her parents—they're a cross-combination of Satan's demons on the human plane! Madeline, where are you?"

Suddenly the room was illuminated by a blinding white light and Priestess Haloise fell to the floor, covering her head with her arms. After a few moments, all of her apprehension vanished, and she rose to her knees, staring into the light as the room around her disappeared. The Heavens opened, reclaimed her spirit, and re-filled it with all the knowledge and wisdom acquired through millions of years of existence before the Creation of Man. Between the flash of an instant, every question Haloise had ever asked was answered, and although she was no longer a priestess, she knew exactly who she was.

When the brilliance faded, she retrieved Madeline's picture from the bowl and lit it on fire to eliminate the potent energy it had created, watching as it burned. "They're searching for her," Haloise said. "In less than two days, spiritual freedom as we know it will either fall under the control of Satan or remain within the Doctrine of the Lord God Almighty. Madeline is the most powerful medium separating the lines of good and evil. I have been sent to lead and protect her by combining the unbreakable laws of the Kingdom with the crumbling laws of Earth."

Haloise then opened her Vodou *Scroll of Demoncide* in search of the human law on the slaying of demons. The moment she found it, the house began to rumble violently, and all the candles blew out, flickered, and reignited as a howling wind encircled the house. Without angst or hesitation, she rushed out the front door into the now-freezing cold and looked up at the sky.

For a human, the sight before her would have been both mesmerizing and frightening at the same time, but for Archangel Haloise di Michael her female body was but a vessel of vengeance, and the Trumpets of War had finally sounded.

"Lucifer!" she screamed to Heaven's number one archenemy. "We meet again, this time in the flesh! The sum of all the Lord's Wrath against you has officially descended upon your blasphemous reign and all who follow it. Prepare yourselves!"

Hurricane force winds raged and whipped through her long-braided hair, and the starry night sky slowly turned a fiery bloodred.

24

MORTAL
DIVIDE

The Cold War was officially over; God had reinstated open warfare, and the top two leaders of the Final War had both descended and ascended from Heaven and Hell to mobilize the early stages of battle.

However, the mortals of the world continued their lives as if nothing was amiss. Years of expectation and speculation, followed by years of doubt, had created a stagnant sense of well-being where the majority of the souls living on Earth had no fear of the Great Beyond, but rather existed without Divine rule as if they themselves were gods.

Lack of belief in the Promised Return of The Second Coming had made it easy for humans to forget that two thousand years of life were but a millisecond in death. They had fancied themselves exempt from the Death Sentence imposed by God for the brutal murder of Jesus Christ, and the rising Rebellion of Satan.

Now, Judgement was imminent, and either the kindness or wrath of compensation for their deeds would forever be upon them. How blissful life must have been for those who dwelled without the threat of consequence; and how devastating life must have been for those who endured the cruelty and disadvantages received for their undying faith and obedience. However, the day was dawning when the inhabitants of the world would no longer have the power to reward or condemn another mortal for their social status or wealth. For the side they themselves had individually chosen prior to death, and the quality of conduct exercised in life, would be the only factors determining his or her position when the door of the Kingdom closed on the other side.

Fortunately, the Day of Judgement had not yet come, as the official battle in the Era of the Ether for souls on the human plane had only just begun. The door was still open, despite the fact the invisible road leading to it was almost impossible to find. Especially if the signs the strays looked for were only the warnings they could hear with their ears or see with their eyes.

Unfortunately, the chance of an undecided or unclean soul's acceptance into Paradise and Eternal Life was unlikely, as was his or her ability to resist the very temptations threatening banishment. For it was humanity's own refusal to accept the Teachings passed down from the beginning of time that had allowed the penetration of Satan and the abandonment of faith; worshiping instead the obsession with Satan's mirage of earthly glamour, wealth, and celebrity idols as the ultimate reward, and forgetting even the body is nothing but dust.

And now, because of that obsession and abandonment, only two days remained before Satan's Central Church of Enlightenment would open its doors and deliver the first mass. If that happened, it would mark the end of life as the mortals knew it and the choice for eternal salvation would no longer be theirs; the allotted time for repentance would expire, the Kingdom's door would close forever, and no soul left undecided would ever be allowed back in.

———

Shortly after 8:30 p.m., the lightning storm from Cincinnati had made its way to New Orleans, and the rain now poured. Rapid and sporadic thundershowers from Earth's atmosphere sent violent electrostatic discharges to strike with blistering accuracy throughout the Orleans Parish, and destroy all structures doomed to land in their paths.

Throughout the streets of the French Quarter, partiers and tourists huddled under eaves and inside already-filled restaurants and bars; their festivities unwillingly and hostilely halted by the sudden freezing storm of hurricane-force water and wind.

Along St. Charles Avenue and Canal Street the streetcars stopped forcedly as rushing waters covered the tracks. Falling telephone wires and traffic lights ignited fires, causing cars and buses to crash and jam in the streets. And chaos erupted as anyone caught outside screamed and fled to any shelter, including the aboveground crypts and mausoleums in the open-to-the-public, tourist-swarmed cemeteries, to avoid the flying debris and drenching rain.

———————

The deafening sharp crackling and low rumble of thunder resounded through the hallways late Friday night at New Orleans State Psychiatric Hospital. "Lights out" for the patients in the children's ward had officially commenced at 9:00 p.m. And apart from the sparse night personnel consisting of only two psych techs, one nurse's aide, and one nurse, the bustling activity from the day was at a standstill.

In the doctors' wing, it was dark and mostly empty except for a faint light glowing from inside Dr. Fields' office at the end of the hall.

Nurse Monroe, recently off duty, wore a pair of full-coverage headphones and sat alone at Dr. Fields' desk next to a small lamp. She had waited all day for the chance to hear what was on Madeline's psychiatry session tapes she'd stolen from Dr. Garrison's office, and now she had her chance. The knowledge that it was a federal crime to break into a doctor's office at NOSPH and steal confidential patient information didn't bother Nurse Monroe a bit. After she'd unburied Madeline's skeletons and combined her findings with the events of the previous twenty-four hours, she would attain sole authority over Dr. Fields' future, and any disciplinary action against her would be the last concern on anyone's mind.

Word about Nurse Monroe's showing at the gala had spread with viral rapidity, and within hours, confirmation of her newfound infamy had circled back around to her satisfaction. Every doctor who had attended the conference luncheon that day knew Dr. Fields had taken her up to his suite at the Hotel Raphael, including her own father. Not that she was surprised; she'd taken every precaution to guarantee her victory didn't go unnoticed, as it was always in her plan for the ensuing public spectacle to enhance her chances for a proposal after the climax of her entrapment.

Nurse Monroe had received an additional, unexpected boost to her delight when she heard that her godmother, Administrator Hamilton, had made a terrific scene at the luncheon about having witnessed Madeline leaving the gala with Nathan Raines.

Dr. Fields had only considered the damage control he would have to execute concerning his indiscretions with Nurse Monroe, but he never expected the embarrassment encountered when he arrived at the luncheon. He had prepared himself to indulge in the same lavish greetings of adoration enjoyed at the gala; instead, his colleagues heckled and castigated him more brutally than the worst hazing which often occurred behind the locker room doors of his country club.

A doctor taking his nurse—who happened to be the daughter of one of the most powerful men in medicine—to bed, would have made for an interesting story at the club. But a doctor having his trophy date walk out with another man—who happened to be his known adversary—on said doctor's night of honor because of having gone to bed with said nurse, only made for the most hostile shades of disrespect Dr. Fields had ever known.

His level of disgrace only elevated when Madeline's absence from the luncheon intensified the allegations against him. Unlike

Madeline had hoped, Dr. Fields did notice her lack of appearance. He'd even called her multiple times that morning to confirm her attendance, as having her show unconditional allegiance to their relationship was part of his plan for rectification. When he called Cristy at NOSPH to see if Madeline had come into work and found Madeline truant there as well, his mind inflamed with anger and jealousy. There was only one place he'd imagined his prized obsession to have been, and that was with his despised nemesis, Dr. Nathan Raines, who'd skipped the luncheon as well. The plunge in Dr. Fields' fortune had infuriated him beyond his capacity for subtle retaliation, and mere damage control was no longer on his agenda.

Cristy, of course, had wasted no time in relaying the details of Dr. Fields' plight to Nurse Monroe. And Nurse Monroe had already spoken to Administrator Hamilton, who'd caught her up on the rest of the news reported on the four-way scandal. All of which had left Nurse Monroe with the feeling of absolute control and vindication as she sat at Dr. Fields' desk preparing to feast on Madeline's most intimate secrets.

As far as Nurse Monroe knew, Madeline didn't have a single friend in the entire world that would protect her. And as soon as Nurse Monroe produced the incriminatory evidence she was compiling against Madeline, she would never have to hear the name "Madeline Knight" again.

Nurse Monroe armed herself with a pen and paper, pulled one of Madeline's session tapes out of a manila envelope, slipped it into the audiocassette player next to her, and pressed play.

As Dr. Garrison and Madeline's voices sounded over the headset, Nurse Monroe listened with hungry fascination:

"March fourteen, year two thousand fourteen, six o'clock in the evening. Dr. Madeline Knight in session," said Dr. Garrison, on tape. "I know that in the past you've made it clear to me that you do not believe the medications I have prescribed would be of any benefit. However, because the symptoms of your schizophrenia are progressing, whether or not you choose to accept that diagnosis, if you want to continue working as a licensed medical doctor I have no choice but to increase your dosages to prevent further relapse."

"I understand," Madeline replied.

Simultaneously on the other side of the children's ward in the patients' wing, Ross was making his evening rounds. Despite the lights-out-status designated for sleeping, the patients' wing was illuminated by gray-hued fluorescent lighting twenty-four-hours-a-day including the patients' individual bedrooms. And because patients not in evaluation slept in unlocked quarters, it wasn't an uncommon occurrence for staff members to find one or two problem cases wandering around after hours. More importantly, keeping a close account of the overly savvy patients who saw the slumbering state of their housemates as a choice opportunity to rob them of any personal belongings he or she coveted, was an all-night job for the psych techs.

But working the graveyard shift on a Friday was not Ross' regular schedule.

When Madeline examined Savannah on Thursday morning, Ross had taken the opportunity to prepare the room for Savannah's exorcism, expecting to perform his extraction after Madeline had finished. And because he'd also seen Haloise that same morning and been relieved of his own demonic attachment, he had felt confident the exorcism would go as planned. But he had been wrong.

When Haloise relieved Ross of his disturbance, she had also granted him immunity from any further satanic possessions. Afterward, when Madeline and Ross administered Savannah's second session, the demonic entities inside Savannah had multiplied in strength and antagonism because the demon assigned to Ross had returned to Savannah. The result was a belligerently fierce demoniac Madeline had to sedate, which had only allowed

Ross to prepare the room without completing the exorcism.

Now, only twenty-four hours remained before Savannah was transferred out of NOSPH, and Ross intended to send her to the next destination minus the un-clean spirits piloting her possession.

After verifying every other patient was in his or her quarters and resting peacefully, Ross assigned the other psych tech on duty to a station far from his own. He then stopped outside Savannah's room, opened his black pouch to confirm everything he needed was in place, opened the door, and entered.

Nurse Monroe continued to listen to Madeline's session recordings while jotting down every word of interest as fast as possible:

"But, Dr. Garrison," Madeline continued, on tape, "even though I understand your obligation to medicate me in the manner you see fit, you need to understand that I'm only submitting to your prognosis in the effort to stay in compliance and continue my job. And I know what your definition is for what you think I have, but like I told you before, my symptoms are derived from a lifetime of continual attacks by Satan to collect my soul. I am well aware of the difference between that and a legitimate mental health diagnosis. I am not schizophrenic."

"Madeline, it's not just my definition," Dr. Garrison replied. "Every manual from which American psychiatrists operate is clear on the definition of schizophrenia. And the basis for my diagnosis depended on whether I could determine if your symptoms matched the requirements, and they did."

"Well, as long as I'm talking to you under the privilege of doctor-patient confidentiality and not as a resident, I don't mind saying I find it pretty disturbing you would choose to ignore my explanation in favor of a manual. Shouldn't you take my personal experiences and professional research into consideration and then conclude for yourself whether I have an illness? Listen, I first started studying psychiatry to protect both my sister's mind and my own from deterioration. Gabriella lived with me for a long time after we left our foster family, and I found we both had similar disturbances and didn't want either of us to succumb to the same fate as our brother. From there I knew it was my calling and went into the field. I wanted to save the minds of those already compromised in order to protect their souls. Now, years of my research has proven that Satan can only take the souls of humans without consent by taunting them into psychosis and substance abuse to weaken their natural defenses against him."

"Madeline, I do hear what you are saying, and I have taken your personal experiences into consideration. But, I'm very sorry to have to tell you that psychosis runs in your family. That's why your brother and sister were also affected. It's hereditary, not satanic."

"It's only hereditary because we lived in the same house. I'm asking you to void my diagnosis. Not only is it detrimental to my record, but I could lose my license, and my work here has yet to be completed. Once Satan takes the mind, his victim's actions are uncontrollable and can't be reversed by conventional methods. That's the reason they can harness superhuman capabilities. Their minds are no longer their own and the limits of our world no longer apply. My patients need my help!"

Nurse Monroe stopped the tape; she had everything she needed. She took off her headphones, stood up, and slipped on Dr. Fields' white doctors' coat with his name on it. She then picked up his one-wood driver out of his golf bag and walked over to a wall covered with dozens of pictures of Dr. Fields and Madeline accepting different awards and large department checks.

Nurse Monroe then reared back, and with all her might smashed every picture repeatedly. "With that filthy half-black rube strapped inside an NOSPH cage," she screamed between strikes, "the title of Mrs. Dr. Fields will finally be mine!" When she finished, not one memento was left hanging, and shattered glass covered the floor.

After catching her breath, she exhaled with satisfaction, dropped the club in the middle of the mess, picked up the phone, and called Dr. Fields.

"Harry," she said calmly. "It's Sherrie. I need to see you tonight."

When Ross entered Savannah's room, he looked over to the seat by the window where she'd been sitting at night when refusing to sleep, but she wasn't there. He looked over to her bed, which was still made, and she wasn't there either. Bewildered, he looked 360 degrees around, and still did not see her.

Suddenly he heard what sounded like an animal snarling echo throughout the room, barely audible at first then becoming louder and interweaved with heavy breathing. He looked up and saw Savannah directly above him clinging to the ceiling with her hands and feet, glaring down at him with glowing red, rabidly-bloodshot eyes.

Before Ross could react, Savannah hissed so loudly the sound shattered his eardrums and sent him into a chaotic state of nauseating vertigo and deafness. With lightning speed, she sprang down on top of him and knocked him to the floor. She then crawled over his body, clutched his head in both hands, and smashed his skull back onto the cement floor savagely, again and again with a cracking series of thuds until he began to convulse in violent seizures.

As Ross lay on the floor bloody and unconscious with his eyes rolled back under his lids, Savannah lifted his head with both hands, shifted her fingers up underneath his chin, and thrust her thumbs upward deep into the soft tissue of his neck. She opened her mouth, threw back her head, and screeched with roaring triumph as she pulled out her thumbs and Ross' blood spewed back up at her with intense pressure, spraying her face and saturating her clothes.

25

POOR
INNOCENT
SWEET THING

There was an endless pane of stinging, icy rain belting sideways and extinguishing what should have been a seasonally warm night when Madeline peeled into a parking spot at New Orleans City Hospital. Her flight home from Cincinnati had been riddled with gut-wrenching turbulence and barely able to land, pressurizing her desire for retaliation, and her capacity for containment was rearing to blow. She had literally been to Hell and back, barely escaping her own death and declaring war along the way. Now, only one hundred feet and a brick wall separated Madeline from the person who'd sent her there, and she wanted Gabriella's head on a spike.

Wearing a tight black sweat suit with her tousled hair in a loose ponytail, Madeline ached with adrenaline-fueled anticipation. She flung open the car door with the wheels still rolling and the motor and headlights still on, ran across the flooding lot, and stormed up the front steps to the psychiatric ward. Pure hatred and turbulence dominated her demeanor and the expression of her face, and after passing through the sliding-glass doors and into the lobby, she forcibly composed herself.

Hardly avoiding a scene but appearing unfazed, Madeline

calmly walked up to the security attendant as water dripped copiously from her clothing and hair. "I need to see Gabriella Jackson," she said.

The attendant stared at her with a perplexed look. "Ma'am," he said, "it's ten o'clock at night; visiting hours are long over. You'll have to return at ten o'clock tomorrow morning, like everyone else."

Madeline dug into her backpack ready to present her credentials and demand entry, but the night nurse recognized her through the glass and opened the door. "It's okay. Let her in," she said to the attendant. "Dr. Knight, come with me."

Madeline followed the nurse back into the same patient processing room Nathan Raines had taken her through just two days before. With every step, the distress of Madeline's sentiment magnified intensely, hindering her ability to filter the negative stimulants threatening her self-control. Knowing that Gabriella was the chief accomplice to the carefully planned and executed trickery she'd suffered over the past week had left Madeline reliving every lie and word of persuasion to the point of internal madness. She only hoped the Chatsworths hadn't warned Gabriella of her escape, and that she would have the opportunity to confront her sister first.

Just before Madeline reached the door leading into the patient recovery ward she felt the strange sensation of tugging on her skin. The air temperature in the already-cold room dropped below freezing, her lips went purple with frost, her skin white, and the tips of her hair hardened with ice. She stopped walking and slowly turned around, breathing heavily through a lack of oxygen as the rumbling chatter of the patients and staff blended into a low-toned hum. The thick vapor from her breath clouded her view, and after brushing it away she saw a cloudy-black mass of distortion hovering over more than half of the patients wandering around the room.

Madeline closed her eyes, squeezing hard and praying it was only her exhaustion and lack of food causing the disturbing visual illusion. But when she opened her eyes, the distortions were now revealed to be demonic entities attached to the patients, and she saw them more clearly than before.

The infected demoniacs, sensing Madeline's unwelcome presence in their plane, stopped, turned their heads sharply, and with fiendishly warped faces and glowing red eyes, snarled at her through gritted teeth.

"Dr. Knight, are you ready?" the nurse asked, jolting Madeline out of the Ether and back into the normal temperature of the human plane.

"Yes!" Madeline said, reconnecting. "Thank you—take me back." Just before stepping through the doorway, Madeline looked back at the patients; they were all roaming about or sitting as usual, paying no attention to her presence and with nothing out of the ordinary affecting them.

Not wanting to attract additional attention when she reached Gabriella's room door, Madeline waited for the nurse to leave before entering. Gabriella was obviously still awake, as the light and television were still on, and Madeline wouldn't be bothering with the courtesy of keeping the encounter either quiet or civil.

Madeline slowly opened the door to find Gabriella leaning back in a chair by the window with her feet kicked up on the table as she scribbled away in a new journal notebook. Madeline's heart beat rapidly but she didn't say a word. Anticipating the spew of lies sure to pour from Gabriella's mouth, she closed the door quietly, turned around, and waited.

Gabriella looked up with a smile. "It's about time you showed up," she said nonchalantly. "I've been waiting all night for you. They wouldn't release me or allow any phone calls until you got back. And I sure am starving because this city hospital food is worse than licking the scraps from the bottom of a pig trough! Let's grab some of those real New Orleans delicacies before we head on out of here."

Madeline grabbed a chair and securely wedged it under the door handle, locking them inside. She then charged at Gabriella with determined authority and backhanded her across the face with full force. Gabriella toppled over backwards, slamming into the concrete wall as the notebook went flying. Madeline stepped forward and knocked the table out of the way, ripped Gabriella up by her shoulders, and pinned her tiny body against the barred window. Gabriella attempted to scream, but Madeline jabbed her knee into Gabriella's stomach, lodged her left forearm up underneath Gabriella's neck, and put her hand over Gabriella's nose and mouth so tightly she couldn't breathe.

"Before we head out of where?" Madeline demanded. "Where is it exactly you seem to think we're going? You lying Judas-Witch! You're no sister of mine; I should smash your head against these bars and let the nurse clean up the mess!"

Breathing hard with emotion, Madeline looked at her own reflection in the window and was disgusted by the uncontrolled violence of the woman staring back at her. She had never offensively harmed either Gabriella or anyone else in her entire life; her role was the protector, not the assailant. But Gabriella's ruthless betrayal was the worst crime Madeline could think of, and the agony of such malicious deceit had killed off any remaining wreckage of the love she had left for Gabriella. But the exploitation ailing Madeline most was that she'd believed Gabriella's lies and allowed her sister back into her life despite every previous act of devious sociopathic treachery warning of a repeat performance.

The softest place in Madeline's soul had always been her love for her brother and sister, and then eventually the patients she extended the same affections in their absence. When she agreed to have Gabriella committed to the state psychiatric hospital in Illinois, it had been the hardest decision she'd ever made.

But separating herself from Gabriella, and the evil corrosion Gabriella carried with her, had been Madeline's only chance at survival. Maxwell had already been in prison for over a year, and the shame and ridicule endured because of her siblings' disgraceful behaviors had left Madeline a social pariah. Their foster parents had already disowned them after Maxwell's infamous public trial, and anyone of medical importance in Chicago had made it clear that Madeline, too, was finished. The board members of the university she attended hadn't even allowed her to finish the school year. They refunded her entire undergraduate and medical school tuitions and gave her the choice to either leave on her own accord and maintain her transcripts or face expulsion on the grounds of moral misconduct by proxy.

Madeline abruptly released Gabriella, then turned away and walked to the other side of the room to regain perspective.

Gabriella, however, was immovably calm and coolly unaffected by Madeline's vile outburst. When Madeline turned back around to address her enemy, Gabriella's innocent face had gone blank and she visibly began to transform. A black cloud of mist whirled around Gabriella's body and slowly dissipated as her entire form distorted. When she settled into her new shape, the daintily beautiful young woman's wide brow had become furrowed and lined, and her once peach-blush cheeks and delicately moist skin were now pale and dry. The left side of her mouth turned up slowly in a sinister half-smile revealing pointed teeth, the pupils of her big green doe-eyes glowed red, and her lids creased at the corners as she glared up at her sister.

"Oooh, anger—I like it!" Gabriella cooed evilly. The other corner of her mouth turned up, she sat down in her chair, and leaned back with absolute contentment, sighing in relief.

"You sent me up there to be slaughtered!" Madeline yelled, frightfully confused and cautiously keeping her distance. "Why did you do it? After everything I've done for you all these years, why did you come after me?"

Back to the same emotionless expression, Gabriella looked over at her journal notebook lying open on the ground. She stood up and slowly walked over to retrieve it, and then remedied the overturned table. After sitting back down in her chair, she closed the notebook and placed it precisely into position on the table. "I can see by your unsavory disposition that your amateur quest to expose our parents did not go in your favor," Gabriella said.

"However predictable, it appears your gullibility has overshadowed your intelligence once again. So, don't stand there and blame me, because I explicitly warned you that if you went up there alone it would be a disaster. And as usual, you wouldn't listen."

While Madeline glared in disbelief, Gabriella rose again from her seat and walked over to the window. She peered out at her reflection, taking pleasure in her terrifying appearance, and then looked up toward the ceiling. She put out her hand and extended her arm to a quarter-size black widow spider clinging to its web in the corner of the window. The venomous arachnid unclenched its long-gnarled legs exposing sharp fangs and the bright-red hourglass on its abdomen, then crawled to the edge of the thick dew-soaked web and descended a silk string onto Gabriella's hand.

"Sent you to be slaughtered?" Gabriella asked, shaking her head. "No, no, no—I sent you to be saved. Saved from the molten depths of Hell you will no doubt now be burning in. And your precious brother, Maxwell the Saint. . ." She paused for a moment, admiring her pet. "That part was my idea—I've always known you so well. We knew murdering him would be all the bait you needed. And it was doing the world a favor; that worthless brain-fried psychopath was even more sick and twisted than all the rest of us put together and you just couldn't see it." As the spider crawled up her arm, she broke off the string, lifted it up, and started playing with it gently like a yo-yo.

"Cut the games, Gabriella! Tell me why you did it. What did they promise you? I know it had to be good, so what was it? What?"

Gabriella turned to Madeline. "Everything you denied me! I never wanted to leave with you back in Salem. Not only did you destroy my family, you stole fifteen years of my life. If I had it my way I wouldn't have sent you to Ohio to join us; I would have sent you to die!"

Gabriella walked over and stood next to Madeline, who shuttered as she eyed the spider. "I've always hated you, just like our mother does," Gabriella said, enjoying the slicing impact of her nasty disclosures. "That's why we both kicked back and enjoyed every moment of your beatings, reveling at the retribution handed down for your blasphemies against our family. Didn't you ever wonder why they never punished me? You are such an insolent fool. You thought you were protecting me by taking the lashings for my mistakes when I'd gone out of my way to disobey them knowing perfectly well you would bear the blame. You are nothing more than a disgraceful slave-of-the-cloth, and I have never been as happy as I am at this moment, knowing you've turned them down and everything I would've had to share with you will now be all mine."

Madeline turned away, fighting back tears. She was a pawn in a sick sadistic game and Gabriella had been a strategically placed double agent the entire time. Madeline had always convinced herself the favoritism toward Gabriella was the sole doing of their parents and had never blamed her sister. She had assumed the horror of witnessing her and Maxwell's endless childhood beatings would have been less traumatizing to the young Gabriella than enduring them—therefore she had been grateful for Gabriella's omission. After all, the omnipresence of pain was a burden Madeline was raised with, learned how to block out, and never allowed to make her cry.

The words she'd just heard come out of Gabriella's mouth, however, were more painful than any physical punishment, and releasing the tears induced by such unabashed cruelty now seemed inevitable. But Madeline stifled her weakness a little longer, because although Gabriella had wounded her viciously, Gabriella had also freed her from having to feel any emotion or responsibility for her sister, ever again.

After embracing a much-needed moment of clarity, Madeline turned back around. "So," she said coldly, "daddy's Poor Innocent Sweet Thing finally reveals her true colors. Even though I now despise the sight of you, I have to say you look much better with your mask off—befitting of course that you would be wearing a hospital gown during the unveiling!"

The spider had since escaped Gabriella's attention, launched a new silk string, and landed on the floor. Madeline stepped in closer and smashed it with her shoe.

"You may have disillusioned me," Madeline continued, "but I can assure you all the good I've done for you and for everyone else in my life was never in vain. Look at yourself; you truly amaze me. Your wasted lifetime filled with selfish deceit and lies hasn't gotten you anywhere. I knew there was a deeper reason I locked you up years ago. I thought then it was to protect your soul, turns out it was to contain it!"

At that moment, the night nurse tried to open the door. When she realized it was jammed, she knocked on the window. When neither Madeline nor Gabriella acknowledged her, she became angered. "Dr. Knight!" she screamed. "Open this door right this second!"

Madeline continued to ignore the nurse, tears welling up again in her eyes. "I've got news for you, Gabriella; it's not you Satan wanted—it never was. Your hopes of indulging in the luxuries of darkness are but useless delusions of nothingness. You mean no more to him than a disposable slave whose mission has failed, and now you're going to have hell to pay!"

"You're wrong!" Gabriella screamed, her emotional shield crumbling. "The only soul that needs to be contained is yours. My parents are coming for me, and when they do it will be you who has hell to pay!"

"That's what you think. You're not getting out of here tonight, or ever if I have anything to do with it. Your seventy-two hours may be up, but I've already taken care of that. So, you might want to get accustomed to the 'pig' food around here, because when I'm done with you the last thing you'll ever do is eat outside a hospital ever again."

Gabriella shrieked and lunged out at Madeline with superhuman strength, knocking her to the floor. Before Madeline could react, Gabriella pounced on top of her and pulled at and ripped out her hair. Madeline tried to fend Gabriella off, but Gabriella began punching and kicking with such machine-gun speed and ferocity, it was no use.

While Madeline covered her face with her arms, the door burst open and two psych techs and the nurse ran into the room. When one of the techs pulled Gabriella off her sister, Gabriella had already transformed back to the same innocent beauty. The nurse quickly sedated her with a hefty tranquilizer and strapped her to the bed. The other tech restrained Madeline as a team of dispatched security officers filed into the room and placed her under arrest.

As Madeline was led down the hallway toward the emergency exit in handcuffs, Dr. Nathan Raines, who'd been alerted of the disruption, rushed after her and took her into his custody.

———————

Nathan grasped Madeline's upper arm and shoved her into his office. She hadn't considered the possibility he would most likely be at the hospital that night; he had been the last thought on her mind when she arrived to accost Gabriella. But working the graveyard shift was Nathan's preferred arrangement, and Madeline knew he was about to pelt her with questions and wasn't looking forward to trying to appease him with the answers.

Once they were securely inside and away from the lurking ears of Nathan's staff members, he launched his interrogation. "What the hell was that?" he demanded. "I could and should have you arrested for what you just pulled. I don't care if you are a doctor— this is my hospital and you will respect it! Now I don't know what you're doing here this time of night, but I'm blocking your access to your sister. I want an explanation, and I want one now!"

Madeline yanked her arm away and walked over to the couch. She wasn't going to exacerbate her sanity further by submitting to a lecture from an outsider with zero intelligence on her predicament. She was sick from exhaustion and still on schedule to process the horrors of the day. She sat down and massaged her temples while deciding her next words carefully.

How could she possibly tell him what he wanted to know? The

reality of her life didn't even register properly in her own brain; how was her explanation going to make logical sense to a man whose profession was judging a person's sanity? Yet the longer she sat in silence, and the longer Nathan stood by the door patiently waiting for a response, the same feeling of safety and comfort she'd felt in his arms that morning withered away her resistance.

"Have you ever reached a point in your life when the results of everything you've ever worked for imploded in your face?" she asked. "Or woken up in a world suddenly transformed into an unrecognizable ruse where the intentions of every person around you were revealed to be nothing more than their own manipulations hidden by lies?"

Nathan walked over and sat down next to her. "Yeah," he said. "A long, long time ago, and I allowed it to ruin me. Instead of confronting my problems, I avoided the pain by rejecting those who'd caused them and pretending they didn't exist. But the only person my loneliness destroyed was me, and I've been living on the edge ever since. You're the first person I've allowed back in."

Madeline looked up at Nathan, searching past the radiance of his eyes and looking for the possibility of truth behind his motivations. She wanted to tell him more but including him in her life would only put him at risk; it probably already had. Now her most important concern was keeping Gabriella under control long enough to decide how to prepare for the Chatsworths' arrival. She knew they were coming to kill her and collect Gabriella by morning, and needed to strategize her next tactical operation.

"Listen to me, Nathan. If you even consider releasing Gabriella tomorrow, my life will be in danger. She was never granted a legitimate discharge from her last hospital. We are not who or what you think we are. I know that's not the answer you deserve. And I can't explain everything to you now, but I will. Under no circumstances can she be released." She took his hands in hers. "Nathan, please?"

He already knew there was more to the Jackson-Knight crisis than either Madeline or Gabriella had revealed, and he intended to discover exactly what secrets they were hiding. However, pushing Madeline for more details before she was ready would only prove counterproductive, and he knew it. "Okay," he said, "if that's really what you need."

Madeline stood up and headed for the door. "I have to go and check on my own patients. I've been out all day."

"Hey, wait!" he shouted, getting up after her. "That's it? You walked out on me this morning! I thought we had something; that this might actually be real."

Madeline had hoped he wouldn't mention their night together; a future wasn't something she was equipped to predict or promise. "We do. It is. I'm sorry; I didn't want to wake you."

"Well, can I see you later? I can call someone in to cover."

Madeline knew she should say no, but felt instant relief at the thought of sleeping in the safety and seclusion of Nathan's protection that night. "That actually sounds really nice," she said. "Call me when you're off; I'll meet you at your place."

———————

While walking back to her car, Madeline's cell phone rang. "Hello?" she answered.

"Dr. Knight? It's Cristy at work. We need you to come in right away!"

"I was already on my way. What's up?"

"It's Ross—he's dead!" she screamed, now crying hysterically. "Savannah DeVears killed him. She's been taken into custody and they're having her transferred tonight!"

Madeline hung up the phone and vomited violently outside her car door.

26

THE CALM BEFORE
THE STORM

Saturday, April 12, 2014 – 12:00 a.m.
Madeline was in shock as she drove slowly through the heavy sleet and hail from City Hospital back to her office at NOSPH. The magnitude of the events she'd seen and experienced over the previous twenty-four hours had shattered her already-limited understanding of the laws of human existence. Therefore, although she prayed the news of Ross' death were untrue, she had low expectations of such possibility.

Madeline had spent her entire life coping with unimaginable instances of solitude and hardship, and the loss and emotional devastation of the previous week should have destroyed her completely. However, because her sufferings were hers to bear alone the ensuing pain had been easier to accept. But if Ross really was dead, not only would the pain be as unbearable as the loss of Maxwell, it would also mean that the satanic infiltration infecting Madeline's life had crossed planes and infected everything and everyone else around her.

Madeline had always suspected that the Savannah DeVears case contained disturbing irregularities indicating a personal connection. Savannah's verbal attacks had addressed private facts about Madeline's early life nobody outside Madeline's family knew of, making it undeniably clear to Madeline that the un-clean entity possessing Savannah intended to extend its influence to her. But dealing with patients under possession had always posed grave risk, and Madeline had taken those risks into account long before designing her residential research around treating demonic disturbances. She had fought against satanic advances directed at herself since childhood, and with the strength acquired by the resulting resistance, accepted the dangers of her job and fought for her patients' resistance as well. Ross had sacrificed everything to join her in that mission, and had given his life in the process.

Madeline's postponing of Savannah's case until after her trip to Cincinnati hadn't been the easiest decision to make, as Savannah's condition had required additional research and diagnosis. The Chatsworths, however, had posed the threat of immediate danger, making Madeline's foremost obligation attending the Central Church of Enlightenment's opening ceremony. And that had been her ultimate choice. Now the consequences of making that choice included both the death of her friend and the transfer of a demonically possessed patient whose treatment had yet to be completed. Madeline was not only devastated; she was overwhelmed with guilt.

Cincinnati, OH – 12:00 a.m.
Inside Pastor Chatsworth's office, Satan sat on his throne next to the fire, while his most trusted confidant, supporter, and personal butler, Lavoy, stood next to him holding a tray of wine.

"Where are they?" Satan asked.

"The Chatsworths are in the air now, my Lorde. En route to New Orleans," Lavoy replied.

"Good. Madeline is the one soul I covet immune to possession. My marriage to her will breed the first of my seed, creating my most powerful ally against God. But she must submit willingly! We had an infallible strategy to disintegrate her mind—where is she!?"

"Trust the process, my Lorde. The primary demon possessing Savannah was strategically unleashed."

"And once again, that wretched, useless, egotistical puppet has failed! I've already retired him for eternity."

"Not failed, my Lorde. This is only the calm before the storm. Madeline is broken. Ross is dead. And we've infiltrated her dreams and injected pure hatred into the hearts of every enemy she has ever known."

"And their King? Where is he?"

"Waiting, close by. As always."

"Forty days was a gift; forty years has been torture!"

"His hands are still tied, my Lorde. We have twenty-four hours left. Madeline must survive on her own before he can reclaim her. We're closing in; nowhere is safe; she has no one."

"Wrong! She had no one. Make sure Madeline never returns to Michael's protection."

"He wouldn't risk eternity to wage war against your army. You cannot be defeated."

"He already has. Use illegal force to control her mind. I will make her my bride!"

After Savannah's second session Thursday morning, Madeline had felt the familiar presence of an unidentified force of evil closing in on her, and she had been correct. But what Madeline did not know, was that Satan had implanted and unleashed the primary demon inside Savannah to assist in making Madeline defenseless against his plot to obtain her soul.

Madeline's imperviousness to evil had long since made her the prime target of Satan's forces, as breaking down the one soul he coveted whom remained immune to his persuasions would ultimately leverage his forces in his war against God. But the one obstacle Satan had to overcome was the inability to affect Madeline directly by means of possession; for him to obtain her soul, she had to relinquish her immunity against him willingly.

Satan had therefore proceeded to attack Madeline with full strength using a multifold strategy meant to disintegrate every aspect of her life. And by carefully planting his soiled spirits in Savannah and sending Savannah to NOSPH, he had ensured a hard hit on Madeline inside her work environment—the only place outside her apartment she felt safe.

First, and most important, was Satan's certainty of the negative effects treating Savannah would have on Madeline herself. Dr. Fields, who was unknowingly under Satan's carefully persuasive guidance, had controlled Savannah's care plan by assigning her case to Madeline, even against the advice of Administrator Hamilton. And, because of Dr. Fields' shameless obsession and intimate knowledge of Madeline's weakened mental and emotional state, he had enthusiastically given her a patient whose lifetime of satanic abuse and resulting deterioration matched her own. Dr. Fields was confident the exposure would instigate a final breakdown, causing Madeline to violate her employment probation and accept his self-serving terms of rescue.

Second, Satan had instructed his demons to rob Madeline of the trusted colleague she had in Ross by corrupting his loyalty and destroying his ability to perform an exorcism. But Ross had been aware of his demonic infiltration, and Haloise had unburdened him of the early stages of his disturbance. Also, by utilizing the Power of the Archangels she was unaware she held, Haloise had also blessed him with future immunity to possession. And when the demons inhabiting Savannah discovered Ross' change of penetrable status, they had killed him at first opportunity.

Third, Satan had boldly encouraged a ruthless spike in Nurse Monroe's jealousy and hatred toward Madeline, as well as an increased desire for Dr. Fields, rounding out Satan's professional attack on Madeline.

But in the end, an unforeseen barricade canceled out Satan's initial efforts, making even the cleverest sources of outside manipulation worthless in his pursuit of Madeline's soul.

Satan was the first of his kind to conduct a physical incarnation into human form—a power only available to him once during his existence. He had waited until the end of his reign on Earth to utilize that power, and had broken and abused every law imposed on his earthly conduct in the process. However, when Satan—the cursed Archangel Lucifer who'd been banished from Heaven—incarnated, the only way to fight him was with another human incarnation of his own kind. And that meant an Archangel from God had to risk eternity in the Kingdom to wage war against Satan on the earthly plane—an Archangel from God who'd already demonstrated the ability to defeat Satan and his fallen angels. And that Archangel, Michael, had chosen the form of Haloise.

The tides of victory had taken a devastating turn for the Prince of Darkness. Now Satan would have to guarantee that Madeline never returned to the Divine safety of Haloise's protection. He had to take absolute control over Madeline's mind, and he had to do it before she learned of Archangel Haloise's existence.

———————

Madeline walked through the doors of the emergency medical treatment facility on the first floor of NOSPH just as the Orleans Parish coroner's office wheeled Ross' body out on a stretcher. She flashed her identification card and stopped the coroner.

The staff from the children's ward had rushed Ross down the emergency elevators in an ill-fated attempt to save his life from the vicious injuries he'd sustained, but it had been too late. Madeline's foreboding instantly materialized and she knew Ross really was dead. She put her hand on his head above the white plastic body bag and rested it there for a moment of silence and respect, but mostly to apologize. She made the Sign of the Cross on his forehead and closed her eyes as hot tears streamed down her cold face.

Madeline had brought a backpack full of personal items into the hospital, and to avoid the invasive search and scan at main security she needed to go up the emergency elevator directly to the doctors' offices on her floor. And because the security code locking the elevators was still disabled from Ross' incident, her access was granted.

The first thing Madeline intended to do was examine Savannah before Savannah's transfer; if it were possible to complete the exorcism Ross had started, Madeline planned to attempt it herself.

On her way to Savannah, Madeline walked past the room where Ross had been killed and stopped to look in. A wall of crime scene tape blocked the doorway and a pool of blood mixed with tiny pieces of cracked bone covered the floor. It was the most graphic sight Madeline had ever witnessed. She could feel the negative energy in the room and somehow knew, action by action, exactly how Ross had suffered there.

Savannah was confined in a patient evaluation room, as those were the only locations equipped with full-body restraints integrated into beds bolted to the floor and two-way mirrors. Madeline looked through the glass in the adjoining observation room to confirm Savannah was still under control, and noticed her coming out of sedation. Savannah's big brown eyes slowly opened, and she looked at Madeline through the mirror even though she couldn't see her. The soul in Savannah had changed. The person Madeline saw gazing back at her through a sedative-induced haze was a frail young girl with no idea where she was or what had happened to her. Madeline knew whatever entity had possessed Savannah had taken all it needed and left on its own accord.

"Dr. Knight," Cristy said. "You need to sign these."

Madeline turned around to find Cristy holding commitment papers detailing Savannah's immediate transfer to a state psychiatric forensic hospital in northern Louisiana. Two psych techs, one pushing a wheelchair and the other with portable restraints, waited to take Savannah away.

Madeline knew she had to sign the papers. Administrator Hamilton had the final word on any case passing through NOSPH; the Admissions and Discharge department had drawn up the transfer order at Administrator Hamilton's request and had a messenger deliver it to her private residence for signature. Madeline's name alongside Administrator Hamilton's was merely a formality needed to verify her acknowledgment of the transfer and the requirement to relinquish all medical reports from Savannah's files needed by the next facility.

Confident Savannah was now of her own mind and body, Madeline signed the papers without hesitation.

———————

Madeline paced slowly around her office, knowing that seeing Nathan Raines that night was not an option; she doubted if she would ever see him again. The All-Seeing-Eye-of-Satan was constantly monitoring every aspect of her life, as well as the life of anyone daring enough to become involved in her affairs. Nathan had been her only chance at reprieve from the danger accompanying her every move, but she wouldn't risk it; she'd brought him enough grief already.

She couldn't go back to her apartment either. The only location now promising safety was behind the heavily guarded walls of NOSPH. She also knew she would be interrogated about Ross' death by hospital investigators in the morning, so rather than have them call on her unsuccessfully at home she alerted the floor's security station of her intent to stay in her office overnight.

Madeline stood in her window distressed and perturbed by the now-flurrying snow, attempting to take inventory of the events of the day. The existence of the never-before-seen Louisiana weather felt like an incoming tidal wave visible from the shore as it approached, even though the death and destruction accompanying it was inescapable. The continuous swarming of supernatural conduct freely developing in the earthly world was incomprehensible, yet impossible to deny. Madeline's dread was mounting beyond her control, and staying immersed in the illusion of the human plane was no longer an option.

A lifetime of suppressed feelings and thoughts flooded

Madeline's mind, and Haloise's prediction from Tuesday night clarified every one of them. Only four days had passed and everything Haloise had told her had manifested in the most cataclysmic way imaginable. Madeline now rejected the possibility of a peaceful future and knew she would never be safe again. Personal plights of self-discovery were no longer the main events in the playbook of her life; staying alive was her new profession.

Madeline hadn't yet reviewed Gabriella's Illinois hospital records she'd received earlier in the week, except for the emergency contact information, and wanted to examine the details before faxing them to Nathan Raines. She retrieved Gabriella's computer bag from the safe where she'd stored the records and sat down on the couch to look them over. After scanning through the first couple of pages, the journal notebooks also in the computer bag monopolized her attention.

Even at City Hospital Gabriella had seemed overly enthusiastic about the new journal she was writing in, and based on her meticulous treatment of the item, it was her most cherished belonging.

Madeline pulled out the journals to see if they contained any information that would be helpful in devising her plan to defeat the Chatsworths. As she flipped through the hundreds of pages of ideologically motivated summations mixed with sociopathic hatred, a sickening regret filled her stomach and she wished she'd looked at the notebooks more extensively upon first discovery Tuesday night.

Gabriella's distinctively tense vigilant handwriting filled every page front and back, leaving no space unused. Dated from the first year of Gabriella's five-year hospitalization up to the past Tuesday afternoon, each excerpt Madeline scrutinized was more diabolical than the last.

January 18, 2010
   These writing exercises are so stupid! I'm not some confused imbecile unable to cope with her "feelings." OK, fine,

I'll do it, but just to keep that old-hag nurse off my back—I have been confined to this latrine of a hospital without any contact from my detestable sister, Annabelle, for almost a year. She has completely ruined my life and I wish I had never stayed with her for one second after she left our foster home. She convinced me otherwise, but that's OK because I've already figured out how to get back at that little witch. –GJ (hmm . . . I love my initials, "GJ" kind of like "GI-JOE," if I was "GI-JOE" I would blow this place UP!)

April 13, 2011

It's been three months since I tried to find my parents to get me out of here and I haven't heard back from them. Where are they? What a joke! I told them it was Annabelle who stuck me here to keep me from telling all her dirty little secrets, and that it was actually HER drinking and drugging that corrupted me. Of course, that isn't true, but they've always believed my lies, so I know they'll eventually get me out. They hate that cowardly tramp as much as I do and will see to it she suffers brutally. Hmm . . . what a thought. Man, I wish I could have seen her hanging from that belt. I would have run up the stairs and held it tight for her until she died and watched gleefully as her big eyes popped out of her ugly head. Ha-ha! Hate her!!! Anyways, speaking of which, it's my little whipping girl's birthday today. I think I'll celebrate for her. I've got the pathetic little weasel who cleans my floors to bring me cocktails at night. Hey, it's cheap, but it works. Plus, it mixes well with my meds! ☺ -GJ

March 1, 2013

Score! Praise the Devil I'm good! I didn't even have to find mom and dad they somehow found me! I'll be out of this fecal-chute in no time. I should seriously get a lifetime achievement award for awesomeness. Mommy always told me I was a queen, and now I will be! I can't believe they want Annabelle there too, though. *Really??!!? It certainly wasn't in my plans, but oh well, I'll make her my slave ☺ And, when Satan's throne is mine and our children control the whole world, I'll have my minions hack off Annabelle's head and say it was an accident! Ha-ha! I seriously crack myself up. I'M. A. GENIUS! –GJ*

March 6, 2014

Peace out, Maxwell! Finally, after a whole year! I know Stefan is a real beast, so that hit had to hurt! Oh well. . . Anyways, just one month left and then New Orleans here I come! Kind of a bummer though that I'll miss the new group of sickos being admitted next quarter. I've truly enjoyed torturing those little wimps and confiscating all their essentials. Easier than taking candy from a baby. I know, I know, mom and dad sent me whatever I wanted, but it's sooooo much more fun to leave these mental cases screaming like lunatics when they wonder where all their crayons and crackers went. Ha-ha. Oh well. "Madeline Knight?" Seriously? What a stupid name! –GJ

April 8, 2014

Glad to be off that tiny plane! I can't believe they didn't fly me first class. But yeah, that wouldn't have looked right. I had to appear as lame as possible, and it worked! ☺ This was way easier than I thought. Belle bought my story in a matter of minutes. She's so tediously pathetic! But I can't believe the snitch actually flew to Chicago. Great. Oh well, I made the call, so they'll take care of her. Belle is as stupid as ever. But that's OK because I've already robbed her entire apartment ☺ ☺ I must have collected at least $10,000. What a moron, she had that loot stashed everywhere. Nice place though. Time to get wasted! –GJ

Madeline tossed the last journal down. A few days before the words would have had more of an impact, but now she had no emotion left to give. She took off her shoes and jacket, turned off the lights, and went to sleep on the couch.

8:00 a.m.

Outside an exquisite penthouse high-rise condominium in downtown New Orleans, several feet of snow covered a balcony that lined the perimeter of the floor-to-ceiling windows of a modern loft-style bedroom.

Inside, the phone next to a double-king-size custom bed rang loudly and jolted Dr. Fields from his sleep. Lying face down on his fluffy pillow, he didn't bother lifting his head when he reached out and picked up the high-tech multiline receiver and held it to his mouth.

"Hello?" he asked groggily.

"It's Florence!" Administrator Hamilton yelled angrily, sharp country spite replacing her elegant Southern accent. "We have a problem, and you're going to help me solve it."

"Good morning, Administrator Hamilton. What can I do for you?"

"I have a dead psych tech on my hands and a bag full of Voodoo-witchcraft-exorcist-paraphernalia that was found next to the patient who killed him. Now, I'm on the block if this goes to investigation. That little black-rube-resident of yours has buried herself this time, and I want her gone!"

"What—Madeline's patient? Are you serious? That's gonna be a load of paperwork," he said, haze fading as he realized the seriousness of the allegations. While Administrator Hamilton continued to bombard him with a slew of profanity-laced accusations, he took a sip of scotch from the glass on the nightstand next to him and checked his watch.

"Now sober up and get over to the hospital so we can clean up this mess! She's done in my facility—done!"

"I'm already well aware of that, Florence. I'm on my way. I'll see you in an hour."

He hung up the phone and looked over to the other side of the bed where Nurse Monroe was sleeping naked. The manila envelope containing Madeline's therapy tapes was sitting on the nightstand next to her with the tapes pouring out and Madeline's personal file lying next to it.

———————

10:00 a.m.
Dr. Fields and Administrator Hamilton walked down the long corridor leading to Dr. Garrison's wing and stopped just before reaching his office door.

"Before we go in, Harry, there's something I would like to discuss with you."

"What's that, Florence?"

"Your little tryst at the gala with my goddaughter. Now, it's going to cost you dearly if you don't make good on your intentions for her. So, I suggest you give her what she wants. Is that understood?"

Dr. Fields broke into a wide grin; he was looking forward to delivering his response and enjoying the finale of this conversation.

When Nurse Monroe came to his condo the previous night to condemn Madeline with the damning evidence she'd compiled against her, Dr. Fields had been amused. He had thanked Nurse Monroe generously for her efforts, as her package would prove to serve him more than her in his continuing mission to blackmail and manipulate Madeline.

But he had already taken care of his problem with Nurse Monroe and wanted to punish her properly for her hearty, cunning attempt to seize him despite multiple warnings against such behavior. Therefore, he'd indulged himself in a gratuitous reenactment of her antics from the night before combined with a little BDSM punishment usually reserved for his "naughty" patients. Nurse Monroe had happily submitted, thinking she'd finally solidified their relationship. She had no idea Dr. Fields had already disarmed her forces and that from that day on he would use her at his disposal, not the other way around.

Never one to let a scandal get in his way, Dr. Fields had spent the entire day, Friday, on his mission for damage control against Nurse Monroe. He'd utilized his newfound friendships with the New Orleans press to turn his disastrous showing at the luncheon into an unrivaled victory to last him many years to come. He knew the only way to avoid Nurse Monroe's expectation of marriage was to hold the position of creditor to her father, and he had succeeded far beyond his expectations. But Dr. Herman Monroe wasn't the only person Dr. Fields had placed in his debt.

He glared back at Administrator Hamilton with a slight twinkle in his eye. He was grateful to be resolving her hilariously presumptuous request for Nurse Monroe before seeking her aid in handling his own request to Dr. Garrison.

"Yes, Florence, about your goddaughter," Dr. Fields replied. "Whereas I respect your attempt to fulfill the desires of the most used split-tail rump in New Orleans, I have to remind you that you should have first considered controlling your own desires . . . for her father."

Administrator Hamilton looked up at him in astonishment and panic loosened her bowels. "What are you talking about, Harry?" she asked, trying to sound as unaffected as possible.

"You know exactly what I'm talking about. The good and powerful Mr. Hamilton has had a private investigator following you and Dr. Monroe for months. A little newspaper-birdmouth from the gala gave me all the details." He reached into his pocket, pulled out the janitor's key to her office, and dangled it in front of her face. "And your little keepsake-video of you two fornicating at the conference hotel in Vegas hasn't made its way back into your husband's hands . . . yet. But it has made its way into mine. Now, we both know where the Walker Hamilton billions you love to flaunt so much come from, and it isn't from lying on your back. So, unless you stick to your own side of the tracks from here on, you'll be back out on your own rump where you started, and I won't be the only laughingstock of the party. Is that understood?"

Dr. Fields knocked on the door to Dr. Garrison's office and he and Administrator Hamilton let themselves in. Dr. Fields had called Dr. Garrison on his way to NOSPH and demanded his immediate presence there as well.

"Arthur," Dr. Fields said, nodding. "It looks like we need to talk."

"You're right we do!" Dr. Garrison replied angrily, looking over at his sabotaged file cabinet. "What's going on here?"

Dr. Fields tossed Madeline's personal file and session tapes onto Dr. Garrison's desk and took a seat across from him. Even though Dr. Fields had instructed Administrator Hamilton to stay quiet, she stood authoritatively by the door in his defense. Dr. Fields then handed Dr. Garrison a clipboard with a thick stack of paperwork almost identical to the paperwork Madeline had signed for Savannah the night before—psychiatric commitment papers to the adult ward at NOSPH with Madeline Knight's name on them.

"These are going to require your signature," Dr. Fields said.

"I'm not signing that! What kind of shuffle-trap are you threatening me with this time, Harry?"

"Look, let's not make this any harder than it has to be. But if you really want me to spell it out for you, I will. You've kept a mentally ill doctor active on our staff without making her managing team aware of it. You've also prescribed mind-altering medications to that same mentally ill medical doctor with no regard for the fact she herself is in charge of the medications of dozens of patients depending on her ability to make rational decisions for them. Now, I don't think we need to get into all the pesky legalities of this situation. You're going to sign the papers, hand over the rest of her file, and we're all going to go on with our lives."

"God damn you to Hell for this, Fields! You knew perfectly well what was going on with Madeline—don't play this game with me!"

"Well, that was before it became public knowledge. You were the one who diagnosed her schizophrenic, not me."

"I made that diagnosis months ago," Dr. Garrison yelled, standing up. "And after our session this week, I'm close to revoking it. I could not, and will not, in good conscience involuntarily commit a healthy patient to a mental institution!"

Dr. Fields stood up calmly and paced with his hands behind his back, thinking. Dr. Garrison waited, shaking, scared, and confused. Dr. Fields then turned around and punched Dr. Garrison in the face with full force, knocking him onto the ground.

While Dr. Garrison lay whimpering as his nose bled, Dr. Fields stood over him.

"It won't be in good conscience," Dr. Fields said. "It'll be under duress. Now sign it!"

27

THE RUNAWAY BRIDE
OF
SATAN

The full moon hung in the black night sky, barely visible through the dense fog enveloping 200 city blocks of old aboveground New Orleans cemeteries. The air was hot and thick, and the smell of death pungent through the wet mist hovering just above the ground. The streets were empty and eerily silent as Madeline, lost and afraid, made her way through the deserted avenues searching for a way out. The encircling energy was nightmarishly surreal, and with its invisible power blocked her in from every direction.

With cold pale skin and thick curly hair flowing to her waist, she wore a ghostly white wedding gown of fitted sheer lace with full-bell sleeves, an open back, and a long-bustled train brushing the ground behind her. Completely bare underneath her dress, she trembled frightfully with no recollection of how she'd arrived in that harrowing place. Everywhere she turned the mist flowed over her path and dissolved only in the way the evil spirits mandated she go. Vulnerable and exposed, she progressed from a walk to a run, turning past the abandoned streetcars parked along the tracks of Canal Street.

Sucking in air but finding no relief, Madeline's breathing increased in intensity and panic ensued. She held up the front of her dress with both hands and ran faster and faster, determined to outrun the Reaper of Death she knew was hunting her.

Suddenly the tunnel of openness ahead ended abruptly. The fog surrounded Madeline fully and spun her around, again and again, until dizzied she fell to the ground in the middle of the dirty moisture-soaked street. When she regained her strength and awareness, she lifted her arms from covering her head, looked up, and saw the mist had faded. She heard a loud creaking to her left and stood up wearily as two enormous iron gates dripping with dew and rotting moss slowly opened, revealing the entrance to a three-story white marble mausoleum.

No longer able to walk, Madeline was involuntarily propelled forward into the Castle of the Damned in an uncontrollable glide. She floated slowly through the gates past a long hallway lined with floor to ceiling crypts and out into the sprawling full-moon-illuminated cemetery courtyard. Hundreds of black crows appeared in the drooping branches of the willow trees and along the rooftops of the freestanding stone tombs. They cawed out loudly, gawking down at her with glowing red eyes, welcoming her fondly yet amplifying her fear.

Having regained her ability to walk, Madeline continued past the cracked and trampled gravestones and through the vapor once again surrounding her. As the sickening feeling of wickedness infiltrated her body, she realized something else besides Death was now following her. She frantically checked over her shoulders as she advanced hurriedly to the other side of the courtyard. And then she saw him.

Appearing through the hazy mist and floating toward her from the gates where she had entered was Satan, wearing a dashing black-tie tuxedo with a white rose corsage fastened to his breast. This was his moment; the deliciousness of the one woman who'd insufferably resisted his temptations for almost thirty years tantalized the bodily senses he'd never before indulged. His pale translucent skin glowed in the moonlight and his visible veins turned from purple to gold. He opened his mouth in lustful anticipation and his silver eyes flickered feverishly, attempting to penetrate Madeline's soul. It was finally time to taste his bride and fill her body with the first of his seed.

At the sight of the humongous, monstrous being who'd haunted her dreams for as long as she could remember, Madeline's body stiffened amongst the inexplicably painful trepidation of the Sands. She screamed out in agony, but no air remained in her lungs and no sound emitted from her lips. She turned from him and ran through the cemetery courtyard and into the other side of the mausoleum. The thick mist flowed in from behind and all she could see were the endless white marble hallways with crypt doors and name plaques lining every wall. Dead roses covered the glass-block flooring, which glowed a fiery red and filled the mausoleum with the only light source from which she could see.

Madeline ran as fast as she could, trying to escape, but every hallway was a dead-end with Satan standing in front of a brightened stained-glass window of images depicting the two thrones of Hell. Each time he was holding a small black velvet box in one hand and motioning with the index finger of the other mouthing, "Come with me."

Repeatedly Madeline turned and ran, trying futilely to locate an exit. At every turn she saw transparent faceless ghosts in groups of threes coming toward her, blocking the way, and forcing her in another direction. Finally, with no unobstructed pathways left, she ran into the sweeping balcony-lined, three-story oval foyer and up the grand staircase to the second floor of the mausoleum.

Pearl-colored coffins on stainless-steel cadaver gurneys lined the hallways at the base of the now-uncovered crypts, and when Madeline reached the end of another corridor of the never-ending maze, for the first time, Satan wasn't there. She turned around to retreat, but the coffin lids had all opened; she reared back, climbed onto the bench in front of another stained-glass window, and bashed it with her fists to break through, but the glass was hard as stone.

Suddenly a name plaque on the crypt to her left halted her fight and caught her attention; she squinted her eyes and looked closer, then widened them in horror. Engraved on the first plaque was: *MAXWELL JACKSON – PROPERTY OF HELL*. And engraved on the plaque next to it was: *MADELINE KNIGHT née ANNABELLE JACKSON – PRINCESS OF DARKNESS-ELECT*.

Madeline pulled on the handle of the crypt bearing her name and effortlessly slid out the drawer. She looked inside and saw her own dead body, cold and gray with a heavy titanium crown fitted securely on her head. She slammed the drawer shut, turned around, and there stood Satan, again blocking her way. Her heart pounded loudly as three transparent ghosts with demon faces floated through him and into her body. She screamed.

––––––––––

Saturday, April 12, 2014 – 11:00 a.m.
The sound of loud pounding on her office door ripped Madeline, still asleep on the couch, from her nightmare. The same cringing anxiety she'd endured upon waking her entire life overwhelmed her body yet again, and the accompanying morning nausea and accumulated bile churned her stomach. But this day, she somehow felt different.

What Madeline perceived as a nightmare felt like reality, and it was. She had visited another time and place existing in a parallel universe subdivided into the realms of the human existence. And now she was half in, half out, stranded in the limbo of the In-Between.

Her office had become a pod in a portal connecting the world of the mortal to the world of the immortal. But the laws of each world could still suck her into their individual vortexes of physicality depending on her need for survival within each. And right now, it was the mortal.

Madeline heard the sound of keys in the door, and before she had the chance to rise, Dr. Fields let himself in. While Madeline tried to adjust to the striking physical changes in her environment, he closed the door and sat down in a chair beside her. She sat up sleepily and faced him bravely, now braless and wearing only black yoga pants and a white tank top.

"I know why you're here," Madeline said flatly.

"I can assure you that you have absolutely no idea whatsoever why I'm here," Dr. Fields replied, taken aback by her unsolicited response.

He had rehearsed this moment a dozen times since Nurse Monroe had so carelessly handed him her "evidence" against Madeline. Nurse Monroe had been so proud to unveil the allegations against Madeline and spoil Dr. Fields' view of her competition. But he had known the truth about Madeline's past and medical diagnosis all along.

Dr. Fields prided himself on a surplus of strengths, and knowing every detail about his young residents' lives was one of them. They were all consistently one-step behind in the game of social and professional life long before they ever knew they were contestants. Dr. Fields required all of his residents to see Dr. Garrison as a condition of their acceptance into his program, and unethically received reports on their sessions regularly.

He had kept Dr. Garrison in a holding pattern for years bought by way of his knowledge of a minor incident involving Dr. Garrison and an accidental encounter with a local prostitute. In actuality, it was an impetuous mistake most men in their circle would find humorous, but not the highly self-righteous Dr. Garrison. He wasn't even a small player as far as the "Boy's Club" was concerned, and had no knowledge of Dr. Fields' own pool of indiscretions, but bowed to him submissively when it came to hiding his own.

And now that all the information both men had kept secret about Madeline was public, Dr. Fields could now use his invasions as leverage in a last effort to obtain her. However, he wanted to give her one last chance to submit to him willingly.

"Madeline," Dr. Fields said, "despite all my generous efforts over the years to help and guide you, you have not only failed me, but your patients as well. Regrettably, I have decided your time here as a resident has come to an end. And, unfortunately, due to the severity of both recent events and your medical status, it has also come to my attention there will be a hearing to revoke your license and deny you entry to the medical board."

Madeline looked at him blankly; she wasn't listening.

"Now," Dr. Fields continued in a prideful, firmer tone, "what I have to say next will never be offered again outside these doors, therefore it's in your best interest to choose your next words wisely. I want you to accept my offer to become my wife. You needn't bother yourself with any of the guilt I know you're feeling about your infidelities with that degenerate Nathan Raines—I've already discovered them. And as you know, I am a very forgiving man. I know you will always be sick, but I can help you. I can take care of you and offer you some semblance of a normal life, despite all your shortcomings. You may never practice medicine again, but you know perfectly well I can make this all disappear and make you the highly admired socialite I know you have always wanted to be. I love you."

He leaned in closer and sleazily rubbed her thigh, caressed her nipple with his finger, and gestured to put his arm around her shoulder in anticipation of her acceptance. But he stopped short when he realized she wasn't looking at him, but rather looking past him.

"Madeline? Madeline!" he said, grabbing her face and turning it toward him. "Do you understand what I'm saying to you? Look at me! What is your answer?"

She continued to disregard his advances while steadfastly looking at the back corner of the office instead. There stood Satan, gazing back at her lustfully just as he had at the mausoleum. He opened the black velvet box and revealed a massive round-cut diamond and platinum engagement ring, and once again motioned silently with his index finger mouthing, "Come with me."

Satan wanted Madeline and he wanted her badly. For him to double his power and multiply the souls he could take without consent, he needed to use his one chance incarnate to marry the most powerful woman alive and breed the first of his generation. Madeline's acceptance of his proposal was an absolute necessity, and the one reason he'd chosen her parents to be his only high-ranking Generals to share in his abilities.

"I've always known what you've wanted," Madeline said as if in a trance. "But you're never going to get it. Not in life, or in death; I'll end it myself before I ever go with you."

Dr. Fields turned around to see what she was looking at but saw nothing. He stood up and looked down at her, enraged; he thought she was talking to him. Even though he hadn't expected her to refuse him so adamantly, he already had a contingency plan securely in place. A plan if played out correctly would end in his victory no matter how long it took.

"Wrong answer," he said angrily. "Nurse!"

The door flung open and in walked Administrator Hamilton, Dr. Garrison, and two large psych techs with a wheelchair and restraints. Leading the ambush was an evilly eager Nurse Monroe with a large needle in her hand, which she squirted for effect showing she was ready to use it.

Now Dr. Fields formally addressed Madeline. "I have here your signed commitment papers guaranteeing a minimum ninety-day involuntary evaluation period to determine which facility will best accommodate you for permanent placement."

Dr. Garrison begrudgingly handed Dr. Fields the papers he had unwillingly signed, which Dr. Fields then showed to Madeline. She didn't even glance at them. Satan had disappeared the second Dr. Fields' strike team entered the office, and now Madeline's senses had returned to the human plane she was still predominately on.

"You know the drill, Madeline," Dr. Fields said. "Either you cooperate, or Nurse Monroe will be more than happy to assist you."

Nurse Monroe stepped in closer, glaring down and itching for the chance to give Madeline what she always thought her favorite toy-mouse deserved.

Madeline looked up and met Nurse Monroe's stare, then held

it there calmly as she slipped her hand underneath the pillow she was sleeping on. She then jumped up in perfect form with her black gun and pointed it directly at Nurse Monroe.

"I don't think so!" Madeline yelled. "Get back—everyone! It looks like you brought a needle to a gunfight."

————————

Madeline burst out of her office gun in hand with her backpack and Gabriella's computer bag over her shoulder. She slammed the door, locked it, and snapped off the key, trapping everyone inside. She knew it would only be two or three minutes before a full-security lockdown, and needed to escape before that happened.

She sprinted barefoot down the hallway coming up to the nurses' station door separating the patients' ward from the doctors' offices. After slyly concealing the gun behind her back, she smiled genuinely at the nurse on duty who was reading a magazine and drinking her usual Saturday morning cappuccino. Without a second thought, the nurse buzzed Madeline through that door and the one leading into the lobby.

Madeline stealthily made her way to the emergency exit leading into the fire escape, hoping the security guards at the front desk didn't see her on the surveillance cameras. She reached into her backpack, pulled out her access card, and then slid it through the electronic door lock—but it didn't work. She tried it again, but it still wouldn't open the door. Panicked as sweat dripped down her forehead, she looked through the lobby doors and saw two security guards coming out of the elevator. With no other options, she typed her personal override code onto the keypad, instantly sounding the floor's alarm as she fled through the doors and down the stairwell.

One of the psych techs locked in Madeline's office kicked open the door, busting the lock and freeing everyone inside. Madeline had ripped her office phone lines out of the wall before leaving, and Dr. Fields had to reach the ward's emergency call box to alert the hospital-wide security squad of her escape.

He ran to the nurses' station and banged on the glass. "Let me in!" he screamed. The stunned nurse quickly opened the door, and Dr. Fields shoved her out of the way, pounded down on the Code Red alarm button, and got on the phone to security. "This is Dr. Harold Fields in the child's psychiatry unit. Implement a Code Red. Secure all exits—patient on the run. Subject in question is Dr. Madeline Knight. I repeat: Dr. Madeline Knight is the subject in question. She is armed and dangerous. Restrain and sedate on contact."

The deafening sound of sirens blared in the background as Madeline raced down the concrete stairs. She slammed into the exit door at the bottom of the South West Wing to open it, but it had already automatically locked.

"No!" she screamed, banging her fists on the door and panting hard as she whirled around contemplating what to do next. Going back up wasn't an option; every other door would now be locked too. She smashed the glass on a nearby fire extinguisher case with her elbow, took out the extinguisher, and slammed it down on top of the door handle—no use. She lifted her gun, turned her head to the side to avoid any blowback debris, and fired three rounds, blasting off the lock. She kicked the door open and ran out into the blistering bright-white blizzard.

Once outside, Madeline quickly assessed her surroundings, unable to see more than a few feet ahead. She needed to get to her car before the parish sheriff's department arrived and barricaded the front entrance, and she'd parked on the opposite side of the facility in the doctors' lot. She raced through the snow around the right side of the building, and as she rounded the corner time slowed down. She stopped hard, sliding backward in the ice as her bare feet struggled to reestablish traction, before falling to the ground.

Jack Lee was standing directly in front of her, leaning against the wall in a black leather jacket over his scrubs. He had a two-way radio in his hand, and was clearly aware of the situation because the details were blaring over the waves. With a look of absolute uncertainty, Madeline picked herself up ready to run, but Jack Lee looked at her calmly and shook his head.

"All this just for you, huh, Madeline?" he asked, cracking a smile. "I always knew my girl had to be trouble."

Madeline looked over her shoulder; she had to go.

He reached into his pocket, took out his car key fob, and tossed it to Madeline. "It's no Benz, but she'll do. It's the silver one down at the end. Now, get out of here."

Madeline handed him the black computer bag and whispered something into his ear, then took off running.

Jack Lee got on his radio. "Dr. Knight is headed down the fire escape on the fourth floor in the North East Wing. I'll get to her before she makes it to the bottom!"

After commandeering Jack Lee's new silver Dodge Challenger SRT392 Hemi muscle car, Madeline peeled out of the parking lot in first gear with the precision of a racecar driver, busting through the security gate and leaving nothing but dirty snow behind her.

28

DEMONS ARRIVE
IN
NEW ORLEANS

Saturday, April 12, 2014 – 11:30 a.m.
A tinted-out black Rolls Royce Phantom sedan pulled up to New Orleans City Hospital and parked in the emergency ambulance-unloading zone. The Phantom's front doors automatically opened and Pastor and Mrs. Chatsworth, both wearing mirrored aviator sunglasses, stepped out into the fresh powdered snow. Pastor Chatsworth wore a heavy black suit with his titanium clerical collar and a long hanging silver cross underneath a full-length black trench coat that trailed the ground. Mrs. Chatsworth, covered in heavy jewelry, wore a matching suit and trench coat with a vintage leopard-fur shawl and black wide-brimmed ladies hat and veil covering her chalk-white skin.

Every person in witness, hospital staff, police officers, patients, and visitors alike, all stopped and stared while shivering in mesmerized disbelief. The Chatsworths were the two perfect illusions of the human race, and looked more intimidatingly enticing than the most famous movie stars ever to have graced the false fantasy of the silver screen. They paraded past their entranced admirers with zero acknowledgment, leaving them frozen and helpless to oppose or condemn their blatant disregard for hospital policies.

Pastor and Mrs. Chatsworth breezed through the front doors with their coats blowing back behind them as if they were the monarchs of the palace. And by utilizing the unlimited powers Satan had provided them, and only them, over the minds of mortals, they were. The air surrounding the Chatsworths emanated pure evil and subdued everyone who saw them with the envy and greed induced by the robust perfume of their satanic essence.

The Chatsworths had given up their own mortal statuses right after the birth of their last child, and walked with the assurance that no human being alive could thwart their agenda or challenge their existence. Even the other Soldiers of Satan in position and waiting to launch the other nine hundred ninety-nine CCE churches required the Chatsworths' authority to turn all gathered souls, and bowed to them submissively in Satan's absence. But still, the ogling admiration of the hospital bystanders allegorically falling at the Chatsworths' feet only stoked their egos all the more.

The moment the Chatsworths walked into the building Gabriella sensed her parents' presence. She abruptly sat up in bed, inhaled the scent of her half-demonic breeders, and smiled knowingly. With no phone privileges and an extended stay on her second hold, she had waited anxiously all night for their arrival, believing unwaveringly that they would obliterate the prison sentence Madeline had maliciously bestowed upon her.

Gabriella's own transformation into an immortal wouldn't be complete until she first descended into Hell and received her vows. But this was the closest she had been to her beloved parents in fifteen years, and the Chatsworths' potent proximity ignited Gabriella's blood into fire. She was long past ready to leave New Orleans and take her rightful place, no longer beneath her parents, but above them. Salivating, she began to spring excitedly off the walls like a caged wild animal.

Pastor and Mrs. Chatsworth brushed ahead of the other family members and friends already waiting in line for visiting hours, and up to the security desk. The muscular and armed security attendant looked up disapprovingly, but then cowered the instant he comprehended the Chatsworths' malevolent appearance and authoritative manner.

"I am Pastor Milton Chatsworth," he said. "My wife, Palamia, and I are here to collect our daughter—Gabriella Jackson."

"Umm, I'm sorry, sir," the attendant said stuttering. "There are no patients on the list for discharge today. We only release wards of the state on Tuesdays. Please take a seat and I will find someone to assist you."

The attendant's unfathomable disregard for Pastor Chatsworth's request left the demon unamused, and Pastor Chatsworth continued to stand in front of the desk motionless.

Unwilling to question the unquenchable guests before him, the attendant picked up the phone as the other people in line slowly backed away. "This is Officer Hayes at the front desk. Can you please tell me who the attending psychiatrist is for Gabriella Jackson?"

"That would be Dr. Raines," the nurse said on the other end of the line. "However, his shift doesn't start until later this evening around nine o'clock."

"Can you please page him? We have a situation."

———

Dr. Fields had wasted no time calling in Madeline's "escape" to the parish sheriff's department. He wanted her caught and brought back to him before she exercised her legal rights against the psychiatric commitment he'd bound her to. But it wasn't as simple as just putting her on law enforcement radar.

If Madeline was caught and Dr. Fields hadn't implemented a plan for her treatment, the police would first bring her into City Hospital for evaluation, as was customary with all psychiatric patients apprehended by the authorities. Dr. Nathan Raines and his staff would then have the first opportunity to administer Madeline's initial assessment. And if that happened, Dr. Fields would lose his right to preside over her medically and suffer the strict disciplinary action sure to accompany a doctor who'd illegally committed a patient involuntarily; Nathan Raines would happily see to that.

Therefore, to prevent such an unfortunate occurrence, Dr. Fields set himself up a temporary command station at the main Sheriff's outpost with the authorization of several of his friends in elected offices. They were more than willing to assist him in capturing the "feverishly violent" convict who'd wielded a firearm in a federal medical facility, as Dr. Fields had enthusiastically informed them. In fact, after Dr. Fields had finished implanting his list of vile lies and accusations about Madeline into the heads of the officers at the station, he had them psychotically rabid and ready to launch a full-fledged manhunt.

A character assassination, however, wasn't the only method Dr. Fields had used to lure several police units into assisting with his underhanded criminal activities. Dr. Fields knew how the minds of men worked—it was going to take a lot more than bad-mouthing a twenty-nine-year-old woman to convince a group of civil servants with a short cap on their already low salaries to break federal laws. A problem he easily remedied by boasting a million-dollar cash reward offered to the lucky officer who captured Madeline first and delivered her directly to him.

———————

Officer Gates, sweet, happy, and pleasingly round with a shiny face and rosy cheeks, sat inside his New Orleans Police Department cruiser keeping warm with the heater blazing and a hot cup of chicory coffee and a brown bag of fresh beignets. He was just beginning his twelve-hour shift patrolling the French Quarter, and liked to indulge in the decadent New Orleans favorite of sweet fried dough fritters every morning. He was just starting to wipe the powdered sugar off his face when an All-Points Bulletin was transmitted over his radio by the dispatcher.

"The Sheriff's department has issued an APB for Dr. Madeline

Knight, AKA Annabelle Jackson. She is a mixed-race female, twenty-nine years old, brown hair, brown eyes, athletic build, standing five feet nine inches tall. The suspect is an escaped patient from New Orleans State Psychiatric Hospital and is armed and extremely dangerous. Do not approach alone. The suspect's home address is 15934 Royal Street, apartment 4PH. All units are to be on the lookout."

Officer Gates was first to respond. "This is Officer Gates, unit 182 NOPD. I'm two blocks from the suspect's residence. I'm on my way there now."

29

BLOOD SKY DAWNING

Saturday, April 12, 2014 – 1:00 p.m.

After evading the minefield of Dr. Fields' NOSPH ambush, Madeline sped away in Jack Lee's car with only one place to go. She was desperate to make it back to Haloise in time to seek relief from Satan's terrorizing ailments, and then gather what she needed from her apartment and flee New Orleans. Her visual and physical perception of the world had been capsized ever since crossing planes into the underworld of the Chatsworths' lair, and the severity of her condition compounded with every passing minute.

Satan had literally shut down the city, freezing Madeline in with a localized subzero ice storm. She turned off the empty freeway and onto the poor-inhabited neighborhoods leading into the Bywater. The inner-city gentlemen who congregated daily on the street islands playing checkers, socializing, and lounging on lawn chairs, now wore thick garments and huddled around makeshift fire pits. As Madeline slowly drove by on the un-plowed snow-covered roadway, the men stopped their activities and instinctually followed her to every stoplight. Without touching the car, they encircled her in swarms while reciting prayers and staring through the windows in mesmerized astonishment. There was a foreign aurora of white light surrounding Madeline's body they had never before seen, couldn't understand, and felt greatly drawn to, responsible for, and protective of.

Frightened and confused yet remaining calm so as not to further alarm her passionate spectators, Madeline cautiously plowed through the mounting blockade of snow. Her new security escorts trailed her on foot until she arrived in Haloise's neighborhood, and then went quietly their separate ways.

Almost every building in the Bywater was covered in white and dripping with icicles. Madeline parked her car inconspicuously down an alley behind a large dumpster and sprinted to Haloise's house.

After Madeline passed through the front gates and stepped onto Haloise's property, the freezing air instantly warmed. No snow piled on the grass or sprinkled the garden, and the sun beamed down brightly, illuminating the house in a colorful glow. But the striking differentiation in weather only jolted Madeline's coping mechanisms all the more. She felt as if she were in a wonderland of ever-changing elements existing without a universal law of operation and slipping deeper into the core of the fantasy. She dreaded that Dr. Garrison had been right about his diagnosis, and that she might actually be succumbing to the earthly illness of schizophrenia.

Satan had fought for almost thirty years to break Madeline down mentally and force her into submission. And if she hadn't escaped Dr. Fields' scheme to have her committed and chemically induced, Satan would have succeeded. But Madeline had escaped, and while her mental health technically was deteriorating, it wasn't from schizophrenia. Her brain no longer recorded an inverted view with the desensitized lens of the human delusion, and she had once again unknowingly crossed planes into another realm of the In-Between. The portal of the Ether she'd entered this time, however, was nothing like the Chatsworths' lair or Satan's mausoleum.

Still barefoot and wearing only her tank top and yoga pants,

Madeline wrapped her arms around her chest, brushing the moisture from her body as she walked up the front steps. Before she had the chance to knock on the door it opened, and Haloise, relieved by her arrival, came out and embraced her.

"Thank God, you're here!" Haloise said. "I've been waiting for you; the shift is now in full effect. The Blood Sky is dawning!" She briskly ushered Madeline into the house, looking up and down the street before closing the door. She then latched and secured the multiple locks and steel barricade she had installed in preparation for Madeline's arrival.

Although Haloise knew her days living in her house were over, she had needed to wait until after Friday night to see if Madeline would fight through Satan's attack and return to her protection. And because Madeline had resisted him, as Haloise had prayed she would, Haloise could now prepare Madeline for the unveiling of the Divine knowledge awaiting her.

Archangel Haloise had not yet fully transitioned out of human form, and still needed to remain in a portal connecting her to the human plane Madeline predominately resided in. And while in her pre-incarnate chrysalis stage, Haloise herself was still exposed and vulnerable to a demonic attack by Satan, who was now aware of her existence. Therefore, she had filled her house with hundreds of flaming protection candles and large bowls of holy water to guarantee maximum protection. Aside for an old television streaming the news in the background, what used to look like a normal living room was now an extension of her altar.

"What are you talking about?" Madeline asked, out of breath and shivering from the cold. "What is the Blood Sky?"

"Madeline, I need you to focus on my words very carefully," Haloise said, picking up a knit blanket from the couch and draping it around Madeline. "The choices you make from here on will alter your existence for all eternity. Before the dawn of the new day, life as all God's creatures know it will no longer favor good but rather evil. The repercussions of such madness will affect not only the spirits of the living, but the spirits of all who've died as well. This overhaul of satanic devotion of the wicked far exceeds what I predicted; the amount of human participation is catastrophic, and it is progressive."

Frantic, Madeline began to pace around the room with nervous anxiety. She'd heard what Haloise had said, however her theoretical processing speed for a statement of that magnitude was having a slow time catching up with the validating facts of her own experiences.

"I can't listen to any more of this!" Madeline erupted. "What choices? What difference does it make what I do? I tried to serve the side of good and what has it gotten me? I'm nothing in this world! All the hidden cruelties and injustices ignored or forgiven because society's so-called 'protectors' are afraid to expose their own sins will continue to go unpunished while destroying the victims. It's not going to take until the morning for humanity to favor evil—they already do! The very cause and career I risked my life to advance the quality of have turned against me; they never supported me to begin with. I don't have a job. I don't have any family. I can't even survive one minute outside this door!"

Madeline still hadn't overcome her confusion long enough to notice the difference in Haloise, or to recognize who Haloise now was. Madeline was tired, worn out, and had exceeded her emotional fortitude. She knew the jowls of Satan's hounds were closing in on her location, and the fight-or-flight responses of her body dominated what was left of her conscious mind. She crossed the room to Haloise and took her by the shoulders. "My only option at this point is to run," Madeline said. "I can start my life over again somewhere else; become someone else. You have to help me—rid me of this curse so I can escape the hell overrunning my life. I can't take it anymore!"

Haloise gently removed Madeline's hands from her shoulders and sat her down on the sofa. She then placed her hand on Madeline's head, just as she had done to Ross days before, and replaced Madeline's rushing fright with a comforting sensation of centering tranquility.

"You must calm yourself, my child," Haloise said. "I am the true Protector, sent to lead you along your journey while continuing to navigate my own. I made my choice sixty of Earth's years ago to risk my freedom and my reward of living eternally in the Kingdom of the Divine because I have faith in the Mission of God. Until you choose which path you will take, the only assistance I can provide you with is a temporary sense of clarity at your Crossroads. Like you, the time I have available to do that has almost expired, as the transformation from my first incarnated state is almost complete. Right now, the only person who can help you—is you."

Haloise walked over to the fireplace mantel and picked up a picture of herself and Madeline standing in front of the Saut-d'Eau waterfall in Haiti. They were both happy and smiling, reveling in the holy energy of the water splashing all around them. There were several other pictures of them together at various locations over the years. As the last of Haloise's human existence began to fade, she took a long moment to absorb the feelings and emotions she knew would soon vanish forever.

"When you came to me years ago," Haloise said, "I always knew there was a special connection between us. It wasn't something I needed to understand, but rather a gift from God not requiring contemplation. I took you under my wings; you accepted me into your heart. You must remember, nothing you have ever done out of the goodness of that heart was in vain. The road you have so tediously traveled was always born in the effort to facilitate the best interest of those around you, even though you have stumbled terribly along the way. It is only true pureness of soul that has provided you with unyielding strength against the evil thrust upon you by the one great Deceiver. This life was not meant for your enjoyment, Madeline; it is a test of loyalty and devotion to be endured. Whoever gives their life, receives it. You must cherish who you are, not turn away from it."

"And who exactly is that?" Madeline asked.

Haloise held the picture for a moment longer and closed her eyes, remembering. She shook her head nostalgically, put it down, and walked to her altar room door. "I think you've always known the answer to that question. If so, then silence your angst and follow me. If not, you will have to exit this house alone and never look back. The Lord only asks once."

Madeline sat on the couch for a moment longer, fumbling with the gauze covering the deep bleeding cut on her right hand. When she looked back up at Haloise, she saw for the first time that the vessel standing before her was not the priestess she remembered. She immediately rose and followed Haloise through the beaded doorway and over to the altar.

They both knelt down and Haloise picked up the bone-handle knife. She clutched Madeline's left hand firmly and cut Madeline's palm deeply down the center. Haloise then squeezed Madeline's hand together as hard as she could, allowing Madeline's thick red blood to pour into a three-inch crystal vial, filling it to the top. After wrapping Madeline's hand in a cloth, Haloise secured the vial with a gold lid and set it aside.

"Now close your eyes and listen carefully," Haloise said. "Feel the knowledge awaiting you. Breathe it in. You must open your heart and accept the words that will guide you that cannot be heard with your ears or seen with your eyes. You, Madeline, are a Chancellor from God, a blessed sheep strategically born amongst the wolves at the highest level of evil to understand the ways of the Darkside in order to salvage souls. Through multiple lifetimes of service to Satan your parents have achieved the top ranks of demon hierarchy. You are their direct opposition."

"'For they are the spirits of devils,'" Madeline said, opening her eyes as scripture not from memory entered her mind, "'working miracles, which go forth unto the kings of the earth and of the whole world, to gather them to the battle of that great day of God Almighty. . ..' This means my parents have the ability to turn souls over to the Darkside on the human plane without the direct assistance of Satan."

Madeline stood up from the altar and walked around the room, absorbing the powerful presence of its newly prominent holiness and rejoicing in the true liberation of her life she'd buried for so long. "I've been defending myself against the powers of Satan since the day I was born," Madeline said. "It has been a relentless struggle draining every atom of strength left within me." She picked up the Holy Bible. "I always hid my Bibles and rosaries; they were forbidden. Somehow my parents would always find them. They could sense God's presence; they were petrified of it."

Haloise walked over to Madeline with a bottle of oil, poured some in her hand, and anointed Madeline's forehead. Haloise immediately flinched back. "Your mind is now penetrable!" Haloise said. "Your body is weak, and we haven't much time."

"I know. My parents offered me one last chance to join them, and I refused. Now, no matter what I do they will never stop raging against me until I'm dead. But I'm not going to waste any more of my life fighting the effects of their blasphemy; I'm going to eliminate the cause!"

Madeline walked over to the altar and picked up the *Scroll of Demoncide* Haloise had read the night before. "If my parents can turn souls without assistance, they fall under the definition of Demons on the Human Plane. They are not subject to civilized law, just as their victims are not subject to the protection of the laws the demons obey. Milton and Palamia Chatsworth are not human, and the definition of Demoncide is the slaying of such beings, ritually, on spiritual ground. That is my destiny. That is why I was sent to them. The days of the wicked mauling God's defenseless flocks are over. It's time to send Satan's Soldiers back to Hell!"

The house began to shake with a steady rumble and the deafening high-pitched sound of squeaking and flapping wings filled the room. "What is that?" Madeline screamed. She ran to the window and pulled back the curtains, looked up, and saw a dense black cloud of bats circling the house. "He knows we're here!"

"Satan isn't the only one closing in on you," Haloise said. "Your parents are in the city. You need to prepare."

While Haloise put together the items Madeline would need to execute a Demoncide, Madeline sat on the couch wrapping her freshly stitched wound in gauze after cleaning out and rewrapping her old one. She then meticulously studied the *Scroll of Demoncide*.

News coverage detailing the police hunt for Madeline flashed on the television, "Dangerous psychiatric doctor on the run amidst record-breaking, below-freezing New Orleans temperatures . . ." the anchor commentated.

Madeline realized she would no longer have the chance to return to her apartment.

Haloise came out of the altar room with a brown leather satchel and a map and handed them to Madeline. "It's less than eight hours until dawn," Haloise said; "I will help you track your parents. There is only one place in southern Louisiana where you can perform a Demoncide."

Madeline smiled. "That's why we live in Voodoo country."

10:00 p.m.

Nathan Raines had rushed to City Hospital earlier in the day after receiving a message saying Gabriella Jackson's parents were in the building and refusing to leave without seeing him. The Chatsworths, however, not wanting to risk a scene that might jeopardize their image prior to the first mass, had already left to search for Madeline before Nathan had arrived.

After unsuccessfully scouring the city, the Chatsworths had since returned to City Hospital, and Nathan had left his graveyard shift in the emergency room to meet with them. He had just watched the news in the staff break room and seen the police search for Madeline. Now, he sat at his office desk distressed and disturbed opposite an exceedingly angered and urgent Pastor and Mrs. Chatsworth.

"As we've already tried to explain to your insolent staff, we are here to collect our daughter," Pastor Chatsworth declared, keeping his composure. "I have hours to keep and a private plane on standby. I want this handled."

"Again, I apologize for keeping you so long," Nathan said. "I made my way up as soon as permitted. However, concerning Gabriella, I have in no way cleared her for release. And I have no plans for doing so until I've properly diagnosed and cleared her for reentry into society. Which right now, she has shown no indication of being prepared to do. And furthermore, I've never even heard of you before today."

"That's ridiculous!" Pastor Chatsworth said, stiffening in his seat and disgruntled by the audacity of the man sitting in front of him. "Need I remind you that I am the leader of the most powerful and influential church in all the world? Any opposition from you deterring my wishes will surely result in your demise."

Nathan Raines no longer allowed anyone to tell him what to do—especially when it came to the happenings within his own hospital. But mostly, he was baffled by the conflicting requests for and against Gabriella's hospitalization, and the sudden emergence of her and Madeline's parents. "And need I remind you, sir," Nathan countered, "that I have no care whatsoever who you are, where you come from, or what sort of authority you think you have. I am the Chief of Staff and managing psychiatric physician at a city hospital, which I control. The only person under whom I take authority is the publicly appointed Judge herself."

Pastor Chatsworth stood up, towering over Nathan Raines; he wanted to rip the young doctor's throat out and could have done so instantaneously. But it wasn't the time. "I strongly urge you to reconsider," Pastor Chatsworth said. "I can personally assure you Gabriella will be better cared for by her family with the support of her church. I want to see my daughter, and I want to see her now!"

Nathan Raines stood up to meet him. He dwarfed Pastor Chatsworth by two inches, and wasn't intimidated by the strikingly flamboyant pastor, or his silent ghost-white wife who stared right through him. "Not only will I not be releasing Gabriella into your custody, but you are in no way authorized, under any circumstances, to see or make decisions for her at this time."

"Well, then you will tell me who is," Pastor Chatsworth demanded, chillingly unsettled by the immovability of a man he thought beneath him. "My daughter has rights."

Dr. Raines took a step back and looked inquisitively at the pastor and his wife. Regardless of how disconcerted he was by their presence, their lack of involvement in Gabriella's care up until that point piqued his curiosity. And they had yet to mention Madeline. The entire situation was surreal and involved the fugitive woman he had quickly grown to love; he needed to wring out the details, so he could try to help her.

"Okay," Nathan said. "If you will allow me to excuse myself, I will try to find a solution to this seemingly mutual problem. Try to make yourselves comfortable while I sort this out."

Nathan exited his office, took his cell phone out of his pocket, and dialed Madeline's number. He had called her at least twenty times already. First when she hadn't shown up the night before, and then incessantly after seeing the news. Her phone had gone straight to voicemail every time, and she hadn't bothered to return any of his messages.

"How did I allow myself to get involved in this kind of mess again?" he asked himself, holding the now-ringing phone to his ear.

———

The snow was now only gently falling, and Madeline was still at Haloise's house awaiting her final instructions. Madeline heard her cell phone ring, and when she saw, again, it was Nathan, her stomach tightened.

She answered the phone nervously. "Nathan . . ." Madeline said. "What's up?"

"What's up?" Nathan asked. "Are you kidding me? Two people claiming to be your parents are sitting in my office demanding the release of your sister!"

"What—my parents are in your office? What are you talking

about—how do you know it's them?"

"Aside from the fact they were pretty clear about it, it wasn't exactly hard to tell! And I'm sorry to say the resemblance is quite disturbing. But never mind that, I've seen the news, Madeline—who are you people?"

"Nathan, wait! Your life is—."

"No, you wait! Every person in this hospital knows about you and that your sister is under my care. How dare you put me in this position—what kind of mind game is this? And where were you last night? This time you owe me an explanation and I want one now!"

"And I'll give you one! But please just keep them in your office. I'm on my way—I'll meet you outside the service entrance and explain everything. But no matter what, don't let them see Gabriella and don't tell anyone you've spoken to me!" She hung up before he had the chance to respond.

——————

While Nathan was in the hallway on the phone, Pastor and Mrs. Chatsworth heard every word of his conversation, and decided to intercept Madeline before she made it to City Hospital. They looked at each other knowingly and hissed through open teeth.

After failing to locate Madeline earlier in the day, the Chatsworths had figured it best to first retrieve Gabriella and use her to bait Madeline out of hiding. But that scenario no longer seemed necessary. Killing Madeline was top priority, and they had to be back in Cincinnati in less than twelve hours to present Satan with her head. They would come back for Gabriella after Madeline was dead, and when they returned to City Hospital, they wouldn't be nice about it; they would take the walls down.

——————

Nathan was now more frustrated and angered than before, yet intent on questioning the Chatsworths further to keep them in place until Madeline arrived. But when he walked back into his office, to his shock, the Chatsworths were gone.

———————

Madeline was relieved. Now that she knew the Chatsworths' location she could concentrate on how to get them onto the designated spiritual ground. She was confident the answer would come as soon as she saw them, so right now the next step was making it to the hospital without being arrested so she could.

"Alright," she said to Haloise. "Time to lead the enemy to perdition." She walked over to Haloise and hugged her long and hard. "Goodbye, Haloise."

Haloise kissed Madeline on both cheeks. "Goodbye, Madeline, for now. Remember, you must do this exactly as the book describes. The Laws of Existence between the Kingdom, Humanity, and the Darkside will always remain in effect, regardless of who we are, what we are, or who or what we become. That is the only way to complete such a task and still save your soul. Between the *Scroll of Demoncide* and the book of *Demonology and Protection*, you will have everything you need. But if you make even one mistake, and the books are not physically combined upon execution, you lose the protection they provide for the disposal of a human body, even if it is demonic, on the human plane—."

"Oh, no!" Madeline said. "The book is at my apartment. There's no way it's safe for me to go back there—it's the first place the police would look!" Haloise had a bigger concern. "What is it?" Madeline asked, as she stood by the door ready to leave. "What?"

"There is one last thing, my child . . . one last thing you have to know before you proceed."

30

THE KING

Saturday, April 12, 2014 – 11:30 p.m.
Madeline was stone serious as she drove back to her apartment in the French Quarter. The blizzard had completely stopped the moment she left Haloise's house in the Bywater, yet heavy gray clouds from the receding storm still blocked out the moon. The New Orleans heat had returned with unrelenting brutality, and gusting winds of hot air melted the snow and ice, colliding with the water and shrouding the city in a bath of rising steam.

It was the eve of Madeline's thirtieth birthday, and what her life would entail after the darkness faded into light, she did not know. But fear was no longer an emotion she registered, and although an ocean of foreign uncertainty eclipsed the horizon, a conscious unburdening of earthly hindrances had provided ultimate relief.

The Quarter was packed with teams of NOPD officers attempting to keep control of the thousands of people venting in a manic frenzy over their mystifying taste of environmental apocalypse. The streets were swarming with locals and tourists alike, all enjoying the blissfulness of their anonymity and naiveté while partying half-naked in the warm-weather snow. Madeline parked in a dark alley on the backside of her apartment building, crept out of the car, and covertly surveyed the scene.

Officer Gates was still sitting in his patrol cruiser stationed outside the front entrance. He had been there all day, and was now comfortably relaxing in the air conditioning while munching on his dinner—a foot-long po'boy.

Moving with the shadows and still barefoot with the satchel over her shoulder, Madeline snuck around to the wall encasing the pool in her complex. She climbed on top of a car, jumped out and gripped the rough bricks, and then heaved herself up over the top, landing softly on bent knees. She ran to the fire escape, scaled the ladder to the rooftop, and with her spare key opened her deck door and disabled the alarm.

Once inside, she moved quickly. The longer she waited, the less likely the Chatsworths were to be at Nathan's office when she arrived. She washed her face and combed her hair back into a long tight ponytail, then changed into a tight black military cargo leather jacket, black leather combat pants, and black tactical boots. After strapping two heavy-duty tactical gun holsters to her thighs, she grabbed the book of *Demonology and Protection,* retrieved her silver handgun from under the front entry table, and deposited them both into the satchel.

Unsure how much money, if any, she might need, Madeline checked all the secret spots she'd hidden her emergency cash, hoping Gabriella hadn't drained her completely. But under every board, behind every outlet, and even in the attic, all her fireboxes were empty. It wasn't the first time Gabriella had stolen Madeline's money, but it would be the last. Fortunately, her safe had fingerprint-engaged locks, and $10,000 were still accessible. She opened the safe, took out two stacks of hundred-dollar bills, and stocked up on bullets.

After shredding the notarized letter naming Gabriella as her beneficiary, Madeline went to her nightstand for one last item. As she reached for the drawer, she spotted the picture of Maxwell lying next to the bed.

Whereas Madeline had been full of regret and sadness the last time she looked at the memento, this time she felt nothing. She had pointedly disregarded every nasty word anyone had ever said about Maxwell, even though deep down she knew it all to be true. Maxwell's innate wickedness was the one reality of Madeline's life she had refused to accept, and the most painful. The knowledge that the brother she had loved more than herself was in actuality openly evil was a harsh accuracy unavoidably substantiated by firsthand evidence—evidence that had traumatized her into absolute denial. Blaming their parents for Maxwell's revolting acts against his own innocent wife and child had been easier for Madeline than comprehending that he was, in fact, the most vile, monstrous descendant of all.

Madeline had blocked out the memory of her last visit to Maxwell and replaced it with the false image of them both smiling in his graduation picture on the university lawn. But now, her clear perception forced the truth to rush back into her mind with the same intensity as it had happened six years prior.

Madeline, twenty-three years old, sat in a chair at the end of a long damp corridor lined with rancid-smelling empty cells, facing Maxwell's private chamber in one of East Pen's old abandoned buildings once used for executions. Maxwell sat on his bed refusing to look at her.

Madeline, wearing a special visitor's badge reading *Annabelle Jackson,* was crying. "How could you do it?" she sobbed. "How? You're going to rot in Hell for what you've done. They were your family—your job was to protect them! You let our parents destroy you and became exactly what they wanted you to become."

Without looking away from the wall, Maxwell spoke coldly. "My wife was nothing but a worthless deserter—a steaming carcass of rotting meat! She deserved the punishment she received and more. She had the nerve, the audacity, to try to leave me. That fink should have known if she tried to take my child I would end her. And when my daughter deceived me by choosing her mother's side, it was the end for both of them. They violated my majesty and I handed down their deaths. I was justified in what I did—

nobody defies the King."

Stunned by the seriousness and delusion in his voice, Madeline couldn't believe what she was hearing. He wasn't the brother she remembered; she didn't know who he was.

He turned his head sharply and looked at her for the first time. With glowing red eyes, he looked possessed. "How dare you question my authority; don't you know who I am? No . . . you wouldn't, you've never known your place!"

He sprang off the bed screaming uncontrollably and reached through the bars, grabbing at Madeline. She jumped back, but the cold brick wall behind her barely allowed her to escape his long fingernails as he scratched at her face, which was just out of reach.

"This isn't you, you're possessed!" she screamed. "I'm never coming here again—I'm done with you. I'm done!"

"Shut up you stupid snitch!" he seethed demonically. "If you had been there when I stuck my shotgun into her mouth and blew her head off, and even attempted to block my way, you'd be dead too—nothing but collateral damage!" Suddenly calm, he stepped back for a moment and gaped motionless with his head cocked back over his left shoulder in a kinked position, then smiled deviously. "I would have looked at you with pleasure and blasted you back to the cesspool you came from. If these bars weren't blocking my way, I would smash your disgusting traitor skull so hard against that brick wall they would have to clean your brains off the floor with a hose."

"Stop—stop!" she pleaded, covering her head with her hands and shaking. "What's wrong with you? This isn't you, I know it's not—it's not!"

"What did you come here for? Did you think you were going to dethrone the King? I'm the King! I'm the King! Do you think you're so much better than me? Do you? We're exactly the same! He's coming for you too—you're gonna hang! He'll never stop until you're his—never!"

Terrified and paralyzed, Madeline watched as Maxwell climbed the latches of his cell door and, cackling loudly, threw his head back and bashed it against the bars, again and again, screeching as blood splattered all over Madeline's face.

"I'll see you in Hell!" he screamed. "I'm the King! I'm the King! I'm the King!"

Several guards unlocked the gates and filed in. One of them escorted Madeline out, and as she turned to look back, the others opened Maxwell's cell door with batons and handcuffs ready. They then proceeded to beat him repeatedly, even after his bloody body lay unconscious on the floor.

———————

After waiting for Madeline in the City Hospital parking lot for less than five minutes, Pastor and Mrs. Chatsworth had been able to pick up her scent more powerfully than ever before; and that change in Madeline's mortal status could have only meant one thing.

Pastor and Mrs. Chatsworth had then quickly tracked Madeline down at her apartment, and parked the Phantom in the middle of the street behind Officer Gates' police cruiser. But, after the unproductive encounter with Nathan Raines, Pastor Chatsworth was no longer willing to tolerate any more roadblocks.

They both exited the car, and Mrs. Chatsworth watched callously as her husband walked up to the side of the cruiser and tapped on the window.

First startled, Officer Gates rolled the window down when he saw who he thought was a man-of-the-cloth. "How can I help you, Father?" he asked.

Pastor Chatsworth reached in and snapped Officer Gates' neck with precision force, killing him instantly.

After rejoining his wife, Pastor Chatsworth kicked in the iron gates leading into Madeline's building, and they calmly walked through the courtyard and boarded the elevator to the fourth floor.

———————

When Madeline recovered from her flashback, she finally

understood, undoubtedly, that the demon of Maxwell had been the primary demon contributing to Savannah's possession. And Madeline was now officially free of the last emotional attachment to her old life.

"They were right," she said, picking up Maxwell's picture. "This fight may have started because of you, but now I'm continuing it for the world's salvation, not yours!" She hurled the picture against the brick wall and huge slivers of glass shattered all over the floor.

Madeline then retrieved the last item she needed from her nightstand drawer—her long shimmering black crystal rosary fitted with a Saint Benedict medal—and started for the door. As she rounded the corner outside her bedroom heading back to the spiral staircase, once again, time slowed down. She looked up and saw the Chatsworths heading up the hallway toward her.

"I tried to give you one last chance," Pastor Chatsworth said. "Now you're going to die! I've always enjoyed torturing you in the past, but this time it's going to be a real treat."

As Madeline turned to run, he stormed up to her with increasing speed and dug his pyramid-shaped nails deep into her shoulder, clawing her back to him. He ripped away her satchel and viciously body slammed her to the floor, then grabbed her by the hair and dragged her face down into the bedroom.

Mrs. Chatsworth stepped in around them and shut the door.

"This time there will be no one to hear you," Pastor Chatsworth said, "no one for you to tell, and no consequences. The sound of your last breath will never be heard outside these walls."

Mrs. Chatsworth walked over and stood in the corner, then turned around to face them. She could barely contain her excitement; it was the moment she'd waited thirty years to indulge in, and she was ready to watch Madeline die.

On his wife's nod, Pastor Chatsworth used Madeline's hair to hold her up and began bashing her head in with his fist, blow after blow. After the third strike, her blood splashed across the room, staining her once-pristine white bedding and champagne-finished antique furniture. But he didn't stop. He couldn't stop. He enjoyed it too much.

When Madeline was one strike away from death, the bulging demon was finally satisfied with the extent of his flogging. He let go of her hair and she fell hard to the ground. Barely conscious, she scratched at the wooden floor trying to escape him.

Pastor Chatsworth then ceremoniously took off his black belt. He yanked Madeline back to him by her hair, brought her to her knees in front of her mother, and bound the whip securely around her neck.

Madeline lifted her head as blood streamed down her bruised, swollen, battered face. She looked at Mrs. Chatsworth, who was now standing over her. "You said you were going to kill me yourself," Madeline choked, blood spewing from her mouth. "But I see you still can't bear to get your hands dirty—still afraid of the burn?"

Mrs. Chatsworth didn't respond, she just smiled signaling her command, and Pastor Chatsworth tightened the noose, pulling hard with both hands.

Madeline gripped the belt as her face turned purple, trying to slip her fingers underneath the leather to free herself. She spotted a large piece of broken glass on the floor next to Maxwell's picture, released her hands from the belt, and sank her body closer to the floor, lessening the pressure. She felt around, clutched one of the razor-sharp wedges, and whipped her hand back, slicing it across Pastor Chatsworth's arm and gashing it open. He let out an agonizing roar, ripped his hand away, and lost his grip on Madeline as black blood splattered across the wall.

Madeline sprang to her feet, snatched up the satchel, and ran down the hallway and out the smashed-open front door.

"Don't let her get away!" Mrs. Chatsworth screamed. "We have to kill her; she cannot survive!"

31

BLUE
SALVATION

Sunday, April 13, 2014 – 12:15 a.m.

Madeline raced down the stairs into the courtyard, through the garden, and out the front entrance. Looking back over her shoulder to gauge the Chatsworths' proximity, she slipped on a thin layer of ice, launching forward onto the windshield of the police cruiser out front. After sliding her bloody face off the smeared glass, she looked inside and saw Officer Gates dead with his head slumped over on his chest.

She pushed herself back and sprinted around the corner to the Challenger, jumped in the front seat and locked the door, then pressed down on the ignition button—nothing. She tried again and again, manically pushing in on the button, but the engine wouldn't turn over.

Pastor Chatsworth smashed in the driver's side window with his elbow, shattering glass in Madeline's face. He reached inside, pulled the handle, and flung open the door. She twisted her body around bending out of his reach, and then kicked him square in the chest with her left leg, launching him painfully back all the way to the other side of the street. She pressed the ignition button hard once more and the engine roared.

Pastor Chatsworth scrambled to his feet and lunged back toward the car. Madeline slammed the door on his hand and dropped into gear, hit the gas, and blasted off with the tires peeling and the door still open, leaving him tumbled over on the ground.

He ran back toward the Phantom where Mrs. Chatsworth was already waiting behind the wheel. She saw him running up the street and stepped on the throttle, smoking the tires as she took off to retrieve him. Without slowing down, she yanked the steering wheel hard to the right, fishtailed into a controlled slide, and hydroplaned around the corner while opening the passenger side door. Pastor Chatsworth clutched the handle as she flew by and in one swift motion jumped in like a diving bat, closing the door behind him.

Madeline looked into the rearview mirror and saw the Chatsworths in tight behind her; the hunt had serendipitously switched back into her favor.

"Come on and get me!" she said, weaving through the sparse traffic ahead. The sidewalks were still covered in fast-melting snow and the streets full of slush. Madeline opened her map and blew through a red light at the major intersection ahead, confident the Chatsworths would follow.

An NOPD officer waiting at a stoplight in the same intersection heard the dispatcher over his radio, "APB update: Madeline Knight, AKA Annabelle Jackson is driving a stolen vehicle—a 2014 silver Dodge Challenger SRT."

Madeline darted through the light in front of the officer followed by the black Phantom, heading for the freeway. He lit up his sirens, sped after them, and called in his catch. "I have the suspect in view and I'm in pursuit."

12:20 a.m.

Dr. Fields stood in the break room of the Sherriff's Department looking out the window into the darkness at his reflection and the reflection of Satan, who hovered behind him. Dr. Fields had been waiting at the station for almost twelve hours, and still nobody had discovered Madeline's location. The always-confident doctor suddenly felt the sharp twinge of anger and concern.

He had demanded every available officer report for duty to expand the hunt and double the reconnaissance infantry available to track his prey. But even for a man with Dr. Fields' power and willingness to sacrifice, taking control of several city and state law enforcement agencies hadn't been an easy feat to accomplish. Convincing the already-over-budget Administration to disperse their resources on a runaway doctor-turned-psychiatric-patient was low on official priority lists. Dr. Fields had needed to utilize diplomacies far richer than just financial rewards and manipulative blackmail to secure their cooperation. And the high price of those rich diplomacies included purchasing a favor from the one being he never wanted to be indebted. However, in the end, he had no choice.

Now, with Dr. Fields' newly acquired obligation and bankrupt reserve account, he was instructed to fix one nonnegotiable stipulation into the heads of his officers: when they apprehended Madeline, they needed to deliver her to him—alive.

Except Satan wasn't going to leave his last opportunity to plant his seed in Madeline's human body and confiscate her soul up to chance; especially after Dr. Fields' last failed attempt at obtaining her.

Today, it was Satan who had sold Dr. Fields his social and financial salvation, and Dr. Fields' lifetime of servitude would forever extend into eternity. But, this time the payment would be the unwilling possession of Dr. Fields' own body, and it wouldn't be charged to a demonic subordinate; the Human Portal would be a Full-Step-In by the Prince of Darkness himself.

"Fields!" shouted a lieutenant. "We've got her; let's go!"

As Dr. Fields confidently turned to leave, the spirit of Satan snatched him back violently by his hair, and with fangs wide open and exposed, frightfully devoured Dr. Fields' soul. A galactic tide of distortion invisibly ripped through Dr. Fields' skin as Satan excruciatingly infiltrated his flesh and took absolute control.

_____

A visibly altered Dr. Fields with a permanently furrowed brow and gritted teeth, joined the squad of police officers as they ran out of the precinct, jumped into their waiting cruisers, and lights-on squealed out of the parking lot.

_____

Madeline was in the lead as she made her way out of New Orleans and over the long bridge highway leading deep into the Honey Island Swamp. The Chatsworths were close behind her and the lone police cruiser behind them.

At the end of the causeway, Madeline abruptly made a last-second maneuver off the highway and blew through a country road stoplight just as a two-trailer semi-truck sped toward the same intersection. The Chatsworths veered off behind her barely making it through, but the police cruiser behind them went breaks-burning as the officer attempted to avoid collision. The semi-truck jackknifed as it approached, hard on the breaks and sliding sideways in the slush as the officer spun-out, landing engine-dead in a ditch.

With the roads now clear and hot with steam, the army of police led by Dr. Fields was quickly catching up, their stream of red, yellow, and blue lights visible in the distance.

Madeline turned off the country road and down a dark backwater dirt trail out of the Chatsworths' view. Mrs. Chatsworth, caught off guard, cranked the wheel, flew over a dirt embankment, and sprayed through the wetness and mud getting right back on course behind her.

Forward visibility went no further than their headlights, and the only foliage lining the trail were trees dripping with moss and thick prickly brush.

"Where do you think you're going?" Pastor Chatsworth seethed. "You can't escape us now!"

Madeline sped up, driving dangerously ahead and rounding the corner, once again out of the Chatsworths' view. When the Phantom's headlights vanished from her rearview mirror, Madeline jerked to a halt and switched off the lights. With the satchel over her shoulder, she exited the car and ran through the trees into the deep marsh of the predator-infested swamp. She was unafraid as she went through the waters, sensing exactly where to go.

The Chatsworths increased speed, catching sight of the parked Challenger just as Madeline disappeared into the darkness. Mrs. Chatsworth slammed on the breaks, sliding to a stop as she whipped the wheel around and parked horizontally in the middle of the trail. She and Pastor Chatsworth ejected without hesitation and charged after Madeline. Their eyes glowed red through the trees, and even though they couldn't see where Madeline had gone, the familiar scent of their offspring filled the air.

The police force following the Chatsworths' tracks turned down the muddy trail. Dr. Fields and his chauffeur were first to spot the abandoned Challenger and Phantom. They parked the cruiser on the side of the road and the others followed suit.

Every officer threw on waist-high rubber waders and heavy yellow jackets with reflective striping. Armed and ready, they unloaded a team of raging bloodhounds, turned on large flashlights and, consumed and entranced by the chase, filed out after the target.

Dr. Fields, with his own eyes now glowing red, waited inside the safety of the cruiser listening to the coverage over the radio; Satan had sent out his dogs, and now waited eagerly for them to bring back his dinner.

Madeline led the Chatsworths further into the swamp, holding her satchel above her head to avoid the water now up to her chin. Once on the other side of the marsh she saw the first destination Haloise had told her to go. Surrounded by a thick foreign mist was a small wood-paneled swamp shack—old, abandoned, and covered with green moss and a thick web of dead vines. It had an A-frame rusted-metal roof, a rotting deck with four steps leading up to the front door, and one small window on each side of the entrance.

"Over there!" Mrs. Chatsworth yelled from the middle of the water. "Do you see her? Over there!"

Madeline ran into the shack, and once she closed the door her scent vanished. But when the Chatsworths reached the shore, they still knew exactly where she was and marched forward ready to attack. They ran up the steps, swung open the door, and stormed inside. Then, instantaneously crippled by the sight in front of them, they stopped.

Madeline held her stance on the other side of the room with her black crystal rosary draped around her neck and her two guns, one in each of her bloody gauze-wrapped hands, pointed directly at them. The room was ablaze with the light of one thousand dripping white candles and adorned with artifacts from every holy religion. The book of *Demonology and Protection* and the *Scroll of Demoncide* sat open atop a brass candle-covered altar next to Madeline, and a series of archaic celestial markings formed a circle on the floor under the Chatsworths' feet.

Pastor Chatsworth stood motionless; he was ready. He had somehow always known Madeline would come back to punish him—and she had. The cowering Mrs. Chatsworth turned to run, but the door had closed and locked behind her. She pulled hard on the handle desperate to escape the torture of the holiest place she'd ever been, but it was no use. When she turned back around, her and her husband's faces began to melt from the stocked museum of clean-spirited religious relics.

Without words or emotion Madeline double-pumped the triggers, shooting Pastor and Mrs. Chatsworth simultaneously, each twice in the heart.

————————

Sunday, April 13, 2014 – 1:00 a.m.
With dozens of flashlights flickering in the darkness and dogs barking in the distance, Madeline walked silently out of the shack.

As she proceeded down the steps and turned in the opposite direction of the search, her brown eyes turned sparkling diamond blue.

Behind Madeline, Satan stood outside the shack door no longer wearing his tuxedo, but back in his colonial suit. He removed the silver watch from his pocket, flipped open the case, and checked the time; it continued to tick loudly, the rhythm now twice as fast as before.

Satan opened the shack door, went inside, and closed it behind him. Through the windows, the bright-white candlelit glow turned to rolling flames as he closed out the Chatsworths' reign—forever.

Satan was confounded—how could this have happened? The one soul he coveted for himself had annihilated his two highest-ranking Generals by way of their own treason against him, and now the Central Church of Enlightenment would never open.

"Noooo—I'm the King. I'm the King. I'm the King!" Satan screamed on his knees as the foundation of the Golden Monument caved in and collapsed from a great location-specific earthquake and crumbled deep into the abyss of the Chatsworths' now-disintegrated lair. And like the results of every deceit Satan had ever promised his followers, his precious property had manifested into a wondrous pile of dust, smoking under hot coals in the cold Ohio night.

He now had to retreat to the drawing boards of Hell and devise a new plan, and he had to act with haste. Millenniums of his available time were now reduced to less than a decade, and his marriage to Madeline would have to wait, at least for now.

Blood-spattered with her face beaten and bruised, Madeline was thigh-high in water as she waded through the thawing, duckweed-covered marsh, making her way to the other side. After navigating through a thick forest of trees and brush, she found herself at the edge of the Old Pearl River. Alligators parted like cavalry, venomous snakes fled the waters and coiled on the shore, and massive hawks lined the cypress trees. All deadly in their own right, the predators of the swamps were now nothing more than yellow watchful eyes parting to make way for the first species they were unauthorized to harm.

Madeline dove into the river, swimming hard through the broken ice and fierce currents of the rushing snowmelt. The engine propellers of approaching police airboats sounded in the distance and a helicopter hovered half-a-mile away in the misty night sky. The storm had cleared, and the clouds had passed, yet the rabid hunters and hounds in pursuit could not detect Madeline's location; her scent was long lost.

Through the steaming fog she could see the sacred swamp island in the center of the river coming within reach. It was the second place Haloise had told her to go—the place that would mark the beginning of her long-awaited freedom.

After traversing the deepest part of the river, Madeline ascended from the waters encased in dripping wet leather and, like the rosary, glistened in the moonlight.

She ran to the other side of the island, knelt under the only tree, and remembered the last thing Haloise had said to her. Before leaving Haloise's house only hours before, Madeline had thought her mission only included the disposal of the Chatsworths—she had been wrong.

"There is one last thing, my child . . . one last thing you have to know before you proceed." Haloise had said, while Madeline stood by the door ready to leave. "One more revelation you must understand about me and about yourself."

A light had appeared above Haloise's head and her body began to transform. Her dark skin turned sparkling gold, her eyes changed to bright turquoise, her long gray hair grew shiny black, and her soft features re-formed beautifully hardened and androgynous.

"I volunteered for this post," Haloise explained, "long ago, to come down from the Heavens and take the form of Archangel Incarnate. We will fight kind against kind and abolish Satan's plan to rob humanity of the right to choose which side their souls will lie. Satan is under the illusion that the more souls he collects the less severe his Final Punishment will be—he is mistaken.

Now, with open warfare re-instated, The Laws of Existence render neutrality obsolete—humanity will choose either God or Satan; Judgement is imminent! It is the Eve of The Day of Revelation: The Great Reveal of the only Stipulations releasing humanity from the Death Sentence imposed by God for the brutal murder of Jesus Christ, and the rising Rebellion of Satan.

As the Execution Date draws near, God will sift-out the worthy and discard the rest, leaving the Damned to suffer Second Death! Our mission is to provide the Lord that opportunity—fairly—kind against kind.

Your parents are the first of the half-demonic Generals of Satan. There are thousands of other Generals and Soldiers of Satan like them of similar strength and dedication. Currently no previously-human souls of equal and opposite body and mind exist, which are the only souls who can fight Satan's Army—power against power. You and one other also chose, long ago, to lead that fight and build God's Army; you are the Daughter and he is the Son. Should you receive the transfiguration this journey entails, the Father will reunite you with your King and 'smite the nations' with the fire from your swords!"

Suddenly the room was illuminated by a blinding white light and Madeline fell to the floor, covering her head with her arms. After a few moments, all of her apprehension vanished, and she rose to her knees, staring into the light as the room around her disappeared. The Heavens opened, reclaimed her spirit, and re-filled it with all the knowledge and wisdom acquired through millions of years of existence before the Creation of Man. Between the flash of an instant, every question she had ever asked was answered, and although she was no longer a doctor, she knew exactly who she was.

"I will reverse Satan's winds and push back his storm," Haloise said, "but your operation is your own. Your transfiguration begins now but will not fully activate until you reach the spiritual ground of which I have instructed you to go, the place marking the beginning of your long-awaited freedom. At this moment, your old life no longer remains."

When the brilliance faded, Madeline rose. "Goodbye, Haloise."

"Goodbye, Madeline. You must trust in the process from here on. Now all events and circumstances will reflect the Truth, and you will know Truth by the thoughts in your mind, not by the words that you hear. Remember, you're not saving the world; you're just buying it more time. It is a mortal sin to forget the end of your life is always on the horizon. Whether or not you choose to accept that fact will either determine your fate, or lead you to your destiny. And as you can see, you have found yours. Be well, my child, and Godspeed."

"Where will I find you?" Madeline asked. "Where will I find my King?"

"We will meet you on the other side."

———

As the lights in the distance grew closer, Madeline could hear the men who hunted her attempting to cross the marsh behind the forest on the other side of the river. One by one as they splashed into the re-infested waters, the men screamed out violently. The rows of alligators and snakes that had parted for Madeline had guarded the shore, and were now ferociously devouring the enemies as they tried to pass. The sound of rapid gunfire pierced the air as the men opened fire against the brave animal protectors that ripped open their flesh and tore off limbs.

Madeline unzipped her jacket and retrieved the vial of her blood and the $10,000 she'd tucked into the pocket. She took off all her clothes except for the rosary and stood naked in the center of the island under the moonlight, unwrapping the gauze from her hands and loosening her hair. As she began to transform, her skin turned a sparkling caramel hue, her hair grew into long flowing tresses of loose curls, and the gashes on her face and body were healed.

She gathered the clothing, money, and guns, and doused them in the blood from the vial, then ran back to the other side of the island and threw the blood-soaked objects into the water. At once, a swarm of alligators appeared and ravenously attacked the items, feasting on the sparse morsels of Madeline's human remains.

She turned around and ran back to the tree just as a herd of beautiful white horses, twelve deep, emerged from underneath the surface of the water, gleaming in the mist. The Heavenly Steeds swam toward the shore on the far side of the island, and the lead mare rose up as Madeline waded out to meet her. Madeline threw her leg over the horse's back and grasped its long white mane in her hands.

Exhausted and safe, Madeline fell fast asleep with her head hanging to the side as her horse swam back out into the water and led the others silently down the river and out to sea.

32

HALF MOON
ISLAND

Sunday, April 13, 2014 – 5:00 a.m.
Nathan Raines sat behind his desk at City Hospital lost in a deep gorge of anger and despair. The morning news played on the flat screen television hanging on the wall in the background, and the news anchor reported:

> *"New Orleans doctor Madeline Knight committed a murder-suicide in Honey Island Swamp. She first shot her parents, then herself—her bloody clothing fragments were discovered, but her body was unrecoverable in alligator-infested waters. Dr. Harold Fields of New Orleans State Psychiatric Hospital, also on the scene, was found paralyzed yet responsive—he was taken to City Hospital for emergency care."*

Nathan clenched his jaw, ground his teeth, and furrowed his brow, never to release them again. Katarina's suicide had put him on the edge of benevolence, kept in balance only by the emergence of the equally beautiful and troubled Madeline Knight, who'd become the perfect replacement for his dead fiancé; Madeline's perceived suicide had pushed him over the cliff of malevolence, and she had since become a deadly obsession in the early stages of full realization.

Consequently, Dr. Harold Fields, the man who Nathan believed to have facilitated both women's deaths, would be the second slaying on Nathan Raines' long execution list.

The buzzer on Nathan's office phone rang, snapping him out of his revenge-induced haze.

"Dr. Raines," said the attendant. "You have a visitor; Mr. King is here to see you."

"Send him in," Nathan replied. He straightened up in his seat and stiffened his glance, waiting curiously.

Jack Lee walked through the door holding the computer bag Madeline had given him. He was dressed uncharacteristically debonair in a black sheen, custom tailored, slim fitting three-piece suit with black shirt and tie, shiny silver-buckled black leather boots, and had his long hair slicked back and tied up in a half ponytail.

"So," Nathan said. "The Kentucky King returns for his Second Coming. Been a long time, Jack."

"Not long enough, Onyx," Jack Lee replied. "Madeline asked me to make sure I delivered this to you." He handed the bag to Nathan and stepped back toward the door. "Read them. She said you would know what they mean and what to do."

The two men had met long ago and knew each other well. This time, however, Jack Lee felt cringingly repelled by Nathan's unclean presence and sickening demeanor.

"So, I hear you're headed home," Nathan said. "Happy Birthday. Soon you'll be richer than me, and back in the saddle again."

Jack Lee didn't respond. As far as Nathan Raines concerned him, there was nothing to say.

Nathan opened the bag and pulled out Gabriella's hospital records and journal notebooks, then set them aside on his desk. His face began to burn and something else in the bag caught his eye. He reached in and discovered Madeline's sterling-silver white crystal rosary, which she'd stashed in the bag before fleeing NOSPH. Nathan grasped it with the tips of his fingers, hurriedly tossed the skin-searing relic to Jack Lee, and turned around in his chair with his back to his oldest friend.

Jack Lee knew about Nathan's association with Madeline, but another one of Nathan Raines' selfish quests cloaked in loyalty concerned him not; Jack Lee knew Madeline was untouchable. And it wasn't the first time Jack Lee and Nathan had collided over a sacred object, but it would be the last. The bad blood between them had ran lukewarm for the past twenty-three years, but the temperature was back to boiling, and the conditions of their cold war were now void under an expired treaty.

Jack Lee turned and left the office, never looking back; he knew they would meet again, but in The Second Coming, the joust with Nathan, his betrayer, would be on the frontlines.

––––––––––

Alone in his office, Nathan opened Gabriella's hospital records and the dozens of journal notebooks. He then closely examined the details of her tumultuous medical incarceration in Illinois, and irately flipped through the pages of her personal accounts of malice aforethought.

As Nathan scrutinized every twisted thought documented from Gabriella's five-year psychiatric stay and the days after her release, his eyes glowed red. And when he looked up from the final page, Satan appeared in the background.

For "New Orleans' Golden Boy of Medicine," the masquerade was officially over. Prince Nathan Onyx Raines, the sole heir to the wealthiest private spacecraft empire in the world, would soon take his rightful place, never to be controlled again.

––––––––––

Dr. Nathan Raines slow-marched down the hallway accompanied by two psych techs whose eyes also glowed red. One tech pushed a wheelchair, one held a bundle of restraints, and all three men stopped outside Gabriella's recovery room door.

Gabriella was in her room, drearily slumped in a chair by the window looking down at two early-shift gardeners who were digging out irrigation ditches on the hospital grounds below.

"Where are they?" she mumbled to herself, distraught and void of all strength. "I know they're coming. Where are you? Someone has to be coming. They always come. I know she'll come. Where are you, Belle? Where are you?"

She turned around when the door swung open and Dr. Raines entered the room with his Entourage of Evil. He had a tray of needles in his hand and stuck the largest into a glass bottle of heavy barbiturates, drawing out a dosage six times greater than the fatal amount.

Nathan Raines had found Gabriella Jackson guilty by evidence engraved from her own hand and had sentenced her to death-by-lethal-injection—to be carried out immediately.

"It's going to be a long, long wait," Nathan said, as the door slammed shut behind him.

Gabriella turned back around looking once more out the window, searching for help that would never come.

———————

After leaving Nathan's office, Jack Lee walked out of the psychiatric ward and into City Hospital's emergency medical center, passed through the swinging doors to the trauma units, went down the hallway outside the patient treatment rooms, and finally entered a large elevator.

Once inside, he pressed the button above the fortieth floor labeled "rooftop." When the door closed, he lifted Madeline's rosary up in his hand, held the matching Saint Benedict medal next to the one hanging around his neck, and smiled.

When the elevator door opened, Jack Lee walked out onto a sky-high helipad just as a sleek, black, tinted executive Airbus helicopter with the gold initials "JLK" landed. The co-pilot immediately exited the cockpit and opened the passenger door,

Jack Lee boarded the aircraft, the pilot re-assumed the controls, and all three ascended into the dark morning sky.

Jackson Lee King, "The South's Most Talked About Man," world-class equestrian, fencing champion, and sole heir to the wealthiest Thoroughbred horse breeding empire in the world, would soon reunite with Madeline once again. He knew she'd transfigured and made it through the storm, and he was out of the desert.

———————

The white horse carrying Madeline docked on the shores of Half Moon Island in the Gulf of Mexico, and along with the eleven others galloped across the spraying white sand to the next destination. After reaching the edge of the bayou ahead, all twelve horses assumed proper formation and bowed their front legs at the feet of Archangel Haloise, who waited on a rock above.

In a flowing gold robe and gold-armor breastplate, Haloise glowed under a halo as bright as the sun and gripped the copper hilts of two flaming double-edged swords with their points thrust into the ground.

Madeline dismounted her horse and made her way up the beach toward Haloise, naked and reborn.

Haloise stepped down graciously and wrapped a long sparkling white robe around Madeline's body, fastening it at her waist. Haloise then touched each of Madeline's shoulders with the blade of one of the swords and placed it in Madeline's raised right hand. Upon Madeline's touch, the sword turned into razor-sharp incandescent steel. Haloise then placed two heavy silver coins into Madeline's raised left hand, and slowly dropped to one knee and bowed.

"My Queen," Haloise said.

The moment Haloise rose back up, the wind began to blow, and she and Madeline turned around as the helicopter carrying Jack Lee landed in the sand. All twelve horses reared up on their hind legs and whinnied out seven times in a trumpeted symphony, then separated into formation.

Jack Lee de-boarded his aerial chariot and walked through the horse-lined pathway to Haloise. Haloise took the second sword from the ground, touched each of Jack Lee's shoulders with the blade, and placed it in his raised right hand. When the flaming blade turned to razor-sharp incandescent steel, she once again slowly dropped to one knee and bowed.

"My King," Haloise said. Haloise then rose back up, took Jack Lee's hand, placed it in Madeline's, and with no words, drifted away up into the pre-dawn morning.

Riding their Heavenly Steeds and wearing unpolished-gold crowns and modern-medieval suits of body armor with silver royal seals embedded in the chests—swords, shields, hooded-capes, gloves, and all—Jackson King and Madeline Knight led their stampede of barding-covered warhorses southeast atop the waters of the open sea.

And as the sun rose over the earth on the first Day of Revelation, revealing a molten-red firmament never again to be blue, The Second Coming of Jesus Christ and Mary Magdalene were ready for battle.

The End of Vol. 1

Coming Soon

THE BOOK OF TIME
VOL. 1
FUTURE HISTORY OF
TECHNOLOGICAL ORBITS
&
THE BOOK OF DEATH
VOL. 2
ERA OF THE ETHER

Available now

GOD'S FINAL GRAIL AND BIBLICAL TESTAMENT
Book I.
DECLARATION

www.godsfinaltestament.com
www.theroyalembassy.org
www.thebookofdeath.net

Melissa Anne Cain: The Second Coming of Mary Magdalene *Literary Biblical Scholar, Scribe, Artificial Intelligence Software & Satellite Technology Hardware Engineer, Alchemist, Martial Artist, Dramatist, Master of Cuisine—Prophet—Founder of The Royal Embassy of Human Completion and Soul Survival & AI-HCSS Laboratory. Raised in the Monterey Bay, California, Melissa Anne is the scion of two families of Founding Fathers— The Daughter of an Aerospace Explosives Chemist & a Radio Wave Hardware Engineer & Code Genius, and the 3rd Great Granddaughter of Honoré Escolle—Master Mason & Founding Father of Carmel & Monterey, California, by way of New Orleans from France during the "Gold Rush to the Gilded Age."*

EDITOR, CO-CREATOR, ANOINTER

Christopher Lee Cain: The Second Coming of Jesus Christ *Literary Biblical Scholar, B.A. Gonzaga University- Journalism, Master of Science: Special Education-California, Alchemist, —Prophet—Anointer, Professor and Co-Founder of The Royal Embassy of Human Completion and Soul Survival & Ai-HCSS Laboratory. Raised in the San Francisco Bay Area, California,*